A Beautiful Surrender

Rachel Mays

ISBN: 979-8-9872089-0-8

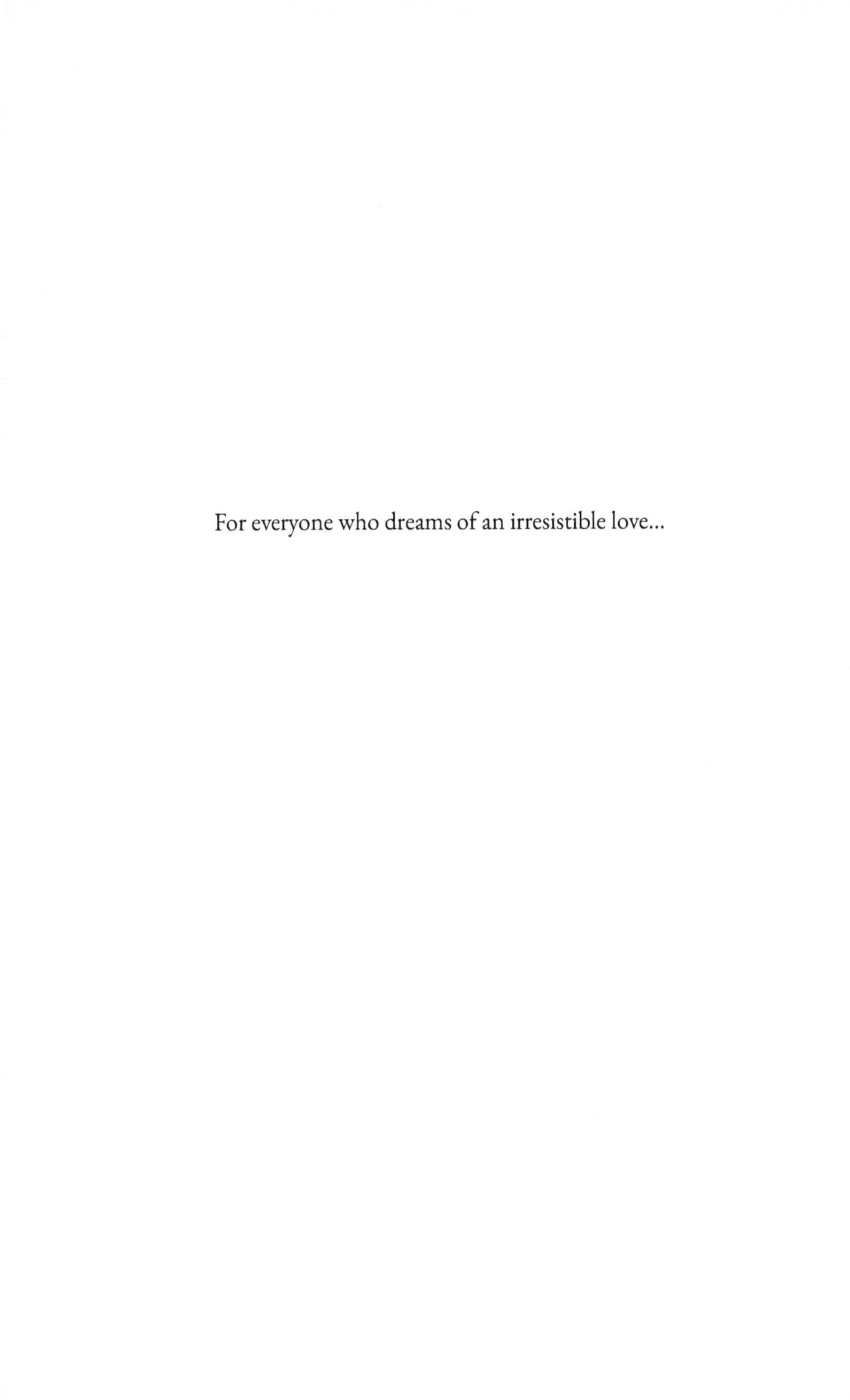

For everyone who dreams of an irresistible love...

Author's Note:

This story contains content that may not be suitable for all readers, including but not limited to, graphic depictions of and references to violence and death. Please take care of your mental health!

Chapter One

ALI

Ali hid behind a cluster of trees, straining to hear anything that might break the silence. A rustle of leaves. A snap of a branch. Her heart threatened to beat out of her chest. It was so loud, she thought it might give away her position.

Breathe, she reminded herself.

It was a chilly fall day. Winter was just around the corner. The wind had blown several strands of blonde hair loose from her braid. She didn't dare sweep them from her face, afraid the motion might attract unwanted attention. After several minutes of silence, she took a chance and peered around the trees. Nothing. Not even a bird or the fluttering of leaves. It was eerily still.

There was nothing beyond the rubble of deteriorated buildings. Their crumbled exteriors were covered in foliage. He could be hiding behind any of the mossy stones protruding from the ground.

Cold washed over her, sinking deep into her bones. Her long sleeve shirt, damp from running, clung to her frozen skin. She could hardly feel her toes in her boots and the tips of her fingers were turning blue. She was desperate to return home. How much longer could she hide out here?

She scanned her surroundings once more and still couldn't spot any movement. She narrowed her eyes like a hawk, but it was no use. The man chasing her was nowhere to be found.

Where had he gone? Should she attempt to make her way back home? It wasn't too far—five minutes, maybe ten.

She cautiously took her first step out from behind her cover. Branches and dried leaves crunched beneath her feet. Before she could take more than three steps, a hand gripped her arm, fingers digging into her bicep. With a rough tug, she spun around and made eye contact with the man who had been following her.

"Gotcha!" Victory was written all over his face. His eyes burned a hole through her and the corner of his mouth perked up, reveling in his win.

"Eli!" She kicked him in the shin and he let go of her arm, doubling over. She brought her hand up to her chest and struggled to catch her breath. He had scared her half to death.

Eli shot her an incredulous look as he hopped dramatically on one leg. The branches scattered across the forest floor almost tripped him and sent him toppling. "Damn, Ali! That fucking hurt." The fire in his brown eyes rapidly disappeared. They glossed over with tears and Ali smirked, knowing she had gotten her revenge.

"You deserved it." She pointed an accusatory finger at him. He couldn't really blame her for defending herself. "Where did you even come from, anyway?" She had been watching and listening so intently.

He cautiously stood up after tending to his sore leg. He winced in pain when he put his weight on it. It would probably bruise but she didn't feel guilty about it in the slightest. It was justified. "It's not my fault you can't hear shit. I found you ten minutes ago when you were stumbling through the brambles and have been stalking you ever since. You were so loud. The reason it's so quiet now is because you scared off every little critter within your vicinity. You're really bad at this, you know?" He chuckled at just how pathetic she was.

Ali rolled her eyes. "I do know. That's why I hate it when you pick this game."

They rarely had a chance to relax and just take it easy. Whenever they did, Eli chose to play hide and seek. It was a childish game. In fact, they had started playing it when they were just kids. Back then, a few other kids had played along, but over the years they had lost interest. They had slowly dropped off until it was just the two of them still playing games in the woods. There was hardly anything else to do in their small village of Andus, so Ali always played along. Even if she knew she was terrible. Even if she knew he would always find her. She was starting to suspect he only chose this game so he could scare her shitless every time.

"Do you want to go again?" he asked with a boyish grin. Eli was in his early twenties now, but in his heart and soul he would always be a kid. Like Peter Pan, he would never grow up. It was something she admired about him. He was carefree and cheerful no matter what was happening around him. Even when she was lost in her own thoughts, he could pull her out and brighten her day.

The wind blew again, and she shivered. She gritted her teeth and rubbed her palms against her thighs. She hated to disappoint him. "I was actually ready to go back home. Aren't you cold?"

"Nope." He placed a hand on her cold, rosy cheek and his warmth immediately radiated through her. She mirrored his movement and covered his hand with hers, although his hand was almost twice the size. He could hold her entire face in his hands. It was so warm and comforting. She leaned into it and basked in the extra heat.

She looked up to smile at him as he brushed the loose strands of her braid back behind her ear. He'd grown so tall over the years. When they were kids, she had grown faster than he did and had been taller than him for many years. She used to tease him about it. At some point though, he grew a foot and then another foot and then another until he became the tower standing here today. His boyish round cheeks had turned chiseled and stubble now covered his face. Lean muscle covered his lanky body. His short brown hair was soft and feathery. Objectively, Eli was quite handsome.

"You're a human heater. Stay close. I might need you," she said as they turned to walk back home under the setting sun.

They walked this path all the time and there wasn't much to see. It was mostly the remains of old buildings demolished centuries ago. Ali loved hearing stories about the twenty-first century and often imagined how this place would've looked back then. Foundations overgrown with weeds outlined the town that had been here centuries ago. Every time they passed, she would pick one of the cement slabs and put a name to it. That one was perhaps an ice cream parlor. Maybe a movie theater, a restaurant, or a salon. She'd seen none of these concepts herself, but that didn't stop her imagination from running wild.

It must've been so exciting living in that time period. The kids who lived here before them probably hadn't played hide and seek in their spare time. They would've had so much they could do instead.

Those places didn't exist now. Their entertainment came in the form of stories passed down through generations and singing songs around a fire. They gathered to eat simple meals as a family. She cut her hair once a year, usually with a rough blade, and kept it in a braid most of the time. It was the most convenient way to keep it clean and out of her face.

They'd been told wild stories about this thing called *technology* when they'd been younger. Hand-held devices that were used to communicate.

A square frame that displayed moving pictures and visual stories. Ali wouldn't have believed it if it weren't for the photos she'd seen in books. The pages were so faded, brittle and falling apart, but it was enough for her mind to take hold. She wished they had those amenities now.

The details of the old world were a little hazy. All they knew was that over time, the oceans had swallowed coastal towns. The rising sea level forced people to move inland. Wildfires scorched the western half of the continent, leaving the land barren and uninhabitable. The small population that had remained dwindled even further due to droughts and famine. When the dust finally settled, the earth was unrecognizable. It had been reborn. Other continents were rumored to exist, but everyone assumed they had also met their demise. They had never come to help.

Very few survived that period. Life quickly regressed and became much simpler. Initially, some people remembered how to make things like automobiles or telecommunications, but resources had been so scarce. They couldn't waste them on things that weren't absolute necessities. Now, that knowledge was long forgotten. A wooden wagon would be considered a luxury today.

They crossed over the remains of a concrete bridge. It was sturdy enough, although the rails had crumbled. It served little purpose since the body of water that used to exist was long gone. They were far from the shore of the lake and this trench was completely dried up.

Eli interrupted her thoughts. "Did I tell you I got another tattoo?"

"Another one?" She raised her eyebrows. Eli had gotten more tattoos than she could count. She had gone with him once and it had made her nauseous to watch as the artist had tapped ink made from berries into his skin. Little dots over and over and over again. It was an extensive process. If he felt any pain, he hadn't shown it.

Eli nodded excitedly and lifted his shirt to show her a new design on his rib cage. An image of a black bird engulfed in flames stretched across his flesh.

"Did it hurt?" She reached out to touch it, and he flinched when her cold fingertips brushed his skin.

"Nah, I was high on gray." He chuckled when she shook her head. He was referring to gray grass, a plant that grew naturally in the area that altered the mental state. It was most similar to alcohol, but distilling alcohol wasn't a luxury they could afford in Andus. Gray grass was readily available and despite its ugly appearance, it made a delicious tea.

He brought his shirt down and grabbed her hand to help her cross over some rubble. The closer they got to home, the more debris appeared. It was a strategic design. It made their village look like a dump, a graveyard, to outsiders, but sheltered in the middle were a few homes and a communal area. Their ancestors who settled here had left the exterior stones for natural protection and used the ones from the middle to rebuild houses camouflaged into the demolished structures.

The town of Andus had a population of a little more than fifty, made up of only a handful of families. It was hard to sustain a population much bigger. It wasn't much, but they were one big family to Ali. It was the only home she'd ever known.

Friendly faces greeted the two of them as they entered the main section of town. Eli grabbed her hand, a show of affection and pride. He loved to show her off, and she let him. The way he adored her made her heart hurt sometimes. She only wished she could return those feelings. She squeezed his hand and let him bask in the moment. The smile on his face was worth putting her own feelings aside.

Dinner was already prepared by the time they arrived. It was always served in the center of town. They each grabbed a bowl full of rice and fish and sat around the fire pit next to their neighbors, who chatted merrily.

"What did you two get into today?" asked a middle-aged woman named Sasha. Her hair was slowly turning from auburn to gray and her skin reflected her years, wrinkled from sun exposure. Her hands were permanently dyed from working with clothing and other rags in Andus, taking bland fabric and turning them into vibrant shades with natural elements. She was an artist in their otherwise bleak village.

"Not much," Eli responded. "Just running around in the woods with this one." He nudged Ali's shoulder with his elbow.

"Ah, to be young and in love," Sasha mused. "I remember when my husband and I used to spend our time doing nothing at all. Just enjoying each other's company. Those are the moments that make life worth living."

Sasha was a widow now and had been for many years, but her words of wisdom were appreciated by everyone around the fire. She carried on with stories of her love life, all the lessons she had learned, the moments that brought a smile to her face and the ones that made her blush. Every single face around the fire pit turned to listen, entranced by her. They ate up her guidance like starving vultures. Sasha had always been a skilled storyteller, and her tales were laced with lessons to learn.

Her words made Ali feel a bit more at ease. Perhaps she could love Eli like that. Didn't she enjoy spending time with him? Doing nothing at all, so long as it was with him? She looked up at Eli's face and took a moment to admire him. The kind and caring man who always put her first. Why was she so hesitant to return that kind of unconditional love?

The crowd groaned when Sasha stood to leave. "You'll have to forgive an old woman. It's past my bedtime."

Eli turned to Ali, his arm now wrapped around her shoulders while she nuzzled into his side. "I'm ready to go when you are."

His eyes bored a hole through her. It wasn't natural, the amount of yearning he felt toward her. She didn't know if she could ever return that intensity, but she resigned to pretend until it became real.

"I'm ready."

Chapter Two

ELI

"Let's get matching tattoos," Eli said as they drank their morning coffee outside his front door. They sat on the one rocking chair he owned, her on his lap. It was chilly, but he had insisted they sit outside. She wore his sweatshirt and a pair of leggings and had pulled his heaviest blanket over the top of them. He held her close and used his own body heat to keep her warm.

"Didn't you just get one?"

"You can never have too many." He looked at her like this was obvious. Ali didn't have any tattoos, so she didn't understand just how addictive they could be, but Eli couldn't get enough.

"What would you get?" she asked timidly. He could tell she was nervous about having a significant amount of ink covering her skin.

"Something small and simple. It's your first one and it'll probably hurt like a bitch." His eyes sparkled. She hadn't said no, and that only encouraged him, leaving the door open to possibilities. He was dying to share this experience with her.

She released a heavy sigh. "Maybe."

"I'll take it!" He finished the remains of his coffee, down to the last sediment of ground beans. Then he tapped her thigh lovingly. "I'm going to shower before we head out."

She stood and allowed him to head back into the house. Without his body heat, she followed him in and sat at the kitchen table.

"Where is your dad this morning?" she asked, her voice elevated as he disappeared into his bedroom.

Eli tore off his clothes and threw them into a pile in the corner of his bedroom. Then he wrapped a clean towel around his waist. "He went out to chop wood. Our stockpile and the neighbor's reserves are getting pretty low. Does your mom need some, too? I'm sure they'll come back with extra." His dad was always the first to lend a helping hand. If anyone in the town needed something, they knew to ask Jack. He was always happy to assist.

"I'll ask her." Ali's voice came from the kitchen.

Eli popped his head out from the bedroom. He smiled as his mind filled with lustful thoughts. "Join me?"

Ali chuckled, but she stood to join him in the shower, nonetheless.

As he dried off his hair afterwards, he couldn't help but feel truly blessed. He didn't know how life could possibly be better than this. He grabbed a pair of jeans out of his dresser and pushed a small box of trinkets to the back of the drawer. Ali didn't know it but inside was a ring his dad had given him, a ring that he intended to put on her finger one day soon. He just wanted to be sure she'd say yes. It was hard to tell with her sometimes.

Ali dressed on the other side of the room, wearing the same jeans as the day before and an old shirt of his that was too small for him. She didn't keep many of her own clothes here, despite how often he suggested it.

One day they'd find a home together instead of staying at his dad's house. One day soon.

They walked through the center of town and down a jagged path. A few trees had burrowed through the rubble and had grown into giants on the side of the path. Their leaves changed to radiant golds and reds and fell to the ground below them. The further they walked down the path, the denser the trees became.

Eli finally stopped in front of what appeared to be a cave, but he knew what lay beyond the entrance. He held Ali's hand and guided her through the dark tunnel. A few moments later, it opened up into a small atrium. The glass ceiling was shattered and natural light shined down on them. The walls were lined with small vials, herbs, and other trinkets.

He could feel Ali's hand shaking in his and tightened his grip reassuringly.

"Eli, I didn't expect to see you so soon." Carter, the man who had drawn all his other tattoos, stepped out from the shadows. "And you brought Allison?"

Eli wrapped an arm around her waist and pulled her close. "Yep, we've got a first-timer." The matching grins that Carter and Eli shared caused Ali to shrink in panic. He gave her a little shake to loosen her up.

"It'll be fine."

"Mm-hmm," she squeaked.

Eli had a design in mind, but she had to trust him. He wanted it to be a surprise. He whispered to Carter, and his friend nodded in understanding. She sat on a stool and bared her collarbone, allowing Carter to clean the skin just below her protruding clavicle. She turned her head away from Carter and toward Eli.

"I can't look."

"Hold my hand," he said, clasping her fingers and intertwining them with his. She flinched as Carter tapped the tool against her skin and the ink sank into her flesh.

She put on a brave face and tried to hide the pain, but Eli could feel her hands turning clammy. "Deep breaths, Ali. You're doing great."

"You owe me so big for this," she muttered, scrunching her brows.

"Anything you want...it's yours." He would give her the world if she asked for it.

Carter made quick work of her tattoo. It took very little time compared to the one he'd just finished on Eli's rib cage. Ali dropped his hand, and he clenched it a few times, shaking out the pain from her tight grip. He was pretty sure she had cut off the circulation from squeezing so tightly. She looked down at the new design above her chest and smiled.

"The sun?" she asked curiously.

Eli simply nodded. He took his turn on the stool and Carter imprinted a new design on his chest in the same location as Ali's. She watched this time, and her face went pale at the sight of his blood.

"I'm glad I didn't watch during mine." She turned away and exhaled, her hands gripping her knees. Eli reached out and rubbed soothing circles across the back of her hand.

When Carter finished, Eli tilted toward her to show off his new tattoo.

"The moon...does it mean something?"

"Did you know the light from the moon is just a reflection of the sun? It means I'd be nothing without you, Ali."

Her eyes glistened with tears. He sat up straight and turned toward her. He hadn't meant to make her cry. That was not the reaction he had expected. She bowed her head and then met his gaze once again. "You have it backwards, Eli."

They spent the rest of the afternoon relaxing in town. Ali sat with some of the older ladies, one of which was teaching them to play a game with dice. Ali was terrible and couldn't get the hang of it. It was a good thing they gambled with pebbles and not real currency because she would've been in major debt.

Eli played a game of ball with the younger kids. They had so much more energy than him and for the first time, he felt old, despite only being in his twenties. He just could not keep up with them. They ran in circles around him and easily kicked the ball away. They tackled him on numerous occasions and overpowered him as he struggled to get back to his feet. By the time they were done, he was drenched in sweat.

He nuzzled against Ali as he sat down next to her, and she cringed from his sweaty head.

"Disgusting," she declared, but she placed a hand on his thigh anyway.

"Are you winning?" he asked.

"Not at all. I think it's time to call it quits."

"I didn't take you for a quitter," he teased, pinching her side as she giggled and tried to escape his clutch.

"I'm not, but I need to go home and get ready for tonight." It was an excuse and he knew it, but she wasn't wrong. It was getting late, and they both needed to wash up and return for dinner. Eli's dad was expecting him to be home soon.

"I'll see you in a little bit?" Eli asked when Ali stood and turned toward her house. "I know Dad is really excited to celebrate tonight."

"Yeah. See you at dinner." He watched as she continued walking in the distance, disappearing into a tiny speck.

Chapter Three

ALI

Ali spent more time in the bath than she normally would've. It was long enough for the water to turn freezing cold, although it hadn't been very warm to begin with. Her mother, Anna, had already left to help prepare dinner and wasn't there to rush her out of the tub, so she took her time. She ran her fingers through her hair in an attempt to work out the tangled mess. Then she gently poured water over her new tattoo, dabbing it dry. She stared blankly at the dirt under her fingernails. No amount of scrubbing that would ever leave her feeling truly clean.

From the window, she could see darkness falling like a blanket over their town. She sighed as she stepped out of the bath and dried off hastily. If she took much longer, she would be late to dinner. In Andus, they all ate together as one big family. It was less wasteful to make meals in bulk, although it typically meant their food was pretty bland. She couldn't count the number of times she'd eaten fish and rice. Only nearly every day of her life. On rare occasions like birthdays or weddings, they'd have a more extravagant meal. Today was Eli's dad's birthday, so there would be a full hog roast with veggies and dessert. She was looking forward to dessert the most.

She yanked a brush through her hair and smoothed it back into a braid, glaring at her naked body in a cracked mirror. Criticizing her body had become a habit. She was scrawny—the result of years of being underfed and spending her days walking along the lake and checking fish traps.

She was malnourished and her knees were too bony. She picked apart the most minute features of her body. She had no reason to be vain. It wasn't practical or sensible, but that didn't stop her. Ever since she'd stumbled upon an old book of photography, she couldn't forget how hauntingly beautiful the women and men were centuries ago.

Her eyes though...if she had to choose one part of her body that she liked it would be her eyes. Those old photographs featured no one with eyes as beautiful as hers. They were a striking shade of brown that made her look and feel fiercer than she was.

And her lips. Eli had told her she had nice lips once. She hadn't known lips could be a desirable feature on a person, but she remembered the way it had felt that day to be complimented by a man. Desired—even if it was just Eli. She had been little more than a child then, and the effect of his words had since worn off. She still appreciated his affection, but it no longer burned inside her.

She grabbed a clean pair of black skinny jeans and a cotton shirt that hung from her lanky limbs. She laced up her black leather combat boots and grabbed her thick tan wool jacket before heading out into the brisk fall evening.

The scent of bonfire smoke hit her as soon as she stepped out the door. It was one of her favorite smells. It always brought back many wonderful memories spending time with family and friends. If the comfort of home was a scent, it would be this one. There was something so comforting about the way the aroma swirled around her, wrapping her up like a warm blanket.

It didn't take long to find Eli waiting for dinner to be served. She could hear his laugh from a mile away, and it brought an instant smile to her face. He was surrounded by a few other older men, including his dad.

"Happy birthday, Jack!" Ali shouted as she snuck up behind them and patted Jack on the shoulder. He embraced her and hugged her tight. Jack had been like a father to Ali ever since hers had died when she was young during a hunting trip gone wrong. It was partly why she had become so close to Eli. That and the fact that he was the only one close to her age. Jack had stepped in to make sure her mom had everything she needed and that Ali was well taken care of.

"Miss Allison, I'm so glad you made it. We were starting to wonder if you got lost. I was just telling Eli here that he needs to lock you down before some other chump comes along." He chuckled and shook her by the shoulders.

It wasn't the first time he'd made a comment about the two of them getting married or having babies or falling in love. It seemed pointless to resist. They probably *would* get married and have kids. The next closest man in age to Ali was seven years younger and the next closest woman to Eli was twelve years older. Eli was the practical option, and marrying her best friend wasn't exactly the worst prospect in the world. Other people weren't so lucky.

"No need to rush things, Dad." Eli nudged his dad and flashed Ali an apologetic smile. Ali didn't know if she was ready for this.

Jack was oblivious to her discomfort and carried on, clapping his son on the back. "Sure there is. I'm not getting any younger!" His belly shook as he laughed and a few of his friends had the decency to look toward the ground, though they were unwilling to reel him in.

Ding. Ding. Ding.

A bell graciously interrupted their conversation. She would get away with another day of no commitments. She wasn't sure how much longer they could delay the inevitable, but she'd take any extra day given to her.

Jack and his older friends hurried ahead to grab a plate, leaving Eli and Ali behind. He shifted uncomfortably with his hands in his jean pockets and avoided eye contact. His confusion was her own doing. Half the time she was sleeping in his bed and the other half she was keeping him at arm's length. Whenever the topic of marriage came up, they both turned to stone.

She grabbed him by the elbow and said playfully, "Take me to dinner, handsome?" She batted her eyelashes at him for good measure, attempting to pull him out of his thoughts.

He snorted. "Do you have something in your eye?"

"Eli!" She smacked him hard in the gut. He was laughing so hard, her hand bounced off his abs. "You are such an ass."

"Oh, that was good, Ali. That was good." He was so out of breath that he could hardly speak. There were tears in his eyes. The teasing was her signal that things were back to normal. The awkwardness from before had dissipated.

"Fine. Find another girl to take to dinner. I'm sure Sarah is available. Sure, she's forty-five years old, but I hear she likes them young." She raised her brows and crossed her arms defensively. He would be so lucky to have her.

"Aw, come on now, Ali. You know I love you." He stepped forward, arms open wide and ready to embrace her, but she took an equal step back. She wouldn't let him win that easily. He paused and a shimmer of playfulness danced across his eyes.

"Don't." She warned him, but he closed the gap in a flash and swooped her up off her feet in a bear hug. He squeezed so tight she could hardly breathe. "Put. Me. Down," she grunted.

"No," he said. "I'm never letting you go. I won't let you leave me."

"I'm not leaving you. Just put me down." She wriggled in his arms, struggling to break free, but his hold was too strong.

"Promise? Promise you'll never leave me?" He loosened his grip and looked down at her.

She locked eyes with him so he knew she was sincere. "I promise, Eli. I'll never leave you. Now put me down!"

He gently set her down and together they made their way over to the dinner table, hand in hand. It all smelled incredible. She added a little bit of everything to her plate and Eli did the same but with double the serving. His plate was practically overflowing. She smirked, but he didn't notice. He was too busy shoveling food into his mouth, his shoulders hunched over the table. Slices of angel cake topped with berries were passed around after everyone had finished their main dish.

Chatter and laughter filled the air. Everyone was having a great time sharing and listening to stories about Jack. The hell they'd raised as kids and then more endearing stories about raising Eli on his own. Eli's mom had died during childbirth, so he'd also been brought up by one parent like Ali. They sat and told stories long after the food had been devoured. Even though her fingers were frozen and her nose was pink from the cold, she couldn't think of any other place she'd rather be than surrounded by these people.

She shivered next to Eli, and he turned his attention to her. He slid his arm around her shoulders and pulled her closer to his side to warm her up. "Do you want to go sit by the fire?"

"Sure." He held out a hand to help her up from the bench. "Always the gentleman." She placed her hand in his and allowed him to lead her to the bonfire. Logs and branches were stacked five feet tall so they didn't have to get too close before her fingers started to thaw.

"Better?"

"Much better."

Before she could take a seat on one of the unoccupied logs, Eli threw his hands up dramatically.

"Wait." He stopped abruptly.

She looked around in confusion, trying to determine the reason for his sudden outburst.

"I know what would make this even better. I'll be right back." He jogged off and left her just as confused as she was before. She sat down and it was only a few minutes before he returned, keeping his hands mysteriously hidden behind his back.

"What do you have there?" She raised her eyebrow. She knew Eli. It was, without a doubt, gray grass tea.

He pulled two mugs out from behind his back. "Tell me you love me." She shook her head, but it was hard to deny him when he was this cheerful. She pursed her lips, refusing to humor him.

"Ali, if you don't tell me you love me, I will drink both of these myself."

She smiled at the thought. He absolutely would. He loved his gray grass. "And I'll be carrying you home."

"I'd like to see you try."

She burst out laughing. He was easily twice her size and there was no way she could possibly carry him. She'd have to leave him out in the cold instead. "Okay, fine. For the sake of my back, I love you, Eli."

He extended one of the mugs with a triumphant look.

She took one sip and her tongue tingled. It was *strong*. "Whoa, are you trying to get me fucked up?"

"No, you're just weak. But don't worry. I actually can carry you home." She glared at him, but he wasn't wrong.

It didn't take long before her whole body was feeling light and floaty. Floaty. Was that even a word? It felt like she could float away. The only thing holding her to the ground was this log. But if she stood up, gravity would cease to exist. Her lips were balloons. They'd help her float away. How would she steer? Would she ever come back down? Maybe she'd live among the stars instead.

Ali, are you okay? Ali?

"Ali?"

That wasn't her voice?

"Earth to Ali—" A deep voice interrupted her trance. She turned to see Eli lying on his back, one arm supporting the back of his head. He was watching her with amusement and chuckled. "I told you. You're such a lightweight."

She opened her mouth to say something and realized her fingers were on her lips. When had that happened? She lightly tapped them. Her lips were not balloons after all.

"I think I'm ready for bed." She stood up, but her legs were like jelly and she stumbled forward, closer to the fire. Eli and his lightning reflexes grabbed her by the elbow to save her. Why wasn't he fucked up?

"All right, I've got you. Let's get you home."

Eli's bedroom was small, but cozy. His bed took up most of the space, along with a small desk. The windowsill was covered in shells they'd collected together. She kicked off her boots and felt his soft rug between her toes. He helped her out of her jeans and top, and she tossed her bra on the floor.

It wasn't a romantic or sexy moment. He'd seen her naked plenty of times. He was just as familiar with her body as she was with his. They were comfortable, brought together by their circumstances. The two had been inseparable for nearly two decades. She didn't know why she was so scared to commit to him. They acted like a married couple already.

He pulled one of his shirts over her head and it was so long that it fell to just above her knees. She reached up to remove her hair tie, letting her long hair unravel.

His bed was more comfortable than her own. It might've been the fluffy pillows or maybe his warm body. Moments later, he slid in behind her and wrapped his arms around her.

He moved in close. So close that their bodies became one. She could feel his breath on her shoulder, his thumb rubbing against her stomach. Some nights they would fool around, but tonight she wasn't in the mood. He ran his hands down her waist and to her legs, playing with the hem of the shirt she was wearing. She felt something grow and press into her ass.

"Ali…" He planted a kiss on her shoulder, while she pretended to sleep, squeezing her eyes shut.

"Ali?" His hand slipped under her shirt. She remained motionless, hoping he would realize nothing was happening tonight.

He heaved a sigh and gave up. His hand returned to rest on her stomach outside of her shirt. "I love you, Ali."

It wasn't like the other times. Things were shifting between them. She'd sensed it for a while now. This wasn't friendly love or familial love. She heard the longing in his voice when he said it and knew it meant something more. Something more than she could give him in return. She winced and vowed to erase that confession from her memory.

Chapter Four

ALI

She could hear Eli's deep breathing before she opened her eyes. His body was so warm. She could lay in his arms forever, enjoying the beat of his heart against her cheek. At some point in the night, she had rolled over to face him. She snuggled in closer, their legs intertwined. When her eyes finally fluttered open, she smiled at the sight of him. He looked so peaceful in his sleep. The hard, chiseled lines of his face seemed softer in the glow of morning light. He was more relaxed. She watched his bare chest rise and fall and her breathing synced up with his. He always made her feel at ease.

She reached up to touch his chest, and traced gentle lines down, down, and down further until she reached that V shape at the top of his briefs.

He stirred, then inhaled sharply and said, "Your hands are freezing." Without opening his eyes, he took her hands in his. "Good morning."

She nuzzled his neck and planted a quick kiss. "Good morning." *That* got him to open his sleepy brown eyes. She hadn't forgotten his confession from last night. The confirmation that Eli had feelings for her beyond friendship. Sometimes she felt guilty for the kisses, the sex, all the time they spent together. She felt like she was leading him on, but did it matter? It wasn't like they had other options. If they were bound to be together, then why not give him what he wanted? She would do anything to make Eli happy.

He wrapped one arm around her back, running his hand through her hair. The sensation was gentle, but he was in total control. He licked his lips and stared down at hers.

Dishes clattered from beyond the bedroom. "Breakfast is ready!" Eli groaned in dismay. His dad always had impeccable timing. His face dropped in disappointment as he tilted his forehead to rest against hers.

"Can we just ignore him?" he whispered. His lips grazed her skin. Ali was inclined to humor him, but it wasn't possible. If they tried, Jack would just shout at them again. She'd stayed here enough times to know that he had zero patience. It wasn't malicious; he just didn't consider that maybe his son would like some privacy.

Right on time, he shouted again. "It's getting cold!" They both laughed and slowly parted. She couldn't help but stare at his body as he got out of the bed wearing only his underwear. His muscles rippled as he pulled on a pair of shorts. There had to be something wrong with her. How frustrating that it felt like she was settling when this perfect specimen of a man was standing in front of her. She desperately yearned to feel a spark, but she just didn't.

When they were younger, she'd thought maybe there was something there, but it turned out she'd just been eager to explore the unknown. She'd wanted to know what it felt like to be with a man.

Eli made her feel safe and comfortable. It was easy with him. Easy, but not passionate. At least not on her end.

He grabbed her clothing from the night before and handed it to her. She should keep more of her own clothing here considering how often she stayed the night. Jack would certainly have something to say about her wearing the same clothes, and if her mom was up when she got home, then she would too.

Ali felt Eli's eyes on her as she changed back into her clothes. He handed her the jacket she'd worn last night and kissed the top of her head as she threw it over her arm before they stumbled out of the bedroom together.

Jack feigned surprise. "Oh, hi, Allison. I didn't realize you were here, too."

He knew. His words weren't convincing at all. Plus, he'd cooked enough eggs for three.

"Good morning, Jack. Smells amazing in here."

"Thanks for breakfast, Dad." Eli grabbed a plate for himself and Ali.

She devoured hers as quickly as possible, almost choking on the toast that accompanied the scrambled eggs. She couldn't give Jack more time to talk about her future as his daughter-in-law. There was only so much she could take. "I can't stay long. I need to stop at home before we check the traps." She headed out the door before either of them could object. She caught Jack looking at Eli with a confused expression. Eli just shook his head, a silent order to drop it.

"I'll see you in a bit," he called after her.

Jack gave Eli a stern look. After she left, Jack would no doubt drill Eli about when he would propose to her. He didn't care for the casualness of their relationship and expected something more serious. That was one conversation she was glad to miss.

One day, Jack would be her father-in-law. Perhaps she should get used to standing up to Jack alongside Eli, but today he could handle the difficult conversation on his own.

It was freezing outside. It would be a brutal day checking the fish traps. They'd been assigned this job many years ago when they were old enough to contribute to the community. In a few months, they'd get their winter break when the lake froze over. It was pure torture to work in the cold and wet, but someone had to do it. She made a mental note to throw on some extra layers before they went out today. She'd have to pull out the thick wool socks stuffed away in her bottom drawer.

She tried to open the front door of her house as quietly as possible, but it was pointless. As soon as the door cracked open, her mom was waiting for her, sitting at the table in the dining room. She hovered over a piece of tattered fabric with a sewing needle, attempting to patch yet another hole in one of her blouses. She didn't even look up when Ali entered the house.

"You should at least tell me when you're going to be out all night so I know where you are, Allison." Her words were sharp, but Ali knew they came from a place of love. It didn't matter that she was a grown adult. She still felt like she had to obey her mom's wishes.

"Sorry, Mom. I meant to give you a heads up, but it got late and then I just forgot," Ali said timidly, hoping her mom would forgive her.

"It's okay. Sit, sit," her mom insisted as she laid down her sewing kit. There was more toast on the table and a jug of juice.

"I can't stay long. I need to change and get to work." Ali tried to rush to her room.

Anna fussed before she could get far. "You have to eat something. Come sit with your mom. I feel like it's been forever since we've caught up. I rarely see you anymore."

"I already ate at Eli's." She went to step around her mom, but she wasn't giving up that easily.

"You spend a lot of time with Eli. Is there something you need to tell me?"

Ali knew her mom wouldn't let her leave without having a conversation. She accepted defeat and took a seat at the small dining table and poured a glass of juice. "Do we really need to do this right now?"

"Is he the one, then?"

She let out a huff of air. "Mom, there is no one else. Who else would be 'the one?'" She put up air quotes.

Anna looked down and contemplated for a moment. Her shoulders sank and her eyes drooped heavily. Ali had never seen her looking so fatigued.

"I don't want you to settle, Allison. I always wanted more for you out of life...more than what I had."

There was an uncomfortable energy in the air. They'd never talked about her parents' relationship before. Not like this. Ali had assumed they were head over heels in love.

"Don't get me wrong. I loved your father. He was a good man and cared for me, provided everything I could've asked for." She gestured around the house. "But just like you, I had no other options. I sometimes wonder if I should've moved with you when you were younger, after your father died. Maybe you would've had more opportunities if we had found a larger town."

Ali had never even thought of leaving Andus. She'd never considered the way life could've been in another town or even that there were other towns. It seemed naïve now, but she had always assumed this was the only way of life.

She crossed a leg over her knee. "Why didn't you? Why didn't you leave?"

Her mother sipped on her glass of juice, staring off into the distance like she was envisioning a different life. Ali wondered what she saw, what had brought on this conversation.

"I had no idea what else was out there. What if I left, hoping the grass was greener somewhere else, only to find a desert? I didn't want to risk it. Now I'm afraid I risked your happiness instead."

"I am happy."

Anna looked at her with skepticism.

"I am," she insisted. "You know Eli. He's an amazing guy. I'd be lucky to marry him and have a family with him."

Ali didn't know if she was trying harder to convince her mom or herself. "I love him enough. Enough to make it work. It's not worth beating yourself up over when it's inevitable. We can't change things now."

Ali took her mother's hand in her own. She hadn't noticed how fragile and worn her mother had become. The winters always took a toll, the small house too frigid to protect the two of them. Even her hair had a frost to it. Her dark blonde hair had slowly turned white.

"What if we could? Would this still be enough for you?"

Ali shook her head. There was no point to this conversation. Her life was set in stone and it did no good to daydream about some other life meant for some other version of her. She knew her mom meant well, but she let out a frustrated sigh.

"I can't do this right now. I'm late for work." She grabbed a piece of toast and rushed to her room to change.

When she came back out, her mom was no longer in the kitchen. She must've left for work as well. Ali let the door slam shut behind her and made her way to the edge of town as quickly as she could. Eli was probably already waiting for her.

As much as she hated to admit, their conversation that morning had gotten her head spinning.

What would she want out of life if she could have anything? Did she even want to be married or have kids? Was it possible to love someone more than she loved Eli? Did she want to spend the rest of her life checking fish traps?

She couldn't even picture a life different from this one. It was all she'd ever known. She had done a terrible job of shaping her own life. She let life happen to her.

What else existed beyond Andus?

Chapter Five

ELI

ELI STOOD BY THE old rusted 'Andus' sign on the edge of town, waiting for Ali. She was running late. He had a feeling her mom had given her a hard time for not coming home last night, but it was nothing compared to the earful he'd received from his father.

"Just do it already," he'd yelled. As if it were that easy. Eli wanted nothing more than to be with Ali for the rest of their lives, but he sensed her hesitation. If he pushed her, would it ruin their friendship?

And then there was her mom. As much as his dad wanted them to be together, it seemed Anna was the total opposite. Most days, he felt resentment radiating from her. The days Ali chose his bed over her own only ignited her disdain.

Didn't she realize Ali was all grown up now and could make her own decisions? She wasn't a child breaking curfew. It was a bit extreme and uncalled for, in his opinion.

He scanned his surroundings again, hoping to see Ali, but she was still nowhere to be found.

Hurry up, he thought.

He tended to get impatient when it came to work. He'd rather get it all out of the way and have some free time, but Ali usually preferred to take things slowly. She'd once told him if they had to work, they might as well make the most of it. She always chose the long way around. Stopping to smell the roses.

In the summer, he was completely okay with it. Her idea of taking their time was to skinny dip in the lake. She'd strip down to nothing and run into the water. "Just to cool down," she'd say. He would always be okay with taking *that* break from work.

This morning was significantly cooler, so he hoped she wouldn't feel like lingering today. He would much rather be back in a warm bed with her, running his hands over her soft skin.

He quickly brushed the thought from his mind. The last thing he needed right now was to get wound up. He couldn't spend all day distracted thinking about her thighs around his waist or his hands cupping her breasts. It would drive him mad.

He spotted Ali in the distance and watched her pick up the pace when she noticed him.

"Sorry. Have you been waiting long?" She was a little out of breath as she jogged the last few steps.

"Not at all."

"You're lying, aren't you?"

He grinned at her accusation.

"It doesn't matter. Let's just get going."

They set off in the direction of the lake. She was unusually quiet today. Eli could sense something was up but he didn't like to pry. Ali always came to him when she was ready to talk. Whatever it was, he was sure she'd share eventually. If she wasn't ready to talk about it, then he'd distract her in the meantime.

"Do you think aliens are real?"

She stopped in her tracks and her eyes widened. "What?"

"Do you think aliens are real? Like, do you think there's life in outer space? Is there another planet out there where we could live that's better than this one?"

She looked at him like he'd grown two heads. Then, she opened her mouth slowly and spoke with uncertainty. "I guess? It's possible."

"Cayden was telling us a story yesterday. Apparently he heard from his dad that they used to have transportation to space, Ali. To *space*! How would they even get up there? Anyway, he said that scientists back then were trying to figure out a way to live up there before everything went to shit here. Guess they should've tried harder."

She shook her head at him, but a smile crept across her face. His mission to distract her had been successful.

"What do you think aliens eat?"

"Eli, you're so weird." She rubbed her hand across her forehead. "I don't know. My intuition says they probably are vegetarians. There's got to be a lot of weird wildlife on other planets, right?"

They made their way to the first trap. "It's empty."

It wasn't a surprise. The fish became less active when the temperatures dropped. But it wasn't great either. Their supplies for winter weren't as plentiful as they'd been last year. They had hoped to get a few more good days in before the lake began to freeze over.

"Maybe we'll have more luck at the next one," she said.

Eli followed her as she made her way toward the next trap. "So do you think alien planets have gray grass?"

"Oh my god, don't talk to me about gray grass," she groaned. "I have a headache from last night and I don't need reminding."

"Aw, poor thing," he teased. "You were quite amusing last night, actually. You should drink gray grass more often."

She moaned again. "What did I say?"

"It's not so much what you said. It's what you did. You were like a statue. You just sat there, feeling your lips and muttering about flying. And then you swayed in your seat like you were listening to music, except nothing was playing."

"That's not so bad. I've been worse."

"Yeah, like that time you stood on the table and flashed everyone your—"

She shoved him off the beaten dirt path, right into a pile of weeds. "We don't talk about that time!"

Eli tried to make his way out of the bramble, but she pushed him down again. He tripped backward over a branch and instinctively grabbed her arm on the way down, pulling her with him. She released a huff when her body hit his chest.

"Are you okay? I'm so sorry." He started checking her body for scratches and that everything was all right. Her hair was covering her face so he couldn't see her reaction, but he felt her trembling. He gently rolled her body off his. No, not trembling. Shaking. She was *laughing*. Of course she was. He was so concerned for her well-being and she was amused.

"I'm fine, Eli," she said between fits of laughter. "You don't need to worry about me."

Once he realized she was okay, he began to see the humor in the situation. He chuckled and shook his head at her, pulling a weed out of her braid. "I thought I might've hurt you. You're so tiny and fragile."

"Fragile?" Her tone shifted to indignation, and she glared at him. "I am not *fragile.*"

"Okay," Eli conceded. She *was* fragile, but he wouldn't argue with her. He got to his feet and helped her up from the ground. "I should push you like you did me."

"You wouldn't dare."

"No, I suppose I wouldn't."

"Fragile," she muttered under her breath as she stomped off toward the next trap. Eli hid his smile.

The rest of the morning dragged on. They checked a few more traps, most of which were empty, but a few had a fair number of fish caught in them. It wasn't ideal, but it was better than nothing. They stopped for lunch at one of Eli's favorite places.

It was an overgrown playground of cement and metal near the beach. Ridiculously tall structures of wood and iron twisted and turned across the terrain. Hills reached toward the sky and plummeted back down to earth. They were completely unsafe to explore. Time had ruined their integrity, but they were a magnificent sight.

His favorite place of all, though, was in the middle. It was a circular platform with ceramic horses all the way around. Ali hopped up on one of the horses with ease and pulled out a sack lunch. He pulled himself up on the one next to her. It was covered in dust and gold flakes were peeling from the pole that connected it to the top of the structure.

He was in the middle of a big swig of water when Ali turned to him. "Eli, are you happy?"

That was a very loaded question. He wasn't sure he wanted to know where this was going. "What do you mean?"

"I mean, is this all you ever wanted? Living at Andus. Checking fish traps for a living. Being with me *till death do us part?*" She emphasized the last bit dramatically. It was flippant, and he choked up a little.

"I'm happy," he said cautiously. "Why do you ask?"

She looked lost in her own thoughts. This had to be what was bothering her this morning. She picked at her food, not eating a bite.

"Are you happy?" he asked her.

She scrunched her face, contemplating her answer. "I don't know. I thought I was. My mom just said some things this morning..." She shook her head. "I just feel like this is all I've ever known. How could I possibly know if it's enough?"

It felt like a punch to his chest. All the air escaped from his lungs. Eli didn't know if there was more out there for him, but if he ever had the desire to explore it, he would want Ali by his side. He picked at the peeling paint in front of him. "You don't know if I'm enough?"

She looked up at him urgently. "No, Eli, that's not what I meant at all. Of course, you're enough. You're more than enough."

"It's all right, Ali. You don't need to spare my feelings. We've always been honest with each other." He meant it sincerely. It was more important to him that she be honest. Suddenly, the thought of marrying her felt like torture. To be bound to a woman who didn't love him back. He would always wish his feelings were reciprocated. A dagger of pain pierced his heart.

"Eli—" She reached for his hand and gave him a pitiful look, which only irritated him more. Her eyes were like glass, pleading with him to understand.

He swallowed the lump in his throat and braced for whatever she was about to say.

But loud shouting in the distance interrupted them. She never finished her sentence. They both snapped their heads in the direction of the noise. They should've been alone out here. No one came this far out of town except hunters and gatherers. And no one ever wandered in this area. Something wasn't right.

Chapter Six

ELI

ELI SLID DOWN FROM his horse and helped Ali down as well. She slipped her hand in his and it felt like fire and ice at the same time. A burning passion on his end and cold indifference on hers. He gripped it anyway as she slid down, her feet hitting the hard floor with a *thump*.

"What do you think that was?" she whispered. She was tense. He could feel it.

He didn't answer and instead led her into the woods toward the voices that stood between them and Andus. They were careful not to make any noise or to be seen. He didn't know who could be in these woods, but it was important that he spotted them before they spotted him.

The voices died down, and it was silent for several minutes. Had the noise been from an animal or their brains playing tricks on them? There was no whisper of the voices they had heard back on the horses, let alone a shout.

As they worked their way through a thick spot of trees, he saw movement up ahead. He looked back at Ali and placed his index finger to his lips. She nodded and followed his gaze.

It was still unclear who they were, but there were three men in the clearing. Eli didn't recognize any of them, so they couldn't be from Andus.

"Who are they?" Ali whispered.

"I don't know."

He studied them for clues. They wore gear like soldiers but traveled lightly. They were armed, but no more than the average hunter. Perhaps they were scouts. Where had they come from though? And what were they looking for? He was torn between wanting to stay safely hidden and wanting to know more.

"Can you hear what they're saying?" Ali was right behind him, so close he could feel her breath on his ear. Her body huddled against him and shielded him from the wind.

"No. I think we need to get closer."

"Is that wise?"

"No, but if you want more information, I'll have to move in. You should stay here."

Her eyes grew wide. "Eli, you're not going anywhere without me."

He looked back at the group, weighing the options. One man muttered something inaudible, and they started to move west.

"Fine. We'll follow them at a distance. Stay close to me and keep quiet."

She nodded in acknowledgment and treaded softly behind him.

The group traveled quickly. It was like they were familiar with this terrain. They had to be from somewhere close, but neither Ali nor Eli knew much about outside civilizations. At a closer look, they all seemed to be very fit and strong. His gut told him they were dangerous. He didn't want to get into a confrontation with this group, and definitely not while Ali was with him. She shouldn't be here, but she was too stubborn to return home even if he told her to. She was brave, even to her own detriment.

They followed the group of men for at least twenty minutes. The temperature dropped even lower than it had been that morning and flurries of snow started to fall. It added an eeriness to the air around them. He couldn't recall the last time strangers had come upon their town. It must've been when he was a child. He vaguely remembered a mother and child seeking refuge after stumbling upon their town. They hadn't stayed long before continuing their travels. Andus hadn't been the sanctuary they'd hoped for.

"Eli, look." Ali grabbed his shoulder and pointed in the distance. It was hard to tell with the snow coming down harder, but it looked like there was billowing smoke a few miles away. It could only mean one thing—there were more than three outsiders in their midst.

"We should head back home." He was already worried about confronting three men. Now there was potentially a whole army they were at risk of stumbling upon. "This is too dangerous. We should get more men to come back to investigate. And more weapons, too."

The knife he carried would only be useful in close combat. He doubted Ali was armed at all.

"We can't do that." She looked at him with disbelief. "We need to know what they're up to. The snow is getting worse. It could be a full storm by the time we get back and ready to head out again. There's no time."

She was right. There was a good chance this storm would worsen in the next couple hours. "What's the plan, then? We can't just waltz in and ask who they are and what they're here for. We don't even know if they're looking for Andus. Maybe they're just passing through."

She considered the possibilities. "We'll get as close as possible. At least find out how many there are. If there are women and children with them, I'm less likely to believe they're dangerous. But if they look like soldiers..."

"If they look like soldiers, then what?"

They were both quiet. Andus wasn't equipped to handle an attack. Neither of them wanted to say it, but they'd be forced to evacuate their home. Eli prayed to god, if there was one, that this gathering was small and non-threatening. Small enough that their village could defend themselves.

It would be even better if they were simply passing through. They could laugh about it afterwards, how paranoid they had been.

"Come on." Ali led the way this time.

They were careful to keep their distance from the trio as they headed south, away from the shore and away from their familiar route. It didn't take long till they were on the outskirts of the campsite. They did their best to stay hidden under the cover of the trees, lying low on the ground. The snow did them a huge favor by reducing visibility. No one would spot them unless they knew where to look. They had gotten lucky.

"How many are there?" Eli asked her, squinting into the camp. By his count, there were at least twenty, maybe even thirty men.

"There's got to be at least fifty," she said with a look of defeat. "And I don't see any children. It's too hard to tell from here if there are any women." She took his hand and turned to him. "What are we going to do, Eli?"

"We have to go back and warn everyone. They need to get out as soon as possible. Maybe...maybe we're overreacting, but we can't take that chance. If they move on, then we can return home."

They both watched the group to see if they could make out any other helpful details. They were definitely armed. Many of the men had gathered in a circle. One who appeared to be their leader was yelling something indistinct. He had very regal air about him and he commanded the other men's attention. They moved into some kind of formation, like they were getting ready to move out.

"They're moving. They're headed straight toward Andus," Eli said in alarm. "Ali, we have to go."

He jumped up and grabbed her by the arms to pull her to her feet. His heart was racing, and Ali's shoulders were tense.

They moved as quickly as they could while maintaining distance, but the army had a lead on them. Unfortunately, they were positioned at the rear of the convoy. It was becoming impossible to cut them off or get ahead of them to reach Andus first. Ali remained quiet. He could tell she was scared and truthfully, so was he. The closer they got, the less opportunity they had to warn everyone.

"We're not going to make it. We have to make it, Eli. Our parents, our friends..." Ali turned to him with a look of frustration. A tear trickled down her frozen pink cheeks, and he reached up to wipe it away.

"This can't be happening." She closed her eyes and pursed her lips, preventing a breakdown.

"Stay strong, Ali," he said.

He took her hand and they started running as fast as they could, which was difficult since the snow had accumulated a few inches. He kept sinking and nearly tripping over his own feet, entrapped by the drifts. It was even more difficult for Ali who was a foot shorter than him. The worst of the snow drifts surpassed her shins.

A roar split the air and Eli's stomach dropped. It was a battle cry.

They were too late.

He couldn't see clearly through the trees yet, but it was evident from the noise that an invasion of some sort had begun. His heart crumbled before he even saw the damage.

When they could finally see through the trees, they both stood in shock.

The air burned orange with fire. It started small but grew quickly until the whole town was ablaze. He and Ali stopped to the side of the main entrance of town where the foreign army was bottlenecked. Screams sounded from inside Andus.

Eli was about to make a break for it when Ali grabbed him by the sleeve of his jacket.

"What are you doing?" she screamed at him.

"What does it look like I'm doing, Ali? Let me go. We can't leave them." He tried to jerk his arm free but she held fast. "Ali, let me go!"

"Eli! You're going to get yourself killed!"

He yanked free and moved out of reach when she scrambled to grab him again.

"Eli, please get back here," she pleaded with him from the edge of the tree line, her face crumpling when he didn't obey. Her hands balled into fists. Only the falling snow obscured him from enemy eyes. "Don't do this."

"I'm not letting Andus fall without a fight." He swallowed a lump in his throat. "You should stay here." There was a high likelihood he wouldn't return. No need for her to endanger herself, too.

He pulled out his knife. It wasn't much, but it was all he had. He might have the element of surprise, too. The invaders weren't expecting anyone to attack from outside of the town.

"Eli, please!"

She was right behind him. So much for staying put. "Just give me a minute," she said. She had one hand on her hip and the other on her head, trying to find a way out of this.

Eli waited expectantly, his patience wearing thin as the battle raged on.

Suddenly, her eyes lit up. "They're all at the main entrance. We can jump the fence near the farms and get in that way. Follow me. Hurry!"

They stomped through the thick snow, taking the long way around this time. Eli had never been to the farms before. It hadn't even occurred to him that there might be another entrance than the one they used every day. It was his fault they'd wasted precious time. Thankfully, Ali's mom had worked on the farms, so she was familiar with the route to get inside from when she'd tagged along as a child.

They made their way to the fence made of logs and mesh wiring. It was taller than he'd expected, almost taller than he was. He interlocked his hands and made a step for Ali. She took the boost and climbed the fence with ease. It was a long jump from the top, but she hopped down without fear. Her bravery was admirable, or maybe she was just too preoccupied to be scared. He placed one foot on a log and then another, pulling himself up over the top, and dropped beside her.

They ran along the rows of crops and through various sheds filled with pigs and chickens. The intruders hadn't gotten this far yet, and it was eerily quiet except for the livestock. Ali made a hard right turn into one of the sheds.

"What are you—"

Eli didn't have time to finish his sentence. It was immediately clear why she'd stopped. This shed was full of tools and equipment. There were some disturbingly long knives used for slaughter. She grabbed a couple and handed him two as well, one for each hand. These would work much better than his pocketknife.

"Ready?" he asked her as she pulled her loose hair back into a ponytail.

"Ready." The fear she'd displayed earlier in the forest was completely gone. This woman was brave and fierce. It amazed Eli how she could turn it on and off like a switch. Meanwhile, his hands were still shaking.

They treaded carefully, sneaking peeks around the corners of build-ings and rubble. It wasn't long before they ran into an intruder. He faced the opposite direction and didn't see them initially. Eli hesitated for one moment, realizing that he'd never killed anyone, but another scream in the distance sent rage surging through him. He lunged without another thought and sliced into the man's back. The man grunted and crumpled to the ground, blood oozing from his wound.

Eli's entire body shook from adrenaline. Ali brushed her hand down his arm, and he clenched his jaw. He didn't have time to process this. They were still under attack.

They rounded another corner, and this time there were two men. They sauntered out of an empty house, hands full of stolen belongings. Eli ran toward them without hesitation this time. He turned his brain off and let his instincts take the lead. He slashed the first one across the leg and plunged his knife into the man's stomach. But the second was quick to respond. He dropped his possessions and grabbed Eli by the throat from behind. Eli couldn't breathe. His throat was being squeezed so tightly. He yanked with all his might on the man's arm, but it was no use. He threw his hands back wildly, swinging to hit the man, but every swing was a miss. His lungs were on fire and blackness crept into the edges of his eyes. He was going to pass out.

It couldn't end like this. He couldn't give up after only killing two men. That wasn't enough of a stand. He needed to fight harder.

Through the muffled noise and scuffling, he heard Ali scream with rage. The chokehold was released and Eli inhaled sharply, oxygen filling his lungs. His hands instinctively went to his neck. It felt as though the man's hands were still there, even though they weren't. He turned around and looked down. The man was bleeding profusely from his neck and Ali stood over him in a state of shock, blood splattered across her front and covering her knife.

"Ali, it's okay. Ali, you're all right." Eli closed the gap between them, and she shivered in his arms. "You did what you had to do. You saved me."

Her chest expanded as she took deep, self-soothing breaths. He took her face in his hands, examining her. Her eyes were blank, like she was locked in a daydream. He brushed his thumbs across her cheeks and her eyelids fluttered closed. After a couple more deep breaths, she opened her eyes again and they had a new glisten to them.

"I'm sorry. I wasn't expecting...I don't know what I was expecting," she said slowly and softly.

"Are you going to be okay?"

"I have to be." She stood straighter; her determination had returned.

"Let's keep going then."

They left the bloody scene behind them and made their way toward a new one.

They were horrified by what they saw next. There were bodies everywhere. Some intruders, but most were people of Andus. People they knew. She saw Carter's body frozen where he'd been slain in a pool of his own blood and trampled snow. Terror and shock were frozen on the faces of the dead. The putrid smell of smoke and blood permeated the air.

Who would do something like this? Why would they do something like this? Andus had always been a peaceful community. It made no sense. His friends, his family, hadn't deserved this.

Ali brought one hand to her mouth. She looked extremely pale, like she might be sick. Eli had the urge to protect this woman at all costs. Had it been a mistake to bring her here? Was it too late to leave?

They weaved their way through the red-soaked battlefield and inched closer to the main entrance of Andus. The noise of combat grew louder.

They snaked between decrepit buildings until they found themselves at the main entrance. This was it.

He turned to Ali. This might be the last time he ever saw her. There was an unbearable weight on his chest as their eyes met. An urgent need. He wrapped one arm around her waist and pulled her in tight against his chest. With the other hand, he tilted her head back and leaned down to kiss her lips. They were cold, but as his lips pressed against hers, they warmed up. His tongue gently slipped out and her lips parted. For a moment, the world stood still as their tongues and limbs tangled.

Then he pulled away and planted one more kiss on her forehead. "I love you, Ali." His lips brushed her skin. He didn't need her to respond. "Let's do this."

She nodded solemnly.

Then they rounded another corner and charged into chaos.

Chapter Seven

ALI

THE SCENE TOOK ALI's breath away almost as much as Eli had just moments ago. She couldn't believe that just that morning she'd been worried that life as his wife wouldn't be enough. Now she might not have a life with Eli at all. That kiss had felt like a goodbye. Like she was about to lose him, and she wasn't ready to do that. Instead, she focused all her energy and attention on the war zone in front of her.

There was so much happening that it was hard to focus on any one thing. Before she could decide where to go first, an intruder rushed toward her, threw his arms around her waist and tackled her to the ground. The man was at least twice her size and it was too difficult to throw him off. She threw a quick punch to his nose, which knocked him back momentarily. She twisted and crawled along the ground, dirt piling beneath her fingernails. Then he grabbed a leg and pulled her back toward him. She screamed as her arms scraped on the rough surface and the tiny scratches started to bleed. Her attacker flipped her on her back so she faced the sky and gripped her wrists while she squirmed beneath him. His hold was too strong, and she couldn't free her hands.

"Save that one," another man with black hair and snow in his beard shouted over the commotion. "Put her with the rest." He went back to wrestling with his own opponent.

Her heart pounded in her chest. When her attacker reached down to bind her hands, she swung her head at his with all her might. It was the worst pain she'd ever felt, but it worked and knocked him off. Her head seared from the impact. She felt like her skull was being split in half and her vision blurred. He appeared to be in an equal amount of pain, so she scrambled to her feet as quickly as possible, hoping to make her way back to one of the abandoned buildings and regain her composure. She could hardly see past the stars in her eyes, and she stumbled clumsily and fell back to the ground. Her chin crashed into the dirt.

"Where do you think you're going?"

The man with the black hair was back, and he pulled her off the ground by the collar of her shirt. The fabric wrapped tightly around her neck, choking her. She dug her fingers into the fabric, trying to make enough room to breathe. Her legs struggled to find balance as he yanked her to her feet.

She swung wildly at him with her knife. Her vision started to clear, but it still hadn't returned to normal and she had all the grace of a newborn fawn. He ducked easily out of the way of her weapon and laughed. He *laughed.* This was the moment she truly felt defeated.

She gritted her teeth and jabbed again, hoping her knife would find its target, but missed once more.

"My, my, you are hopeless. Just a pretty girl with no brains or brawn. What a pity. I'm sure we'll find a place for you, love."

It disturbed her to know they didn't intend to kill her. She didn't want to know what sinister things they had planned instead.

She swung once more and this time he caught her by the wrist. He was right. She didn't have the strength to match him. He dug so tightly into her skin that she dropped her weapon and fell to her knees.

"Ali!" She turned her head to see Eli running in her direction. He sliced through one intruder and then another. He was a natural fighter, but it wouldn't be enough. He ran into two men and sank his knife into the one on his left side, allowing the one on the right to take advantage of his vulnerability. His assailant knocked him over the head with the hilt of a sword and Eli dropped to the ground, out cold, one hand still clinging to his knife. Blood trickled from his hairline down to his face.

"Eli!" Ali panicked. He was the one person she'd thought she could depend on, and now she was very much on her own. Her lip quivered and her heart shattered to see him lifeless like that.

The man knelt on his back and pushed him further into the snow and mud. Eli let out a soft groan and Ali let her tears fall freely.

"We can use him as well. Make sure you bind his hands tightly. Don't want that one on the loose." Ali's captor turned his attention back to her. "Why are you crying, love? We haven't even done anything yet." He mimicked his partner, raising the hilt of his sword and bringing it down with force. Everything went black.

When Ali regained consciousness, she was lying on a wet floor. It was dark and it took a moment for her eyes to adjust. She wasn't alone. There were several other people who were also bound and gagged. The cloth was so dry it made her mouth feel like a desert. Her head swiveled on her neck and she fought against the gag. She felt like she was choking. Like she was dying. She couldn't breathe.

She tried to sit up, but it was difficult with her hands bound behind her back. It took a few tries, but eventually she was successful and propped herself up against the wall. She searched for Eli but could only see women and children. Most of the women appeared to be young as well. Her stomach dropped. Her mom was nowhere to be found.

Though she tried to remain calm, panic bloomed in her chest again.

She knew they hadn't wanted to kill Eli, and he wasn't here. Maybe her mom was somewhere else too.

A little girl next to Ali met her eyes, petrified. Ali used her shoulder to nudge the gag in her mouth. It was tight, but it was loose enough to roll down and out of her mouth. She licked her lips to get rid of the cotton mouth feeling.

"Are you okay?" Ali asked the child.

She nodded tentatively, and tears welled in her eyes.

"Are your parents here?"

The tears fell, and she shook her head in dismay.

"Everything is going to be fine." Ali knew she shouldn't make promises she couldn't keep, but the young girl looked so terrified.

She contemplated how to get to her feet in this condition, but before she could make any moves, a door opened and blinding light poured in from outside. All she could see was a shadow of a figure, followed by several more. And then several more. They filled the room and grabbed whichever woman or child was closest, then led them back out the door. Ali watched in horror as the numbers dwindled.

The quiet was unnerving. It had been so loud before she'd been hit over the head. The silence spoke volumes. It said, "You've been defeated. We broke you."

Andus had fallen.

This wasn't the rushed pace of combat—it was the aftermath. They took their time.

A man grabbed her by the elbows and pulled her up. Ali shook out of his grip and spat in his face with fury.

He grumbled inaudible words and replaced her gag with unnecessary force, then had to practically drag her out the door. She certainly wouldn't make it easy for him. The world spun and she stumbled, but the man kept her upright.

He removed the rope binding her hands and repositioned them so her hands were in front. Then he tied them to a long string that connected her to other people from Andus.

Prisoners. Hostages. What would become of them?

"Move, move!" Loud shouting erupted from the front of the line and the rope jerked forward. Ali welcomed the numb feeling that took over. It was better than the devastation that threatened to drown her.

They made their way to the entrance of Andus. The clearing that had been used for celebration just a day ago was now unrecognizable. Smoke filled the air while the surrounding buildings burned, and lifeless bodies littered the ground.

She gasped in horror when she spotted one body splayed on the ground.

Jack.

She stopped in her tracks and sobbed uncontrollably. A rough hand on her back forced her to keep moving forward, leaving Eli's father behind. Her eyes filled with tears and her vision blurred again. This was too much to process.

Bodies were lined up in the street as if the people had been killed execution style and it left a bitter taste in her mouth. Each of their bodies lay in a row, guiding the prisoners to the entrance of Andus. Sasha's body was among the fallen.

The hostage procession caught up with the executioner, and Ali couldn't look away from the grisly scene. It became clear they had gathered anyone over a certain age to kill and anyone below was being taken. She and Eli had been spared because they could be used. These people...they could not. Their lives held no value to these intruders.

People she'd known her whole life kneeled on the ground, trembling with fear and waiting for their turn. Ali's ears filled with screaming and crying that intensified with each swing of the executioner's sword.

Her lips quivered in utter ruin when she finally caught sight of her mom. She kneeled in line with the rest. She was alive, but her time was dwindling. She caught Ali's eyes and her look of dread dissipated. "Stay strong, my beautiful child," she said. Her words were soft, but each one hit Ali like a blow to the chest. "I love you."

"I love you, too, Mom," Ali whispered. She tasted salty tears as they streamed down her face.

The executioner moved on to Anna, who sat upright with determination and tenacity. Ali couldn't watch. She swiftly turned her head when he brought his arm up to swing. She held her breath and knew when it was done by the gasps and cries that rang out.

The executioner didn't pause. Didn't give them time to grieve. He moved on to the next person with a swift swing of the sword. Another body fell. Another round of screams from the crowd.

Ali closed her eyes and let the rope tug her along. She was completely shattered, a ghost of herself. This life didn't feel like hers anymore.

This was the end of everything.

⚜

Snow fell for hours, covering the ground with several more inches before it finally stopped. It made traveling immensely difficult. Numbness started in Ali's toes and spread through the rest of her body. The rope cut into her wrists and rubbed them raw. She could already see irritated red marks forming.

Exhaustion made her steps slow and her eyes heavy. The sun was only just setting, but it felt like it had been days since she'd last slept. The trauma of the day's events wore on her body and mind.

The other women and children in line had to be feeling the same way. Their pace slowed multiple times throughout the evening, and each time, an invader shoved them forward aggressively. She witnessed a couple children stumble over their feet and fall to the ground. The invaders were quick to grab them and prop them back on their feet. They showed no mercy. They were ruthless.

They were a rather quiet group. No one had much energy left. No one wanted to rehash what had happened. Most of them were trapped in their own heads, wishing to wake up from this nightmare.

They traveled farther than Ali had ever been before, way beyond the route she'd shared with Eli. She didn't recognize any of the scenery any-more. They'd left behind familiar paths and trudged through overgrown forest. The trees encroached upon her, pressed in and suffocated her. The branches, although leafless, kept out most of the sunlight. Darkness loomed over them as if warning of things to come.

The leaders of the pack came to a halt as night fell. Their final des-tination would apparently be a multi-day trek and this was where they would stop for the night. Ali and the other prisoners huddled together, their shared body warmth the only relief they got from the cold air. The older women attempted to shield the kids by circling around them. Ali hadn't spotted Eli yet, although her gut told her he was still alive.

Her eyelids drooped as she sank into the nook of a tree. She didn't trust this group of soldiers enough to let her guard down, but she doubted they could do much worse to her. After a few minutes of sitting, drowsi-ness took over and she could no longer fight it. She hadn't realized how tense her muscles were until they relaxed between the other captives.

Closing her eyes, she surrendered to exhaustion. If only she could wake up and find this was all a dream.

But it wasn't. It was a nightmare, and it was only just beginning.

The sun hadn't even risen when people stirred. A couple men came around to wake the prisoners and hand them food and water. So much had happened yesterday that she hadn't realized until this moment just how hungry she was. She hadn't eaten in almost a full day. She took a bread roll from a man who looked even younger than herself. Was he here by choice, or had he been forced to join this invasion force?

He looked too young to be corrupted like this. Had he killed people? Did it terrorize him the way it did her? She tried not to think of the people she had murdered the day before. It had been self-defense, and she would do it again if she had to.

All her muscles ached and even eating the bread was a chore. Her jaw was clenched and her head was pounding. She took small sips of water, afraid that if she drank too much, she might vomit.

They didn't give her much time before everyone was standing and prepared to move out. She stretched to loosen up her tense muscles, but it was no use. Her legs were like solid logs, and it took a strenuous effort to move them forward. The cold air assaulted her skin as the group spread out along the rope. She desperately hoped that today's hike would be shorter than the day before.

They trekked through the woods, the weeds thick, and brambles sliced at her legs. The trees moaned in the wind, singing a solemn song. Mourning that which had been lost. It was the only sound that accompanied their hike.

After what felt like hours, she spotted the black-haired man with the beard again and made eye contact. Ali had never hated anyone in her life, but she despised him. She wanted to claw his eyes out like a feral beast.

He smirked and fell back to walk next to her. "So glad to see you again, love. Are you enjoying the walk?"

He chuckled, amused with himself, but Ali found him entirely unfunny. She refused to acknowledge him. His voice left a bitter taste in her mouth.

"What's your name?"

More silence.

He bit his lip and ran his eyes over her. "I'll just call you 'love,' then. I'm General Colin, but you can also call me 'love' if you'd like."

He leaned in closer and the stench of sweat and blood made her want to vomit. It was repulsive.

"Are you pouting, sweetheart? Mad we sent your little shit hole up in flames?"

His smile made her skin crawl. Again, she did not respond.

"Maybe you're just not the talkative kind, hmm?"

He brushed his fingers across her cheek, and she cringed. His touch boiled her blood.

"Oh, we are going to have fun with this one," he said as he strolled away. Ali didn't like the way he said that at all.

They stopped again around mid-day. They were served the same food they'd eaten for breakfast, a bread roll and some water. Ali supposed she should be grateful they were feeding them at all. She kept hanging on to the fact that they meant to keep the survivors alive. It was the only thing that calmed her nerves. As long as she was alive, then there was hope. If she was alive, then she could fight. She could escape. She could dream. Hope was all she had right now.

Ali found herself next to a line of men. It was the first group of men she'd seen since yesterday and she searched frantically for Eli. It didn't take long to spot him since he towered over most of the other young men and boys. She moved closer to him and pulled her fellow captives along with her.

"Sorry," she muttered as their rope tightened. "Eli!"

He looked up, and she'd never seen him look so dreadful. His face was bruised and swollen almost beyond recognition and his light brown hair was soaked in blood.

"Ali." His voice was hoarse, and she wished she could cradle him and tell him everything would be all right.

"They killed them. They killed them all. I couldn't stop it."

His eyes were dark, and she could see the dismal scenes replaying over and over in his mind.

"You did everything you could. You can't possibly take the blame for this. We were doomed from the start. There were too many of them." She tried to reassure him, but she wasn't sure it did any good.

"I...I could've done more. If we had gotten there sooner...if—" He was lost in thought. "My dad is gone, Ali." Tears carved a path down his dirt covered face and his jaw clenched.

"I know."

He looked up with furrowed brows.

"I saw him. My mom is gone too." Her voice broke when she recalled her mom kneeling on the ground, waiting for the strike of a sword. "You still have me, though. I need you just as much as you need me. We'll get through this together."

"Will we?" He hung his head, and the silence looming over them was suffocating.

Truthfully? She wasn't sure, but it felt better to hold on to hope than to give up.

They sat in uncomfortable stillness a little while longer, both feeling too weighed down to speak. People shifted around them and rose to their feet. She dreaded whatever would come next. Oh, how she wished she could just stay here with Eli and mourn all that they'd lost in such a short time. They needed time to grieve.

Their journey in the afternoon was just as tedious as the first half of the day. This area had no trails, so much of the path was swampy and overrun with thick weeds and bushes. They had to pass through multiple pools of freezing water. Ali tried not to think about the snakes or other critters that lurked beneath the water and tall grass.

It was early evening when their path turned to crumbling asphalt. Within minutes, their destination came into view. Her jaw dropped when she spotted the stone walls over the tops of trees. The walls must have been two or three stories high. It was a mighty fortress covered in vines. She'd never seen anything like it. She couldn't see what lay within those walls, but she knew she was about to find out.

"Stop here." The captors paused at the general's command and gathered fabric out of backpacks. A chill ran up her spine when she realized what was happening: they were blindfolding them. Her heart raced, and she fidgeted with fear.

One of the men slipped a black bag over her head. It smelled like sweat and must and it immediately became hard to breathe. Her hands were pulled by the rope that bound them, and she followed blindly. Each step was more difficult and more terrifying than the one before. There was no way to navigate her surroundings while her hands were tied. Tree branches sliced at the skin on her arms and caught on her pants.

"Watch your step," someone said, voice muffled through the blindfold.

Ali did her best to feel out the steps with her foot before transferring her weight with each step.

The ground felt slick, like wet stones. Based on the echoing of voices, she thought they must be in a tunnel. She felt claustrophobic even though she couldn't see anything. The opening wasn't very large at all.

At one point, the person in front of her stumbled and she collapsed on top of them. The person behind her helped her up as they both fumbled around in the dark.

Eventually, they reached a second set of stairs heading back up and she could feel cold air hitting her skin again. The breeze blew around her and that feeling of being trapped in a small space disappeared. Her shoulders relaxed just a little.

Voices rang out. Lots of them. The buzzing of conversation made her feel like she was home again, except she knew this wasn't home. Her home was gone forever. This was her hell.

The bag over her face was unceremoniously removed, and the daylight blinded her.

"Welcome to Rysburg."

Chapter Eight

ELI

Someone yanked the cover off Eli's head. Agitation flared inside him. His emotions were all over the place. One minute he felt sad and hopeless, and the image of his dad's lifeless body replayed in his mind. The next minute he was on fire and wanted to destroy everything in his reach even if it killed him too. He was spiraling.

"Welcome to Rysburg."

Eli had never heard of it, but he knew without a doubt that it was a hellscape full of demons. Monsters without souls.

He scanned his surroundings, but it didn't seem like hell. They were in the middle of a street with vendor carts and shops along the sides. The air was filled with laughter and the smell of baked goods. It looked like a normal village with normal people. Mothers with their children and young couples smiled as they went about their day. There were men doing business, exchanging coins for supplies. People chatted merrily as if twenty people bound in ropes and soaked in blood hadn't shown at their doorstep. They were oblivious.

Absolute monsters. They knew the destruction and harm they had caused, and they didn't even care. Eli held each and every one of them responsible, from the youngest baby in his mother's arms to the oldest walking around with a cane. They were all guilty.

Eli and the others were led through the streets, and most people didn't even glance their way. The few who did, immediately averted their eyes when Eli looked at them. If these people didn't acknowledge the prisoners, then they wouldn't have to admit they were complicit.

Eli was keenly aware that their buildings were much more pristine than the ones at Andus. This wasn't a decimated town that had been patched together to be *good enough.* This town oozed wealth and stability. Where Andus had piles of rubble and dust covered streets, Rysburg had freshly painted doors and sparkling windows. The people weren't wearing rags with holes in them. They wore clean pants and dresses. They wore sturdy coats that protected them from the cold and boots that actually kept the damp out. How many towns had they ruined in their pursuit of finer things?

They walked under an archway and through a large wooden door into a cold and sterile holding room. It was empty except for the prisoners who lined up against the bare walls. His eyes met Ali's, and she gave him an encouraging nod in solitude.

Once the door to the outside had slammed shut, they shuffled through a secondary door, a few at a time. They started with the men. Every half an hour, they took a few more while the rest of the captives waited anxiously to find out their fate.

At last, it was Eli's turn to go through the door. A guard released the rope from his wrists, and his shoulders sagged with relief. He hadn't realized just how tight the ropes were until now. Bruises were already vibrant on his skin. He rubbed his wrists, massaging the throbbing flesh.

He gave the guard a menacing look. For a moment he considered fighting him, tearing into him like a maniac, but he'd never make it out alive. The guard led him and two others through the door and pointed to a rack of plastic bins in the corner.

"Strip," he said in a bored tone. He acted like this was a frequent occurrence. "Toss your dirty clothes in a bin."

The two other boys in the room looked around nervously, not sure what to do. They were so young, and Eli could see the fear in their eyes.

He was determined to set a brave example for them. Grabbing the back of his shirt, he yanked it over his head, making it a point to glare at the guard as he tossed it into the bin. He wanted to gouge the man's beady eyes out.

The strings on his shoes were nearly frozen and took a moment to untangle. Then his shoes landed in the bin with a loud *thunk*. He unzipped his pants, still glaring at the guard.

He couldn't physically hurt the man, so he hurled mental insults at him instead, picturing all the ways he'd like to attack the man.

His pants dropped to the ground, and he bent over to grab them. Lastly, he stepped out of his underwear, roughly tossing them into the bin. If this asshole thought he would be ashamed or humiliated, he was entirely wrong. Eli wouldn't let him have that satisfaction. He stood tall and proud.

The two boys followed his lead and did their best to mimic his courage.

"Through the door." The guard pointed to yet another door. Eli made his way across the room and resisted the urge to bash the guard's head against the wall. Fury swelled, threatening to burst out of him if he didn't get it under control.

Somehow, the next room was even more sterile than the others. The floor was grated and wet. After the three of them were inside, the door closed with an ominous *bang*. It sent vibrations through Eli's chest and against his ribs. He caught movement in the corner of his eye and another guard stepped out from the shadows with a hose in hand.

"Stand still. It's going to be cold."

Eli stood tall, chest puffed out. The arctic water pierced his skin like a thousand icy needles. He stood his ground even though the injuries he had sustained in the attack screamed in protest. The guard wasn't careful about his aim, either. Eli just barely squeezed his eyes shut before water sprayed his face. The pressure was so immense he had to raise his hands to protect his eyes and wipe the water from his mouth and nose.

"Hands down."

The guard's voice was as cold as the water coming from the hose. His callousness infuriated Eli, but he lowered his arms back to his sides and clenched his fists.

The water shut off for a moment. "Turn around."

They all obeyed his commands without protest. The water blasted across his skin again, and his muscles tensed involuntarily. At least when he faced away, he could hide his grimace of pain as the water ran over his wounds. He dropped his head and focused on the freezing, dirty water draining through the floor.

This town was the epitome of luxury. There was no way they couldn't figure out how to make warm water run through that hose. No, this was just another way to torment their captives. A mind game built to break them.

Eli refused to break.

When the guard was satisfied with their cleanliness, he yelled at them to hold their arms out. Eli winced as they clasped a thin metal band on each of his wrists. It was like a bracelet, but one that he could not take off and one that probably signified he belonged to Rysbug. The guard distributed clean underwear and nudged them through another door, where they were guided down a staircase and through a maze of holding cells, most of them empty. There were small windows no more than a foot wide and they were few and far between. It was cold, dark, and damp down here.

One by one, they each got their own individual cell. Eli shivered at the thought that these cells may have been full at one point. How many villages had they decimated before Andus? Would he be here long enough to see them full again?

The guard forced Eli into his own cell. It was small. There was a chamber pot and sink in one corner and a small cot on the other side with fresh clothes and shoes. Not a single thing to help pass the time. They spaced the prisoners out far enough with empty cells between so they couldn't even talk to each other. Another form of torture, to have them sit here, in the dark with nothing to do. It was enough to make someone go crazy.

Eli grabbed the black sweatpants and gray T-shirt and threw them on. His hair was still dripping wet, and they hadn't bothered to give him a sweatshirt. He curled up on the cot that was too short for his height and pulled the blanket up over him. It was incredibly thin as well. His body ached and shivered while he did his best to warm up and relax. It would've been nearly impossible, except he was completely drained of energy from the past couple days.

He tossed and turned, his anger fueling him and keeping him awake and alert. He heard other prisoners cry every once in a while, but his own tears never came. Instead, he focused on his fury.

Chapter Nine

ALI

THE LIGHT IN THE room blinded Ali and made her head throb again. She felt nauseous from worrying, and it took what little energy she had left to keep from gagging.

She wasn't sure how long she'd been waiting in this room. It felt like it had been hours, but she thought perhaps her mind was misconstruing time. The minutes passed slowly in this eternal hell.

They started with the men. They took them through a door from which they never returned. She dreaded the mystery hidden beyond that door. Ali had always been more afraid of the unknown than anything else. It made her feel powerless, like she didn't have time to prepare for what lay ahead.

She looked around at the scared faces. Some were vaguely familiar and others she knew well. Every single one of them looked as depressed as she felt. *Hopeless.* She had lost her mom and she could almost guarantee that everyone in this room had lost someone they loved, too—a parent or grandparent or maybe even a sibling. All the happiness had been stripped from the atmosphere. The light in their eyes had been extinguished.

Tears threatened to fill her eyes again at the memory of everything they'd lost. She pressed her hands into her stomach, squeezing tightly against the pain in her core. She dug her nails into the skin of her palms, distracting her and preventing her tears from spilling over like a waterfall.

After the men were gone, they took the women in groups of three or four. She didn't know it was possible for the room to feel even smaller than it originally did, but as their numbers dwindled, the walls pressed inwards, suffocating her.

Finally, it was her turn.

A guard cut the ropes from her hands and led her into another room.

"Remove your clothes and toss them in the bins," he said with a sinister grin. He was enjoying this too much.

Her stomach flipped again, and she swallowed hard. The other women in the room looked around nervously at each other, fear growing in their eyes. No one wanted to make the first move.

The guard stepped forward and grabbed one of them by the chin, guiding it up so their eyes met. "Did I stutter? Take. Off. Your. Clothes." He released her face aggressively, pushing her back a few steps. She stifled a cry. "Before I do it for you."

Ali knew he would. He would hold her down, rip off her clothes, and leave her feeling bare and empty. The gleam in his eyes said he would enjoy it, too.

Ali reached down to untie her shoes. Her fingers were shaking so badly, partially from the cold and partially from distress. She fumbled with the strings that were laced tightly on her boots and finally managed to undo the knot.

The man stomped her way and stopped in front of her. The sound of his heavy boots was a threat in their own right.

She slowly looked up and met his dark eyes, and he let out a dramatic sigh. He rubbed his brow and said, "I expected more from this group. I'm not sure what use the scouts thought we'd get out of you when you can't even untie your shoes."

He bent down until his face was so close she could feel his breath. His pupils were a black abyss, endless and empty. Then he swiftly put one hand behind her knee and yanked her leg out from underneath her. Ali landed on her tailbone, and pain shot up her spine. He squeezed her ankle, grabbed her boot, and pulled it off in one callous motion, then repeated it on the other side.

He tossed her boots in the plastic bin and turned back to face her. "Faster, faster." He made a circular motion with his hands, hurrying them along. "We don't have all day."

Ali was motivated to keep his hands far away from her, so she unzipped her jacket and shook it off her shoulders. She lifted her shirt over her head and avoided making eye contact. Her jeans were damp from snow and sweat, but she wriggled them off her body, trembling in the cold air.

She inhaled deeply and unsnapped her bra, tossed it into the bin and slid her underwear and socks off in one quick swoop. She felt his eyes crawl over her and it gave her goosebumps. Heat rose to her face, and she stared at her toes.

From the corner of her eye, she caught the motion of the other women, but she gave them their privacy, even if he wouldn't. She held her hands together to keep them from shaking and blocked what bits of her body she could.

After everyone was undressed, they were herded through another door.

"How many more are there?" the next guard asked in a deep voice. He was younger than the first guard, maybe a couple years older than Ali, but he spoke to him like an equal.

"Why? Got somewhere to be?"

The new guard grinned. "Yes, someone is waiting on me. She's got a nice body and a feisty bite. And when I grab her and put her to my lips," he licked his bottom lip and raised his brows, "she makes my head spin." He laughed, and it was the first warmth Ali had felt in days. She envied his ability to feel happiness.

The first guard slapped his shoulder in amusement. "It doesn't matter how much you love the bottle, Nik. She'll never love you back." He turned and headed back. "Just a few more groups to go. When we're done here, I'll meet you at the bar. Friends don't let friends drink alone."

"Friend is a bold word," Nik yelled back at him. He grabbed a hose and focused his attention back on the women. "Spread out. Uncross your arms."

He didn't gawk at their bodies the way the last guard had. Instead, he looked bored as he sprayed them down from head to toe. The water was freezing cold, and her nipples hardened but she kept her arms pressed to her sides. This was the most dehumanizing experience she'd ever endured.

She distracted herself by watching the dirty water run down her legs. She hadn't realized how much blood and filth had accumulated during their trek. As much as the water stung, she was glad to be clean.

The guard, Nik, moved closer and took his time rinsing each of the women. As he moved toward Ali, he aimed the water at her shoulders and slowly moved the hose down. She'd been naked in front of Eli before, but she had never felt this exposed. The blast of the water stung against her newly tattooed skin. He took a suspicious amount of time over her breasts and then her midsection. She looked up when he got to her groin.

To her surprise, he wasn't looking at her bare body. He was staring at her face.

Her breath caught and her heart skipped a beat. His eyes were a steely blue that contrasted his disheveled dark brown hair and the stubble covering his jaw. Moisture clung to his bangs and cheeks. His features were strikingly sharp, like a cold, hard, impenetrable fortress. He was an unwavering mountain, and he had all the confidence she lacked in this moment.

She'd never seen a man so stunning before, except for in those old photo albums. No one, man or woman, in Andus had come close to his level of attractiveness. A shame that his heart didn't match his exterior, because there was no doubt he was a monster like those that had attacked her home.

His gaze was penetrating. So much so that she might've been more comfortable if he *had* been gawking at her body and not her soul.

"Turn around." His voice was deep and, for lack of a better word, soothing. His words calmed her beating heart despite the mouth that spoke them. They were slow and deliberate, and for some reason, she wanted to hear more of them.

She turned, obeying his command. He grumbled something inaudible and pushed her hair over her shoulder. Her chills had nothing to do with the temperature. She was hyperaware of his fingertips grazing her nape.

The water trailed over her back and down her body while she struggled to breathe. For a moment, she felt lightheaded. When he moved to the woman on Ali's right, she carefully snuck a look at his profile.

The fringe of his hair swung softly in front of his eyes. The sleeves of his shirt were rolled up to his elbows, and she admired the muscle and veins protruding on his forearms. His hands were rough and calloused. She guessed that this likely wasn't his main job in Rysburg. He probably did something else with his hands to have developed that rugged exterior.

Or perhaps his rough hands were the result of a hobby? He was tall. Not quite as tall as Eli, but maybe just an inch or two shorter. He also wasn't as lanky as Eli. His shoulders were broad and strong.

He glanced her way and caught her staring. She should've been terrified, and part of her was, but she also couldn't look away. He was enchanting.

He clenched his jaw and looked away, moving on to the final woman. She squeezed her fists and realized that her hands were clammy. She was sweating even though the room was frigid.

Nik finished and went to hang the hose back on the wall. His arms weren't the only muscular part of his body. She stared at his backside as he walked away, impure thoughts trickling into her mind. She shook her head to rid them. Now wasn't the time for intrusive thoughts. It made no sense to be thinking about him like this. She did her best to calm her conflicting feelings.

It was only because she'd never seen a man so handsome. At least not in real life. That was the only reason she was having a hard time keeping her eyes off of him.

"Hold out your hands." The women did as he said, and he placed a metal band on each of their wrists. They were cold and rubbed against her already irritated skin. She itched to take them off the moment they touched her.

Shifting nervously on her feet, she waited while he dug into a bin of freshly washed underwear, his calloused fingers brushing her hand as he passed them to her.

He opened the door on the opposite side of the room and waved them through. As she passed him, she tried not to notice his muscular arms leaning against the door frame. Her skin heated and she desperately hoped he wasn't ogling her body the way she was his.

Her eyes adjusted to the difference in lighting. There were several cells in front of them and the guard led them down a hall to the left, where a maze of cells spread out. He brought each of the other two women to their cells and took Ali to one in a far corner. She couldn't retrace her steps if she tried. It must be by design that they didn't want them to know the way out.

Clothing was laid out on a small cot, and she wasted no time grabbing it to cover up. The thin gray T-shirt and black sweatpants swallowed her small frame but she was grateful to have clean clothes again.

A small window at the top of the cell revealed that daylight was nearly gone. She'd survived another day, and she would continue to do so.

Day by day, she would keep going. She would keep fighting.

She glanced around her cell. There was nothing else to do, so she lay down on the cot. It wasn't much worse than her bed back home, but not as comfy as Eli's. Stiff, but it wouldn't stop her from sleeping. No, what would stop her were the thoughts racing through her head. Replaying the events of the past forty-eight hours. That uneasy conversation with her mom. A normal day with Eli. Andus under attack. Her mom being murdered. The long trek to Rysburg. A brutal intake process.

And steely blue eyes that demanded her attention.

Chapter Ten

NIK

THE SUN SET BY the time Nik was finished with his duties. He hadn't expected it to take so long, but they captured more people than the scouts had estimated. He and the other guard rounded up the plastic bins and took them to be sorted. Judging by the state of these prisoners, there wasn't much that would be salvaged off their backs.

They had taken in roughly fifteen or twenty prisoners. He was surprised by how little they fought back. It was like all the fight had been sucked out of them before they'd arrived, which was probably for the best. It would've been completely useless for them to try to fight. It was always harder to watch the ones who still had fight left in them. They eventually broke, but it was always a painful journey.

A lot of them looked too young to fight, but there were a few grown adults in the mix. Their labor would be useful this winter. Rysburg was still recovering from a nasty virus several months prior. It had wiped out a large percent of the workforce before they had gotten it under control.

Nik couldn't help but size up each of them that had come through. He mentally sorted them into the jobs for which they'd be best suited. The youngest ones would likely weave or sew, possibly help in the daycare. Safer jobs that took little muscle or endurance. The older ones would help in the greenhouses or on the farms. Eventually, if they assimilated, the sturdy men could help with scouting missions, hunting, and war efforts. But they'd have to earn that trust first.

In all his years working in the prison, he'd seen *very* few people assimilate. Not that it was a surprise. Demolishing villages created animosity. Nobody truly expected them to join Rysburg's community. They would simply use the prisoners for their labor until old age or disease claimed them.

Nik's breath was visible in the frigid air. He was almost to the door of the pub when he heard footsteps running up behind him. Before he could turn around, a pair of hands landed on his shoulders, shaking him gleefully.

"Just the man I was hoping to see."

"Hello, Marcus." Nik was a little less enthusiastic. Marcus wasn't necessarily a friend. They had worked together for many years. Nik didn't have many friends, though, so he tolerated the man's company, no matter how grating he could be. "Glad you could make it."

"I wouldn't miss it! Spending time with my pal." He patted Nik's back in emphasis. "Where else would I be?"

Nik narrowed his eyes with a little more annoyance than he meant to. "At home with your wife, maybe? I'm no expert in relationships, but I think I'd want to spend more time with my new wife if I were in your position."

Nik knew what it was like to go home to an empty house and a cold bed. He wouldn't take it for granted if he ever found someone to hold and cherish.

Marcus gave him a serious look. "Nik, do you want to spend time with my wife?" He laughed when Nik's jaw dropped. Not *at all* the point he'd been trying to make. "Man, you are tense tonight. Let's get you a drink."

They stepped into the Spotted Salamander, the lone pub in the town of Rysburg. It was primarily visited by lowlifes and young men. It was perfect for Nik. A bit crowded tonight, but that was normal for the end of the week.

Marcus spotted two open stools at the dark wooden counter and squeezed through the crowd while Nik followed. The pub was full of guards, likely celebrating their victory. Nik had heard there were a few losses, but overall the mission had been a success.

One of the men called out to him, "Nik! Where've you been? We missed you out there!"

Nik shrugged his shoulders. "Not cleared yet for battle. Doc's orders."

Nik was also recovering from the virus that had swept their town. One of the scariest times of his life, and that was saying something since he'd been through a lot of missions and seen a lot of death. It had knocked him on his ass, but he had miraculously pulled through with some rest. The doctor had been monitoring his breathing before he cleared him to go on missions again. It was frustrating for him to stay back while his comrades risked their lives. He was forced to watch over the newcomers instead. Day shifts spent monitoring the greenhouse workers and night shifts were for walking the halls of the prison.

"Ahh, what a pussy." The soldier rolled his eyes and turned back to his table.

Nik's lip curved in a snarl and he moved to grab the man from his chair, looking for a fight.

Before he could get too far, Marcus threw out his arm to stop him.

"As much as I'd love to see you kick his ass, I came here for a drink, which I won't be able to enjoy if you get us thrown out. Don't listen to him. He hid in the back the whole time. I'm pretty sure I saw him rub his sword in some blood just so he could pretend he contributed. Man is useless in battle and has no room to speak."

The fire in Nik's eyes simmered slightly. It was hard being excluded from such an important mission, but Marcus had a point. Nik had contributed far more than this guy ever would. He was the first to volunteer for every mission, and he gave his heart and soul to build and protect this town. He had more kills to his name than this man could count.

"Yeah, I guess you're right." Nik was confident he'd get another shot to throw a punch. The Spotted Salamander often got out of control on the weekends. Bar fights were more common than not.

They settled into their seats, and Marcus raised a hand to wave at the bartender. "We'll take two ales, please." When the bartender left to grab two glasses, Marcus turned back to Nik. "Of course, I'm right. I've literally never been wrong."

Arrogant son of a bitch.

The bartender came back with their drinks and waited for payment.

"You're getting this, right?" Marcus asked with a wink. "It's the least you could do for those of us who had to work hard this week."

Nik huffed and pulled some coins from his pocket. "Yeah, I've got it." Then he cursed him under his breath.

Marcus paused, about to take a sip. "What was that?"

"Nothing." Nik hid a smirk behind his glass.

A few drinks later and Marcus was slurring his words while Nik's head spun.

"So...what did you think about the newcomers?" Marcus nudged Nik in the side with his elbow.

"What do you mean?"

"You know...did you check any of the women out? God, I love my job." He chuckled, and Nik was repulsed.

"Some of those were literal child—"

"Not those! God, Nik. I might be a pervert, but I'm not a sick fuck. No, the older ones. Don't tell me you didn't take a mental picture of Blondie."

He lowered his mug from his lips. "No. What the fuck is wrong with you?"

Marcus's face flushed. "What the fuck is wrong with *me?* What the fuck is wrong with *you?* You can't tell me a bunch of naked ladies were in front of you and you didn't take notice of any of them."

"Yes, I can." Nik stood, feeling a bit lightheaded. He'd had enough to drink and enough of Marcus's chitchat.

"Aw, come on, Nik."

Nik walked through the crowded pub and to the door before Marcus could stop him. The cool air on his cheeks was refreshing after sitting in the stuffy room for so long. His balance was off as he tried to walk home and when he reached into his pocket, he realized he'd made an unfortunate mistake. He had left his key at the office in the prison.

Shit.

He took a deep breath and tried to settle his queasy stomach. He hadn't intended to drink so much, but the only thing waiting for him at home was a cold, dark, lonely bedroom. The ale had sounded so much more enticing and the bartender had kept them coming. The ground spun, but he did his best to pick one spot and focus. He was tired and drunk and all he wanted to do now was go home and pass out. This was *super* inconvenient for him.

Nik inhaled one more deep breath and then shuffled toward the prison. The streets were quiet tonight. It was cold and most respectable folks were safe and warm at home. Only the scoundrels like Nik stayed out this late.

He was thankful that he didn't pass anyone on the way to the prison. He had no desire to chat after Marcus had left him in such a foul mood. In fact, he only had to interact with one person.

Tonight was Sam's shift to watch the prisoners. When Nik stumbled in through the door of the office, Sam jumped out of his seat in alarm and dropped a tattered book.

"Holy shit, Nik. You scared me half to death. I thought you were a prisoner that somehow escaped." His face was white, like he'd seen a ghost. "I would've either died in an ambush or died for failure to control the prison." He sank back in his chair and dragged his hands along his face.

"Sorry, man. Left my house key here by accident." Nik slurred his words.

Sam watched with a raised brow as he stumbled around like a toddler learning how to walk. The desk was full of clutter, and he had to shift a few things before he spotted them. "Got 'em."

He started toward the door and a noise that sounded like a woman's screaming reached the office. He paused in his tracks. "What was that?"

Sam didn't even look at him. He bent down to grab his book. "Hmm? Oh, it's one of the prisoners, I think. Nightmares or something. They were all still in their cells when I checked a while ago." His dark eyes peeked over the top of his book. "No point in investigating every squeak."

"Do you mind if I—" Nik pointed his thumb over his shoulder in the direction of the cells.

He waited patiently for Sam's approval. He was clearly drunk and unsteady on his feet. Sam had every reason to deny him, but without any keys to the cells he was completely harmless.

"Knock yourself out, man." Sam gestured toward the darkened halls.

Nik wandered the prison, following the panicked shouts as they got louder and louder. It was dark except for the beams of moonlight coming through the small windows, but he'd walked the halls many times and was familiar with the layout. At last, he came to the cell in the far corner. The woman inside was thrashing about in her sleep. Nik remembered her. A small, fragile-looking thing with long blonde hair and hypnotizing brown eyes.

He had tried his best to be respectful of the women in the showers, but he was still a man, after all. He'd be lying if he said he hadn't glimpsed her body; thin, but soft and enticing. Something about the way the water had glistened on her skin had made him salivate. He'd looked away before he had gotten a boner from her naked body. There was no way one of these pathetic prisoners could have that power over him.

He watched her for a few moments. Her tiny hands gripped the blanket as sweat appeared on her brow. Between the shouting and whimpering, her breathing was heavy and strained.

He gripped the bars of the cell door and leaned forward as much as he could. "Hey."

She didn't hear.

"Hey!" he yelled a little bit louder, rattling the bars.

Her eyes popped open, and she gasped. Then she blinked and slowly looked around, as if remembering where she was. Nik watched her grip on the blanket relax as reality sank in. She looked over at him, confused by his presence. She looked pitiful to Nik. Pitiful, but beautiful.

"You were having a nightmare."

"Oh." It was barely more than a whisper. She clutched at her throat. "Can I have some water?"

"No." He was too drunk to stumble to the kitchen and even if he wanted to, it was probably locked.

She raised her brow, clearly not expecting that response. She stood and had to grab her sweatpants to keep them from falling off of her hips. She held on tight and inched closer to the door and closer to Nik. He removed his hands from the bars and stepped back. It wasn't necessary. It wasn't like this tiny woman could hurt him, but he'd rather not be within her reach.

She was close enough that he could make out the features on her face. Her big eyes, pupils dilated in the dark. Her pale, flawless skin and fluffy red lips. "What are you doing here?"

He was mesmerized by the way her lips moved in his drunken stupor.

He actually had no idea what he was doing here. Standing in front of her now, he felt somewhat foolish. He had only come here for a key and now he was staring at a prisoner's lips. His brain was melting, turning him into a bumbling idiot, and she was staring at him with such poise. He wasn't accustomed to this shift in power dynamics.

He needed to leave, and quickly, before he said or did something stupid. He quickly scanned the rest of her body, his eyes catching on her lower half.

"Those pants look completely ridiculous."

Too late. He had said something stupid.

Her eyes flickered in surprise as he turned to go, and he was pretty sure he saw a soft smile cross her face. Meanwhile, his cheeks burned red.

He practically *ran* from the prison, from Blondie. His surroundings were nothing more than a blur. All he saw was her face. Her eyes. Her lips.

He would spend the rest of the evening trying to forget about those lips.

Chapter Eleven

ALI

Ali woke up sweating, tangled up in the thin blanket she'd been provided. It was the worst night of sleep in her entire life. It was impossible for her to distinguish between what was real and what was a dream. Like the guard who had come to her cell in the middle of the night. Had *that* been real?

As she rolled over in bed, she was met with a blinding light beaming in from the high window in her cell. She squinted her eyes to guard against the harsh sunlight. She had no sense of time in this place. Was it morning? Afternoon?

She tensed when she spotted a tray of food and water at the door. Someone had been to her cell while she was sleeping. The thought of someone sneaking in while she lay unconscious unnerved her.

Her toes turned painfully cold when they touched the floor. She could've sworn she had some socks on, but she must've kicked them off in the night while twisting and turning. She threw back the blanket, searching the bed for her missing socks before slipping them on and approaching the tray.

Cold vegetable soup. That's what they had left her to eat. Or maybe it had been warm at one point and she had just slept too long. She grabbed the tray to take it back to bed when she noticed something else had been left.

She picked up the monochrome bundle of cloth and let it unfold. Another pair of sweatpants, at least four sizes smaller than the ones she currently had on, and a smaller shirt as well. Her lips curved into the slightest grin.

So it had been real.

She had a blurry memory of Nik standing with his hands on the bars of her cell. He had looked flustered and was having a hard time forming words. It had been charming, in a way. Then he had looked down at her with those dark eyes, making her knees weak, and mocked the way her clothes hung from her body. It was a kind gesture to provide these substitutes.

A kind gesture for a monster, anyway.

She shook her head and blinked away the memory. That was not a memory she wanted to relive. The butterflies in her stomach felt traitorous. It was hard to not think of him, though. There was nothing else in the cell to distract her, and rather than reliving all of the horrifying things that had happened in the past few days, her mind kept taunting her with visions of his face and questions about his character.

She couldn't tell if it was a blessing to not be reminded of recent horrors, or a curse that she couldn't get him out of her head. Perhaps she'd suffered a head injury in the attack.

A commotion sounded somewhere down the hall, but it was too muffled to tell what it was. Several voices blurred together, and at first it was impossible to make out distinct words. Then one voice moved closer to her cell.

A loud, booming voice could be heard now. "Let's go, ladies and gentlemen. Time for a tour. Everyone be ready in five minutes."

A tour? Ali was curious to see beyond her cell. She changed into the smaller clothes as quickly as possible and gulped down the cold soup. It tasted terrible, but she choked it down anyway. She wasn't sure when her next meal would be, and she needed the energy.

She was ready by the time a guard came to unlock her door and motioned her down the hall where others were filing out of their respective cells. The guards shuffled them through the halls and into a larger common area with an opening to the sky in the middle. The ground had a dusting of snow, and the outer walls were made of tan stone overgrown with vines. Around the perimeter, there were a few simple benches and a few more around a fire pit in the center. The sun peeked through, giving it a majestic feel. If they weren't in a prison, it would've been quite beautiful.

"Listen up!" The nervous chatter surrounding her died down when the man spoke. "You will be allowed out of your cells periodically, assuming good behavior. Work is mandatory. You'll earn your keep here."

Their keep, she thought with hostility. As if they had chosen to be here and their captors were so gracious to offer a place to stay. How kind of them...

In addition, you'll also be let out for meals and for some free time on the weekends. Again, this is for those who exhibit *good behavior only.*" His emphasis on good behavior made rebellion come alive in her.

The guard extended his arm to show off the open space in which they currently stood. "This is the courtyard where your meals will be served and where you can spend your free time." Then he took a few steps backwards and motions for them to follow. "This way."

They made their way along another hall and she spotted the biggest kitchen she'd ever seen in her life. So many ingredients, pots, pans, utensils. It was more than she could've ever imagined. Everything was spotless, too. How did they keep it so clean?

"Some of you may be assigned to the kitchen. In that case you'll be working here with one of our chefs. Let's keep moving."

The guard walked fast and didn't give them much time to take in their surroundings. Ali supposed they had the rest of their lives to explore their small enclosure.

The next opening was very similar to the shower room they had entered through. Grates in the floor for drainage, but this one had individual shower stalls and a mirror on one wall lined with sinks. Shelves of clean towels and washcloths lined another wall. It wasn't glamorous, but like the other rooms, it was spotlessly clean. She was grateful for that. "These are the showers. You'll be allowed to rinse off once per day for no more than fifteen minutes. Any questions?"

Ali looked around her. Everyone was too nervous to speak. They all glanced at each other, waiting for someone to make a sound, but no one did.

"Right. Well let's go back to the courtyard then. If you think of anything at all, just ask me or one of the guards on duty."

The group shuffled back in the direction they'd come from. Besides the guard giving the tour, a few others had appeared in the back to keep watch. Now it was their turn to take the lead.

"You'll be given half an hour now to spend in the courtyard. The other guards and I will be making rounds to give out your work assignments."

Ali found Eli in the crowd and approached him tentatively. The last time they had spoken, he'd been in a dark place. She couldn't blame him, but she wanted to gauge his mood before she spoke. He looked distracted, but otherwise okay.

She reached out to touch his arm. "Hey."

"Hey," he said in his husky voice. It always amazed her that this man could be the perfect juxtaposition of masculine and sensitive. He was a bright beacon of light most of the time, but when something upset him, it was obvious. It was written all over his face.

"How are you feeling?"

"I'm fine, Ali. I'm...adjusting." He looked around and took in his surroundings. "I just still can't believe this happened. This doesn't feel like my life."

"I know exactly what you mean." She slipped her arms around his waist and hugged him close.

She felt his chin rest on top of her head. "I'm glad you're here. I don't know what I'd do without you."

A man cleared his throat and interrupted their reunion. He had a clipboard in hand and a pencil. "Names?"

They both gave him their first names.

"You'll be assigned to the greenhouses." He appraised Eli's giant body and added, "You might be a better fit for a more physical position in the future, but you have to earn that responsibility." He scribbled something down and walked off toward the next person.

"Greenhouses. Fun," Eli said sarcastically.

"At least we can be together." She could only handle so much change at once. She didn't know what she'd do if Eli was suddenly ripped from her, too.

They spent the remainder of their free time snuggled together in the cold. His arms were the safety that she'd missed. He was her home away from home.

"Free time is over," a guard yelled over the hushed chatter.

Ali lifted her head from Eli's chest. She knew that voice, the one that had caused her insides to melt and her chest to constrict. How long had Nik been here?

His eyes flickered in her direction, and she had this gut feeling that he'd been watching for a while now. When he looked at her, the hairs on her arms stood on end. It felt like he wasn't just looking at her, but *through* her. She felt just as naked now as she had during their first encounter.

She tore her eyes away from him and rose to her feet. Eli held her hand as they made their way back through the halls and to their cells. His cell looked no different from hers. Same tiny bed and next to nothing else. She was sure his legs dangled off the edge uncomfortably. She was aware of Nik watching the two of them carefully as he locked Eli back in his cell.

"I'll see you tomorrow, Ali."

"Bye, Eli."

She wasn't sure if it was a good thing or a bad thing that her cell was in the far corner. It meant that after each person got locked back in their cell, she got closer and closer to being alone with Nik.

"In you go, Ali."

Her jaw dropped when he said her name. She hadn't expected him to pick up on it when Eli said goodbye. And his voice...his voice somehow simultaneously made her pulse rush and scratched a part of her brain that she didn't know existed.

"It's Allison." No one called her Ali except Eli. It was so unnerving to hear this stranger refer to her by that nickname.

"Hmm, and is Eli your boyfriend, Ali?"

There it was again. That unnerving feeling. Except it wasn't as unpleasant as she expected it to be. It pulsed through her, making her feel alive. That numb feeling bled through her pores, and her body awakened.

Her eyes turned to slivers. She reiterated, "It's Allison, and no. He's a friend. Why do you ask?"

"Call it boredom." He shrugged and gestured to the cell she was supposed to enter, but his eyes made it hard to lift her feet. Those eyes might be her undoing if she couldn't stop getting lost in them.

She walked into her cell and turned around to watch him lock up. He had large hands. What would it feel like to have those hands all over her? How much of her waist could he hold? He could probably cup her breasts entirely, and her ass cheeks. He could cradle her head, fingers laced in her hair.

She squeezed her thighs together as her thoughts turned to arousal.

Her body was a traitor and her mind was an accomplice.

He finished with the lock and jiggled the door for good measure. Then he stared directly at her with those stupidly gorgeous eyes, dropped his glance quickly and looked back up to her face. He seemed to be weighing his next words. With a smirk, he said, "These clothes look much better on you, Ali."

She was left stunned and confused.

•••••

The rest of the day was torture. She was looking forward to working tomorrow just so she'd have something to do. For several hours, she lay on her bed and stared at the ceiling. Her thoughts alternated between reliving her mom's death and envisioning what her life would look like here. She was in a perpetual tornado where the past and the future swept her up and wouldn't release her. She was going to go insane.

She spent another hour pacing back and forth and painted a vivid picture of Nik's eyes in her mind. And then she tore it down in shame and flopped down on the bed again.

Dinner was the best reprieve from solitude. She picked out a spot to eat while Eli grabbed a couple bowls of pasta. They were small and entirely flavorless. She never thought she'd miss fish and rice, but she yearned for the comfort foods of home.

She should've savored that last dessert—savored it all. She had taken her life for granted.

They'd been celebrating Jack's birthday. Ali dropped her fork in the bowl with a clatter. He would never celebrate another birthday.

She laid her bowl on the bench beside her, no longer hungry.

"What are you thinking about?" Eli asked when he noticed her expression change.

"Everything."

"Ali..." He rested his hand on her knee, and she looked up. "I'm not done fighting. I've been thinking about this all day. I don't know how yet, but I *will* get us out of here."

He sounded so sure of himself. She didn't see how that would be possible, but she trusted him. And she had to admit, she preferred this version of Eli to the one who had been too depressed to speak. If this gave him a distraction, a sense of purpose, then she would support him. And on the rare chance that he might succeed, then they would both escape this place.

She covered his hand with her own and he slid his fingers between hers. Instinctively, she looked around the courtyard. It didn't hit her right away what she was looking for, but then she felt a sense of disappointment when she didn't see him.

It wasn't *what* she was looking for but *who*.

Nik.

She squeezed Eli's hand by accident, but he misinterpreted the tension. "It's all going to be fine. I promise." He smiled at her in that innocent, boyish manner that she loved. She tried to ignore their matching metal bands that definitely said it would *not* be okay.

"What do you think work will be like?"

"I don't know but, I think it could be worse. I overheard some of the other guys talking earlier. They have to clean out horse stalls. They have to pick up *shit*." His face scrunched in disgust, and they both burst out with laughter. For a moment, things felt normal again.

Indeed, it could be worse.

Ali dreaded going back to her cell. She couldn't stand to be alone with her thoughts again. As soon as she got back, she jumped into bed and closed her eyes, willing sleep to come. When she did fall asleep, it was anything but restful. Just like her thoughts earlier in the day, her mind bounced back and forth between past and future, nightmares and fantasies.

Chapter Twelve

NIK

NIK WAS UP AND out of bed before the sun rose. Today was the first day working with the new prisoners. He had to get to the prison and escort his team to the greenhouses. Thankfully, he would just oversee their work. He'd never had a green thumb. He had once tried to grow some flowers around the exterior of his house and they had all died within a week. After that, a sweet elderly neighbor offered to tend to his landscaping while taking care of her own. He returned the favor by bringing her meat and produce from town.

Sam waited for him at the prison, looking far too cheerful for this early in the morning. Nik was glad it was Sam he was working with and not Marcus. Marcus was such an ass. It was hard to be around him for long periods of time. Sam usually kept to himself and didn't get in anyone's business. Most of the time he just doodled in a notebook he always kept with him.

"I've already rounded everyone up that's coming with us," Sam said, standing in front of a group of six people. Nik's pulse quickened when he realized Ali was one of them. And that guy, her *friend,* Eli. This would either be fun or a disaster. Maybe a little bit of both.

On their way out, they stopped by the office to grab some sweaters and hats, passing them out to the prisoners. It was a ten-minute walk to the greenhouses and winter was now in full force. Though it was warm in the greenhouses, it wouldn't be on the walk there.

Ali took the sweater and hat from him, and he held on just a little too long. Long enough to draw her eyes to his and for her to tug at the extra layers before he loosened his grip. He tried not to smirk when her eyes blazed with annoyance. For some reason he was drawn to her.

Sam led the way while Nik covered the back. People often cowered from Nik, and he tried not to notice the way their group moved closer to Sam and edged away from him. He'd been told once or twice that he was intimidating, which was an excellent quality for a guard. It wasn't on purpose. He just towered over most people and unless he made a conscious effort to smile all the time, his face turned sharp and vicious. He had no incentive to change this quality about himself. It was a good thing that people left him be.

Nik watched Ali and Eli closely, trying to make out their conversation from afar. He couldn't explain why he was so interested in learning more about this woman. He just was. And that another man was so close to her only piqued his interest more. Maybe he was just competitive. What did that guy have that Nik didn't?

He had the urge to work his way between them. After all, he could do it. He was ranked relatively high in their guard and being respected in Rysburg meant he could get away with a lot. If he asked the right person, he could have Eli moved to work in the kitchen or with the cattle, anywhere but here, although he'd have to come up with a reason. A sinister thought crossed his mind. Wouldn't it be more fun to tease and torment Ali while Eli watched? If this guy wanted her, wouldn't it be more fun to take her from right under his nose?

A rare smile stretched across his cheeks.

Sam unlocked the door to the greenhouse. It was full of tomatoes, peppers, onions and many other vegetables and spices. The metal framing had somehow remained standing through the end times. The glass had been replaced through the years with whatever they could salvage from other villages. Now they had three large greenhouses that helped feed the couple thousand inhabitants of Rysburg. They also bred poultry and cattle. They used to have a larger fleet of horses, but a particularly harsh winter had taken out half of their herd a few winters ago. They were still recovering.

Nik knew they were lucky in Rysburg to have so many resources. Or rather, they made their own luck. It was a vicious world, and they did whatever they had to in order to stay on top. Protecting his people was his number one priority, and he wouldn't apologize for the things they did to stay secure and thriving. Every time he started to feel guilty, he'd take a trip to the opening in town where kids often played ball. He'd watch them giggle and run without a care in the world and remind himself that *this* was what they fought for. For generations to grow up, protected from the cruel realities of the world outside their borders. He fought to protect their innocence.

He had to remind himself of that again as he peered at the prisoners.

Today their job was to plant corn. They had a rotating schedule of crops and switched to something else whenever one was harvested. It was nice to have variety, and he'd been told it was good for the soil.

Sam explained their duties for the day and showed them where the tools were, as well as the seeds.

Nik stepped forward to interrupt. "I think the potatoes could use some fertilizer. Don't you agree, Sam?"

"Uh, sure." Sam gave him a questioning look and scratched his short black hair. He turned his attention back to the prisoners.

Nik pointed at Eli. "You. Follow me."

Nik took him a few rows over and plenty far away from Ali. "This row and the next will need to be fertilized. You can spread it with your hands. I'm afraid we're all out of gloves."

He had apologized, but he didn't mean it in the slightest. There probably were gloves somewhere around the greenhouse, but he wouldn't look for them. He thrust a bucket of horse manure into Eli's hands.

Eli clenched his jaw but said nothing. He took hold of the bucket and turned to work. Nik frowned. He had hoped it would be more fun taunting Eli but he submitted far too easily.

Nik returned to the empty row waiting to be planted with corn. The other prisoners were busy spreading seeds and covering them with fresh dirt. He patrolled the aisle, pretending to watch them, but he was only really interested in watching one.

When he made it closer to Ali, she flashed him a menacing glare. "Was that really necessary?"

"Excuse me?"

"Why did you do that? Why would you separate Eli from me and make him work with horse shit? Is this some sort of punishment or something? You're insecure? Having a power trip?"

Nik straightened in indignation. She was *bold.* He moved till his face was inches from hers and he could see the flecks in her eyes. She leaned back, but he leaned forward to maintain their proximity, so close he could breathe in her scent.

"Oh, Ali. If I was punishing you, you'd know it."

He leaned back to take in her body language. She was frozen solid and sufficiently startled.

Good.

He walked around her, slow and threatening. "Are we going to have problems, Ali?" Her name tingled on his lips, ensnaring her and reeling her in.

Her shoulders tensed, and when she spoke, it was just above a whisper. "No. No problems here."

"Perfect."

He grazed his hand along her back as he headed back toward Sam and he felt her shiver beneath his fingertips.

Oh, yes, toying with her would be fun indeed.

He spent the next few hours pacing back and forth, taking extra time whenever he passed Ali. Sometimes she caught his eye and other times she ignored him. Either way, he felt her magnetic energy pulling him in.

They took a break around midday for lunch. Eli had rejoined the group and sat next to Ali. They chatted so naturally, like nothing had happened.

Nik felt a bit neglected, forgotten even. And he refused to be forgotten.

He handed out sandwiches to the other prisoners before stopping in front of Eli and Ali. He handed one sandwich to Eli, who grumbled, "Thanks."

He extended his arm to hand Ali the other one, and right as she reached for it, he snapped it back. She rolled her eyes and huffed, agitated by Nik's childish behavior. He didn't care. He was having too much fun.

He extended it once more and this time let her grab it.

"You're not going to say thank you?"

She took a big bite and purposefully ignored him.

"You're welcome, babe."

Ali's face flushed, and Eli turned to her with a questioning look. Nik wandered away and left them to sort that one out.

The friendly chatter they enjoyed before now looked more like bickering. Nik smiled to himself. Annoying Ali and pushing Eli away at the same time? Two birds with one stone.

They finished lunch and Eli went his separate way again. Nik decided to follow him and see how his work was coming along. He was surprised to see he was almost done. When Eli caught him watching out of the corner of his eye, he scoffed.

"Is there something else I can help you with?"

"Nope. Just checking on how things are going over here."

Eli hesitated. "You should leave Ali alone." It was a threat, but a completely empty one. He had no power here.

"I'm afraid I can't do that. It's literally my job not to leave her alone." Nik crossed his arms and focused on Ali, a few rows over. She was working diligently and wiped an arm across her sweaty brow. He was struck by how naturally beautiful she was, even covered in dirt and sweat. He couldn't take his eyes off her.

Eli followed his gaze, clearly uneasy. It was so much fun getting under his skin.

"You see, the thing is, I'm kind of fascinated by her. I'm sure you understand. You seem to be quite fascinated as well. But Eli, I don't share. And mark my words: I tend to get what I want."

Eli rose to his full height and took a step forward. He was just slightly taller than Nik, but Nik didn't back away. Eli clenched his fist but wavered, visibly struggling to reel in his anger. Getting into a fight on his first day outside a cell would be a terrible idea.

"You'll never have Ali. She's a fighter. She'll claw your eyes out before she ever lets you touch her."

Nik grinned at the thought. He wouldn't mind if she did. The idea of Ali going feral over him made his muscles weak.

"Oh, I didn't tell you the best part. She's going to want me. She's going to choose me. She's going to *beg* for me."

Eli was about to put hands on Nik, but Nik grabbed him by the shoulders. "I wouldn't, man. I can and *will* make your life hell."

If looks could kill, Nik would've been dead. Eli let go of him and took a step back. Nik gave him a condescending tap on the shoulder and walked off, leaving Eli fuming.

He felt Ali's eyes on him as he passed, but she looked down and shook her head. He didn't think she could hear what had been said, but she obviously wasn't impressed with their near altercation.

That was okay. He was confident in his ability to win her over, and he had all the time in the world. He couldn't explain his attraction to her. It made no sense. It couldn't be her looks. Although she was gorgeous, there were plenty of beautiful women in Rysburg. And she was objectively inferior to him. She was a prisoner, for god's sake. But even he had to admit he hadn't been able to shake her from his mind. He was infatuated. Maybe if he just scratched the itch, he could forget about her.

They finished their work late that afternoon. They headed for the prison in the same manner they had left, Sam leading the way with Nik in the rear. Everyone was quiet and worn out from the day's work. It made Nik happy to see that even Eli and Ali weren't talking. It was only the first day and he'd already driven a wedge between them.

"I'll take it from here," Sam said as they reached the door to the prison.

Nik gave Ali one last glance, but she paid him no attention. "Yeah, I'll be back later tonight." He was working a double shift today but had been given a few hours to sleep before returning to the prison to keep watch overnight. "See you, Sam."

Nik turned his back on the prison and Ali. For now.

Chapter Thirteen

ELI

Eli was thrilled the workday was finally over. He had been dreading it, but he never could've anticipated just how bad it would be. That guard, Nik, had it out for him, and his obsession with Ali made Eli sick. He was scared for her. That she might wind up being hurt by this guy, taken advantage of. But he was also scared for himself. That this guy might be right and might get everything he wanted. He seemed charming enough and good looking, too.

Ali was too smart to fall for that shit, though. Right? But she hadn't flinched when he called her "babe."

Eli felt like he was missing part of the conversation. What had gone down between them in just a few short days?

He stripped out of his putrid clothes that reeked of sweat and horse shit before hopping in one of the shower stalls. He scrubbed as quickly as he could to remove the filth from his hands and arms, but the gross feeling all over his body wouldn't be scrubbed away so easily.

Ali wasn't speaking to him. He'd thrown some accusatory questions her way when they'd been left alone at lunch.

"What was that? Who is he? Are you guys friends or something? You can't be friends with the enemy, Ali."

He'd be lying if he said he didn't feel betrayed. She'd told him nothing was going on and he was overreacting. That they had only spoken once or twice and he was reading too much into it. Her voice had been defensive, though. Like she was hiding something from him. He knew her well enough to know when she wasn't being honest.

The water shut off automatically right at the fifteen-minute mark. Eli rubbed his wet head on a towel and wrapped it around his waist before grabbing his clean clothes from the counter. He didn't wait for his body to dry completely before pulling them on and heading back to his cell.

Afterward, he sat on his bed, staring at the wall. Contemplating life.

He couldn't live this way. He *wouldn't* live this way.

How could he get out of this place before he lost his mind?

He knew one thing for certain: if he was in this prison, he'd never escape. He'd have to pay more attention to the greenhouses. Their route to and from them. What were the ways out of Rysburg? Where was the tunnel from which they'd entered? Were there escape routes from the greenhouses themselves? The one guard hardly paid him attention, which he could use to his advantage. Nik, however, couldn't take his eyes off Ali. How would Eli get them both out if he was always watching?

It seemed so foolish to think that he could escape, but these cells provided no other form of entertainment than to daydream. The cold, hard stone surfaces taunted him and the iron bars mocked him. They knew he was locked in here for eternity, even if he was unwilling to admit it. He moved from the bed to the ground and did a few push-ups. His sore muscles protested, but his willpower was strong. Anything to take his mind off of Ali and their dismal fate here.

"Did we not work you hard enough?" His thoughts were interrupted by Sam, who watched with amusement as Eli finished his last push-up. He slipped a key into the lock of the cell door, and it creaked as it swung open. "It's time for dinner."

Eli followed him to the kitchen and grabbed a tray of unrecognizable reddish-brown mush. It was chilly in the courtyard but unusually sunny for this time of year. He found Ali sitting alone on a bench, her head hanging low. Guilt sank in for the things he had said earlier that day. He always hated it when they fought. She was his best friend, and he could never stay mad at her. Fighting with Ali was a punishment to himself.

"Hey." He tapped her shoe with his foot.

She looked up but said nothing.

Eli sighed. He *really* must've fucked up. He was about to start profusely apologizing and begging when she slid over and made room for him on the bench.

Ali remained quiet while they ate, and he could hardly stand the silence. It made the sound of utensils against plates even more grating.

"I'm sorry, okay?" He tilted his head in her direction, hoping to make eye contact.

"You said some really shitty things today." She finally looked at him, and he half-wished she hadn't. Her gaze bore through him like a dagger.

"I know."

"Do you believe me when I say there's nothing going on?"

"I do. Forgive me?" He pushed his lip out and pouted, showing off his best puppy dog eyes.

"It's not funny, Eli. You're all I have here. If you can't trust me..." She stared into the distance. Her mind was elsewhere. "I just don't want to lose you too."

"You haven't lost me." He placed a hand on her knee and rubbed it with his thumb. He knew she was thinking about Andus and about their parents, but he was still here and wasn't going anywhere. "I didn't mean to come down on you so hard. I just felt out of the loop, I guess. We've always known everything about each other and for the first time, I felt like you were keeping something from me. I was wrong to jump to that conclusion and I really am sorry. I do trust you."

Her eyes met his, searching for sincerity. She seemed satisfied with what she found and pushed her half-eaten tray of food away. "I forgive you."

"You're not going to eat that?"

"I'm not hungry. Maybe I'll go on a hunger strike," she said half-jokingly, but he was concerned she was being serious.

"That's a terrible idea. If we do ever get the chance to get out of here, I need you in top shape. Not weak and starving."

"Do you really think we're ever going to get out of here?" Her voice was skeptical. She looked up at the sky, waiting for a prayer to be answered. She was almost angelic, the way the warm sunlight hit her pale skin. It only made her frown more devastating.

"Yes, or I will die trying."

Ali whipped her head in his direction.

"I'm serious, Ali. This life"—he waved his arms around at their surroundings—"isn't a life at all. I will do whatever it takes to escape. And you're coming with me. You can always depend on me."

"Where will we go?" She was humoring him. He could tell she didn't believe they would ever actually escape, but she would entertain his wild ideas.

"Anywhere you want."

"Neither of us has any idea where we're going."

"We'll figure it out along the way. What about someplace sunny and warm?"

She considered it for a moment and whispered softly, "I think I'd like that."

Then she nuzzled her head into his neck, resting on his shoulder. He could sense her despair and knew she didn't share his optimism. He wrapped an arm around her back and pulled her close. If only he could take the pain away. If only none of this had ever happened. He had failed to keep her safe before, but he would never fail her again. Her hopelessness only drove him to be more committed to saving them both.

He *would* find a way.

Chapter Fourteen

ALI

ALI COULD HARDLY KEEP up with her rollercoaster of emotions. She had started the day feeling cautiously cheerful that work might help distract her and give her something to look forward to. Instead, she'd been taunted by Nik, had fought with Eli, and then had to listen to his pointless dreams. It was a cruel reminder that her life was over. It didn't belong to her anymore; she was someone else's property. She felt guilty for even having a moment of happiness. Tears burned her eyes when she thought of her mom.

She'd been foolish to think her life would return to any sense of normalcy. How could she think she could go about her day with a new job and create a new routine here? Was it that easy for her to forget who these people were and what they had done?

She punched her pillow and flung her body down on the bed. The pillow muffled her anguished screams. Her muscles tensed as she let out everything she'd been holding in. Then the energy drained from her body, and her tight grip on the pillow slowly released. She took slow breaths, attempting to bring her heart rate down.

Rolling over, she stared at the cracks in the stone ceiling. She wanted to clear her mind of all thoughts and emotions. She concentrated on the stone and the way it swirled unevenly. One looked like a cat. If she squinted, another one looked like a boot. This was her new form of entertainment to keep from losing her mind. Or maybe this was the behavior of someone who already had lost her mind.

She spotted a man's face on the surface. A hard jaw with a bristly beard. His eyes glared back at her. He reminded her of someone she didn't want to think about.

Nik.

His cocky grin had infuriated her after his treatment of Eli today, but it had stirred something else in her too. Something she didn't want to admit. It seemed like the harder she tried to forget him, the more she couldn't keep her mind off him.

She placed her hand on her chest when her heart started beating rapidly again. It pounded against her chest like a drum. Taking deep breaths, she slowly brought her hand down further, feeling her soft breasts through the thin fabric of her shirt. She swallowed hard when she remembered the way he looked when their eyes met. There had been a hunger in them that made her feel dangerous. That she was strong enough to survive. Her nipples hardened, and she bit her lip.

Why did her body insist on reacting this way?

And why couldn't she stop?

Her hand traveled further south, and she lifted the hem of her shirt. Her fingertips playfully slid across her skin. The metal band rubbed uncomfortably until she adjusted to a different angle. She pictured Nik's hands grazing her skin, and it made her breath hitch and her leg muscles tighten. If she thought about him just this once, maybe she could get him out of her system.

She slipped her hand underneath her shirt and cupped her breast, rubbing her thumb over her nipple. But it wasn't her thumb. It was Nik's mouth, his lips covering her and sucking gently. Her head lolled to the side and her eyes fluttered shut.

Her other hand loosened the tie on her pants, sliding down between her thighs. She massaged her clit for a moment before spreading her fingers to her slit. She gasped when she discovered how wet she was. Her eyes popped open, and she was thankful to be in the corner cell where no one could see or hear her. It had been so long since she'd been turned on like this. She had forgotten what it felt like. Heat radiated and covered the skin across her chest and arms, up her neck, and to her cheeks.

She closed her eyes again and softly moaned as she slid one finger inside. She relished in the growing intensity, slowly sliding her finger in and out. She imagined Nik's mouth on her neck, traveling to meet her own lips, his tongue dipping in and sliding across hers. She imagined his fingers exploring her, pushing deep inside her. God, what she wouldn't give to have him touching her. She needed more. She slid a second finger in and moved a little faster, her toes curling and thighs tensing.

Her breath was labored, and she rocked her hips against her pulsing fingers. She was desperate but wanted this to last as long as possible. She moved her fingers slowly and took the time to rub her arousal over her clit before dipping in again. Pleasure built in her core. She pictured Nik grabbing her hips and thrusting inside her, his muscles tensed, a look of pleasure on his face. The thought of his cock throbbing inside her was enough to push her over the edge. Her mouth formed a perfect, speechless O and she squeezed her thighs together as her walls fluttered around her fingers.

She panted as she recovered from her orgasm, then she removed her fingers and wiped them off. That had certainly helped her relax and had eased her frustrations. She sank into the bed, ready to fall asleep.

"That was amazing," a voice growled from the door of the cell.

Ali bolted up in her bed and stared in shock, letting out a horrified gasp. She hadn't even heard him approach.

"How long have you been standing there?"

"Long enough." His smirk was enraging.

"What are you doing here?"

"What do you mean?" He was holding a plate in one hand and a fork in the other. He waved the fork around at the prison walls. "This is my job."

"It's your job to sneak up on people and invade their privacy?" She was fuming, but also still turned on. She could feel the cum between her thighs and clenched again. She had *just* been thinking about this man's hands and mouth all over her and here he was, hers for the taking. The way he looked at her and treated her...she didn't think he'd say no if she offered.

She swallowed hard. She wouldn't go there. Fantasizing about him was supposed to be the end of her fascination with him.

"It's my job to make sure you're behaving." He grinned and held back a laugh. "I'm gonna have to keep a closer eye on you."

Her cheeks flushed, and she covered her face with her hands, willing him to disappear. Or better yet, maybe she could disappear far, far away from here.

"Don't be embarrassed. We all do it." He lifted the fork to his mouth, and she realized he was eating cake. Chocolate cake from the looks of it. Her stomach growled, and she recalled the half-eaten dinner she'd thrown away.

"I don't need to visualize you jerking off." Her mouth watered at the sight of the cake. Or from the thought of his hard cock in his hand. No, it was the cake. Definitely the cake.

He swallowed and licked the chocolate frosting from his lips, and she remembered her vision of his lips on hers. "I wouldn't mind if you did." He shrugged before a devilish, knowing smile formed. "Ali, were you visualizing my dick?"

She didn't have a chance to object before her cheeks flushed again, betraying her. She didn't want to give him the satisfaction. "You're disgusting."

He threw his head back and laughed. Despite the embarrassing situation, his laughter made the corner of her mouth perk up. It was a calming sensation. When he had his laughter under control, he leaned his head against the bars. "Oh, Ali. That is so hot. I promise, the real thing is better than anything you could imagine."

She exaggerated a sigh of frustration, but he wasn't the only one that thought it was hot. His reaction made Ali squeeze her thighs together. She watched him lick the frosting off his fork. He had to be doing that on purpose. It was giving her visuals of his tongue in other places. Licking other things.

"Do you want some?" he interrupted her fantasies.

"What?" She was flustered.

"Do you want some cake?" He pursed his lips together, holding back another laugh. He pointed to his chest. "I already know you want some of *me,* but I might share the cake too if you ask nicely."

His smile was both charming and infuriating. She wanted to smash his face in the cake...and then maybe lick it all off. She hated the way her body and heartbeat were reacting to this man.

She should have said no. She should have told him to leave her alone, but she didn't want him to leave. Not really. "Yes, I would like some."

She stood and walked over to the bars on shaky legs.

"Ask nicely." He wasn't laughing anymore, and his eyes had turned dark beneath his long lashes. Being this close to him made her body tingle.

"Fuck you."

"If you ask nicely, I might let you do that, too."

The effect on her body was instantaneous. The thought of his body up against hers, his cock inside her, made her knees buckle. But his cocky grin made her want to punch him in the groin. She gritted her teeth.

He took another bite of cake, taking his time cleaning the fork with his tongue. She had to look away before she threw her hands through the bars and grabbed him by the shirt. Her stomach growled again, and she shook her head and gave in...just a little.

"Please." It came out as barely more than a whisper.

"Please what?" He watched her lips with such intensity.

She pressed her teeth together so hard it made her jaw hurt. "Please, can I have some cake?"

He surveyed her body, his eyes coming to a stop at her hard nipples visible through her thin shirt. She watched his throat bob as he swallowed, her own throat tightening with a desire to kiss his neck, right where that vein pulsed. He swiped his thumb across the top of the cake, gathering a scoop of frosting. "Open up."

Fucking asshole.

She shook her head and leaned back from the bars

He sucked the frosting off his thumb. "None for you, then."

Then he gathered more frosting on his thumb and waited for her to make a move. She hated the way her body rebelled against her brain, but she stepped close to him once again.

Her jaw dropped in obedience, and he put his thumb in her mouth. She felt filthy and delicious all at once. She closed her lips around his knuckle and licked the frosting off, relishing the taste and texture of his skin, committing it to memory. She wanted other parts of his skin in her mouth.

They locked eyes while she continued to suck every bit of frosting off of him. Warmth built between her legs once more, and she wished he would open the door and close the space between them.

He kept his thumb in her mouth far longer than necessary, watching her with hungry eyes. A low moan escaped him when she swirled her tongue over him one last time and popped him from her mouth. Ali felt dizzy with lust and they both stood in silence for a few moments. Their shallow breathing was the only sound in the cell.

Then Nik brought his thumb to his mouth, savoring the taste of her.

Oh god, she thought. It was a good thing there were bars separating them, because she feared the things she might do without them.

"Nik," she whispered, her voice full of want that grated against her ears. She couldn't take her eyes off of him. She couldn't even blink, afraid that he would disappear if she did. That this would be just another dream.

He reached through the bars, brushed the loose strands of hair behind her ear, and trailed his thumb back over her bottom lip. She flinched but allowed him to continue. "Can you do me a favor?"

"What?" She was full of nervous energy.

He licked his lips and flashed a grin. "Will you think about me again tonight? When you touch yourself?" His eyes lowered to her core. Did he know how wet she was? Could he sense her arousal?

Her lungs constricted. She would *absolutely* think of him later tonight. But now that he was asking, she didn't want to. She wanted to ignore his request just to piss him off.

"Answer me," he growled.

Her eyes fluttered at the sound, and she pressed her body into the bars. Closer. She needed to be closer to him.

"I won't make any promises."

What had come over her? She'd never behaved like this, but something about him made her feel brave and unashamed to go after what she wanted. It was wrong, but she had an innate desire to please him despite his position.

She reached through the bars to touch his chest, but he backed up. He was dangling himself in front of her, close enough to torment but just out of reach.

"Not yet. All in due time," he assured her. "I only want you to touch yourself tonight, Ali."

Unbearable longing swelled between her thighs. She nodded in understanding.

"Good girl." He winked and turned to leave. "Oh, and Ali?"

Her shoulders tensed, and she squeezed the bars, waiting for his next request.

He smiled when his eyes met hers. "I'm going to want a recap in excruciating detail."

Her jaw went slack as he turned the corner and disappeared.

Chapter Fifteen

ALI

ALI WOKE UP WITH hair in a mess and blankets jumbled in a knot. She had done as Nik had asked and thought of him while touching herself last night after he had left. She had come several times before passing out, exhausted and overcome with gratification. She hadn't been able to help herself. Every time she'd climaxed, she thought about Nik appearing at her cell and desire had pooled in her all over again.

One time hadn't been enough to forget him. Neither had five. Maybe it had been the boredom. Maybe it had been his piercing blue eyes and casual smile, the rumble in his voice.

She thought about the way he'd asked for details and squirmed in bed. She didn't have time for this. Judging by the position of the sun, it was almost time for work. Someone would be at her cell any minute. Maybe it would even be Nik. She tensed, suddenly feeling uneasy about her salacious thoughts of him.

Hopping out of bed, she changed into her work clothes. She ran her fingers through her hair and smoothed it back into a braid, then brushed her teeth and dreamily replayed the image of sucking on Nik's thumb. His eyes had been so intense. She could only imagine how intense they'd be if she were sucking his cock.

She gripped the side of the sink as another wave of hunger ripped through her abdomen. It was enough to bring her to her knees.

The rattle of her cell door snapped her out of it. She spit the water in the sink and wiped her hands on her pants.

"Time to go." But it wasn't Nik's voice. She didn't even try to hide her disappointment.

Sam misunderstood her dismay. "Chin up. Trust me, there are worse jobs you could have. The greenhouse isn't so bad. And there are worse guards you could be working with." He continued as he unlocked the door and let her out, "I don't think I'm that bad."

She gave him a friendly grin. He was right. So far, Sam had been the kindest person she'd met here. He was incredibly polite. He said little, but he also didn't sneer or look down on the prisoners either.

Sam led the way down the hall. "Unfortunately, I can't say the same thing about Nik. He's a bit of a hard ass. Always grumpy, too."

Ali let out a soft laugh. There was a darkness to Nik, even while he was taunting her. She'd never been scared of the dark, though.

Sam continued to let out the members of their work group and they made their way to the greenhouses. Still no sign of Nik. Ali hated that she was disappointed. He had gotten her worked up the night before and then hadn't shown up today. It was probably a trait of these villains in Rysburg. Setting expectations only to fall short of meeting them.

What was she doing? This was a total betrayal to her people. The light of day and cold air made it easier for her to see and think clearly.

"Are you all right?" Eli asked as she aggressively buried seeds. She was taking out her frustration on her assigned tasks. The poor crops had done nothing to her, but they were an easy punching bag. She threw the tiny specks into the hole she had dug and then covered it with dirt, packing it down tightly. Too tightly.

"Yes." It came out a lot sharper than she meant it to. "Sorry, I just didn't sleep well."

He sighed. "I get that. My mind has been racing since the day we got here. It's hard to turn it off. Even harder with nothing to do in those miserable cells."

She felt a fresh pang of guilt. Eli could never know about Nik. The confusing feelings she had toward him. The things they had said and done. It would break his heart.

Where did this leave them, after all? She no longer felt bound to him, but she still felt loyal to him. She had never been in love with him the way he loved her, but he was her best friend.

She cleared her throat. "Yeah. I've had a lot on my mind, I guess."

She was thankful that Eli got to work with her today. It was one good thing about Nik being gone. He wasn't here to separate them. It would also be easier to get him off her mind if he wasn't around.

They spent most of their day chatting like they used to when they'd checked the fish traps together. It was easy to forget they were even captives when she was with him. Her best friend always provided the best distraction.

He seemed at peace, if just for a moment. Was he hiding his true emotions from her? Trying to protect her from seeing the pain he was in? They had both lost their only surviving parent. It had to be killing him, too.

Ali thought about all the things she would've told her mom over the past week. She would've told her that other towns did exist. That they could've gone searching for more than their simple, quiet life in Andus.

But what could she say about Nik? The prison guard who got under her skin and ignited something inside her that she couldn't extinguish? Her stomach turned, and she closed her eyes wearily.

She let Eli distract her for the rest of the day. She didn't want to get lost in her thoughts again. It was too painful there. She just wanted to feel numb. It was too bad they didn't have gray grass here.

After lunch, they pulled weeds from between the crops. Her arms grew tired and sweat glistened on her forehead. Eli tried to wipe it, but he only made it worse, adding dirt to the mix. They shared a lighthearted laugh over it.

Somehow, throughout the day, she had finally managed to forget about Nik. Eli held her close as they walked back to the prison that evening, snow crunching beneath their feet. They took turns trying to catch snowflakes in their mouths. Eli was way better at it than she was.

They made it back to the prison and waited their turn for the showers. Eli went first and quickly hopped out after a few minutes, looking like a wet dog. His hair dripped and his shirt clung to his body, beads of moisture dotting the fabric.

"See you at dinner," he said as he walked toward his cell.

Everyone else had finished up and Ali was left alone in the showers. The warm water was incredibly relaxing, and the pressure massaged her shoulders. They weren't given much time, but even she could admit that the showers here were better than her bathtub in Andus. She scrubbed the dirt from her forehead, her arms and underneath her fingernails. By the time the water shut off, she was feeling quite refreshed.

She thought she heard feet shuffling, squeaking against the hard floor. "Hello?"

No response.

Chills raced up her spine. She was sure she'd heard something. Cautiously, she pulled back the curtain and peeked her head around the stall. Her stomach turned when she realized she wasn't alone.

"We should stop meeting like this," Nik said, a smug grin on his face. He looked good, wearing his signature black T-shirt and black jeans. He crossed his arms over his chest and waited, leaning against the wall.

Ali gripped the edge of the stall, searching for her towel.

"Then stop stalking me."

"Watching," he retorted. "We've been over this. It's my job to observe you." He took slow steps in her direction, the sound of his boots splashing on the wet floor, puddles previous prisoners had left behind. Her heart pounded in her chest with each step as she shifted to stay hidden behind the stall wall.

"Can you grab my towel?" She pointed to the folded towel just out of her reach.

He picked it up and held it out for her, and she quickly wrapped it around her body. He wasted no time stepping close to her once she was covered. She didn't know why it mattered. He'd seen her naked already and he'd caught her with her hands down her pants. A nice gesture, nonetheless.

His dominating presence forced her to take a few steps back, colliding with the wall. He slipped through the curtain and closed in until they were separated by only an inch. She had the urge to run from him, but also to run her hands up the front of his black T-shirt and down his bare arms.

His fingertips played with the hem of her towel, lightly grazing the skin on her thighs. She squeezed them together to combat the throbbing between her legs.

Nik gave her a knowing and hungry glare.

"Well," he started. "Did you think of me last night?"

She was speechless and entranced by the pads of his fingers trailing further up her legs, lifting her towel dangerously high. She instinctively reached for his hands and he paused. When she loosened her hold, he began feeling his way up her legs once again. She couldn't swallow. Her heart raced and she let out an incoherent whimper.

"When I ask a question, you're supposed to answer." He moved his hands to her hips and pressed his body against hers. His thigh nudged between her legs, separating them and exposing her. She could feel his muscle pressing into her pussy and she resisted the urge to grind into him.

She let out a soft sigh. "Yes. Yes, I thought about you." She placed her hands on his chest and felt the hard ridges of muscle beneath his shirt. He had the body of a god. So many firm and solid surfaces. She wanted to run her fingers over every single one of them. It was unfair that someone this crass could be so attractive. She thought she heard him choke back a moan.

"What did you do?" He licked his lips and his eyes swept her body.

Ali hesitated. She had never done anything like this before. She felt self-conscious describing how she touched herself. "I—"

Nik could clearly sense her timidness. "You...slipped your hand in your pants? Between your legs?" He wiggled his own thigh to emphasize that pulsing between her legs.

Ali startled, then nodded. Did he know just how badly he was tantalizing her?

"And then?"

She bit her lip. He was doing things to her body while hardly touching her. She had the urge to wrap her legs around him and let him drive into her.

"I rubbed my clit...and my fingers, I put them...." She gulped, unable to finish her sentence.

Nik moved his hands up further over her breasts, alternating between sharp squeezing and gentle massaging. Her legs trembled. They might've given out if it weren't for his lower half pinning her against the wall.

"Keep going," he whispered in her ear.

Her eyes rolled back in her head, and she struggled to continue. "I...ah...I was really wet. You make me so wet."

How could someone so wrong for her make her feel so good?

He growled and grabbed her by the thighs, lifting her up. Her eyes were directly in line with his now, and she wrapped her legs around his waist just like she had wished for moments ago. He gently tugged at the top of her towel and untucked it, letting it fall and gather at her waist. His chest rose and fell as he inhaled deeply at the sight of her breasts. She moved her hands to his biceps that were flexed from holding her up and dug her nails in. He hissed and nuzzled his head in the crook of her neck, kissing along her collarbone.

"How wet are you now?"

So. Fucking. Wet.

"Nik," she panted. She was going to lose it. The soft strands between her fingers felt amazing as she ran one hand through his hair. She gripped it to the point of pain, pulling it back to bare his neck.

His breath caught, and he smirked. "You're feisty."

She leaned forward to gently graze his throat with her teeth. Her body still fought between lust and denial. If she was going to give him pleasure, she would also give him pain. It was the only way for her to feel in control while she spiraled.

He let out an agonized moan. He took her other hand and moved it along his chest, down toward his cock. She inhaled sharply at the size of him. "This is what you do to me, Ali." He cupped her hand over him so she could feel just how hard he was. Her arms fell limp.

She bucked her hips to grind against him, but he held her in place, taking his time. She felt *empty* and needed to be filled.

"Tell me what else you did." He studied her. She watched as he licked his lips, wishing his tongue was on her lips instead.

"I, um, pushed my fingers inside." She took a deep breath and tried to ground herself in the moment.

"Show me."

Her head fell back, and he sucked on her exposed neck. She didn't care how obscene it was. Slowly, she moved her fingers to her pussy, spreading herself wide with two fingers. Nik pulled the towel from her waist and let it drop to the floor. She was completely naked, his plaything. He leaned back a little so he could get a full view.

When her fingers swept over her entrance, she let out a shameless moan. She was *dripping* wet. She slipped in two fingers with ease and felt her legs quiver. Nik gripped her thighs in response, keeping her steady. She pushed her fingers in and brought them out slowly.

Excitement radiated through her as she watched Nik's reaction.

His eyes were wide and his fingers were digging into her skin. His brows pinched together in concentration. "You're so perfect."

She clamped around her fingers at his praise. There was no sign of the cocky, arrogant guard. He was fully mesmerized by her, drowning in her beauty. He couldn't look away, couldn't even blink as she brought her fingers in and out. He took one hand and cupped her breast, thumb rubbing circles over her pert nipple.

She pulsed in and out as slowly as she could bear, her thighs pressed into his waist. His hands shifted to her ass, fondling her. She hitched her fingers inside and rubbed the sensitive walls, the heel of her palm pressed against her clit. The pleasure was overwhelming, and she didn't think she could handle any more as she buried her fingers deep inside. "I'm going to come," she breathed.

He unexpectedly pulled her hand out and pressed both wrists together over her head. She let out a frustrated gasp as he left her feeling empty, but he pressed his abs into her core. She rocked her hips into him, desperate to feel him, to be filled again.

"Beg."

"What?" Her brain stopped functioning. She could only think of the pressure building between her thighs.

"Beg. You want to come? Then beg me."

She looked into his eyes and tried to rock against him again, but he pressed into her, holding her still.

"Beg, Ali."

"I...please, Nik. Please, I want to come."

"How badly?"

"What?"

He huffed out a laugh at how delirious she was, then leaned forward and licked the shell of her ear.

"How badly do you want to come?"

Ali gritted her teeth. "Go fuck yourself."

"I'd really rather watch you fuck yourself." She could feel his smile against her cheek. "I know you want to. I can feel your body shaking."

He held both wrists in one hand and moved the other down across her tattoo, along the side of her breast and stomach. Her body was screaming for release. All she had to do was ask.

"Please."

He released one of her hands so she could continue touching herself. She didn't hesitate to bury her fingers again.

Then, he licked one of his own fingers and slid it in between hers, and she cried in pleasure.

His lips crashed into hers unexpectedly, silencing her, and she felt like she was falling apart. His lips were just as soft as she'd imagined, but he kissed her with such force. She nibbled at his bottom lip and he let out a soft laugh, his breath warm on her face. And his tongue. *His tongue.* He was slick and doing ungodly movements with that tongue.

"Come for me," he whispered, lips still pressed against the corner of her mouth.

That was all it took for her to unravel. She bit down on his lip *hard* as her pussy clenched around their fingers. He groaned in a mix of pleasure and pain.

When she had stopped convulsing, he broke their kiss. He pulled his hand out, up to his lips, and licked his finger clean.

Ali was speechless.

"You taste even better than I expected."

He lowered her legs and let her slide back to the ground, then he bent down to retrieve her towel. The sight of him kneeling in front of her was enough to arouse her again. He rose slowly, leaving gentle kisses on her thigh, her hip, her stomach, and up to the sensitive skin under her breast. Finally standing fully, he left one more quick kiss on her lips. "Your towel."

"Thanks." She looked down and was a little mortified to see her cum on his T-shirt from where she'd been grinding into him. He didn't seem to mind, though.

"Let's do this again sometime." He tilted her chin up and kissed her again, his tongue moving in when her lips parted. He tasted like heaven, and she felt sad and confused when he stepped back and turned to walk out of the showers.

"That was it?" she called after him.

He teased, "Don't be greedy, Ali. You're so obsessed with me."

Her hands acted before she could think it through. She grabbed the tiny bar of soap from the shelf in the shower and chucked it at his head.

He flashed a toothy grin and easily stepped out of the way, the soap missing him entirely.

"Have a good night." He waved and then disappeared.

What the fuck just happened?

She felt frazzled and in need of a cold shower. She was keenly aware that it didn't matter what she thought about him when he wasn't around. It didn't matter that she felt like a traitor when it was just her and her own thoughts. Because whenever he turned up, her brain melted and she became a lustful fool.

No one would ever understand what was going through her head. They wouldn't understand why she was fooling around with a Rysburg guard. She didn't even understand it herself.

Chapter Sixteen

NIK

NIK BOLTED OUT OF bed the next morning. He'd had a hard time sleeping last night and wasn't afraid to admit that he looked forward to seeing Ali today. She'd become the highlight of his day. *Dear god,* the way she'd looked while she was fingering herself. How it had felt when she quivered in his hands. He gritted his teeth when he remembered her wet, tight pussy around his finger. The noise that escaped her lips had almost sent him spiraling right beside her.

He had sped home to his own shower, stroking himself vigorously. He could've just fucked her then and there, but he was enjoying the wait. It was going to be explosive when he did finally have sex with her.

He had to force her beautiful body from his mind so he could focus on getting ready. While brushing his teeth, he noticed his lip was sore and slightly swollen from where she had bitten down. It just made him think about her orgasm, and his dick turned semi-hard again. It was so hard to keep her out of his head.

He couldn't remember the last time he'd been this excited about someone or something. For so long, it had felt like he was going through the motions of life. Wake up, go to work, come home, go to sleep. Repeat until old age claimed him. He'd been in a perpetual fog and Ali was the sunlight that had broken through.

There was a bit more pep in his step that morning. A noticeable difference from his usual saunter. His elderly neighbor even said as much on his walk to work. "Good to see you, Nik. You look cheerful."

"Thanks, ma'am. I'm doing pretty good." He waved her off. "Have a good one!"

He rushed to Ali's cell as quickly as he could, wanting to be the one to walk her to the greenhouses. The thought of holding her hand on the way rose unbidden to his mind, like a newlywed couple still in the early stages of their relationship when everything was fresh and exciting. That would never happen, but it was fun to fantasize. Sam would think he'd lost his mind and question whether he should be in charge of the prisoners. He was definitely taking advantage of his position.

Nik made it to her cell just as she was pulling her shirt over her head. She pulled her hair through and let it flow down her back, combing through it with her fingers. He leaned against the door frame and watched for a moment. She was beautiful. Mesmerizing. He'd never met anyone like her. "Good morning."

She spun around and her timid grin took his breath away. Her cheeks flushed, and he knew he wasn't the only one who had been thinking about their encounter yesterday. She had no reason to be embarrassed or shy. She was a goddess in his eyes. He had an insatiable need to learn everything about her, inside and out.

"Good morning," she said nervously.

He opened the door for her and allowed her just enough space to sneak by, rubbing against his chest. She was intoxicating. He needed her like he needed air.

There was an awkward silence as they walked toward the jail's entrance. He didn't feel comfortable talking to her while others were present. And then, of course, there was Eli. Nik hated that he couldn't just get rid of him. Send him off to work with another group. But it would raise questions and he didn't have a good excuse to do so.

Nik watched them with envy as they walked side by side, chatting like the old friends they were. If only Eli knew the things Ali and Nik got up to in their free time. It didn't take long to have her begging for him. He couldn't help but grin at the thought.

There would come a time when Nik could rub it in Eli's face, and he couldn't wait. Not yet though. He had a feeling Ali wouldn't like that, and he had to tread lightly if he wanted a repeat of last night's events.

Every so often, Eli looked back at Nik. Nik took every opportunity to flash a taunting grin. He couldn't help it. All he could think about was Ali's legs wrapped around him, her chest rising and falling with needy breaths. Eli responded with a puzzled look every time.

Once they made it to the greenhouses, Sam assigned duties. He had Ali and Eli harvesting crops along with one other person whose name Nik hadn't bothered to learn.

"I think this one," he pointed at another nameless prisoner, "can help harvest the tomatoes and that one can water the plants over there." He pointed Eli in the opposite direction, far away from Ali. Maybe he couldn't reassign Eli completely, but he could at least keep them separate here in the greenhouse.

Eli rolled his eyes but made to follow Nik's orders. It was so satisfying when he didn't put up a fight.

Nik's smug smirk disappeared when his eyes met Ali's. She was clearly not amused. He raised his brows at her and gave a quick wink. She shook her head and turned to begin her work.

"You enjoying yourself?" Sam asked him as they moved toward the corner to observe the prisoners. Sam took a seat on a wooden stool and Nik hopped up on the counter next to him, scratching his forehead.

"What do you mean?"

"I don't know. You just seem to get a kick out of annoying that guy."

"Do you have a problem with it?"

"No. By all means, do whatever you want." He bit into an apple and pulled out a sketch pad with a bored expression. "If there's something I need to know, though…" He gave Nik a questioning look. "If he's dangerous or causing trouble, then you have to tell me."

Nik shrugged. "It's not like that. I'm just having some fun."

"All right. We could all use more entertainment around here, I suppose." He didn't question Nik again after that and Nik thanked the gods that Sam was so easygoing. He'd let Nik torment Eli as much as he wanted so long as the work got done.

Halfway through the day, the prisoners had filled several barrels full of tomatoes. Nik was charged with taking the barrels to the stockroom. He wasn't fond of leaving the greenhouses, but it had to be either him or Sam. Since they couldn't let a prisoner leave on their own. Since Sam had taken the last batch, it was now Nik's turn.

Nik loaded them up on a cart and hauled them off to their storage. When he came back, he looked around at their group. Something wasn't right. He saw the two no-name prisoners harvesting tomatoes and filling new barrels, but Ali wasn't where she was supposed to be.

"Where's Ali?" he asked Sam.

Sam didn't look up from his sketch pad. "Who?"

"The blonde one." Nik was agitated. How the fuck was Sam not paying attention? What else did the prisoners get away with while he wasn't watching?

"Oh yeah, she went over that way to help water the plants." He waved his hand over in Eli's direction and Nik huffed when he saw the two of them, their heads together. Still inseparable. Maybe Nik had underestimated Eli.

He stomped off in their direction. They had to have heard him approaching. Eli caught him out of the corner of his eye but quickly looked back down. Ali ignored him altogether.

"And what are we doing here?" He kept his tone light and airy to hide his irritation.

She stopped what she was doing and stood up straight. "We're watering the crops."

"Pretty sure I gave that job to him and not you."

"Does it matter?"

Nik didn't like the tone of her voice. It didn't matter if she was the most beautiful woman on the planet. He was in charge here, and she was challenging his authority.

"Yes, it does. When I give an order, I expect it to be followed." It was hard to reprimand her with her big brown eyes. They looked so innocent.

"I think you're being a bit ridiculous—"

"Ali, just drop it," Eli interrupted in a mutter. "It's fine. I can work here on my own. It's not a big deal."

Nik gave her a frustrated tilt of the head and waved a hand at Eli. "See? Even this fool knows what's good for him."

He grabbed her by the arm to pull her back to her designated working area, but she wouldn't go easily. She tugged her arm back out of his clutch.

"Why are you doing this?" Her voice was louder now, and they were attracting attention from the others.

Great. Just what he needed.

"Why are *you* doing this?" It wasn't a clever retort, he had to admit, but he was growing tired of this. If one prisoner acted out, it would threaten the whole system. They needed to understand who was in charge. And he needed to be respected. There was no room for insubordination.

He put a forceful hand on her back to guide her in the right direction, but she spun around and pushed him away. Now he was getting angry. She had disregarded his commands *and* put hands on him. If the prisoners thought they could get away with that, there would be a full-on revolt.

He grabbed both of her wrists and pulled her close. "How can I make myself more clear, Ali? You *will* do as I say."

Her eyes grew big. A mix of fear and animosity shone back at him. He didn't want to frighten her, but she wasn't giving him much of a choice.

Then she did the worst thing she could've possibly done. She *spit* in his face.

"Ali!" Eli yelped, standing up from behind her.

Nik closed his eyes, trying to tame the anger rising in him. He breathed heavily as her saliva rolled down his face. "Come with me."

He didn't give her a chance to object this time. His fingers dug into her wrists as he dragged her along.

"Stop," she cried out, her heels digging into the dirt. "You're hurting me."

"Does it look like I care?" he asked, loud enough for the others to hear, but he loosened his grip.

They passed Sam and the other prisoners, who watched in silence. Everyone had seen what had just happened, but he couldn't let her win. That would be a sign of weakness, and he was *not* weak.

Rysburg was not weak.

"Where are you taking me?" Her voice was shaky and higher than normal. He almost felt guilty for the fear he was inducing. *Almost.*

He took her to the edge of the greenhouse and made a sharp left turn through a hallway that connected the greenhouses. She'd never been this way and her eyes searched frantically, taking in her surroundings and finding no comfort. No one to save her. He threw open the door to a dark and dusty shed, full of tools, seeds, spare gloves, aprons and other miscellaneous things. He pulled her arm so hard she flew into the room and up against one of the walls, careful not to knock anything down.

"What is wrong with you?" His anger was out of control.

She cowered from him like an injured animal.

"I'm sorry." It was barely more than a whisper. "I...I wasn't thinking. I just wanted to be with Eli. I didn't think...I didn't think that would happen." Her eyes were big and remorseful. Maybe he wasn't the only one who acted on impulse.

He put his hands on his hips and paced back and forth, pondering what to do next. His temper was cooling but he couldn't just let her get away with that.

No, there had to be consequences.

He let out a loud sigh. "I can't let you treat me like that, Ali. You don't get it. The people here...they have to view me as an authority figure. I can't let you walk all over me. I'll lose my job if they don't think I'm capable."

She hung her head and shifted her feet on the dirty floor. "What happens now?"

"I don't know," he grumbled.

"What would usually happen? If it weren't me, what would you do?"

He hesitated. If it were anyone else, he would've handled it in front of everyone. Would've made an example out of them. If it were anyone else, he would still be irate right now. "Anybody else would be swatted for that. The standard is ten lashes."

She considered for a moment, picking at the dirt under her fingernails. "Do what you have to do."

Nik clenched his jaw and tilted his head, questioning her, but she nodded reassuringly. He had to do something, but could he put his hands on her like that? With barely more than a whisper, he said, "I don't know that I can."

"You said you had to punish me, right? And this is the standard? Then do it. You have no reason to treat me any differently than any other prisoner here."

"I could think of one reason," he retorted.

She looked him in the eyes, and there was a resolve there that startled him. For a woman who appeared so fragile on the outside, she was fiery and strong on the inside. He was drawn to that fire. "Do it."

Nik dragged a hand through his hair. Judging from the determination on her face, he wouldn't talk her out of it. "Turn around. Put your hands on the table."

Her breath hitched as she turned and bent slightly forward, placing her palms flat on the wooden table. He walked up behind her and gripped her shirt, untucking it from her pants. His hands moved around to her front and untied the string holding her pants up. They fell to her ankles the moment he let go.

"I didn't want to have to do this," he muttered.

"I know."

He ran his hand across her skin before pulling back. He brought his hand down with an authoritative force. The sound of the slap lingered in the air for a moment, along with her gasp. It only took seconds for her skin to turn red and irritated.

"Are you okay?" he asked.

"Yes. Just get it over with." There was a hint of fury in her voice. Neither of them wanted to drag this out.

He brought his hand up again for a second smack.

She squirmed against the table, and her fingers tensed and dug into the wood as he made contact.

He inhaled deep and prepared for a third hit. This wasn't the first time he'd doled out punishment, but it was the first time he'd felt as if he were hurting himself too.

She jumped as his hand came down a fourth time. And then a fifth. Her legs were trembling and he thought he heard a soft cry escape her lips.

He cupped her ass with one hand and massaged the skin. Her flesh was hot and sensitive. "You're doing great, Ali. Just five more."

She whimpered but didn't fight back.

After spank number six, he took the time to massage her ass again. He couldn't help but notice how smooth and soft she felt. She was so petite. He loved the way he could fit her in one hand. Like he could break her or save her, depending on her mood. Make no mistake, she was absolutely in charge here, not him. He never would've laid a hand on her if she hadn't suggested it—insisted on it.

He went through a couple more hits, seven and eight, alternating between spanking and rubbing her sore skin. Her muscles became more relaxed, and her moans fluctuated from pain and anguish to something else. Acceptance?

His hand came down for a strong number nine. Once again, she jerked and let out a yelp. He took his time running his thumb over the curve of her ass. He moved his hand further south and back up, easing her pain.

She melted into his hand and his cock stirred as he watched her body react to his touch. She wavered on her feet and pushed into his palm. He trailed his fingers lower, between her cheeks and closer to her core. She rocked her hips just a fraction of an inch.

Nik didn't want to remove his hand from her perfect body.

She tilted her hips even further and they both sucked in a sharp breath. She had rubbed her slick center against his fingers, and he was shocked by how turned on she was. Nik moaned and Ali turned to look at him, waiting for his reaction. Her fuck-me eyes were going to drive him crazy.

He could. He could fuck her hard right here. Nothing was stopping him. She'd made it pretty clear that she wanted him as well. Except this didn't feel right. He didn't want her first memory of his dick inside her to be alongside his punishment.

It took all his self-control to pull his hand back, and she whimpered in disappointment. He ran his thumb over his damp fingers, appreciating the way her body squirmed. God, he'd love to see her bent over his bed, legs spread.

Then he raised his hand and brought it down fast for one final smack. He wanted the imprint of his hand to remind her for days to come. She cried out in pain and maybe a little bit of pleasure. Did it even count as punishment if she enjoyed it?

He bent to retrieve her pants and tied them back in place as she stood up straight. Her legs trembled, and he couldn't tell if it was from agony or arousal. He spun her around and noticed the tears in the corner of her eyes. His hands slid up her thighs and rested on her hips.

"Are you all right?" he asked as he wiped her cheek with his thumb.

She was breathing heavily, but otherwise looked fine. "I'm okay."

She slowly raked his body with her eyes, and he felt an overwhelming wave of compassion. He lowered his mouth to hers and kissed her gently. She held still initially, confused and scared. But after a moment's hesitation, she moved her lips with his and wrapped her hands around his neck, pulling him in close.

Nik responded by sliding his arms behind her back and holding her body against him. He might've been the one to hurt her, but he wanted to be the one to comfort her too. He didn't want her to fear him. She pulled him so hard that he tripped over his own feet and pushed them both into the table behind them, fumbling clumsily. Her hands pulled at the top of his jeans, threatening to dip inside, to grip him. He slid one hand lower, over the top of her ass, and she flinched.

"Please don't make me do that again," he whispered in her ear, her hair tickling his cheeks. He kissed her neck, just below her ear.

"I can't make any promises," she countered mischievously.

He groaned as she nibbled on his bottom lip, tugging him between her teeth, and his dick shifted in his pants. She had a wild power over him and he was all too willing to let her take control.

She bit a little too hard and he jolted, bringing his hand up to feel his slightly swollen lip.

"You left your mark. It's only fair I leave mine."

She was right.

When he traced the teeth marks on the inside of his mouth, he was vividly reminded of her mouth on his. That was a feeling he would gladly have permanently imprinted on his lips.

Chapter Seventeen

ELI

Eli felt guilty from the moment Ali had spit in Nik's face. She'd been so determined to work with him. He could've told her no, but he was selfish and had let her stay. All of this could've been avoided if he had acted more wisely. He'd sworn to protect her and once again he had failed.

Nik had been cold and venomous when he'd returned to the greenhouses. Eli had been genuinely scared for her when Nik had pulled her away by the arm. He was easily twice her size and the way he'd gripped her wrist made it seem like he would snap her in half.

Eli didn't like or respect the guy. But if he wanted to find a way out of Rysburg, it would be best to not draw extra attention. He didn't want to be on anyone's radar, but Ali seemed to draw Nik's attention no matter what she did.

It still made his stomach turn to think about Nik's warning. That he would make Ali beg for him. It seemed ludicrous, but it worried Eli nonetheless. Should he worn Ali that Nik had labeled her a target of his desires?

She wasn't exactly Eli's property, but up until a week ago she was supposed to be his wife. And she was still his best friend. He still loved her. He was allowed to be worried about her. He was allowed to have an opinion on her life. Was he allowed to intervene or would she get mad if he brought Nik up again?

Every minute she was gone made him more anxious. What was Nik doing to her? Would he hurt her? Would he force himself on her? Eli felt sick at the thought. He didn't like that they had left the greenhouse and sought privacy. He wrung his hands together and shifted nervously, pacing back and forth as he waited for them to return.

It was too difficult to focus on his work. His mind was consumed with thoughts of Ali. He startled when water overflowed from one of the planters. He'd held his watering can in one place for too long.

After about fifteen minutes, they walked back through the rows of crops. Ali walked a little funny, like it hurt to walk. But she kept her distance and moved to her designated row, staying far away from Eli. Despite his best efforts to catch her eye, she remained focused on her work and kept her head down. It was impossible to tell if she was okay.

Nik, on the other hand, looked smug as ever. He strutted with his head held high and sat next to Sam. They exchanged words that Eli couldn't hear and laughed like they didn't have a care in the world.

It was excruciatingly difficult to take his mind off Ali for the rest of the day. He kept throwing glances her way, hoping her expression would give something away. Anything. She remained stone-faced and didn't look his way.

He threw himself into his work and busied himself to make the time pass faster, but it hardly helped. When their work was done, he wasted no time running to her side. She was walking a little easier now, but he didn't miss the grimace on her face as she moved.

"What happened?" he asked immediately.

She hesitated before responding, "Nothing, Eli."

Nik paused his conversation with Sam to watch the two of them interact. It infuriated Eli that he couldn't have a single moment alone with Ali, that he didn't get the same level of privacy they did. How could she be honest with him when Nik was breathing down their necks?

"Bullshit. Obviously, something happened." He lowered his voice and moved closer. She still wouldn't look him in the eyes.

"Well, yeah. Something happened. But I really don't want to talk about it, Eli." She frowned and tossed her dirty gloves into a pile with the others, then continued walking toward the exit.

"Did he hurt you? What did he do?" He studied her face, no visible signs of abuse, then wondered what her body looked like beneath her clothes.

"Nothing. I'm fine." She crossed her arms, folding into herself like she could feel him assessing her and wanted to hide.

He wasn't paying attention to her responses. "Did he"—he gulped and pinched his brows together—"*do* anything to you?"

She stopped in her tracks and looked horrified. "No!" Then she did her best to soften her expression, taking his hand in hers and squeezing once. "I don't want to talk about it. I promise I'm okay, though. Can you let it go?"

Eli didn't want to let it go. He wanted to know exactly what had happened and just how bad his response should be when he finally got his revenge on the people of Rysburg, especially toward Nik. His mind played all the worst scenarios. It would be better if she just told him. He hated not knowing what had happened, but she was convincing. If she said she was okay, then he believed her. He nodded. "All right, but if anything ever does happen...you'll tell me?"

There was a flicker of something in her expression that he couldn't identify, but she quickly hid it. "Of course."

He held her hand the rest of the walk home, warming her fingers as best as he could. They were both shivering by the time they walked through the prison door.

He insisted she shower first. She likely needed to wash away the misery of the day more than he did. As she left, she gave him a halfhearted smile and continued toward her cell.

When it was his turn, he let the hot water of the shower ease his tension and wash away his worries. He was tired. Tired of every day feeling like a struggle. And now it felt like his one source of support was pulling away. Of course, she was dealing with her own shit. They were all working through their issues in their own way, but he needed her.

He could only hope that she needed him too.

Chapter Eighteen

ALI

IT WAS A WEEK later before Ali could no longer feel the stinging sensation on her bum. She was cautious not to upset Nik or disobey any more of his orders during that time. He was so confusing. She'd never dealt with anyone who was so hot and cold. The brutality of his swing had hurt, but the gentleness of his hand had made her stomach coil.

She should hate him for treating her like that, but for some reason she only felt more called to satisfy him. She didn't want to let him down again. It was pathetic.

And then there was Eli, who was watching her like a hawk these days. It felt like he was waiting for her to break. Every morning he'd give her a look full of concern and every day she'd roll her eyes when he wasn't looking.

Her frustration with him was entirely misplaced. It wasn't his fault she was hiding things from him. She was angry with herself for doing and feeling things that required hiding. She'd never kept anything from Eli before, and she hated the way it felt. He was such a gracious and selfless best friend, and she didn't deserve him.

Maybe she could tell him. Would he understand? Doubtful. Eli resented Nik and Nik seemed to enjoy getting under Eli's skin. They weren't going to be friends any time soon.

And what exactly would she tell him? She didn't even know Nik. Not really. She felt sparks whenever he was around, but she knew nothing about his life, his dreams, his hobbies. He was a mystery, and maybe that was part of what appealed to her. That and the threat of danger. She was drawn to him despite her common sense.

He made her feel good. Made her feel alive. The attack on Andus had shattered her and made her feel numb, but Nik left her body and soul flickering with hot flames.

When Sam appeared at her cell door, she felt a pang of disappointment. "Good morning. We've got a special project for you today."

When he noticed her raised brows, he clarified, "Don't worry. It's nothing bad. It might actually be a nice break from the greenhouses."

A special project sounded mysterious and daunting.

Sam waited until they had all gathered at the head of the prison, not just the folks who worked in the greenhouses but everyone from Andus, and a few faces she only recognized from their mealtimes. People who had been here longer than she had. A sense of guilt crept in as it occurred to her she hadn't taken the time to get to know any of them during meals or free time.

There were also a few other guards, the ones who took the other groups to various job assignments. And Nik. She gulped when she caught his eyes, and he winked in her direction. She glanced up at Eli quickly, but he didn't seem to notice.

"Do you know what this is about?" Eli asked her.

"No idea."

The people huddled close so they could hear Sam. "Today you're all being recruited to help with our Survivors' Day party. The town square needs to be set up with tables and decorations and the chefs will need help preparing food. We have a lot to do today before the celebration tonight."

Sam led the way to the town square while the prisoners followed. The rest of the guards surrounded them, keeping them herded together like cattle.

"What is Survivors' Day?" a young girl named Theresa asked. None of the prisoners knew. They all shrugged, equally as confused as little Theresa.

The town center appeared before them, and they were separated into smaller groups to work. The older and stronger prisoners moved large tables, big enough for dozens, to the center of the square. Ali was tasked with setting up decorations.

A few women from Rysburg hovered over piles of decorations, passing them out and commanding the prisoners where to put things. One woman thrust a pumpkin into Ali's hands. It was larger than her head and incredibly heavy, but she hauled it toward the table as directed.

The pumpkin thudded on the center of the table and another younger teenage girl, Carly, helped to place candles and smaller items around the main centerpiece.

"It's kind of pretty," Carly commented as she tied a ribbon in a bow on the stem of the pumpkin. Her eyes were tired and sad.

"How are you doing?" Ali remembered Carly from Andus. She had worked a lot with Ali's mom in the gardens. What was she doing now?

"I'm okay. They have me working with the children," she said as if she could read Ali's mind. "It's not so bad. They might be the best part of this place. Still so kind and unhardened. They don't look at me differently like the adults do."

Ali summoned a weak smile. It was reassuring to know that Carly had found a flicker of light in Rysburg. She never should've been forced to live through this. None of them should've suffered this fate.

Ali glanced up to find her own flicker of light staring at her from across the square with his beautiful blue eyes. Her eyes darted back to the table, feeling uneasy after meeting his gaze.

Carly left to get more ribbons and candles while Ali smoothed a tablecloth. She walked back to the front of the square to pick up another pumpkin, but this one was even heavier than the last.

"Would you like some help with that?" Nik's voice surrounded her.

"No," she grunted. "I can do it myself."

She could hear Nik chuckling behind her as she struggled to get the pumpkin to the table. Okay, maybe she should've accepted his help. She was only a foot away from the table when she felt the pumpkin slip.

Nik reached out to grab it and easily lifted it up on the table before turning toward her. "You're welcome."

"I didn't say thank you."

He bit his cheek and smirked.

Why was his arrogance so attractive? She couldn't handle the way he was undressing her with his eyes, so she diverted his attention. "What is Survivors' Day?"

He tilted his head. "Did you not have Survivors' Day?"

"Clearly not." She crossed her arms, but when his attention went to her chest, she dropped them again.

He gave a subtle nod, contemplating all the ways their lives were different. "It is what it sounds like. It's a day to celebrate those of us who survived the end of the world. Those of us who continue to survive this god forsaken planet. According to the stories, this used to be called 'Thanksgiving,' a day for people to express gratitude. But when society collapsed, everyone was just thankful to be alive. It became a new tradition. A reminder that we're all lucky to be here."

"You're lucky to be here," she corrected him. "Some of us won't be celebrating."

He placed his hand on her chin and brought it up to him. She tried to pull away, but he only held her tighter. "You're a survivor too, Ali."

He looked like he wanted to kiss her, but he obviously knew better than to do that in the middle of all these people. It felt like her chest was caving in. It hurt to want him.

He released her face and walked away, passing Carly as he went. She approached Ali with more candles and ribbons in her hands. "Are you okay? Was he bothering you? That man looks terrifying."

Ali stifled a laugh. She had no idea.

Once they had finished with the decorations, they moved on to cutlery, setting the tables for the dozens of people who would celebrate that night. Even the napkins and tablecloths were ornate with subtle browns, reds, and creams. At the end of the day, the scene was beautiful. The candles flickered and lent a warm glow to the town square.

Ali wished she'd had an invitation of her own.

⁂

As she lay in bed that night, she could hear the sounds from the middle of town echoing through the halls of the prison. It sounded like a massive celebration. She tried to peer out her window by standing on the bed, but she couldn't see what was going on outside.

She lay back down and brought the blanket up around her shoulders. She'd just have to use her imagination and picture what the celebration must look like.

The food had been brought out and arranged on the tables before they'd left. Roasted chicken, potatoes, corn, and so much more. They'd worked until the very last minute, carefully perfecting the smallest of details. They had only been shuffled back to the prison when the first party guests arrived.

Ali closed her eyes and listened to the faint music that occasionally broke through the loud conversation. It made her miss their celebrations at home. They may have been on a smaller scale, but they still held so much importance to her.

Just as she drifted to sleep, she heard feet shuffling outside her cell. She raised her head and squinted toward the sound.

"I thought you might be asleep," Nik said.

"I'm awake." She climbed out of bed and approached the cell door. Nik was scrambling with a key to unlock her cell. "What are you doing?"

The door creaked open, and he grabbed her by the waist. "Come with me."

He led her back toward the entrance of the cells but opened a door that revealed a set of stairs. They climbed upward and an icy breeze blew around her. They were on the roof with a full panoramic view of Rysburg. Off to the side of the building, she could see the town center illuminated by fire. She smiled as she spotted the stage where musicians were playing.

"Pretty good view, hmm?"

It would be no use to deny him. The second she'd set her eyes on the scene below them, her mouth had formed into a wide grin.

"It is," she admitted.

More stunning than the party were the stars above them. This was the first night in a long time that she'd seen them. She didn't feel so confined up here, alone with the sky. A shooting star blazed across the sky, and she gasped.

"I brought you something."

She turned to look at where he was standing behind her. A small blanket had been laid out and on top of it were two plates with a slice of some dessert she hadn't seen before.

"What is it?" she asked, kneeling to inspect it.

He kneeled beside her and held out a fork.

She took it from him, her fingers grazing his. "I don't have to beg this time?" she asked with a hint of sarcasm.

Nik's laugh made her squirm. That familiar tug in her belly returned. She didn't even have the energy to fight it anymore.

"No begging. Unless there's something else you're hungry for."

She rolled her eyes but dug her fork into the dessert. It was fluffy and delicious, and a moan escaped her lips as she swallowed.

"It's pumpkin pie."

"It's fucking heaven."

Nik laughed again and pulled her on top of his lap. He held her chin and pressed his lips against hers. His touch was soft yet demanding. His tongue danced across her lips, and she could taste the pumpkin on him as well.

"*This*...is fucking heaven," he declared.

She shook her head. He was ridiculous. She tried to move from his lap, but he kept an arm around her, locking her in place. So she stayed and ate her pie in silence, taking in the exquisite view surrounding them.

When they finished, she leaned her back against his chest and he wrapped his arms around her. They listened to the music playing below and took turns pointing out the shooting stars that appeared with a frequency she'd never seen before. It was magical.

Her cheeks were rosy and freezing but the rest of her body was kept warm, tucked into his. He brushed his lips against her temple and pressed a kiss to her skin. Her heart raced and yet she felt so at ease in his arms.

"Happy Survivors' Day, Ali."

Chapter Nineteen

ALI

The next morning, Ali stood from her bed to get ready for work and wobbled on her feet. She felt a little lightheaded and unsteady. Admittedly, she hadn't been eating much. She wasn't doing it on purpose. Eli was right; it would be incredibly stupid to let herself get weak just in case the opportunity ever arose to escape. But that didn't mean her appetite had reappeared out of nowhere. She had so much on her mind and the anxiety was crippling. She vowed to eat more today, even if she didn't feel like it.

She splashed cold water on her face and wiped it away on the back of her hand. She pulled on a clean pair of underwear and jeans. They fit even looser than they had the day she arrived in Rysburg, which seemed impossible, given how malnourished she'd been.

Her hands shook. She gripped the bedpost to steady herself, but the room kept spinning. She managed to pull a long sleeve shirt on before the sound of footsteps echoed through the hall.

Nik came to retrieve her from her cell today and an involuntary grin stretched across her face. She always felt butterflies when he showed up at her door instead of Sam. Heat rushed through her when his eyes explored her. It felt like she was his ultimate desire. Like there wasn't anything else in this world he would rather look at than her.

And she felt the same. After their night on the roof, it was impossible to deny that there was something between them. She loved to gaze at his muscular arms under a black T-shirt. She liked the way it hugged his abs and recalled what it felt like to run her fingertips over his flexed muscles. She cursed the days he wore a jacket or a long-sleeve shirt over them. And his jawline was just so kissable.

But her favorite part of all was his eyes. When they caught hers, it was like he really *saw* her. Like somehow, just by looking at her, he knew exactly who she was. It was comforting and unnerving all at once.

"Good morning," he said in that deep voice of his. His eyes sparkled, and he flashed a small grin.

"Good morning." She made her way to walk toward the door but wobbled and had to reach for the wall for support. Nik's reflexes were like lightning, and he grabbed her around the waist to prop her up. She wiped the sweat from her brow and let him bear her weight. He was just so comfortable.

"Are you all right? What's wrong?" He frowned and pressed a hand to her forehead. "Ali, you're burning up."

"What? No, I'm fine." She swatted his hand away. "I just didn't eat enough."

Nik took a step back and assessed her. Like he was waiting for her to keel over. Why did the men in her life keep expecting her to break? "Mm-hmm," he grumbled. "If you say so. Can you work today?"

"Yes. I told you, I'm fine." She sat down at the edge of her bed and took a moment, waiting for the floor to stop moving. Her head felt heavy, like it was going to topple over.

"Here," Nik said, kneeling on the ground before her. He pulled a leg toward him and slipped on her boot, lacing up the strings. She had to grip his shoulder as he tugged. The force made her wobble.

"Does it need to be that tight?" she asked while his hands worked on the other boot.

"Tighter is better." He smirked and raised his eyes quickly before looking back down at her shoestrings.

Ali shook her head, but couldn't stop the grin from forming on her face. The innuendo, his hands on her legs, his head between her knees. Her head started to spin again.

He stood and pulled her up gently. He stared at her longer than necessary before deciding to trust that she was okay to work. "Let's go."

He stayed close after that—not that she was complaining. She liked it when his arm brushed up against her. She liked it when her fingers brushed up against his.

Even after they met with Eli and the others for their trek to the greenhouses, Nik stayed closer than he normally would. Within arm's reach but out of Eli's line of sight. How lucky was she to have two men protecting her, even if they were overbearing? She snuck several glances back at him on their walk and every time she was met with his simmering gaze. Eli went on about who knew what. She had stopped listening ten minutes ago.

Nik finally gave her some space when they made it to the greenhouse. He must've been satisfied that she'd made it there without incident. The cool air helped clear her head. Perhaps it had been just a fleeting moment of dizziness.

By midmorning, she knew that wasn't true. She felt even worse than she had back in her cell. Black crept into the corners of her eyes, and she was too weak to lift even a watering can. Her fingers wrapped around the handle, but the weight was too much for her shaky arms. She attempted to lift it, and everything went cold and dark.

Her eyes fluttered open to see several people surrounding her, including Nik by her head and Eli at her feet. Nik had her head propped up in his lap while Eli threw him daggers with his eyes. Everyone else stood at a distance, their gazes suffocating her.

What had happened?

"Ali? Ali? Look at me." Nik cupped her cheek and patiently waited for her to open her eyes completely. She struggled to focus, but when she did, she studied the wrinkles in his forehead. He looked so concerned. She felt the need to press a hand to his face and soothe those creases of distress, but then remembered that everyone was staring at her, including Eli.

"Are you okay?" Eli said softly, doing his best now to ignore Nik. His hand gently gripped her ankle, his thumb rubbing comforting circles against her skin. His face had lost most of its color, but he looked relieved to see her awake. She had no idea how long she'd been out.

"What happened?" she asked, shivering from a cold sweat. For a moment she considered sitting up, but she didn't think she could support herself. She decided against it.

"You passed out," Nik answered, placing his hand on her head again to check her temperature. "I thought you said you were fine." It sounded like a reprimand.

"I thought I was." Ali shivered again, and he pulled her body closer to him. The dizziness subsided and she started to sit up, but both Eli and Nik pushed her back down, looking at each other with contempt. The animosity between them was visible. Tangible. They were both possessive creatures prepared to claim her.

Gods, what had she gotten herself into.

Sam hurried over with a glass of water and knelt, handing it over. Her hands shook when she tried to grab it and she nearly sloshed water all over herself.

Nik took it from her hands and insisted, "Here, let me help you."

She sipped the water cautiously, her stomach churning. The only thing that could be worse than her current predicament would be to vomit in front of everyone. She scanned the small crowd surrounding her and suddenly felt very self-conscious.

Nik read her expression so effortlessly. "Everyone, get back to work. We've got this." He gestured to Eli. "You, too."

"Like hell I am."

It pulled a small chuckle from Ali. He was so stubborn.

Nik looked like he was about to argue, but Ali interrupted, "Nik, it's fine. He can stay, right?"

She gave him her best pleading eyes, which was quite difficult when she could hardly keep them open. That look had always worked on Eli, but she could tell it wasn't having the same impact on Nik.

"No." It wasn't his usual cold or commanding response. It was soothing. He turned to Eli and, for the first time in Ali's memory, he addressed him without his normal frigid armor. "You can't do anything for her right now. I've got her."

Indeed he did. Another shiver made its way through her body. He had unexpectedly taken every bit of her that she was willing to give. And she was surprised to discover just how much of herself that meant.

Eli looked at her, expecting her to protest. She didn't have the energy for it, though. She didn't want to hurt him, but she knew she was about to.

"It's okay, Eli. You don't have to stay."

She expected Nik to gloat, but he stayed quiet and gently brushed her hair away from her temple. Eli's face scrunched in a mixture of anguish and disgust. He stood abruptly and turned to leave, giving her one last look before shuffling away, shaking his head. If she had any strength left, she might've reached out to him, but she couldn't seem to lift her arms.

The ground disappeared as Nik lifted her. He held her close to his chest, and she welcomed the warmth of his body. She nuzzled her head into his shoulder. She inhaled and his scent dazzled her. It only took seconds to place.

Pine trees.

Her eyes drooped and her grip loosened, settling softly on his chest.

The rhythm of his breathing and the jostle of his steps rocked her into a deep sleep, so much so that she didn't feel the harsh cold of winter when they stepped out from the humid greenhouse.

Chapter Twenty

ALI

When Ali opened her eyes again, she was lying in a large, firm bed with fluffy blankets, between sturdy wooden bed posts. The white comforter covering the bed had floral designs sewn into it by hand. Definitely not the familiar cot she slept on every night in her cell. She blinked and placed her palms on the bed, willing the room to stop spinning. She still felt nauseous.

The room had a golden glow to it. Sunset crept through the thin drapes that covered windows on two of the four walls. It gave her a sense of comfort despite not knowing where she was. This place was warm and inviting.

She studied the room. A bowl of water with a rag sat next to her on a nightstand. There was a large wooden wardrobe, one side hanging open. She could see men's clothing inside. Books and small trinkets covered the surface of two matching bookshelves. A chaise lounge stood in the corner, and she recognized the jacket hanging off the arm.

Nik's jacket. This was Nik's room. And Nik's bed.

She held her breath and studied her surroundings. She felt like she was seeing something she shouldn't. Like she was invading his personal space. She wasn't supposed to be here.

Shifting to her side, she tried to press up on one elbow but had to fall back down immediately. Her body was too weak to prop herself up, and the room spun as soon as she attempted it.

Cold sweat broke out on her forehead, and she wiped at it. Her pillow was slightly damp from her fever.

His pillow. This wasn't her pillow. She was lying in his bed where he slept every night. So where was he?

Her mouth watered, and she realized how thirsty she was. And hungry. She must've passed out for several hours if the sun was already setting. She had missed lunch and dinnertime was quickly approaching. She wasn't sure if she could keep anything down, but she had to try.

The door across from her creaked open softly, and she saw Nik's hair peek around the corner before the rest of his body followed.

"You're awake." He opened the door the rest of the way and walked into the room. "You've been out for hours. I was getting worried."

"You were worried about me?" Her voice was scratchy, like it hadn't been used in days. She placed her hand on her neck and massaged her swollen lymph nodes.

"Hang on," he said as he slipped back through the door. She could hear him on the other side, shuffling things around. "I'll make you some tea," he shouted loud enough for her to hear.

The kitchen must be connected to his room. She was so curious to know more about his home. She hardly knew much about him at all, but it felt like this house would share his secrets. It would divulge everything she needed to know. She wanted a grand tour, but that would have to wait. She settled into the bed and pulled the blankets up further.

After a couple minutes, he returned with a steaming cup of tea. She tilted the pillow against his headboard and adjusted herself. It was only a slight incline, but it was all she could manage without getting nauseous again.

"Here you go."

She took the cup from him with shaky hands.

"Thank you."

The tea was delicious with a hint of citrus, and it felt amazing on her sore throat.

"Feeling any better?" He placed the back of his hand on her forehead and watched her with his steely blue eyes.

"Not really." She let out a sigh and sank back into the bed. He grabbed the cup out of her hands, clearly concerned she might spill it. Her arms snaked back under the blanket where they were nice and warm. Even being out in the open for a few minutes gave her the chills.

He reached into the bowl of water and pulled out the rag, dabbing gently at her hairline. Her eyes fluttered shut at the touch. He was good at this. At taking care of someone.

"How am I here right now?" she asked. "I find it hard to believe Rysburg doesn't have a dedicated infirmary."

"We do." She shivered as he ran the rag across her arm and then let it drop back into the bowl of water. "Would you rather be there?"

"No. I just...I don't understand how I can be here...in your house. This is your house, right?"

"It is." His eyes were softer than normal. Maybe it was the lighting...or maybe she was delirious. "I might have paid off a guard or two."

She scoffed. Not that she wasn't grateful to be in this comfortable bed, but the idea of him spending his money to keep her close was ludicrous. "And how much did I cost?"

"Do you want the real answer or do you want me to say something absurd like you're priceless to me?" He placed a hand over his heart and tilted his head affectionately.

Ali grumbled some expletives, and he laughed. "Are you hungry?"

"Oh my god, yes." Her stomach growled right on cue despite the nausea churning there.

"I've got some soup on the stove right now." His voice was low and sultry and penetrated her bones. What an odd twist of fate that had led them to sharing this intimate moment together. She should get sick more often.

"Sounds perfect." An invasive thought crossed her mind. She didn't know when she'd get this chance again. "Do you cook?"

He tilted his head, and the sunlight hit his exquisite jawline in a new way. He was stunningly gorgeous, especially in this light and in this room. "I do."

"What's your favorite color?" she pressed. She'd start with the easy questions.

His lips turned up in amusement. "It's green."

He said nothing else. He was waiting for her. Playing her game.

"How old are you?"

"Twenty-six."

Only two years older than her.

"Do you live here alone?"

"Are you planning on sneaking in and killing me?" he responded playfully.

She squinted her eyes and waited for his legitimate response.

"Yes, Ali, I live here alone. Does that surprise you?" He chuckled, and the sound was music to her ears.

"Maybe a little. Truthfully, I expected a playboy like you to have a woman to come home to." It was hard to believe a man this attractive was sleeping alone every night.

He scoffed. "What makes you think I'm a playboy?"

"Aren't you?" He'd been chasing after her so ferociously, she had assumed he was like that with all the women.

He shook his head and gave her that penetrating glare. He leaned in closer to her and whispered darkly, "No, I don't bring women home to bed. I've saved that position for you." He winked and goosebumps covered her body. Then he leaned back again and eyed the ground thoughtfully.

It took a moment before she found her voice again.

"What about siblings? Parents?"

She loved that he wasn't stopping her. Her brain was racing with questions to ask next.

He swallowed, and she watched his throat bob. "No siblings. My parents are both dead."

Same, she thought, but she didn't want to ruin the mood. Not when she was opening him up like a book.

"Why did you become a jailor?"

"Technically, I'm not. I'm a guardsman. I go where I'm needed. I just so happen to be needed at the prison right now." He licked his lips and paused, shifting his weight back and forth uncomfortably. "My dad was a guardsman. He expected a lot out of me growing up, especially when my mom got sick. I was expected to be the man of the house while he was gone, but it felt like nothing I ever did was good enough for him. He treated me like a servant more than a son. Initially, I wanted to be a guardsman to be like him, to prove that I could be everything he expected of me. But the older I got, the more I wanted to do it to spite him. I wanted to be better than him. I wanted to be chosen for the missions he was overlooked on. I wanted the titles and recognition he never earned. I wanted him to stand in my shadow for once. I wanted him to see me."

Nik picked at his fingernails before speaking again. "It didn't matter in the end. He died before we ever served together. A heart attack not long after my mom died. I was already in training, though, so my fate was sealed."

It was a lot more than Ali was prepared for and a small part of her regretted prying when she saw how uneasy it made him. He had gone out of his way to take care of her while she was sick, and she returned the favor by opening up old wounds.

She was saved from coming up with the perfect, comforting response when he spoke first, clearing his throat. "I'm going to check on the soup."

He strode out of the room, shoulders hunched.

Ali turned to her side and stared into the room, slightly darker now. When he came back, he had shaken off the confession, but his playful grin hadn't returned.

Ali got a few sips down while propped up on her elbows. She took a break and let the broth and noodles settle in her stomach. She could already feel the life returning to her cheeks. Her fingertips were no longer corpse-like. They were warming up rather quickly.

Eventually she found the strength to sit up fully in Nik's bed, the blankets still tucked around her lower half. There was a cloud of awkwardness in the air as they both ate their soup silently. The only sound was the clinking of spoons against their bowls.

"So..." he started in a husky voice. "What's your favorite color?"

His lips stretched thin in a sly grin and she let out a half-stifled laugh. She could recognize his attempt to ease the tension for what it was.

"Blue," she responded. Her fingers traced the floral design on the comforter. "Did your mom sew this?"

He nodded silently. "For my last birthday before she passed."

"I bet she was lovely." Any woman who poured this much time and love into a gift surely would be. It reminded her of her own mother.

"She was."

He stood and took the empty bowl from her hands and returned to the kitchen. By now, darkness was flooding the room and Nik lit a lamp in the corner. He gave her one of his T-shirts and drawstring shorts to sleep in. Her own clothes were filthy from the greenhouse and damp with sweat. While she changed, he switched the sheets on the bed for fresh ones. Of course, his clothes engulfed her. His shorts hung well below her knees and his shirt draped loosely over her shoulders, but it smelled like him.

She slid back into the blankets and blissfully accepted the way the large, soft bed enveloped her. She was feeling much better after eating, just exhausted. Some sleep would surely help her recovery.

"Do you need anything else?" he asked.

She scanned the room. A glass of water. A fresh wet rag to wipe her sweat in the middle of the night. Extra blankets at the foot of the bed.

"No, I think I'm all set." An unexpected thought crossed her mind. "Where will you sleep?"

"I can sleep in the living room." He watched as her eyes squinted in confusion, in disappointment. He tilted his head down. "Unless..."

She gulped. She hadn't thought this through. Her instinct absolutely wanted him to slide under the covers with her, but the voice in her head filled her with self-doubt.

She shouldn't be doing this, but fuck, he looked so good. And it'd be so nice to fall asleep with his arms around her.

His eyes darkened as she scooted to one side of the bed and made room for him. He pulled his shirt up and over his head, and her jaw dropped. Oh *gods,* those abs.

She pressed her thighs together and bit her lip, eagerly waiting for him to get into bed. She wanted to run her fingers over those ridges again, but this time without the dreaded fabric. He turned around and she watched as he unbuttoned his jeans.

"Turn around," he commanded her as he looked over his shoulder, hands paused at the waistband of his pants.

"Why?" She smirked. "You've seen mine. Show me yours."

He fought a smile but shook his head and proceeded to undress. Ali watched hungrily. His abs were heavenly, but his ass was sinful. She might've let a small whimper escape her lips because he scooped up a pair of shorts and covered up quicker than she would've liked.

Before getting into bed, he put out the oil lamp. She could make out the outline of his figure as her eyes adjusted to the darkness. She held her breath as he lifted the covers to hop into bed next to her. His body felt warm and strong, his chest pressed against her back. He roped one arm around her waist and laid his head on the other. Without a shirt, his skin was warm against her flesh.

She squirmed and pressed back into him, her ass nudging his pelvis. His arm tightened, holding her still.

"Don't do that," he said in a strained voice.

If she had more energy, she might've turned around and wrapped a leg around his waist, but her fatigue was overwhelming. She used all her self-control to relax into him, letting the heat of his body and the steady rise and fall of his chest soothe her to sleep.

❦ ❦

Ali woke in the middle of the night with sweat pouring from her body. Nik's arm was still draped across her, holding her tightly against his chest.

His legs were tangled in between hers, and it took everything in her to ignore the aching between her legs.

She needed to move. She needed to get away, right now. She felt sick, and she couldn't be sick. Not here. Not with him.

Her stomach rolled uneasily and she inched away from him, out of his clutch. She let his arm drop to the bed gently and his continuous soft snoring let her know she hadn't disturbed his sleep. She hobbled to the door, hunched over in pain, and found the bathroom door just outside his bedroom.

She didn't bother to find a light. The soft starlight lit up the room just enough to make out the shape of the toilet. She hit her knees on the hard floor and retched into the chamber, her body shaking with sickness.

Hair clung to her neck and her forehead as she continued to be sick, gripping the edge with white knuckles. She felt like she was dying. She had survived so much, but this would be her ultimate demise. It really was a cruel world.

The bed creaked, and she heard Nik's footsteps. A candle illuminated his figure through the crack in the door.

"Are you okay?" he asked before kneeling beside her.

She tried to wave him off. He'd done enough already. "I'm fine. I didn't mean to wake you. Really, go back to bed."

He huffed out a small breath. "I'm not going to leave you like this." He reached out with a glass of water that he'd brought from the bedroom and pressed it to her lips.

Her body trembled so badly, she thought she might be sick again. She pushed the cup away.

Nik traced circles over her back, his strong hand soothing her and calming her unsteady breathing. He pulled her hair back while she retched again.

"I don't want you to see me like this," she moaned.

"There isn't a single part of you that I wouldn't want to see," he whispered.

Her body slumped and Nik guided her to the floor, laying her head in his lap. He continued to rub her back and brush the hair back from her face. He lifted the back of her shirt and slipped his hand under, rubbing his hand over her smooth back. It simultaneously gave her chills and comforted her.

She dug her fingers into his thigh and closed her eyes, desperately seeking rest. She prayed her stomach would settle enough that she could sleep. Her body fought against the exhaustion that ravaged her. His hand stopped moving as he pressed his palm into her back.

"You're burning up again."

She murmured indistinctly.

"Do you trust me?"

She nodded into his lap and he lifted her up, turning her around to face him. He stood and moved to the bathtub, turning the water on and allowing it to warm up. He grabbed the bottom of her shirt, and she knew what he was about to do. She lifted her arms so he could slide it off. He gave her a hand for balance as she stepped out of her shorts and then helped her into the bath. The lukewarm water quickly cooled her down as he poured a cup full over her hair and down her back.

After a few minutes, she stood. He wrapped a towel around her and then held her in his lap. She studied his face and then traced his lips with her fingertips.

"You confuse me," she said, and the words came out as delirious as she felt.

"How so?" His lips moved beneath her touch.

"I think I was supposed to hate you..."

If he felt anything, he didn't let it show. His breathing remained steady as his blue eyes bore through her. "But you don't?"

She shook her head, and her eyes fell closed.

She wasn't sure how long she'd been passed out, but she felt him stir beneath her. He carefully stood and picked her up off the floor, cradling her in his arms. She draped an arm around his neck and leaned into his strong body as he carried her back to bed.

Chapter Twenty-One

NIK

A TINGLING FEELING IN Nik's arm woke him up. His limb had fallen asleep sometime during the night. He carefully lifted his head off his arm to allow the blood flow to return. Ali didn't move. Her body simply lifted and fell with every deep breath she took. She needed this rest. She'd been here a couple days now, slowly recovering.

Despite the grislier moments of taking care of a sick woman, Nik had loved every minute. She was here, with him. He got to spend uninterrupted time with her, and it was perfect. He felt a bond slowly forming with her, more than just the physical connection.

She looked so beautiful with her blonde hair falling over her shoulders like a golden waterfall. He brushed her hair off her shoulder. The T-shirt hung off her small frame, exposing her bare skin. He brushed his lips against it. She smelled sweet, like flowers, mixed with the scent of his own shirt. He liked the way they mingled. Like he was all over her.

She shifted slightly in her sleep, and he let out a heavy sigh when her lower half nudged his groin. She rubbed against him and reached a hand back toward his thigh. She knew exactly what she was doing to him. She did this every time he hugged her from behind. This time, he didn't have the heart to stop her. He ran his fingers along her thighs and lifted her shirt ever so slightly. She wasn't wearing any shorts, so he could feel the soft skin of her ass pressing into him. He gave her a squeeze before moving his hands to her hip bones. He was the luckiest man in the world.

His cock hardened as he pulled her close to him. It didn't take much for her to get him going. He ran his hands up her arms and watched as the hairs stood on end. She inhaled and shivered. His lips brushed her shoulder again, and she turned to look at him.

"Good morning," she said sleepily.

He moved his palm along her abdomen. "Good morning. How are you feeling?"

"Much, much better." Turning to lie on her back, she slipped her fingers between his and his chest tightened. Such a small act, but it radiated through his body. He yearned to slide between her legs and cover her with his weight.

"You look a lot better." Her cheeks were rosy once again and the unpleasant clamminess had disappeared from her forehead.

"The sickly look I had before wasn't doing it for you?" she teased, smiling in such a way that it lit his entire room. It brightened even the darkest corners of his home.

"Oh, it was doing it for me," he countered and pulled on her waist, dragging her body on top of him.

This was exactly how he wanted to wake up every day—with this stunningly gorgeous woman on top of him, grinding into him and making him hard as a rock.

She rolled her hips over the top of him, and his breath hitched. She was doing that thing again, where she ran her fingers over his chest. It tickled but in a sexy, satisfying way. He adored the way her eyes lit up while she explored him.

He dipped his hands beneath her oversize t-shirt. She leaned forward and placed her hands on either side of his face. The casual intimacy was killing him. He gulped as she bent down and nuzzled his neck, alternating between tender kisses and ravenous sucking.

Was this real? Was she real or was he dreaming?

His hands were all over her. Across her back. Down her sides. Wrapped around to her ass so he could press her body into him, tucked tightly against his cock, only his thin shorts separating them. He shifted his hips so she could feel the length of him. Her body was trembling, still weak from the bug she'd caught.

She leaned back and lifted her shirt over her head. Her hair fell down and draped across her chest. His cock throbbed at the sight of her. He groaned as she swept her hair to one side, giving him a clear view of her chest, that little tattoo above her breast. His heart raced, and he moved to grasp her soft and supple mounds. He palmed her breasts and pushed them up, causing her to inhale sharply. He used his thumbs to play with her nipples.

She was a freaking goddess.

She gripped his wrists and threw her head back, digging her pelvis into his rock-hard shaft. This angle, her on top, it took his breath away. Black fireworks exploded, darkening his vision. He needed release, and he needed it soon. Pain seared through him as he bit his cheek to prevent an embarrassing, premature unraveling.

"You're gorgeous." His voice was weak and raspy. "Fucking perfect."

She lifted her head and stared down at him with a wicked grin. She rolled off the side of him and he groaned in her absence. He *needed* her. He leaned toward her to pull her back but she pushed his hands away. "Please," he begged.

Using one hand, she pushed him flat onto the bed and placed the other hand on top of his shorts. His dick twitched at her gentle touch, imploring a more rigorous hold. She moaned as she stroked him through the loose fabric, feeling every thick inch of him. He thrust into her hand at a controlled pace.

He watched as she shifted her hips greedily and sat back on her heels. He knew what she was feeling because he was feeling it, too. He brought his hand to his waistband and pulled, letting his shaft spring free.

"Oh," she whispered in surprise, eyeing his cock. His size had caught her off guard.

He didn't know how much more he could take. He needed her now.

She slid one leg between his, straddling his lower thigh, and bent down. *Fuck,* she was incredible.

Nik had never felt anything more exhilarating than Ali's tongue on the tip of his cock. Nothing would ever excite him more than the sight of Ali's mouth around his dick, her lips stretched thin. She swirled her tongue and his whole body stiffened.

She made long, fluid movements over his length, using her hand to cup his balls. He could feel her arousal on his thigh as she rocked her hips against him. Her legs tensed around him.

He watched her build up her own orgasm while sucking him off, and he couldn't help but think that there was nothing hotter than this magic she was performing.

He wouldn't last long like this. He pulled her hair back and watched her work. He let out a guttural moan, and she brought her mouth up with a soft *pop.*

"No, please don't stop." His voice was full of desperation. He was so close.

She stroked him lazily and smirked.

She was wicked. A tease. It was only fair after the things he'd done to her.

She rubbed her thumb over his sensitive underside.

"Ali…" he pleaded.

It was frustrating, being at her mercy like this. He liked being in charge. When she dipped her head again, he wove his fingers through her hair and pulled her in close and made quick, small thrusts into her mouth. She moaned, and the vibrations sent an earthquake through his body. He hissed and pumped into her until he crashed over the edge, spilling into her. She stared him right in the eyes while she swallowed every last pump and licked him clean afterwards.

Nik was breathing heavily as she pulled herself up to lie beside him. Her fingers wandered across his body. She played with the hair on his lower abdomen and kissed his shoulder.

Then Ali tilted her head toward him. "Are you hungry? I could eat some breakfast."

"I could think of one thing I'd like to eat," he replied suggestively. He grabbed her by the waist and swiftly pulled her under him, nuzzling her neck. She laughed but made no attempt to stop him.

He didn't need food. He needed her. He needed her thighs wrapped around his face, her cum dripping down his chin. He needed her screaming his name.

A knock at the door interrupted them, and they both froze.

Another knock, harder this time, and Sam's voice rang out. "Open up! I know you're home, Nik."

He groaned and rested his head against her forehead. He wanted to scream. He wanted to cry. The most stunning woman was lying beneath him completely naked and turned on, and Sam was at his fucking door. He had the worst timing. What was he doing here, anyway?

Ali brushed a hand against his cheek before he reluctantly rolled out of the bed. Whatever Sam wanted, he hoped he could get rid of him quickly and get back to the gorgeous blonde in his bed.

He pulled his shorts back up and threw on a sweatshirt as he stumbled to the door.

"Can I help you?" he asked as he swung the door open to meet Sam.

"Hey, sorry to show up here so early and unannounced. Listen, is the prisoner still here?"

"She is," he answered cautiously.

"Is she feeling better?"

He thought for a second. If she was still sick, she could stay a while longer. But he also didn't think it would be wise to lie, especially to Sam who always had his back. "She is."

"Good. I was informed the prison would have an inspection later today. You need to get her back there as soon as possible. I know you have your little crush on her or whatever, but it's important you get her back to her cell immediately."

Dammit. Nik really didn't want her to leave yet, but it didn't seem he had any other choice. "Thanks for the heads up. We'll be back soon."

Sam gave him a quick nod and trudged off through the snow.

He returned to the bedroom to see Ali changing back into her clothes. She must've overheard their short conversation. He was overwhelmed by a sinking sensation in his chest. A void that only she seemed to fill. He couldn't explain the way she made him feel whole.

She sat on the edge of his bed, lacing up her boots. Of course, this could never last, but he'd take whatever stolen moments they could share together. He let out a heavy sigh.

"Raincheck on that breakfast?" he murmured.

She wrapped her arms around his waist and even though she was so much smaller than him, he felt oddly safe there. Protected.

"Sounds good," she said as she pulled away.

Chapter Twenty-Two

ELI

SEVERAL DAYS AFTER ALI returned to the prison, she and Eli sat around a bonfire. She hadn't spoken about her time away, and Eli didn't ask. He was too afraid to drive a wedge further between them.

The fire did little to combat the brutal temperatures that had fallen over Rysburg. Eli's cheeks were bright red, and he thought he could see frost on the tips of his eyelashes. The skin across his knuckles had cracked from the dry cold.

It was absolutely ridiculous that they made the prisoners eat meals outside while they practically froze to death. Assholes.

It wasn't right, the way they treated them. Ali shivered next to him and ate her soup in misery. Looking around the fire, there wasn't a single face that was happy about their current situation. But they all put up with it. There wasn't much they could do.

Surprisingly, the younger ones handled it best. They ran around the courtyard playing games, the movement keeping them warm and entertained. Eli caught the eye of the two kids who had lived next door, Jamie and Kristen, and waved to them. They waved back without a care in the world. He admired their resilience.

"Let me take your bowl back," Ali said as she rose to her feet.

"I can do it." He reached his hand out to take hers instead. He wasn't sure if she was still feeling sick or not, though she had shown no signs of passing out again.

"No, really. I want to stand and walk. It might help me warm up a bit." She gathered up their bowls and utensils and walked back toward the kitchen.

The air around them was still tense. He was tiptoeing around her. He didn't know how to ask what was going on with her anymore. The last time he had brought up Nik, it hadn't gone well. She seemed to be shutting him out, but it only made the situation worse if he tried to get her to open up.

She had been gone for days, though, and it had eaten him up. There was a bond between the two of them that he couldn't deny. Ali was on a tightrope and the closer she got to Nik, the further she got from Eli.

Eli moved closer to the fire, its blaze flickering before his eyes. Ali's absence chilled him in more ways than one. He hated that she was adjusting so well to this new home. She was strong and confident, and he was weak and second guessed everything. She was leaving him behind and he'd never felt more alone, even when she was sitting next to him. He was losing his best friend. He was losing everything.

Eli knocked over a piece of wood with his shoe and watched the embers glow. His hope of getting out of here was getting more bleak as the days passed. And if he did find a way, would Ali even want to go with him?

She should, given that she was a prisoner...but he had his doubts.

His stomach dropped when he looked up to find Ali talking to Nik near the entrance of the kitchen. A bitter taste filled his mouth.

Nik's words haunted him. He was so confident he could win Ali over, and Eli was starting to think he was right.

He watched them talk, and it rattled him to the core. She wasn't afraid. She wasn't nervous or timid. She wasn't annoyed or frustrated. She was enjoying it. She was fucking *enjoying* their conversation. He hadn't seen her smile like that in quite some time.

It wasn't supposed to be like this. It was supposed to be him and Ali together against the world. She was supposed to confide in him. She was supposed to trust him. But there she was, touching Nik's arm while he grinned like the smug asshole Eli knew him to be.

He felt sick. And depressed. And hopeless.

Eli stood and took a few steps in their direction. His body moved quicker than his thoughts. He had no idea what he was going to say or do, but he couldn't sit still anymore. He couldn't watch them...watch them what?

Become friends? Something else?

Whatever this was, he wouldn't sit by while they flaunted it in front of him. His hands shook as he got closer, and he clenched them into fists. Nik made eye contact first, and he mouthed something to Ali. She turned around and gave a feeble, unconvincing smile.

She would've walked to meet Eli, but Nik grabbed her by the arm, keeping her at his side. The rage that ran through Eli was indescribable. His eyes narrowed and he could feel his ears burning red.

"Get your hands off of her," he hissed before he reached them.

Nik rolled his eyes and looked bored, which made Eli even angrier.

"Calm down, man. She's more than capable of taking care of herself. She doesn't need you."

Eli knew he only meant in this context, but hearing that Ali didn't need him sent him spiraling. It was what he was afraid of, after all. He lunged through the air and in the blink of an eye, both he and Nik hit the ground. Nik never saw it coming. Eli had caught him so off guard that he was able to connect his fist with Nik's jaw at least twice before anyone realized what was happening.

"Eli!" He heard Ali scream, but it sounded distant. Like an echo, a faint whisper in the wind. He was alone with Nik, and he was going to tear him apart. Nothing else existed. He'd make him regret the day he set his sights on Ali.

Blood trickled down his knuckles, and he felt a tug on his shoulder, but he shook it off. Nik seized on this moment of hesitation and grabbed Eli's wrists, flipping him onto his back, then Nik hit him hard in the face. He thought he heard his nose crack, but he felt nothing.

The only thing he felt was fury.

When Nik struck again, Eli tasted blood. Eli struck him in the stomach when he reared back to hit him again, and he hinged forward. Eli took advantage and shoved him off. He found himself on top of Nik again, but it was only for an instant.

Nik used the momentum and kept rolling, forcing Eli back to the ground. This time he shoved the side of his face into the ground, straining his neck. Eli tasted the dirt beneath him. People had gathered around them, but they quickly stepped out of the way as the two of them tussled on the ground.

"Stop fighting," Nik growled, keeping Eli's face pinned.

Eli couldn't. He didn't know how. Rage coursed through his veins. He was a wild animal that had been backed into a corner for too long. He swung wildly at Nik but failed to make contact. With his face forced to the ground, he couldn't see where to strike.

"Eli!" Ali was screaming again. He saw her out of the corner of his eye and could see she was crying, her hands covering her mouth. He didn't want to look at her. This was her fault.

"Stop!" Nik snarled as he shoved Eli into the ground with his forearm. The pressure was cutting into Eli's neck, restricting his oxygen. "You don't want to do this, man."

Yes, he did.

It was stupid, but his sense of self-preservation was long gone. All he knew was the hatred and wrath bubbling inside him.

Finally, his limbs gave out and he had no choice but to lay still and accept defeat.

Several other guards shuffled their way through the courtyard and pulled him rigorously to his feet, letting Nik tend to his wounds. Eli's own blood continued to trickle down his face.

"What in the hell is going on?" a menacing voice demanded and the whispers and chatter died down. Eli recognized the man as Colin, the general who had led the attack on Andus. He didn't have the energy to be frightened. The only reason he remained on his feet was because the guards held him under the armpits. He'd given up.

Colin turned to look at Nik. "What happened?"

Nik's eyes shifted. He looked like he was debating telling the truth. Eli had no idea why he didn't immediately blame him for the brawl. "He, uh, we just had a disagreement."

"A disagreement? Not what I saw." Colin's eyes met Eli's, and he felt his spine go cold. Turns out he did have the energy to be frightened.

 This man was a cold-hearted killer.

Ali was still crying and looking at Nik, clearly expecting him to do something. But Nik looked resigned. He knew his place, and Colin outranked him.

Chapter Twenty-Three

NIK

NIK COULD FEEL ALI's glare. She expected too much from him. Maybe if Eli had stopped fighting sooner and hadn't drawn so much attention, but now that Colin was here? There was nothing he could do. They'd both have to stand and watch whatever horrors Colin decided to inflict. He stood tall and straight as Colin came to a stop in front of him.

"Nik, I'm disappointed in you. Letting a prisoner draw blood? We can't allow that." Colin's voice was calm, and it made his words even more unnerving. Nik had a terrifying effect on people, mostly due to his size and brooding expression, but it was nothing compared to the fear that Colin instilled. He *enjoyed* watching people suffer. It was his favorite pastime.

"Now, what shall we do with you?" Colin paced back and forth in front of Eli, contemplating ways to punish him. He was known for being ruthless and his discipline would likely be unbearable. He barked at the two guards keeping Eli on his feet, "Tie him up against the wall."

The guards obeyed him, and Eli shuffled nervously as they tied his wrists to two torches embedded in the stone wall. His arms stretched uncomfortably, and he had to stand on his tiptoes.

Nik could hear Ali sobbing and it made his stomach turn to acid. He looked down, afraid to meet her eyes.

Ali, don't watch, he begged her silently.

But when he looked over, she was staring at Eli in horror. Nik grimaced. She didn't need to watch this. She'd been through enough. Both of them had. Nik would be the first to admit he didn't like Eli, but even he didn't want to watch *this.*

The rest of the crowd shifted uneasily, not knowing just how ruthless Colin could be.

Colin ripped open Eli's shirt, exposing his tattooed back to the cold air. He pulled out a whip from inside his jacket. Eli's torso expanded with each deep breath, waiting for the inevitable.

The prisoners watched with a mix of anticipation and horror. Nobody spoke a word while Colin paced back and forth. He got a sick sense of satisfaction out of it. Teasing his vengeance. He would draw this out as long as possible. It was like he could smell the terror in the air.

The man thrived on the fear in their eyes.

Colin cracked the whip in the air and the sound made several people jump, including Eli. He looked terrified and Nik felt a pang of guilt.

But it wasn't his fault Eli was in this position. He tried to get him to stop. He did everything he could.

It was going to get much, much worse. If only Colin would get it over with.

He cracked the whip in the air once more with a sinister grin. It was sickening to watch. He got off on terrifying people.

The next crack of the whip landed in the middle of Eli's back. He hissed and his face contorted in pain. His hands strained against the rope binding him to the wall. His whole body thrashed like a trapped animal before he stilled and readied himself for the next blow.

Nik had trouble swallowing the lump in his throat. He and the other guards watched with stony faces. It would be a sign of weakness to turn away or show any sign of disgust or sympathy. Instead, he snuck glances at Ali, hoping she would look away. Hoping these images wouldn't haunt her for the foreseeable future. It made him nauseous to see her fidgeting with shaky hands and wide eyes. She shouldn't be watching this. He couldn't even comfort her the way he wanted to.

Another crack of the whip. And another. And another.

This went on for several minutes, and each crack elicited more nauseated looks and groans from the crowd. It was hard to watch. Eli's back turned from stripes of pink, irritated flesh to dark red gashes cut deep into his skin. His tattoos were unrecognizable, and blood started to trickle down his mangled back.

Colin turned around to the crowd with a look of irritation. "Why are you all so quiet? This is prime time entertainment here. Ungrateful bastards. Can I get some applause or something? Or do I need to beat every one of you?" He pointed a finger at the crowd, pausing on several prisoners who flinched and retreated from his attention.

The other guards threw quick glances at one another and slowly brought their hands together in approval. Two or three of the prisoners joined in, terrified they would be next.

Nik sighed and clapped apathetically. He braved a glance in Ali's direction and the anguish hit him like a rock. Watching Eli take a beating was painful, but he knew the hurt he caused by giving his approval, even if it was just for show. She looked more broken than ever. Her cheeks were pink from the cold and her eyes bloodshot from crying. He wanted nothing more than to hold her. To let her cry on his shoulder.

He held her gaze, trying to speak without words. To apologize for everything, but she didn't believe the remorse in his eyes.

He turned away from her judgmental glare, afraid that he might throw up if he watched her any longer.

"How about you, love?" Colin pointed to Ali, and Nik's entire body turned to ice. "Ah, I remember you, sweetheart. You look so pretty when you cry." He ran a thumb across Ali's cheek and Nik flinched, stepping closer to them. He wouldn't let Colin hurt her.

But Ali was more than capable of taking care of herself. She stepped out of Colin's grasp and gave him a cold glare.

"Aw, don't be that way, love. Is this your friend? Your lover? Should I slice him open like I did your mother?"

He might as well have sliced Nik open. Nik hadn't asked about Ali's family. He knew she didn't have one. Not anymore. He hadn't wanted to think about *why* her family didn't exist. To acknowledge that Rysburg had taken that from her. Colin had taken that from her.

Nik missed whatever Colin said next, but he seemed to grow bored with her and returned to his punching bag.

"Turn him around."

The guards untied Eli's arms and turned him to face the crowd.

Colin shook out his arms and dropped the whip to the ground. Then he landed a punch to Eli's face followed by a second and a third. Eli's skin was blue and purple, his eyes already swelling. The general punched him again and again and then threw a few more into his stomach for good measure. In his grand finale, he grabbed Eli behind the head and yanked it down into his knee. There was a sickening sound of bone crunching, and Eli fell to the ground.

Several people gasped. Several others cried. Ali ran forward and Nik moved instinctively, ready to stop her or protect her, but it wasn't necessary. Colin was already walking away. Without his direction, the guards made no move to stop her.

Nik knelt to assist her. "Here, let me help him up."

"Get away! I think you've done enough," she snapped and pushed him square in the chest.

"Ali," he protested.

"I don't want your help!" She cradled Eli's head in her lap and cried over him. Blood streamed from his broken nose.

A few of the other prisoners stepped forward to help her, easing between Nik and Ali. He felt a heavy weight on his chest.

"Please..."

Two men lifted Eli, walking back toward the cells. Ali followed them, not bothering to make eye contact with him on the way out.

Nik was left kneeling on the blood-soaked ground. Hot tears filled his eyes as he watched Ali walk away.

Chapter Twenty-Four

ELI

Wind brushed against Eli's face as he whipped in and out of the trees. The sound of Ali's laughter filled the air. She was incredibly fast, and his legs pumped hard to keep up with her. She had left him in the dust, with only the sound of her voice to guide him.

She effortlessly hopped over fallen trees and dove under tree branches, the same branches that snagged Eli's clothing and left small scratches on his cheek. He couldn't feel the sting they left behind, too mesmerized by her voice.

"You're too slow. You'll never catch me," she teased.

It only ignited his motivation to push harder.

He put everything he had into chasing after her. His legs resisted the strenuous effort.

They were almost at the edge of the woods. He could see the opening in the distance. Their finish line. He was within arm's distance of her, closing *the gap. Her hair trailed behind her and tickled his arm. Just a few more inches. He could almost taste victory.*

But she pulled farther ahead only fifteen feet from the finish line. She threw her hands up in the air as she left the tree line and entered the clearing.

"Yes!" she exclaimed. "Ha! I knew you couldn't beat me!"

He laughed at her triumphant display. She'd won their bet. "I let you win."

"Bullshit." She laughed and danced in circles around him, taunting him for his failure. She hummed a boastful tune while gliding through the wildflowers. Their aroma filled the air.

"Fine. You won, fair and square. What do I have to do?" He grimaced and waited for her sentence. The last time he won a bet, he'd made her lick the sand on the beach. She'd gagged and struggled to wipe the dryness from her mouth, doubling over and dry heaving. Surely, she'd get her revenge now.

Her dancing ceased, and she stopped in front of him. She tapped a finger to her lips, considering his sentence. Then her cheeks flushed as she grinned at him.

"Kiss me."

Eli's heart stopped beating. He'd never kissed a girl before. They were barely more than kids. Standing there in front of him, she was the epitome of perfection.

He took a few steps forward, his arms dangling nervously at his sides. He didn't know what to do with his hands. They suddenly felt clammy and heavy like logs. He settled on gently placing them on the sides of her waist, the heat rising in his cheeks.

She laughed softly and put her hands behind his neck, and he shivered. Her delicate fingers tickled every fiber of his being.

He leaned in close, his nose bumping into hers, and they both giggled. Her breath puffed against his face, inviting him to come closer. And then...her lips were on his. Soft and sweet.

He felt his own cheeks radiate with heat and pulled away. "I was supposed to kiss you."

"You were taking too long."

She released her hold on his neck and turned to dance through the wildflowers, carefree and full of light.

Chapter Twenty-Five

ALI

ALI WAITED IMPATIENTLY OUTSIDE Eli's cell while a healer checked his wounds. He had been completely unconscious when they'd brought him back, incapable of speaking or acknowledging her. Terror threatened to suffocate her. She'd already lost everyone else. She didn't know how she'd cope if she lost him, too.

Despite their troubles adjusting to this new life, Eli was her number one priority. It was time she started acting like it. She hadn't believed her eyes as she'd watched Nik and Eli's altercation. What in the world had they been thinking?

The images were burned in her brain. Eli falling limp under the whip. And Nik fucking *clapping*. Disgust filled her, and more tears fell down her cheeks. How could she possibly cry anymore? How could there be anything left in her?

Her tears dripped off her chin and hit her hands, still stained with Eli's blood. It had dried there, and she couldn't tear herself from his side long enough to wash them. She needed to be here when he woke up.

Her head pounded. A delayed effect from the sobbing and the fatigue. She had no idea what time it was. Very late in the evening. It felt like the healer had been here for hours. He'd occasionally leave to get more clean cloth, water, medical devices she didn't know the name of. It felt like an eternity.

Eli's cell was mostly silent. Every so often, she heard a soft groan, but it died so quickly she thought she was imagining things.

Ali slumped to the ground and put her arms around her knees. She so desperately wanted to see him, to make sure he was okay. Logically, she knew this wasn't her fault. But if she hadn't been talking to Nik, then Eli never would've fought him. She was the one who had let Nik in. She squeezed her eyes shut, trying to erase the image of him clapping.

Why would he do that?

She let her head fall back against the wall behind her and dug her nails into her skin. She reveled in the pain for a few moments before her muscles relaxed.

She must've dozed off because a hand on her shoulder startled her awake.

"You can see him now," the healer said. His eyes had a friendly light to them, an encouraging glimmer. She didn't feel worthy of his sympathy. He grabbed a bag of belongings and left down the hall, leaving her alone with Eli.

He was lying on his stomach, his back covered in some sort of ointment with fresh bandages. His head rested on top of his pillow, his hands tucked beneath it. The room smelled like blood and burned her nostrils, leaving her nauseous.

"Eli?" she whispered as she entered his cell. She wasn't sure if he was sleeping.

A low grunt echoed through the air.

Hesitantly, she approached his bed. She didn't know how to talk to him like this, especially when a part of her blamed herself for his situation.

She sat down slowly on the edge of the cot, trying not to jostle him. "Eli, I'm so sorry. Are...are you okay?"

As soon as the words left her mouth, she realized how absurd they sounded. Of course he wasn't okay. He was never going to forgive her.

Eli looked at her with a blank expression. There was an emptiness there she'd never seen before. "No."

She licked her lips. Her mouth was incredibly dry all of a sudden. The oxygen was sucked out of her lungs, and she couldn't replenish it. "It's going to be okay. We'll get you the help you need and you'll heal just fine."

There was a good chance she was assuring herself more than him. He didn't look like he was buying it. The physical wounds would heal, but some wounds were invisible and harder to make whole.

"Ali, when are you going to understand? Nothing here is fine. Nothing here is okay. The only way you or I will ever heal is if we're some place far away from this god-forsaken town."

She sucked in a gasp of air, struggling to hold back tears, and reached for his cheek. But he pulled away, wincing as he strained his muscles and tender flesh. "I'm sorry, Eli. I don't know what you want from me. I'm...I'm trying here. I'm trying to make the best of this situation."

"The best of this situation? Ali, you went and made friends with the enemy. That's hardly making the best of the situation. That's just accepting defeat. I thought we would be in this together, but I'm completely on my own out here."

Friends. He said it with such disgust. What would he say if he knew they were more than friends? Ali couldn't admit that to him. She didn't need to, though. As far as she was concerned, Nik was no longer in the picture. She would recommit to Eli and to helping him. To getting out of here. It would be how it was always supposed to be. Eli and Ali taking on the world together.

"You're not alone. I'm here."

"Maybe you shouldn't be." He closed his eyes and missed Ali's look of sadness. "I'm tired. I think it's time for you to go."

The finality in his tone struck her in the gut. Ali picked at the bloody skin around her fingernails, debating if she should argue with him. Debating if she should stay anyway. But the best thing for Eli would probably be to get some sleep, so she stood and walked to the door of the cell. "I really am sorry, Eli."

She gently closed the door to his cell and stepped into the hall. She flinched when she caught a dark figure lurking out of sight. Of course there was a guard watching them. They would never be left alone in an unlocked cell.

The figure stepped into the light, and she broke into tears when she saw it was Nik. He was looking at her with such pity and remorse.

She couldn't handle any more today. She was entirely spent. She had already decided she was done with him, but here he was. He wasn't done with her.

Ali covered her face with her hands, and her body shuddered in despair.

Nik took a few steps forward and wrapped her up in his arms. He held her, not saying a word.

She hated it. Hated him. But she couldn't step away. She didn't want to be anywhere near him, but there was also no place she'd rather be. It was so confusing, and she couldn't think about it right now. So she just wept in his arms while he soothed her.

He took her hands in his and grimaced at the blood that still covered her. It covered her shirt too.

"Ali, I'm so—"

"Don't. Just don't."

She didn't want to hear his apology. Didn't want to hear his excuses.

He dropped her hands and wrapped her back in that warm embrace. Her legs trembled as she gave in and clung to him. When she couldn't stand any longer, he picked her up and carried her back to her cell.

⁂

Ali woke the next day with pink, puffy eyes and a migraine. She was physically and mentally exhausted. Her body ached, and she didn't think it was possible to tear herself from the bed. It had been well past midnight when she'd returned to her cell. She had tossed and turned all night long, waking up multiple times and crying herself back to sleep.

Everything felt so wrong.

This place constantly toyed with her emotions. Nik made her feel warm and welcome. He gave her a sense of belonging. Everything felt okay when she was with him, but yesterday was a cold reminder that none of this was okay. She was still a prisoner. Rysburg was still responsible for the death of her family and the destruction of her home. Eli had been right about everything, but now he hated her.

She had hit an all-time low. She didn't think she could handle much more.

Nik kept his distance that morning. He didn't come to fetch her from her cell and he kept a noticeable gap during their walk to the greenhouse. He didn't eavesdrop like he normally did. Although there was nothing to listen to. Eli was still in bed, healing from the abuse he'd suffered.

Even the cold couldn't get to Ali. She was numb.

Ali stared vacantly as she planted seeds. She didn't see Nik approach her from the side.

"Ali?" he said softly.

It startled her out of her trance, and she froze. She didn't know how to respond. She didn't know if she wanted to. It felt like her body was shutting down on her. Failure to function. She blinked the haze from her eyes and turned to face him.

Why did he always look so handsome? The roughness of his jawline and his rigid muscles juxtaposed the tenderness in his eyes. He waited for her to say something, but she couldn't form words. None that felt right.

"Are you okay?"

She chewed the inside of her cheek and sifted her fingers through the dirt. She couldn't stop the images from flooding her mind again. Eli getting whipped. Nik clapping. Her throat closed, and she struggled to breathe. Her chest heaved, and she began to hyperventilate.

"Hey, hey, it's all right. Breathe, Ali."

Nik reached to rub her back but she didn't want to be comforted. She didn't deserve to be comforted.

He was a villain, and she was a traitor.

She stepped out of his reach and found her voice again. "I don't want to talk to you."

She barely recognized the sound of her own voice. It sounded fragile and raspy. It belonged to someone else, someone weaker than her. This place had broken her in ways she'd never expected.

"I tried to get him to stop. He just came at me out of nowhere. I had no idea he'd react like that."

"Yes, you did. I've watched you torment him ever since we got here. You're constantly antagonizing him. Does it really surprise you that he finally stood up for himself?"

"Looked like he was standing up for you, not himself. He's obviously jealous." Nik winced, immediately regretting his choice of words.

"Well, there's nothing to be jealous of...not anymore." She turned back to the empty holes in the dirt, filling them with seeds.

"You can't be serious." He no longer looked timid and empathetic. He looked angry. And she thought she saw a hint of hurt as well. "Ali?"

"Why did you do it?"

"I told you, I tried to get him to stop. I was just defending myself."

"Not that. Why did you clap? Do you hate him that much?"

"I don't...I didn't have a choice. There are certain expectations I have to live up to as a guard."

"Expectations," she huffed. "And if it had been me? What *expectations* would you live up to if it were me?"

He stepped closer, his chest pressed against her back, pinning her to the planters. He didn't care that they were in the middle of the greenhouse where anyone could see. His presence engulfed her, dominated her entire being. She had to ignore the pulsing between her legs at his nearness.

"I would kill anyone who laid a hand on you."

A hand grazed her arm, but she shook her head and spoke firmly. "Don't."

He took a step back, and she felt his absence immediately. She refused to meet his eyes again, afraid she might give in and let him in. He stood in silence, watching as she dug through the dirt. She didn't even know what she was doing with her hands. She only knew that she had to keep busy or she might fall apart.

"I'm not giving up that easily. I'm not giving up on us," he whispered before turning away.

Ali did her best to convince herself that Nik meant nothing. This thing between them meant nothing and he would get over it.

Even as she thought the words, she knew they weren't true. He meant something and even if he could get over it, could she? She couldn't tell if she was doing the right thing. Was the right thing supposed to hurt this much?

He left her alone for the rest of the day. But every time she looked his way, she found him watching her. He did an amazing job of masking his emotions. He was stone cold. No one except her would suspect the sadness and anger he was feeling right now. To everyone else, she was sure he looked like the usual Nik. Solemn and intimidating. Even Sam carried on chatting cordially while Nik listened, uninterested.

Ali jumped in the shower quickly after work, hoping to visit Eli before dinner. One of the guards was kind enough to open the cell for her, and she watched as he slept peacefully. But his snoring was unconvincing. He wasn't actually asleep. He just didn't want to be bothered by her. She couldn't blame him. It would take some time to heal their friendship, but he was worth it and she was willing.

She sat down on the bed and held his hand. "How was your day? Mine was pretty uneventful. Especially without you. I didn't realize just how boring work could be when your best friend is missing."

The sound of his snoring stopped, and he just breathed heavily. Apparently, he was interested in what she had to say, even if he didn't want to acknowledge her yet.

"Everyone misses you, actually. They're all worried they'll be forced to spread manure since you're not there to do it. You've underestimated your value."

She thought she saw the corners of his lips tug into a grin.

"I spoke to Nik today."

Eli flinched, but kept his eyes closed.

"He's not going to be a problem for you anymore. I'll make sure of it."

His shoulders relaxed, and he sank back into the bed.

Ali's eyes burned again. God, how many times had she cried in the past few weeks? She inhaled through her nose and steeled herself. This was the last time she would cry. She was so sick of feeling weak; it was time to be strong. It's what she promised her mother after all.

"I hope you feel better soon. I need my friend back. I can't do this without you." She leaned down and kissed him softly on the forehead, then left him alone for the evening. She'd get him to open up eventually. She just had to keep trying.

When she stepped out of the cell, she found Nik waiting once again. The man really didn't give up. She and Nik were similar in that way. He was fighting for her while she fought for Eli. Which of them would break first?

She moved to step around him, but he blocked her path. "Just give me one minute, please."

"Shh." She glanced back at Eli's cell, then crossed her arms over her chest and waited for him to continue.

"I'm going to be out of town for a couple days. I just...I just wanted to let you know that. The timing couldn't be worse." He ran his hands through his hair, clearly struggling to get the words out. "I just don't want you to think that it has something to do with you. You're not pushing me away or anything. I'm still here and I'm not going anywhere. Maybe...maybe when I get back, we can fix this."

She highly doubted he could fix this. Everything about her life was broken beyond repair.

He spun and took a few steps away, but abruptly stopped. Then he turned back to her and grabbed her cheeks, pulling her in for a passionate kiss. It took her breath away. His lips were so soft and inviting. Before she could second guess herself, she gripped his T-shirt and leaned into him.

It had only been five minutes ago that she'd told Eli he had nothing to worry about, and she was already going back on her word.

The thought of Eli was enough to break the kiss, and she pulled back from him. This wasn't right.

Nik ran his thumb over her chin and across her bottom lip, staring into her eyes. "Don't write me off yet."

Chapter Twenty-Six

NIK

THE LAST THING NIK wanted to do right now was leave town. Not while Ali was still upset with him. He needed to make things right, and leaving town now would only give her time to solidify her decision. She couldn't just decide it was over.

He didn't really have a choice, though. He had missed the mission to conquer Andus; he couldn't miss another one. They needed to return to Andus to go through the damage. It's what they did after every town they decimated. It was the reason their town flourished while so many others failed. They could scrap valuable materials and goods in addition to the labor.

Most of the time Nik didn't give it much thought, but knowing that he was returning to Ali's home was unsettling. It felt like an invasion of her privacy, especially now when she wasn't speaking to him. She had seen him play the role of a dutiful guard. He knew that by traveling to her hometown, he'd be forced to face certain demons. Demons that he wasn't ready to face.

They left early in the morning, before the sun had risen, in a small group that included Nik and a dozen other guardsmen who looked equally dispirited to be heading out in the freezing cold. It had taken almost two days for them to trek from Andus to Rysburg with the prisoners, but their group was determined to do it one day. No one wanted to sleep out in the open in the middle of winter. They all would rather be tucked in bed right now with a warm blanket, protected from the wind and the snow that had begun to fall. It was a lot easier to accomplish when they weren't dragging prisoners along for the ride, although the large horse and wagon slowed them down a bit. They had to stick to main trails instead of a more direct route through the woods.

For the first few hours of their journey, everyone was too tired to carry on much conversation. They were all still half asleep, and their feet trudged along purely out of muscle memory. Nik preferred the silence. There were very few people he actually enjoyed conversing with. He just wanted to get this done and over with so he could return and convince Ali that he was sorry and worthy of her forgiveness.

Lunch was a quick stop, merely fifteen minutes. It was long enough to rehydrate, pass out sandwiches, and eat them on the go. Snow turned to sleet and then back to snow an hour later. His clothes were soaked and they'd only been traveling for a few hours. He was thankful to be moving constantly because it meant keeping warm.

It was late in the evening when they finally arrived at Andus. Nik surveyed the destruction as they walked through the entrance of the town. It was dark and hard to make out a lot of details, but he could see crumbled stone and charred walls. It was more demolished than he had expected.

"What happened here?" He turned to the guardsman next to him. "Were you here?"

"Yeah, I was here." He looked around, surveying the destruction. "Just the usual. Came in, rounded them up, and left. It wasn't a very exciting trip, to be honest. They didn't put up much of a fight. I mean, they *tried,* but it was clear from the start they weren't prepared to handle a threat like us."

"Why does it all look so…" He searched for the right word. "Dilapidated?"

"It was like this before we got here. Looks like they built their houses right into the rubble. Pretty interesting design, actually. Haven't seen anything like it before."

The man turned and went through the singed door of a concrete building. Their shelter for the night.

Nik tossed and turned most of the night, kept up by thoughts of Ali and the cold air. He shivered and clenched the thin blanket around his body. His muscles ached terribly from the trip, but it was impossible to rest. He listened irritably to the snoring of his comrades. It must be nice to sleep so peacefully.

When at last he fell asleep, nightmares of Ali haunted him. He dreamt she was still here, with the village burning around her. Her feet were stuck to the ground and she couldn't move. Flames swallowed her and he screamed, trying to reach her, but every step he took forward sent him three steps back. He couldn't get closer. He couldn't save her.

Then Colin appeared and Nik fell to his knees. He easily surpassed Nik, who crawled on all fours, desperate to get to Ali. Colin walked up to her, circled behind her back and then drew his sword. Through the flames and smoke, Nik watched as he slowly slit her throat. She grasped at her neck, drawing in her own blood. His own fingernails bled as he clawed at the ground, but he couldn't save her. He had promised to kill anyone who harmed her, but he was incapable of keeping her safe.

He shuddered awake and felt tears pouring down his face. The sun peeked through the dirty windows of their shelter while he wiped under his eyes. He prayed no one would stir for a little while longer, but his hopes were dashed when the first person stood and stretched. Once one person woke, they would all follow, and it was best not to be the last one to be ready.

They were each assigned different sections of the town to salvage. In the daylight, Nik could see the center of town had been burned beyond recognition. He swallowed bile as he recalled his nightmare.

He was assigned to the northeast corner and set off, hoping the day wouldn't take long. He was thankful that Andus was so small. Between the dozen of them, they could easily get it done in a day.

The sun gleamed through the feathery clouds and it offered Nik some warmth and the slightest hint of optimism, chasing his nightmares away. The snow from the prior evening had already started to melt and splashed beneath his boots. The first door he stumbled upon appeared to be a home. A sign hanging next to the door was scorched from fire, but he could make out just a few letters that appeared to be a surname.

He suddenly wished that he knew Ali's last name, so he could tell whether or not this home belonged to her.

It was probably for the best that he didn't know her full name. That way, he wouldn't be tempted to pry into her old life. He opened the door that hung flimsily on its hinges and entered a family room. It smelled like dust and decay, like it had been abandoned for far more than just a couple months.

He noticed some sturdy furniture, a bookcase and end tables. They could save the lumber from that and repurpose it, but he'd need help carrying it out. The couch and chairs were too shoddy to save. He pulled a mirror and some iron-wrought decor off the walls and slipped it into the large bag he'd brought. Not much else was worth saving. There was a rug with so many holes in it, he wondered how they didn't trip on the frayed edges.

The kitchen had a few utensils and accessories they could use. No food or spices. It looked like everything they had was spoiled. Nik wondered if it was actually for the best that they'd been captured. It didn't look like they would've made it through the winter on their own. He'd have to come back for the table and chairs as well.

This home only had two bedrooms. Much like the couch in the living room, the furniture in both was too worn out to take back. The wood was cracked and wouldn't hold up if they tried to use it for anything else. There were tattered blankets and clothing as well. He only managed to pull out a few shirts and pants that were in decent shape.

The solo bathroom of the home was almost entirely unusable. These trips always made Nik realize how lucky he was to be born in Rysburg. They had everything they needed and extra. Of course, most of it was taken from towns just like this one, but he still felt very fortunate. He didn't know what it was like to go hungry, and he never would. His home was furnished and much more comforting than the ones he sorted through on missions. These felt like half empty boxes with nothing but the essentials.

He left the first home and carried on, plundering three more homes before his rucksack was bursting at the seams. He heaved it back to their meeting point at the entrance of town and tossed it into the cart.

"I'll need a hand grabbing some wood," he said to the other men who were sitting and chatting, already finished with their sections. A few stood and followed him back to the homes to break down the furniture and bundle the wooden pieces.

It took no time at all to finish with the help of several men. Nik sat down by the cart and opened his small backpack to pull out his lunch. It was late afternoon, and he hadn't realized how hungry he was. Despite the freezing cold, sweat formed on his brow from all the heavy lifting.

"Didn't really get much here, did we?" one man asked.

Nik turned to look into the cart and it did look less full than usual. He'd been on four or five similar missions, and this was the lightest he'd seen the cart.

"They're practically barbarians out here. Have you seen how scrawny they all are?" A second man laughed at their expense.

A vision of Ali's tiny, bony frame came to mind.

Nik bit his cheek and focused on his lunch. He didn't appreciate their comments, but he had no interest in getting into an argument. Let them think whatever they want.

"The epitome of poverty," snorted the first man. Apparently seeing people less fortunate than them was comical.

Nik finished the remainder of his sandwich and stood; he needed to go for a walk and put distance between them before he lashed out.

He rounded the front of the horse and cart when he spotted their mission leader marching in their direction with two other men struggling to keep up.

"What's wrong?" Nik asked.

He leaned in close, shaking his head with irritation. He spoke softly but furiously. "Someone else has been here."

"What do you mean? How do you know that?"

"There were weapons...or tools, I suppose. They had farming equipment that they used against us when we were here before. We saw it all. Axes, knives, scythes. We left them, knowing that we would be back to collect, but now they're all gone."

"Weapons?" Nik tried to wrap his head around it. They had weapons. That would've been the most valuable thing they could've salvaged, but they were gone. Who would've taken them? Who would've been here before them? Who the hell knew there was a deserted town here? Or did they stumble on it by accident?

"This isn't good. Colin won't be happy. Neither will Jameson." Nik's leader ran his hands through his hair. No, Colin would not be happy, and Colin was scary when he was unhappy. Just ask Eli.

Once the rest of the men had returned to their meeting point, the mission leader filled them in on what he'd found, or rather what he didn't find. Everyone shifted uneasily, knowing this would be seen as a mission failure.

They argued about whether to stay in Andus for the night. There was no way they could make it back to Rysburg in the daylight; the sun already hung low in the sky. And while none of them were keen to sleep out in the open, they were even less enthused to stay and meet the people who had beaten them to the weapons. In the end, they agreed to head home immediately.

The journey back was even more quiet than the one there, if that was possible. No one wanted to vocalize what they were all thinking. They were all curious about who had been there before them. Who had beaten them to the *weapons,* of all things? Just what exactly did they intend to do with them?

For so long, Rysburg had been at the top of the food chain. No one wanted to think about an unknown predator. A monster waiting in the dark. They were all skittish. A rustle of leaves, a bird chirping, branches cracking under ice and snow. They jumped at every sound.

If it weren't for the darkness limiting their visibility, they would've walked all night. No one would sleep tonight.

When Nik returned to Rysburg, it was almost dawn. The sun was just beginning to peak out from the east. He headed straight toward the prison, desperate to see Ali's face again. He couldn't let it go.

He grabbed the keys from the security room, not even bothering to greet the guard there. It wouldn't have mattered. The guard had fallen asleep on duty. Whoever showed up to relieve him would ream him for it.

He darted toward Ali's cell and made no attempt to muffle his footsteps. He hoped she was awake. He needed to talk to her now, before everything was lost.

"Ali," he said through the bars of her cell.

She stirred, turning to face the door. "What time is it?" The sunlight was a muted blue through her solo window. She rubbed her eyes and sat up in bed.

He unlocked the door as quickly as he could. He just needed to be near her, to hold her. To make promises he wasn't sure he could keep. What could he possibly tell her to make her believe he was on her side?

"Come with me," he said as the door sprang open. He intended to take her back to the prison roof where they could talk in peace.

"No," she said, flinching back from him. He'd taken a few steps into her cell, and the sight of her retreating from his presence caused him to falter.

"Please," he urged. "Please, let me make this right."

"You can't." Tears filled her eyes again, and it killed him to know that he had caused them.

"I'm so sorry. You have to believe I never wanted any of this. I never wanted that to happen. I will do anything, anything for you, Ali. Just give me a chance."

"Anything?"

He struggled to swallow the lump in his throat. She was considering the price he would have to pay to earn her forgiveness. And he would do *anything* she asked of him.

He nodded eagerly, dropping to his knees at her bedside.

Ali took his cheeks in her hands, and they locked eyes.

"Eli can't be here anymore. This place...it's going to kill him."

Nik shook his head, unsure of what she was asking. "What do you need me to do?"

"I want you to get him out. Get him out of Rysburg." Tears streamed down her face and Nik clutched at his chest. He felt her pain as if it were his own. "Please."

"And what about you?" Nik asked, not sure he wanted to know the answer. She wouldn't let Eli walk off on his own.

She brushed her thumb over his face. Her lips trembled and she inhaled sharply, preparing to give him his answer.

Before she could, he leaned forward and closed his lips over hers. He didn't want to know.

"I'll fix this."

Chapter Twenty-Seven

ELI

ELI SWUNG HIS LEGS over the side of the bed and gritted his teeth when his side throbbed in pain. It felt like someone was stabbing him repeatedly. He'd been told that he'd likely cracked a few ribs in the beating and that they'd take the longest to heal.

He'd been in his bed for over a week and he was fucking tired of it. He wanted a hot shower. And food. And a walk in the fresh air. He admitted he was grumpier than normal but being cooped up would do that to a person.

Ali still checked on him daily, sometimes two or three times, and he continued to ignore her. It was easiest to pretend to be asleep, but he knew it wasn't believable. No one slept that much in a day. She just couldn't take a hint. There would be a day when he would move on, but he wasn't ready to do that yet.

Eli slid his toes over the cold concrete. It felt foreign. He hadn't stood up in so long. The poor healer had been on bathroom duty the entire time, and Eli had never felt more helpless or mortified. He wanted his independence back. What semblance he could have inside a prison, at least.

He started to stand and clutched at his stomach when he shifted his weight to his shaky legs. It was amazing how much muscle and strength one could lose in just a week of immobility.

"What are you doing?" a voice squeaked from outside his cell.

Eli rolled his eyes and ignored Ali, just like he had every other time she'd shown up.

"Can I get some help over here?" she yelled down the hall when he didn't respond to her.

He muttered through gritted teeth, "I don't need help."

But his heavy breathing said otherwise. It was a chore to place one foot in front of the other. He didn't even know where he might go—he just knew he wanted to *move*. He grabbed a fresh set of clothes from his bedside table and glared at them. There was no way he'd be able to lift a shirt over his head or step into new pants, not with each muscle in his body screaming in resistance.

Ali rushed to his side and gently wrapped an arm around him. She retreated when he groaned, unsure where to touch him, where she was least likely to hurt him. She didn't realize the pain she had inflicted ran much deeper than his bones.

The healer was quick to respond and opened his cell with a look of exasperation. "What are you doing? You're not cleared to be out of bed yet. You're going to injure yourself even further." The healer gently pushed him back toward the bed and forced him to sit back down. Then he grabbed the clothes out of Eli's hands and began undressing him. "If you wanted help, you should've called for me."

Eli's eyes burned and he swallowed against the lump in his throat. He felt so weak and defeated. Nothing was going right for him. He caught

Ali's look of pity and couldn't even blame her. He pitied himself too. He allowed the healer to change his clothes without a fight.

Before replacing his shirt, he applied a fresh bandage to his back. He was unable to see the damage, but Ali looked nauseous, so he figured it must still be gnarly. The ointment helped to numb the pain.

"How much longer until I can do this myself?" he asked as the healer slipped on his shirt.

The healer inspected the bruises on his chest and side, pressing gently. "It'll likely be at least another week, maybe two. You're healing pretty quickly, but you can't put more stress on this. It's still going to hurt, but you should be able to move around more freely soon. Be patient."

He sighed, then winced as the deep breath irritated his side. The healer cleaned the wounds on his face and added a fresh layer of ointment there, too. He didn't know what his face looked like either, but he was sure it was mangled by the way everyone stared. It felt like the swelling had gone down, at least. He could breathe through his nostrils again as the bone had been set back in its place.

"I'll be back in a few hours. If you need anything in the meantime, *call* for me," the healer reprimanded.

Eli rolled his eyes.

The healer exited the cell and took his bag of medicine with him. Eli didn't miss the glance he gave Ali, a nonverbal warning to keep him in bed.

"I brought you breakfast." Ali approached his bed, staring at him with puppy-dog eyes. A cheap trick, but Eli's stomach growled when he caught the scent of the sausage and breakfast potatoes.

He reached his hand out to take the bowl from her. Her eyes lit up and he was quick to tear her back down. "This doesn't mean anything. It just means I'm hungry." He shoved a spoonful of potatoes into his mouth and stifled a moan. The delicious bites settled his belly, and it made him feel alive for the first time in days.

Ali sat on the edge of his bed and stared at her hands. Her mouth curved down in a frown and if he weren't so mad, he might've felt sorry for her. How had she managed to make *him* feel sorry for *her?* It should've been the other way around.

It was getting harder to ignore her. Being isolated was for him, and the only human contact he got these days was the healer and Ali. Was he doing more harm to himself than good?

He cleared his throat and poked at the sausages. "What's new?"

She whipped her head in his direction, startled that he was making conversation. But her mouth perked up and her eyes widened. "Nothing really. Work is quiet, meals are boring. Honestly, time seems to be standing still since you've been gone. It's not the same when you're not with me."

He nodded along as if he totally understood what she was saying. He didn't, though. She was free. She wasn't stuck in a cell all day and night. He couldn't think of anything else to say, so he filled his mouth with more potatoes.

"Listen, Eli, I feel like I need to be honest with you—" she started, but before she could finish, Sam interrupted.

"Eli! You're awake. I have someone here who'd like to see you." A man he'd never seen before appeared next to Sam. Dark skin and dark hair; he was even more stoic than Sam. He gave a curt nod to Ali, a greeting and a dismissal. He could tell by the way Sam regarded him that this was a man of high position.

Eli didn't know which was worse, having Ali confess whatever was on her mind or entertaining this new stranger. He didn't want to be alone, but both options also sounded awful. He'd rather the healer come back to keep him company.

"Ali, can we have a moment with Eli? Alone, thank you." Sam excused her.

She stood and approached the door of the cell cautiously, clearly uneasy about leaving Eli alone with this new person. She kept her eyes on all of them until she disappeared behind the walls of the cell.

"Eli, I want to introduce you to Jameson, our Head Commander." He waved a hand in the new man's direction.

"Head Commander? You're in charge here?" Eli had an unexplainable knotting in his stomach. He could only think of negative reasons why the head of Rysburg would come to his cell. Was he angry about the fight? Was he here to punish Eli further? Would he be exiled?

Exile didn't sound half bad, actually. That wasn't a punishment. It was a reward.

Jameson stuck out a hand to shake Eli's. He didn't seem angry; he stood tall and regal, and his expression gave nothing away. Eli's eyes flicked to Sam, but his face had that same bored expression he always had. Jameson dropped his hand when he realized Eli had no intention of shaking it.

"What can I do for you?" Eli cringed at his question. It was the polite thing to say, but he didn't want to do anything for them. He wasn't offering them anything in good faith. He only wanted to know what the hell they wanted, and how to get them out of his cell.

"I heard about the incident in the courtyard last week," Jameson said.

Eli tried not to scoff and roll his eyes.

"It may surprise you, but I rarely condone such behavior. I've spoken with General Colin to let him know of my distaste for his methods. However, he has never failed at protecting our town, and I give him more freedom to use his own discretion to keep the peace."

Keep the peace was a horrible way to describe what had happened to Eli. There was nothing peaceful about it.

Jameson continued, "I think in your case, he may have gone too far. I would like to offer my apologies. Nik has told me this was all a misunderstanding and that you never meant to do any harm. He spoke very highly of you, actually, and insisted that you deserve one of our more prestigious positions. We need an additional guard at the gate if that interests you. You'd need to be trained, of course, but we can wait until you're healed properly. And I have to know that we can trust you. Nik has spoken on your behalf, but you'll be supervised until you've proven yourself." He continued on, but Eli was lost in his own thoughts.

What was Nik playing at? Was this a game to him?

"So, what do you say? Are you interested in a new position?"

Eli had to keep himself from laughing. This was crazy. Just a week ago, he had the shit beaten out of him and now they wanted to welcome him into the fold? Did they think he'd forget how they treated him if they gave him a fancy new job?

He would never forget.

"No." He stifled another burst of laughter when Sam's head snapped in Jameson's direction. He clearly hadn't expected that response. Neither of them had. He no longer looked bored. Jameson, on the other hand, remained stonefaced.

"No?" he asked calmly. "You'd rather dig in the dirt and spread manure?"

"Yes."

Jameson exchanged a brief look with Sam, who looked bewildered and shrugged his shoulders.

"Okay, then. I suppose we are done here." He turned to exit the cell and thrummed his fingers against the frame. "Well, I hope you get better soon."

Sam was on his heels as they left.

A wide grin spread across Eli's face, and he chuckled.

The joy he got out of turning them down would power him through the rest of the day.

Chapter Twenty-Eight

NIK

NIK TOLD HIMSELF HE was giving Ali her space. He was letting her calm down. Truthfully, he was avoiding her. He was scared to see her. He was scared that if he tried to approach her, she might turn him away. He didn't want to give her another chance to tell him it was over.

Their short time apart only made things more painful. He had no idea what he would say when he saw her again. He'd been working on a plan to get them out of here, himself included. He knew it wasn't part of the deal, but hell would freeze over before he let her leave without him. If Ali was going to leave, then so would he.

The more he thought about it, the more appealing it sounded. To have a fresh start where he didn't have to be a ruthless guard, where he wouldn't have to kill and steal. He should've thought of it long before, but then he never would've met Ali.

He stopped at the Spotted Salamander for a drink. He had spent a lot of time there ever since the fight with Eli. The buzz of conversation was like a siren's song. It made him feel less alone, even if he didn't talk to anyone but the bartender—a polite "thank you" every time she refilled his glass.

He was alone in the bar. It wasn't even noon before he had his first drink, but he cut himself off after one. He had other things to do today and couldn't sit here for hours. But the one drink was necessary to get him through the day. After draining his glass, he paid his tab and left the empty bar behind him.

The middle of town was buzzing with people shopping for gifts. The snow was gently falling, and it made for a romantic setting. Couples walked hand in hand and parents attempted to reel in their energetic children. Most of them failed. It brought a smile to his face as the kids ran amok.

The holidays were approaching. Nik wanted to buy something for Ali, even if she wasn't speaking to him right now. But if he showed up with a gift in hand along with a way for them to escape, then maybe he'd have a chance. Maybe he could earn her forgiveness.

He wasn't used to buying gifts for people. His parents had passed away years ago and without any friends, he didn't have anyone to give presents to. He usually spent the holidays alone in front of the fire with a bottle in his hand. He'd accumulated some wealth, being a bachelor with barely a hint of a social life, so he sought out the most valuable gift he could think of for Ali. She was worth every penny.

There was a small jeweler in the center of town that always had dazzling pieces, most of them salvaged from nearby towns. He started checking out the rings, but he didn't know what would fit her. She had tiny hands, and these all seemed like they'd be too big. And did a ring symbolize something more? Something too much, perhaps? It definitely didn't say *I'm sorry, please forgive me.*

He moved on to the necklaces. Many of them were large and gaudy. They didn't suit her at all. His eyes swept over the jewels so quickly he almost missed it. A small silver chain with an amethyst gem set in a rose. It was perfect. Simple and subtle. He picked it up and rubbed it with his thumb. It would look beautiful around her neck.

"That's a wonderful choice," the woman working the stand said to him. She'd been watching him browse for the last fifteen minutes. "I take it this is for someone special?"

"Yes." Ali's eyes flashed before him. He missed those big brown eyes. The way she'd looked at him before it had all gone wrong. He'd give anything to wrap his arms around her waist again. "I'll take it."

The woman took the necklace from him and put it into a small velvet bag.

"What's up, Nik, my buddy?" Hands landed roughly on Nik's shoulders, and Nik groaned. "Who the hell are you shopping for? You got a girlfriend you didn't tell me about?"

Nik turned to face Marcus, the last person he wanted to see, second to Colin. "Hey, Marcus. Are you getting your wife something, or are you still telling her your presence is a present?"

Marcus laughed louder than necessary. "You're a smart ass, you know that? But that's a good idea. I don't need to get her anything at all except myself!"

Nik gave the woman some money and took his purchase, hoping to get away from Marcus as quickly as possible. Unfortunately, Marcus followed him, uncaring that Nik was obviously trying to get rid of him.

"Will you be at the bar tonight? I could use a wingman."

Nik didn't even bother to hide his disgust at the fact that Marcus was requesting a wingman when he had a wife at home. "No. I'm busy."

"Busy? With what?"

"With..." Nik looked around waiting for a good excuse to fall out of the sky. Then he spotted his exit across the street. "With Sam. Yeah, he needs my help with something. In fact, I need to go chat with him right now."

Nik could feel Marcus's eyes following him as he crossed the street. He wanted to head straight home, but now he was forced to make more small talk. Socializing was exhausting and he didn't have the energy for it.

"Hey, Sam!" He made a show of it and was delighted when he looked back to see Marcus heading off in the opposite direction.

"Hey, Nik." Sam was browsing some sketch pads. He had one in hand but put it back in a drawer with a heavy sigh. Paper was an expensive item around here, but Nik knew how much Sam liked to draw. "I was hoping I'd run into you."

"You were?" They didn't speak much outside of work.

"Yeah. You know, when you recommended Eli for the position, I would've assumed you'd already spoken to him about it. He was totally caught off guard. Turned down the job. Right in front of Jameson, of all people." He turned to look at Nik, expecting an explanation.

"He turned it down?" Nik was genuinely surprised. This was a terrible turn of events. That position was supposed to help Eli. It was supposed to get him closer to escaping. Having someone positioned on the wall would've helped them immensely. How could he turn it down?

He thought Eli would've loved the opportunity to get away from Nik. Although perhaps he was sticking around for Ali. He hadn't talked to Eli beforehand because he didn't want to be punched again, but that might've been a mistake. Maybe it would've been better to give him a heads up. His initial plan to get them out took a hit.

"Yes, he turned it down. I don't think Jameson was pleased at all."

Great. Nik was setting records for how many people could be upset with him at once.

"I'll talk to him. See if I can get him to change his mind. I really didn't consider that he might turn it down, but then again, he is a total idiot." He chuckled, but Sam wasn't amused. When Sam didn't respond, he continued, "All right, well, I'll see you around."

His house was quiet when he reached it. His living room was covered in darkness, and it wasn't the first time he'd felt entirely alone and empty in his own home.

Nik hadn't always been so closed off. He used to have friends. He'd been quite popular as a kid and, in his teens, he'd been highly sought after by the young ladies in town. It wasn't a singular incident that had changed him overnight.

First, it was his mom getting sick. He had spent less time with friends so he could help take care of her and take on more responsibility around the house.

Then his dad died, and although their relationship had been tumultuous, his death had affected Nik more than he wanted to admit. He didn't know how to talk about his conflicting emotions with the people around him, so he put on a fake smile while he was out with friends but then came home to an empty house just like this most nights. It had taken its toll. He'd grown accustomed to being alone. It was easier than keeping up the facade around others.

He'd had a girlfriend at the time, but he'd built walls faster than she could break through them. He'd known he was pushing her away, but he hadn't been able to help himself. It had felt right to be alone and wrong to let anyone in.

That's why Ali was so intriguing. She was the first person he'd met in a long time who he actually wanted to open up to. He wanted to know about her, but he also felt compelled to share about himself. It was a terrifying and blissful feeling. Like jumping off a cliff. He couldn't let go of that feeling. Couldn't let go of her. He was a different person when he was with her.

He had a glimpse of what life might look like with her in it. Sharing a house. Sharing a bed. Chatting in the mornings with a hot tea, snuggling close on the sofa, perhaps a child in the spare bedroom. For once, he'd let himself have hope for a future where he didn't have to grow old alone.

Nik skipped dinner that night. His stomach was so knotted, he didn't have an appetite. Instead, he went to bed early. The scent of Ali lingered on his pillows even weeks after she had been there, and it was all he had of her for now. He'd get her back, though. He was sure of it.

Chapter Twenty-Nine

ALI

Ali's days dragged on without Nik or Eli to keep her company. Eli still kept her at a distance, although he had stopped pretending to sleep when she visited him. It was an improvement. Their conversations were awkward and forced, but he was healing physically and she hoped he was healing emotionally, too. She was optimistic.

Nik, on the other hand, continued to watch her from the corner of the greenhouse every single day. It had been weeks since he had showed up at her cell after his mission and they hadn't spoken since.

Her chest tightened at the thought of him.

"Don't write me off yet."

Well, she hadn't. She was hovering in limbo, unsure of which way she'd tumble. She still got butterflies in her stomach when she saw him. And she still felt a pang of guilt when she visited Eli.

Sometimes he'd open his mouth like he was about to say something and then abruptly turn and walk away, face flushed and unsure of himself. It was endearing how flustered he had become, but it pained her too, this invisible wall that had been put up between them. She wanted out of Rysburg more than anything, but she also just wanted to hear his voice again.

Ali missed him. She shouldn't, but she couldn't help it. She missed his strong hands and commanding presence that made her feel safe. She missed his eyes, too. Occasionally she'd glance his way and catch him staring. His eyes spoke when he couldn't. He missed her, too.

Ali was lying in bed, enjoying an afternoon off of work. It was the week of their Winter Solstice Festival. With no one to supervise them, even the prisoners had been given a break. It would've been even better if they'd been invited to some games or celebrations. She'd overheard Sam describing the traditions and they sounded delightful. The exchanging of gifts. A massive feast featuring hot cider and cookies. Games, singing and dancing. It all sounded so appealing. Instead, she was making shapes out of the concrete on the ceiling for the hundredth time. It was getting hard to find new ones.

The bars to her cell rattled, drawing her eyes away from the ceiling. A guard she had never seen before nodded at her as a greeting. Nik rarely came to her cell anymore. "Surprise! You and the other prisoners are invited to the New Year's banquet."

"A banquet?" Ali asked, somewhat excited that she'd get to join in the festivities after all. It was hard to keep the eagerness out of her voice.

He nodded. "Well, not so much 'invited' as 'required to serve food and drinks,' but same thing. Here's your uniform. Get dressed. You're needed at the hall in twenty minutes." He tossed a delicate white cloth at her.

The thin fabric slipped between her fingers. It was silky but so light-weight, she was sure there must be more to the outfit that was missing. She held it up and watched as it unraveled, dropping to the floor. It was a mix of silk and lace, most of which was sheer. A singular loop connected to the waistband was meant to go around her neck, leaving her back completely exposed and just barely covering her breasts. The skirt was more opaque at the top but faded into a transparent fabric by the time it hit her knees.

She gaped at the *uniform* in disbelief.

"It's pretty, isn't it?" the guard asked with a crooked grin, pressing his cheeks up against the bars. He flashed his teeth, and it made her nauseous. The dress wasn't pretty. It was obscene. "Can't wait to see it on you. Go ahead. I'll wait."

He was polite enough to mock closing his eyes. Whether he could see anything or not, Ali wasn't sure, but it didn't matter. He'd see most of her body anyway in just a minute. She tugged her T-shirt and pants off and slipped into the gown as quickly as possible. At least this uniform wasn't too big for her. It fit her perfectly, leaving no uncomfortable gaps. The bits of skin that were meant to be covered stayed safely hidden. "Okay, I'm ready."

He turned around and made no effort to hide his reaction. His eyes grew wide, and he smiled disturbingly. Ali crossed her arms, trying to cover what the dress did not.

"You should take your hair out of that braid. You'd be even more sexy."

"I think I'll leave it," she spat. She didn't feel sexy. She felt objectified. "What about shoes?"

He tossed a sleek pair of sandals through the bars. They featured a thin sole and a gilded band slung between her toes and wrapped around the back of her ankle. She would surely freeze to death.

Ali pulled a sweatshirt over her head and followed him through the halls of the prison.

She was surprised to see Eli amongst the group being escorted to the banquet hall. This was the first time she'd seen him out of bed. What a cruel way to be reintroduced to the world. Was his uniform as atrocious as hers? He wore sweatpants to cover up.

"Hey, you're working tonight?" she asked him.

He looked down at his feet. "Obviously."

"Oh." This was all still so awkward. "I didn't think they'd let you. How are you feeling?"

"I'm fine. A little weak, but it feels good to finally be out of bed."

"Right. Well, try not to work too hard. I imagine you'll be sore tomorrow."

"You're not my mother, Ali. I know my limits." He didn't look at her as he spoke, and the words cut through her.

She hesitated. Everything was so fragile between them, but she wanted him to know she was here for him. "If...if you need anything tonight, ask me. Don't be a hero. Don't act like this isn't affecting you or you aren't in pain. Ask me for help, Eli."

He finally turned her way. "I will," he said softly.

They stepped through a back door of the building in the center of town. It took them through a hallway and into a kitchen much larger than the one they normally saw in the prison. It hadn't occurred to Ali just how many people would attend this banquet, but there was enough food to feed hundreds. Chefs were running around, pulling things out of wooden stoves, cutting various vegetables and organizing appetizers on shiny silver trays.

Through the loud noise and clatter of kitchen utensils, she could hear music coming from the cracks in the doors lining the opposite wall of the kitchen. She was curious about what awaited them on the other side. Such a shame that she had to be a servant rather than a guest. Already, she felt a sense of elegance and sophistication that she'd never experienced before.

They were given a place to remove their coats and sweaters. She stuffed her belongings into a cubbyhole next to Eli's. She couldn't hold back laughter when he removed his top and sweatpants. He was shirtless and his pants were made of a similar fabric to that of her gown, flowy and slightly transparent. She could see his lean legs poking through. His back looked much better. Scars were forming now, but the black of his tattoos helped disguise the red and shiny skin.

"Stop it," he said, but he also smirked. "They're ridiculous. I know."

"I think you look...ethereal." She snorted, unable to keep a straight face. For a moment, everything was normal again. She was joking with her best friend, and it felt good.

Eli's eyes lingered on her. He scanned her body up and down and raised his brows. "You look—" He ran a hand through his hair. "Fuck, Ali, you look like everyone is going to be looking at you. And they're going to see *all* of you." He looked around her like he was trying to find some hidden fabric, but all he found was more bare skin. His face flushed. She was reminded of the man who'd been in love with her months ago. Was he still in love with her? After everything they'd been through? "Ali—"

"I know." She shrugged. There was nothing they could do about it. He didn't need to get into any other fights on her behalf, though she suddenly worried that he might. "I'll be fine," she reassured him.

The head chef rounded them up and began passing out trays. They were to intermingle with the guests silently. Seen and not heard. Ali took a tray with tiny bite sized snacks. A fluffy mixture she didn't recognize on top of toasted bread and green garnish placed delicately in the center. It smelled amazing, and she hoped she'd have time to sneak a bite at some point during the night.

She pushed through one of the swinging doors and into the main ballroom. It was so stunning she forgot to keep moving for a moment.

The music was louder now, and she saw it was coming from a small band with string instruments. The walls were made of marble and columns lined the room from floor to ceiling with vines swirled around them. Ornate chandeliers filled with candles hung all around the room. The cool dusk light beamed through stained glass windows and created a magical green and blue atmosphere, like an underwater paradise. It was beautiful.

Someone bumped into her, and she almost dumped her entire tray. She gathered herself and tentatively stepped forward into the mass of people. There must've been a thousand people present. She had severely underestimated the number of people in Rysburg.

Ali weaved through the crowd, pausing near groups of people while they swiped appetizers from her tray. She mostly came across couples, which was to her advantage. The women gave her a quick look and sneered, turning to their friends to whisper insults. Meanwhile, the men were too conscious of their partners to stare for long. They only peeked out of the corner of their eyes.

It wasn't until she came across the first group of bachelors that she felt truly uncomfortable. They didn't hide their gawking at all. Some of them went as far as putting a hand on her shoulder or on the small of her back while they grabbed a bite to eat. They made crude comments, and she felt inferior and insignificant.

She was grateful when her first tray of food ran out so she could go back to the solace of the kitchen. She slammed the tray down on the table and several heads whipped in her direction. Her cheeks flushed in embarrassment. They all quickly returned to what they were doing, uninterested in whatever tantrum she was about to throw. This might've been her first time being treated this way, but it was clear they were used to it. If she was hoping someone might check on her, she'd be waiting a long time.

She grabbed a new tray and took a deep breath before exiting the kitchen for a second round. She did her best to stick to the groups of couples and avoid a repeat of the vulgar men. Her only goal was to get through this night without feeling completely degraded.

"May I?" a familiar voice came from behind her shoulder.

She spun around and locked eyes with Nik. He wore a dark blue button-up shirt and black slacks. His normally tousled hair had been combed back. He looked sleek and handsome, but she preferred him more rugged in a black T-shirt. This one didn't cling to his muscles the way she liked, but it did bring out the blue in his eyes. But there was purple there, in smudges underneath his eyes. He must not be sleeping well. His brows pinched together, and he looked sad to be so close and yet feel so far away. The same sorrow echoed in her heart.

She extended her tray so he could grab a bite.

"Thanks." His eyes dropped to her chest as he took one of the tiny appetizers, but he quickly cleared his throat and averted his eyes.

Her cheeks flushed, but her lips curved into a smile. His feeble attempt to be courteous was appreciated, but she also liked to see him squirm. The power she sometimes felt over him was divine. Chills ran up her spine and heat rolled across her chest and down between her legs.

"You're welcome." She turned, needing to get away before she did or said something she'd regret. She felt his eyes on her as she made her escape.

Chapter Thirty

NIK

"You look like you've seen a ghost." Sam interrupted Nik's train of thought. He'd been watching Ali almost all night long. Spotting her in the crowd whenever he could. Her blonde braid was a stark contrast against the sea of black coats. His heart raced every time he got a glimpse of her full body in that gown. It took his breath away and he would gladly surrender his life with that last bit of air if it meant he got to lay eyes on her.

It didn't even bother him that other people were looking. He wasn't the jealous type. Unless it was Eli and then it was mostly just jealousy of how well they knew each other. Eli had decades of knowledge that Nik would never have. A lifetime of experiences he'd never shared. Would Nik ever know her as intimately as Eli did?

No, others could look, but what lay beneath that dress was for him and him alone. Even now, when they weren't speaking, he knew she belonged to him just as he belonged to her.

She couldn't hide it, though she tried. The pink on her cheeks and between her breasts said it all. He had the urge to whisk her out of this hall and back to his bed. To see the other places she was flushed. To run his hands over her skin and feel the warmth beneath his fingertips. Feel her shudder from his touch.

"Has she forgiven you yet?" Sam asked, pulling Nik out of his thoughts.

"What?" Nik turned in alarm.

Sam sighed dramatically and took a sip of his drink. "Nik, we work together every day. You're not hiding anything from me. It's painfully obvious something is going on there. Not to mention the time you took her to your *home* of all places rather than the infirmary. I haven't seen you two sneaking off or whispering around the greenhouses lately, so I know something isn't right. I'm not blind. Don't insult my intelligence."

Nik swirled his drink and tried to read him. He didn't look mad or disapproving. He just looked bored, like this was all factual information that everyone knew and unworthy of his attention. Small talk. That's all it was to him.

Did everyone know?

"Um, okay. She's still not talking to me." He felt like his head was spinning.

"Then why the hell are you still standing here? If I have to watch you pining for the next month, I'll lose it. It's pathetic, Nik, and pathetic doesn't look good on you. Go fix it."

Did Sam really just call him pathetic? Sam had always been the quiet one. Non-confrontational. But his stillness was deceiving. He saw more than most. Perceived more than most.

Nik downed the rest of his drink and placed it gently on a nearby tray. He grabbed another glass and quickly downed it as well, letting it burn his throat and light a fire in his veins. "Okay. Yeah, I guess I'll go fix it."

He still wasn't sure what he was doing. He didn't even have a plan, but step one was obviously talking to her. Last time he'd seen her, she'd been over by the string band, but she had probably moved on by now. He scanned the crowd and weaved in and out of bodies pressed too closely. Some people gave him disgruntled looks as he gently nudged them out of his way. A few hurtled curses his way as their drinks sloshed in their hands.

"Sorry, sorry," he repeated.

Where the hell had she gone? He paused. The crowd had steadily grown during the night. It was getting more difficult to move and nearly impossible to see anyone beyond two feet in front of him. Looking to the side of the room, he had an idea.

There was a grand marble staircase leading up to the second-floor balcony. If he could just get a better vantage point, he'd be able to find Ali. He squeezed through irritated guests again as he made his way to the stairs. Some shoved back, but he paid them little attention.

It was a breath of fresh air when he made it up the first few steps of swirling white and gold. His shoes clicked against the hard surface of the stairs. He hadn't realized just how stuffy the air was among the crowd, but here with his head above the rest, he could breathe freely.

The hall was *packed*. It was easy enough to spot the servers, though. They were the only ones moving in and out of the room. Dressed in white, they wove through the crowds with trays in hand. Everyone else was hardly moving because they had nowhere to go.

He spotted her after a few moments, in the far corner of the hall serving a group of young men. He could tell from her body language that she was uncomfortable, and they were enjoying every minute. Her shoulders hunched as she extended the tray to serve them. She made a face at one man as he sneered. He could only imagine the things they were saying, and it made his blood boil.

Nik descended the steps, prepared to come to her defense when, on the last step, he looked over and saw one of the young men grab her ass and pull her closer to him. Her tray clattered to the floor, and the food went flying as she tried to shove him away. Another one grabbed her wrist in retaliation.

Nik didn't know how he moved so fast, but one second he was on the stairs and the next he was gripping the man's shirt between his fists and pushing him against the wall.

"Touch her again and I'll kill you."

The man turned to his friends and laughed as if to say, *is this guy serious?*

Nik shoved him into the wall again and the man snapped his attention back to Nik. His friends inched closer, prepared to put up a fight, but they were no threat. He'd take them on too if he had to, but right now he only had one target.

"Fine," the man huffed. His friends relaxed a bit as Nik let him slide to the ground. He straightened his shirt and muttered, "Freak."

Nik didn't care to argue with him. Ali was headed back to the kitchen, visibly upset, her dress flowing behind her. He ran after her, sticking close to the edge of the room where it was easier to move.

He swung the door of the kitchen open and glimpsed her exiting a door on the opposite side of the room. "Ali!" he shouted. "Ali, stop!"

She didn't.

He chased her through the kitchen, almost running into a couple workers who dodged out of his way at the last moment. The hallway was dark, and he had to squint before his eyes adjusted. He could hear her muffled noises, but had to walk to the end of the hall and make a left before he spotted her, leaning up against the wall and crying into her hands.

"Ali," he said softly. He approached slowly, afraid he might scare her off if he moved too quickly. Then he took her hands in his and gently lowered them away from her face, interlacing his fingers with hers. She closed her eyes, and he watched as tears rolled down her cheeks. "Look at me."

She squeezed her eyes even tighter and shook her head.

"Please. Please look at me," he said softly.

She reluctantly opened her eyes and looked up at him. "I hate this."

"I know."

"I hate it here," she sobbed, her eyes glassy.

"I know."

"I hate you."

Nik's breath caught and she squeezed his hands, fighting an internal battle. He knew she didn't mean it, but it stung just the same.

"No, you don't."

She leaned into him, wrapping her arms around his back. He felt her hands slide over him, and he held her close as she cried into his chest. "No, I don't."

Nik rubbed her bare back as she wept, her skin cool against his warm hands. He gave her all the time she needed until her tears stopped and her breathing evened out. Then he kissed the top of her head and held her tight. They stood in a silent embrace for what felt like an eternity, but it would never be long enough for him. There was no amount of her that would ever be enough for him.

"I got Eli a job on the wall, but you need to convince him to take it. He's stubborn, but it'll be easier to escape if he's in a more favorable position. I promised you I would fix this, and I meant it. I meant every word."

Her hands traveled over his stomach. "I believe you."

That small confession was all the encouragement he needed.

"I brought you something," he whispered in her ear.

She pulled back enough to look at him in the face, her eyes still glistening and pink. "What is it?"

Nik watched her lips as she spoke, and he desperately wanted to kiss them, to taste them again, to feel her tongue against his. Her cheeks turned rosy as she noticed his gaze, and it only made him want her more.

He reached into his pocket and pulled out the velvet bag from the jeweler. The shadow of a smile crossed her face, and she gave the bag a curious look. She reached for it, but he snapped his hand back playfully. He loosened the strings that held it shut and pulled out the amethyst rose necklace, letting it unravel and hang before her. Its purple reflection sparkled in her eyes.

"Do you like it?" he asked. He'd never seen her wear jewelry. She probably didn't own any, or if she had, it had been left behind in Andus. He hoped this suited her taste.

She held the pendant in her hand, lips parted in awe. "It's beautiful."

"Turn around. Let me put it on you." He was grinning like a fool. It felt so good to be close to her again, to see her smile, tentative though it may be. She turned around and pulled her braid over her shoulder, exposing her neck. A lump in his throat formed as he gazed at the soft blonde tendrils delicately falling at the base of her neck, the vertebrae of her spine jutting all the way down her bare back, the soft white fabric fit loosely over the curve of her hips. She was stunning. He was hit with an overwhelming sense of longing. He'd been drowning for weeks and had finally breached the surface, air filling his lungs once more.

Nik focused on the necklace and pulled it around her, clasping it and letting it fall onto her neck. She shivered when he tenderly ran his fingers down her back, leaning in close to her. She tilted her head to one side and gasped when he gently kissed her exposed neck. Her skin was so delicate.

"You're so beautiful," he whispered, lips moving across her skin. He rubbed his chin across her shoulder, the soft bristles tickling her, making her tense and press into him.

"Nik." Her voice was unsteady, and she rolled her head back, resting against his shoulder. His hands were on her waist, brushing against the soft skin. He moved one hand up across her stomach and slipped it into the thin fabric, cupping her breast. He half expected her to stop him, to push him away again, but she didn't. His touch turned greedier.

She adjusted again to meet his lips, and he moaned into the kiss. He felt her lips curve in a smile, and it took his breath away. The way she moved against him and slid a hand into his hair drove him wild. This was all he needed in life. He only needed her.

"I want you," she said, hunger in her voice. She spun around and grabbed behind his neck, pulling him in for a passionate, ravenous kiss, like she too had been drowning and he was her only source of oxygen. He let his hands travel to her hips and gathered the fabric of her skirt until he could slip his hands underneath. He groped at her thighs and picked her up, wrapping her legs around him.

The sudden motion broke their kiss, and she gasped at him like he'd stolen the air from her lungs, her eyes full of want and need. He pushed her up against the wall, using it to prop her up. She reached behind her and pulled at the fabric behind her neck, bringing it over her head and letting it fall at her waist. Nik drank her in. Her chest flushed like it always did when she was aroused. He liked it even better with his necklace draped across her, the dark violet contrasting against her pale skin.

He palmed both breasts in each of his hands, massaging gently. His cock hardened, and he pushed his hips into her, letting her know just how badly he wanted her. "God, you're fucking perfect." She rolled her hips at his praise, and he gritted his teeth. His eyes rolled back in his head. "Fuck."

Her slender fingers unbuttoned his shirt, and he watched in a trance as she fumbled in a rush. There was nothing about her that he didn't love. He was obsessed with all of it, every bit of her. She pulled the bottom of his shirt out of his pants and unbuttoned them as well.

He pushed up the skirt of her dress and hissed.

No panties. He was the luckiest man alive.

He moved his thumb across her clit, and she jolted. God, he loved how sensitive she was. His perfect girl.

She settled as he rubbed circular motions, and her breaths came in soft gasps. She'd all but forgotten what she was doing with his pants. Her hands hung loosely on his waistband. Goosebumps covered her arms, and he had the desire to cover her whole body with his.

Nik reached down to his pants and picked up where she left off, letting his cock free. He felt her thighs tense around his waist as he pulled back just enough to slide along her entrance.

An impatient moan escaped her lips, and she braced herself against the wall. He made slow, languid strokes along her slit, toying with her clit. His jaw clenched as he felt her wetness cover the head of his cock, down his shaft. He'd waited so long for this. He slid up against her with precision and restraint.

"Oh my god," she said breathily, using her thighs to pull him closer.

"Tell me how badly you want me," he said as his thumb played with one of her nipples and she arched her back at his touch. His mind threatened to explode, watching her squirm and writhe in his hands. Her body frantically searched for him, trying to connect in the most intimate way possible.

"I want you so badly. Please." Her words were slurred, like she struggled to form full sentences. "I need you."

Not want, but *need.* He needed her, too.

Their eyes met and he pushed into her, just an inch, watching as she embraced him, enjoying the way their bodies connected. He pulled back out and then pushed in again, a little further this time. Wrinkles formed on her forehead as she struggled to adjust to his size. It took everything in him to restrain himself. The way she pulled and rocked her hips and begged to be filled. He slid out an inch and pushed forward further, almost fully sheathed. He hissed as she squeezed around his cock; the sensation was mind-blowing. He pulled out one more time, and she gripped his arms in frustration.

"Please." The word caught in her throat. A guttural noise full of desire.

He buried himself in one powerful stroke and she inhaled sharply. Her jaw dropped, and she looked so lost in satisfaction. He took her bottom lip in his mouth and bit gently.

It felt right like this, with his body pressed against hers. She was soft and warm, and he never wanted to leave her embrace. He wanted her to keep her arms around his neck, one hand trailing through his hair for all of eternity.

He was panting now. He pulsed in and out of her as she bit down on his shoulder, experiencing too much and not enough all at the same time. The sound of her soft gasps echoed in his ear, and it set him on fire head to toe.

With every stroke, he felt her clenching, yearning for him to fill the emptiness he left behind.

"Oh my god," she murmured in his ear.

He turned his head to find hers and braced her neck with his hand, controlling the tempo at which they kissed. He traced her lips with his tongue and explored her mouth, memorizing the way she felt and the way she tasted. She was sweet but fiery, like cinnamon.

An unbearable craving built in his core, and he picked up his pace, driving into her. He was so close now.

"Nik," she whined.

"Fuck. You feel so good. I fucking—" Love you? Was this love? "I wanna feel you come."

Her eyes rolled back in her head, and she whimpered. His hands were all over her, an urgent need to feel every inch, from her soft breasts to her round ass. Her small hand clenched his wrist in a death grip while he swirled her clit. He relished the way she held onto him for dear life.

Her eyes squeezed shut and her face scrunched in unadulterated ecstasy. He felt the walls of her pussy flutter around him, and her thighs quivered uncontrollably. She let out a few high-pitched moans before her body relaxed, all energy expended.

A few more pulses and Nik unraveled in bliss, spilling into her. His body collapsed into hers and they both crashed against the wall. He kissed her temple and massaged her thigh while they both came down from their high. Her eyelids flickered dreamily, and she caressed his arm.

They stood in silence. What was there to say? This was everything Nik had wanted, and now he had her. His cock twitched thinking of how lucky he was to be inside her, that she had let him in, and not just physically. He slid out, and she sighed in his absence.

"I need to get back before they realize I'm missing." She glanced back toward the kitchen door and pulled the fabric of her dress back over her head and around her neck.

Nik cursed the New Year banquet for not allowing them more time together.

He kissed her on the forehead before she turned away.

"Ali..." He didn't know what he wanted to say. There were no words to communicate how much this meant to him. How much *she* meant to him. His eyes raked over her body and settled on her face. Her smile lit up the dark hallway and melted his heart. "I wish you didn't have to go."

"I know. I'm glad we had this…if I had left before…I'm glad I got to be with you."

He choked back tears. She was talking about leaving for good. This was her way of saying goodbye. The fire from the torchlight twinkled in her eyes as she smoothed her dress. Meanwhile, he looked frazzled, his pants and shirt still unbuttoned.

He opened his mouth to tell her he had every intention of coming with her, but she'd rendered him speechless. She placed a delicate kiss on his lips, and he leaned into it, forgetting all else. This wasn't the end. This was their beginning.

Chapter Thirty-One

ELI

It took everything in Eli to not spill drinks on all these ungrateful assholes. The liquid bubbled in tiny, slender glasses. This was nothing like the gray grass they had back home. It was sparkling and smelled fruity. They didn't even know how good they had it here.

The party attendees grabbed drinks off his tray without even acknowledging him. Like it had just popped up out of thin air. They didn't want to see the unpleasant servants they kept. It was a dirty secret and if they ignored him, they could ignore their own sins and complacency.

He watched as they got sloppier and sloppier with each tray he brought out. At one point, he dared to drown a glass himself to see just how strong it was. It was delicious but burnt his nostrils. *Strong.* He needed to see Ali's reaction to this.

His heart hurt when he thought of her. Their brief conversation earlier was the closest to normal he'd felt in weeks. Maybe it was time to forgive her and move on. It was telling that she was the first thought that came to mind when he experienced something new and wanted to share it. She'd always be his best friend.

Eli scanned the ballroom, but it was packed. With her height, it was highly unlikely he'd be able to spot her. So he waited until it was time to grab a new tray and headed back toward the kitchen, through the crowd of people. He bumped into multiple shoulders as he went and made no effort to apologize. More than one person hurled an insult, but he just grinned in satisfaction.

The kitchen was a breath of fresh air. He had no idea why anyone would want to be squished together so tightly in that ballroom. Surely they would start clearing out soon and he'd be free to go home and rest.

Home. He shook his head in disgust at the idea of "home" being an empty cell. It had a bed, though, and his body ached. He was no longer used to standing for long periods of time. His healing wounds had depleted his energy.

Servers walked in and out of the swinging doors, dropping empty trays and picking up fresh ones. Other servants were quick to grab the dirty trays and glasses, wash them and then replace them to be filled with yet another round of food and beverages. The chefs were as busy now as they'd been when the prisoners had first arrived. There were no signs that this party would slow down any time soon.

Eli shifted the drinks around in an effort to look busy, waiting for Ali so they could sneak a drink together. A few more of these and he might not feel the pain, might not mind working a while longer. No one paid him much attention. He was wondering how long he could procrastinate when Ali burst through the door, looking distraught. Her eyes were red, like she'd been crying. She crossed the room in a few quick steps and exited through the door on the other side.

His immediate flame of concern grew worse when Nik followed shortly after her, yelling her name. He looked frantic, like he was responsible for whatever was bothering Ali. If he hurt her, Eli would kill him.

Eli stepped around the counter to follow them but was stopped by one of the chefs. He waved his hands dramatically and pointed Eli toward the door, gently nudging him in the opposite direction. "Go! What are you waiting for?"

Eli looked at the door to the hall where Ali and Nik had disappeared. He wanted so badly to follow and give Nik a piece of his mind, but there was a short balding man in a white apron preventing him from making his move, waving his hands in frustration.

He hesitated before taking a few steps backward. He turned around to go back to the ballroom with a fresh tray of drinks, shooting glances back at the door on his way.

Right before he reached the swinging doors, another server stepped through, almost bumping into him. The drinks swayed before settling on the balanced tray.

"Here," he said quickly. "I'll take that and you take this one." Eli traded trays with the new arrival and turned back. The other servant gave him an odd look, but didn't argue. Eli tossed the tray on the counter and hurried toward the hallway before anyone could stop him.

It took a moment for his eyes to adjust to the dark hall, lit only by a few flame torches spread far apart. He heard sounds coming from the end of the hall and tiptoed toward it.

As he got closer to the end of the hall, he could make out a few words.

"I want you so badly. Please," Ali said. "I need you."

His stomach turned, and he didn't need to move any further. He shouldn't be listening to this, but it was hard to drag himself away. He'd misunderstood. Something else had upset her, not Nik. He was the one comforting her now, a task that used to be Eli's.

Their heavy breathing washed over him. He placed a hand on his chest, his heart pounding painfully against his ribs. His blood froze in his veins. He had heard more than enough. It was very clear from the kissing and sucking noises, the ruffle of clothing and shoes against the stone floor, that Ali wasn't done with Nik. She wasn't done with him at all. She had flat out lied to Eli.

Eli walked back toward the kitchen with his head hung low. He struggled to swallow the lump in his throat. How could he be so blind? How had he not seen this coming? He'd noticed their flirty banter, but it never occurred to him that she would've gone this far. What did she even know about him?

Nothing. She couldn't possibly know anything.

Eli moved through the kitchen. Rage coursed through him, and he swept a tray of glasses clean off the counter. They crashed to the floor, several of the glasses shattering on impact. Their shards flung out in all directions and a few people jumped away to avoid having their ankles sliced. Heads whipped in Eli's direction as he shoved his hands through his hair.

"What do you think you're doing?" The same short, bald chef from earlier looked furiously at him. He grabbed a broom from the corner of the kitchen and hurried over to Eli. "Clean it up. Clean it up. Unbelievable."

The chef thrust the broom into Eli's hands and continued to reprimand him, his words jumbled and fuming. The man's agitation did nothing to lessen Eli's fury. He swept the shards of glass into a dustpan and dumped them into the trash.

"Ridiculous. Completely unacceptable." The chef pulled out more clean glasses to replace the ones Eli had broken. "Try not to break these," he said as he placed them on the tray and filled them.

Eli just stared at him with indignation. "No."

He was done with this. He would not do this anymore. What would they do? Beat him again? Been there, done that.

"What did you just say?"

"No," Eli repeated and tilted his head to the side, daring the chef to ask him again.

"You don't get to say 'no,' boy. You're here to work." The chef turned red in the face, clearly fed up with Eli's behavior.

Eli rolled his eyes. They couldn't force him to do anything. He'd take whatever punishment they threw his way.

The other workers in the kitchen turned away, not wanting to be part of this tense conversation. Eli could tell they were still listening intently, though. It was hard not to eavesdrop when the entire kitchen had gone silent. The bustle of chefs preparing dishes had ceased, and the chatter quieted.

"Pick. Up. That. Tray." The chef spat out the words. A vein in his neck pulsed in rage while he bit back an angry tirade.

"No." Eli turned to leave, but before he reached the door, Nik strutted through, his hair and clothes disheveled and his lips swollen. Ali nearly ran into him when he stopped in the doorway, her hair no longer neatly pulled back and her dress crooked. A new piece of jewelry he'd never seen before hung around her neck.

"Is there a problem here?" Nik asked.

Ali attempted to flatten the stray hairs in her braid, her eyes on the floor. She could try all she wanted, but the marks on her neck and the sweat on her brow would be harder to conceal.

Eli's eyes flitted from Nik to Ali and back to Nik, unsure which person he was most angry with.

"Ah, yes, there most certainly is a problem." The chef darted forward to complain to Nik. He pointed an accusatory finger at Eli and carried on. "This young man is refusing to serve the party after he *trashed* the place and—"

"Trashed?" Ali looked up.

The chef looked furious at her interruption, his cheeks flaming red. He turned to Nik and did his best to ignore the others. "Well, he broke some glasses, but—"

"That's a far cry from '*trashed,*' Dimitri," Nik interrupted.

Eli curled his hands into fists. He didn't need Nik coming to his defense. He didn't need Ali's either. She was still half hidden behind Nik and refused to make eye contact with Eli. Her eyes instead focused on straightening the strap of her dress. She fidgeted with it, like there was no way it could possibly cover enough of her body. Like it revealed the secrets she meant to hide.

Eli moved toward the door once more. He'd push Nik out of the way if he had to. He couldn't take one more minute of this place. He was going back to the prison. Hell, if he had more clothes on, he would find the exit to this hell hole right this second, but he'd probably die from exposure.

Death didn't sound so bad right now.

"You know what? Eli has had a hard week or two. Still recovering from an injury."

Eli rolled his eyes. They almost beat him to death but downplayed it to a simple injury.

"Why don't I escort him home? I'm sure you don't need him anymore. Right?" Nik challenged the chef.

"Well, not if he's going to act like that," the man grumbled, but he walked away, leaving the three of them alone.

"Eli?" Ali questioned softly, clearly unaware of what was bothering him. Appearing in the kitchen with Nik was damning, but if only she knew just how much he'd heard. Moans that he'd only heard come from his bed in the past. He couldn't shake the sound from his mind. It clawed at his brain, just behind his eyes.

"Don't, Ali. I'm not interested in talking to you." His voice was louder and more strained than he intended. He could hardly stand to look at her, and he bit his cheek to keep his temper at bay. He glared at Nik instead, wishing he could light him on fire with just his eyes.

Nik didn't mirror his fury. His expression was a mix of sympathy and annoyance. Like Eli barely fazed him, but he did pity him.

Ali looked back and forth between them and her mouth opened in understanding. She touched her fingers to her lips.

When she spoke, her voice was little more than a whisper. "I'm sorry—"

"Sorry? Ali, you're not sorry. You never were. I hope the two of you have a happy life together. What little life you're able to enjoy while you serve him like his bitch."

Tears glistened in her eyes, and Nik stepped forward. "That's enough. You're done here." He grabbed for Eli's arm to escort him out of the hall, but Eli shook him off.

"Don't fucking touch me." Eli shoved him to the side and grabbed his things out of the nearby cubbyhole. He threw on his coat and shoes and stormed out of the kitchen.

Nik didn't attempt to put his hands on him again, but he followed closely, supervising his walk back to the prison.

Eli could see his breath in the freezing cold air of midnight. As they left the music and chatter of the hall behind, the air turned still. The calm before the storm. The bright stars against the ink blue sky might've been beautiful under different circumstances.

Eli remembered watching the stars with Ali when they were young teens. They used to count them, seeing who could get the highest, before they'd lose track and start over. She would giggle innocently when he held her hand. He still remembered late nights and stolen kisses on the sandy beach under a sky just like this one. He clenched his jaw and blinked back tears.

That all felt like a distant dream now. Like he'd made it up in his head. The harder he held onto the memory, the fuzzier it became, replaced by an older Ali holding Nik's hand instead.

The crunching of snow was ever present behind him. "I don't need a babysitter," he spat back at Nik.

"Could've fooled me with how childish you're behaving."

Eli turned so abruptly that Nik almost collided with him. Nik rolled his eyes in that condescending way he liked to do. "Are we really going to do this again? It didn't work out so well for you last time."

Eli looked around theatrically and spread his arms. "There's no one here to interrupt us this time. I don't know. Could be fun." His voice hit an unnaturally high octave. He hated that Nik had this power over him, but he'd finally snapped. Nothing would be more satisfying than pummeling him into the ground.

"Why does it matter to you what Ali does?"

Eli squinted. The answer was so obvious and so hard to explain at the same time. She meant everything to him. She was all he'd ever had. All he'd ever really known. She was an extension of him. He shook his head, too flustered to respond, and continued walking.

Nik jogged to catch up. "What is it? What is your deal? Are you in love with her or something?"

Eli spun around once more. "Of course I'm fucking in love with her. And you? You don't even fucking know her, so what are you doing?" The rage he'd been holding back was seeping through the cracks.

Nik waved him off. "Love. Infatuation. That's my business, quite frankly."

Was there ever a time when he wasn't a condescending, sarcastic douchebag?

"You don't deserve her," Eli snapped.

"*Deserve?*" Nik's face twisted in disgust. "No one *deserves* anyone. And if you love her like you say you do, you wouldn't play these bullshit games with her. You can't just take away love when she doesn't act the way you expect her to. I don't think you love her at all. I think you love the version of her that you made up in your head."

He shoved Nik back a few steps. What did he know? He knew nothing about Eli and Ali's relationship, the things they'd been through. They had so much history together.

Eli gritted his teeth. But Nik wasn't entirely wrong. It was a childish reaction to keep pushing Ali away anytime she upset him, rather than talking about it like adults. Like friends. Like family. His anger was on the verge of exploding.

He lashed out at Nik. "And what about you? What do you *deserve,* Nik? You think you deserve to sit here in your luxury town with extravagant balls and slave labor to put food on your table? You deserve a lavish home and a woman who can't afford to tell you 'no?' You think you're better than me?" Eli had so much resentment toward Nik that went beyond his attention to Ali.

Nik was in Eli's face now. "You think Ali doesn't want me? You think I forced her or something?" His nostrils flared, clearly angered by Eli's insinuation.

"You said it yourself that you would get what you want. How do I know you didn't play dirty?"

Nik took a step back. "Would you listen to yourself, man? I'm not *playing* anything. And I didn't have to *trick* or coerce Ali into anything, either. She is free to make her own decisions."

"Does she know that?"

Nik's lack of response was telling. He just continued to stare at Eli, scandalized. Something like recognition dawned on his face, and his shoulders slumped.

Eli huffed. "That's what I thought."

This entire evening had exhausted him. He wanted to crawl into bed and forget any of it had happened. He stalked away from Nik, who was still lost in thought. If he was a better person, he might've felt bad for the guy. He clearly hadn't considered that Ali might not want him at all.

Eli didn't believe that, though. He only said it to get under Nik's skin. Ali didn't do anything she didn't want to do. But then again, Eli wondered just how well he knew Ali. Was Nik right? Did he have his own version of her in his head that didn't truly exist? Or had the version he knew just morphed into a different person? Grown up to become someone else?

"Wait." Nik was jogging again and fell into step with Eli, who sighed. He just couldn't get rid of him. He exhaled sharply as his feet hit the ground. "Do you want to get a drink?"

"A drink? Are you fucking serious right now?" Eli laughed humorlessly. Why on Earth would he want to get a drink with Nik? Still, the thought of having something to dull the pain was more enticing than going to his cell and staring at the ceiling while his mind raced in anger.

"Dead serious."

"Fine," he spat.

Nik led him to a bar that he'd passed many times before. The rusting metal sign above the door said "the Spotted Salamander." He followed Nik through the old wooden door. The place was entirely empty except for the bartender behind the counter, who was sitting and drinking from her own mug. Apparently, since everyone else was at the ball, she had decided to drink on the job.

"Evening, Marlena."

"Nik? I didn't expect to see you here tonight. Or anyone, for that matter." She hiccupped and then pulled out two more mugs. She pointed at Eli. "Haven't seen your face before. Who's your friend?"

"We're not friends," they both said in unison.

She smiled. "Of course not. What can I get you?"

"The strongest thing you've got."

She hopped excitedly and motioned toward the back. "I know just what you need." She headed toward the back storage and left them sitting together at the bar.

"I'll make a pact with you," Nik said, breaking the silence.

"A pact?" Eli questioned. What kind of deal could he possibly want to make with Eli?

"Yes." Nik nodded. "I'll make sure Ali knows she's not under any pressure and you have to let her make her own decisions and stop holding them against her."

Eli turned to face him, expecting the usual frivolous expression, but he looked quite serious.

"Why are you doing this? Why not just let me walk away so you can have Ali to yourself? I wouldn't be in the way anymore."

Nik inhaled sharply. He opened his mouth several times to speak but closed it, holding something back. Eli thought he understood. He chuckled and shook his head. Ali wouldn't be happy without Eli in her life. No matter how rocky their friendship was right now, he was the only family she had left. Nik didn't want to be the nail in the coffin of their friendship.

Eli's stomach sank a little. This wasn't surface level infatuation. Fuck, the son of a bitch actually cared for her.

Marlena came back with a clear bottle in her hand and poured the liquid into three small glasses. She grabbed one for herself and they took the other two in hand.

"Cheers to a new year," she said merrily.

"To a gentleman's agreement," Eli responded.

Nik nodded in understanding and clinked his glass against Eli's. Marlena was already throwing hers back.

Eli brought it to his lips and drank it in one sip. It burned more than anything he'd ever tasted. He felt like his lungs were shriveling. He coughed and coughed as Marlena and Nik chuckled.

"What was that?" he choked out.

Nik raised his glass and drank it swiftly, wincing as he swallowed.

"Moonshine."

Chapter Thirty-Two

ELI

ELI DID HIS BEST to keep his side of the arrangement. After the initial aversion to Nik's deal wore off, he realized this would ultimately be beneficial to him as well. He didn't want to be the immature and juvenile person Nik had painted. He'd always thought more highly of himself than that and he wanted to prove it to himself more than anyone else. And he did really love Ali. It bothered him that his actions of late hadn't reflected that.

His conversations with Ali were strained and uncomfortable at first. She kept looking at him like he was going to snap and perhaps she had every reason to believe that. After all, he had caused quite a scene at the banquet a couple weeks ago. Not one of his finest moments.

"I can't believe today is your last day working in the greenhouse," Ali said between bites of her lunch, sitting on an overturned bucket. She rocked back and forth like a child. Eli expected the bucket to give out any second. "What am I going to do without you?"

Eli had taken up Jameson's offer to guard the gate after Ali nearly forced him into it. This would be good for them, to have some space apart. And now that he'd calmed down a bit, it made sense to join the guard. The position would give him more access and knowledge than he would ever get in the greenhouse. They could finally make a proper plan to escape. Ali said she would go with him, but he couldn't help but question how serious she was with Nik lingering in the background.

"I think you'll find someone to keep you company." He looked past her to the corner where Nik and Sam were sitting, eating their lunch.

Ali followed his gaze and turned back, face flushed.

"Right." She picked at the bread on her sandwich and stared at the ground, no longer rocking back and forth. He shook his head. Once again, he'd made things awkward. They would never repair their friendship if he didn't learn to keep his comments to himself.

"It's fine, Ali. How many times do I have to tell you?" He tried to reassure her, but he also understood her hesitation. She didn't understand Eli's sudden change of heart, and he wasn't keen to fill her in on the details of his conversation with Nik. Sure, it would help her understand where he was coming from, but it would also improve Nik's image, and Eli was still petty enough to keep from doing something like that. He was still hoping she'd get bored of him and would realize what a mistake she'd made in sleeping with him.

"Are you sure? Because Nik—"

"Ali." He stopped her. "I'm trying my best to be okay with this, but I really would rather not hear his name."

"Sorry." She stared at the ground again, and Eli sighed. How would they ever get past this?

"You don't need to apologize." If anyone should apologize, it was him, but he was too stubborn. The best he could do was bite his tongue.

"What do you think it'll be like? Working as a guard?" she asked, effectively changing the topic.

"Boring," he joked. "How badly does this gate need protecting? I imagine I'll just be sitting around all day."

"Sounds riveting." She smiled, and he returned the gesture. It was nice to see her smiling again. Could they find a new normal between them? One where she was happy and he was content?

"Might not be the most exciting job, but I think it'll be for the best."

It would be. He was sure of it. But as the rest of the day passed, he couldn't help but second guess his decision. He watched from a distance as Nik flirted with Ali and she smiled even larger than she had during their lunch break. He felt like his heart was ripping into pieces, knowing he didn't evoke that level of happiness in her anymore.

If he left, he wouldn't be able to intervene. He wouldn't be able to keep an eye on her and prevent her from making mistakes. But they were her mistakes to make.

If he stayed, he'd be subjected to their banter and stolen glances. It was excruciating. Of all the things he'd been through, letting go of Ali was one of the hardest. Other things had been done *to* him. This was a pain he willingly inflicted upon himself. A blade that cut to his core and bled him dry, but he held the knife.

Eli covered the last row of crops with topsoil and wiped a dirty hand across his forehead. He might miss Ali, but he wouldn't miss this work.

"You're lucky I didn't have you spreading manure today. Thought it would've made a good going-away present, but unfortunately, we didn't need to fertilize today."

Eli caught a glimpse of Nik out of the corner of his eye and grimaced. "I'm so disappointed," he said sarcastically.

"You're doing the right thing," Nik said, reading Eli's body language. It was clear he was struggling with the decision. "Hell, maybe you'll even manage to escape."

Eli raised his brows in shock. He couldn't tell if Nik was serious. Had Ali filled him in? How much did he know? He played coy. "Highly doubt it."

"Not with that attitude," Nik mocked.

Eli grew nervous. What had Ali told him? Were they working together?

"I'm trying to help you," Nik said.

"Yes, you've helped so much already. Thank you."

"You're welcome." Eli could've smacked the grin right off of his face, but they'd been there before and it hadn't worked out well. He hated seeing Nik's smug face. It aggravated him more than anything else.

Nik started to walk away, but Eli stopped him. "Why? Why are you helping me?"

Nik thought for a moment. "I'm not the villain you think I am. And despite how I feel about you, I know you mean a lot to Ali. There isn't much I wouldn't do for her."

His answer gutted Eli, but he knew it was true. "I figured you just wanted to get rid of me."

"That's a bonus." He grinned and turned on his heel, leaving Eli to clean up his area. Eli chuckled as he picked up his tools. If Nik wasn't such a pain in his ass, they might have been friends.

Chapter Thirty-Three

NIK

NIK SAT AGAINST THE trunk of a tree as Marcus pulled out his canteen. Water spilled from the top as he sloppily brought it down from his face. Their reconnaissance mission had been unsuccessful so far. After they told Jameson about their first mission and the missing goods, he had hastily thrown together a second mission to scout the surrounding area. The commander was determined to squash any potential foes before anything bad happened. They were assigned partners and designated areas to search, and Nik had been fortunate enough to be stuck with Marcus.

So far, the only adversary they had come across was a rabbit that spooked both of them when it sprang out of the bushes and a rogue tree trunk that tripped Marcus and nearly made him face plant into the ground. They hadn't come across a single clue as to who might've ransacked Andus, and Marcus started grumbling. If they didn't find anything today, they'd be out here day in and day out until they did.

Jameson would not let this go. He was a ferocious leader and a big reason Rysburg had lasted this long and had so much to be thankful for.

Nik was just as cranky. He missed Ali. Marcus wasn't thinking of his wife, though. It was the conditions that bothered him the most. It was still winter, and Nik's thick coat did little to prevent the cold from reaching his bones. His fingers were purple and they matched his lips, both of which were numb. He cupped his hands and filled them with his warm breath.

"Where to next?" Marcus asked, rubbing his hands against his thighs and doing his best to stay warm.

"The other crew is heading counterclockwise, so we'll continue to move south and then west until we meet up with them." Nik studied a small piece of paper with rough landmarks sketched out to help guide them in their search.

"Hopefully they're having more luck than we are."

"Hopefully," Nik answered dully.

They stood after a few minutes of rest, ready to move on. They both flinched in alarm when twigs snapping sounded in the distance.

"What was that?" Marcus whispered.

Nik brought his finger up to his mouth to silence him. He listened intently, ears strained to make out a sound, any sound other than the light breeze.

Nothing.

His face relaxed. "It was probably just an animal." He grabbed his backpack from the ground and slung it over his shoulder. "Let's move."

But he looked back at the clearing as they continued, and the hairs on the back of his neck stood on end. He couldn't shake the feeling that they were not alone.

Marcus carried on complaining for the rest of the afternoon. The air was too cold, the path too unsteady, the food they packed too bland.

Nik felt the early markers of a migraine coming on. If they came up empty-handed today and had to search again, he prayed he would be assigned a different partner.

"Stop." He abruptly threw a hand out to Marcus, who froze.

"What is it?"

Nik scanned the forest. The white snow made everything blend together. Every surface was covered in a glistening blanket. "I thought I saw something."

Knew. He *knew* he'd seen something. But when he eyed the trees, nothing moved except the branches waving softly in the breeze. The shadows could've been playing tricks on him, but his heart raced. Something didn't feel right. The pit in his stomach grew.

"Must've been my imagination." His senses remained heightened as they continued walking through the forest.

They happened across a black creek, vibrant against the snow. Nik double checked his map and observed their surroundings. They were still on the correct path, but something was wrong.

"The water is supposed to be shallow enough to cross here." He stared at the rushing water; it had to be at least ten feet deep.

"Your map lies," Marcus griped.

"We've gotten more snow than usual..." He ground his teeth. Cold enough to snow, but not cold enough to freeze the river. And warm enough to raise the water by several feet as the snow in the surrounding areas fed the river.

"We can't cross this. It's too flooded." Marcus crossed his arms in defiance, like a child. How he'd made it through guard training, Nik would never know. He complained about every little nuisance.

Nik rubbed his throbbing temples.

"No one asked you to."

If he had to spend much longer with Marcus, he might snap. He pulled out his map again and traced their path with his finger. "We can walk downstream a bit. There should be an old bridge a few miles ahead."

They walked along the edge of the river in silence. That feeling returned—someone was watching them. Maybe he was being paranoid, but something just didn't feel right, and his intuition had never led him astray. But he scoured the forest and couldn't see anything out of place. They hadn't heard any suspicious noises in a while, either. So he carried on and kept his eyes peeled.

"Let's move into the trees," he told Marcus. If something was out there watching, it would be better if they weren't out in the open.

They reached the bridge and started to walk across. The cold air felt even harsher in the open, with no protection from the woods. The wind carried a cruel tune that nipped at his ears and nose.

Halfway across the bridge, Nik stopped in his tracks. His stomach tensed and he pulled his sword out of its sheath, his knuckles white as he gripped the end.

He had *definitely* seen something.

Marcus stood to his side with his sword drawn as well, shooting quick glances at Nik, waiting to follow his lead. Shadows moved in the woods ahead. Nik hoped for a moment that they were fellow Rysburg guards, but when they entered the opening, he immediately knew they weren't. He sucked in a ragged breath. This...this was what he had been wary of. This was the cause of the uneasy feeling he'd had all afternoon.

He counted five men as they walked forward menacingly, dressed in leather and protective gear, prepared for battle, each one of them the size of a full-grown man. They wore black masks, so he couldn't see their faces. That wasn't something they did in Rysburg. No, these were not friends. Their steps were a slow and controlled show of intimidation. They kept their gloved hands at their sides, weapons left in their sheaths.

He didn't know how well Marcus could fight, but perhaps they could take them on their own.

Marcus's eyes flashed back behind them and he jumped, turning to face the other direction. Nik didn't have to look to know they were surrounded on both sides. He closed his eyes for a moment and clenched his jaw, then turned to look over his shoulder and counted another five men. Their odds of getting out of this alive dropped significantly.

Nik had spent his entire adult life as a member of the guard. Fighting was not a foreign concept to him, but every single time, he and Rysburg had the element of surprise. They always did the attacking. He'd never been the one to be ambushed. He knew as well as anyone that playing offense was better than being on defense. No time to come up with a plan. No intel to work with. They didn't have the upper hand this time, and Nik feared it might cost them gravely.

One man stepped forward out of line and Nik gripped his sword tighter.

"Drop your weapons," he ordered, his voice low and threatening. The man was calm. He knew he was in control.

Nik did his best to remain calm, too.

Neither he nor Marcus moved. If they wanted him to drop his weapon, they'd have to make him.

"Don't make me say it again," the man threatened.

He watched their resistance for a moment longer and then whistled.

Something flew through the air. Nik spotted it from the corner of his eye, but he didn't have time to move before the arrow struck him in the thigh. The sharp tip sliced through his flesh, and his muscle throbbed in pain. With a snarl, he dropped to his knees. He used one hand to cover the entrance to his wound and felt warm blood slip through his fingers.

"Drop your weapons," the man repeated.

Marcus looked at Nik for guidance. They were clearly outnumbered; there was no way for them to fight their way out of this. The muscle in Nik's thigh throbbed in agony. Reluctantly, he released the sword in his other hand and pushed it a few feet away. He pulled out the smaller knives he had tucked away and tossed them, too.

Alive and captured was better than dead.

Marcus swallowed, throat bobbing, and tossed his sword and knife out in front of him as well.

"Get on your knees."

Marcus kneeled beside Nik, who was having a hard time putting weight on his left leg. He grimaced as he tried to straighten up, but pain shot through his thigh. The man came closer until he was standing in front of them both, looking down with hatred in his eyes, the only thing left uncovered by his mask. The rest of his men followed him onto the bridge and circled Nik and Marcus.

"Who are you?" Nik asked.

The man didn't respond.

Nik looked to his side to find Marcus breathing heavily with tears in his eyes. Marcus liked to put on a tough exterior, but he was just an ordinary man, terrified to find himself on the brink of death.

A couple months ago, Nik would've felt numb in this situation. A couple months ago, he'd had nothing to live for. He would've accepted this fate without much of a fight. But his eyes burned now as he thought of Ali. Life was cruel. It offered hope and then smothered it like a fire at the end of the night.

The man nodded to his men, and then a hard fist connected with Nik's cheek bone. Fists were all over Nik and Marcus, beating them into the ground. Hitting his face, his arms. Once he crumpled to the ground, the kicking began. Shoes connected with his legs and back.

It was particularly painful when they hit his wounded leg. That spot radiated pain throughout his entire body, pulsing unbearably.

Blood ran down his face from a cut on his brow. He struggled to breathe as the punches and kicks kept coming at his stomach and ribs, sucking the life out of him. Dizziness swept over him, and he was too weak to hold up his head, let alone stand. Each time he tried to gather himself, another kick landed. Another fist connected.

Nik curled into himself and brought his hands up to protect his face from their boots, but they carried on, cracking his knuckles and kicking his head. He heard Marcus's moans, nearly drowned out by the sound of fists hitting them nonstop. One hard hit to the ear and he could only hear half of what he'd heard before; a buzzing noise took the place of their voices.

The hits kept coming and his body went limp. The faint humming faded as he blacked out and gave in to the darkness.

When he returned to himself, he had no idea how long he had been knocked out. He blinked his swollen eyelids and swallowed the bloody spit in his mouth. His lips were dry and cracked and his face lay in an icy pool of blood. His surroundings hadn't changed. They were still on the bridge. He opened his eyes more fully and could see Marcus lying next to him. His chest didn't move and his eyes remained open and glossed over. *Dead.*

He might've yelled in shock, but his jaw was in too much pain and it came out more like a gargle.

"Welcome back to the living. Guess it's your lucky day."

Nik moved his head slowly to see the man standing above him, but black spots blurred his vision.

"Your friend here gave out before you, so you get to send the message back to your people." His voice was a low growl, an attack of its own accord.

He nudged Nik with his foot and pain seared through his body. Every muscle ached and he must've broken a bone or two. He looked at the wound in his leg and saw the arrow had broken off when he'd passed out. Now a jagged fragment stuck out of his leg, drenched in blood.

The man leaned down close to his face. "Did you really think you could go around terrorizing villages and no one would stop you? No one would notice the wreckage you left behind?" He grabbed Nik by the back of his head, fingers laced in his hair, and pulled him back to stare into his eyes. Nik had to grit his teeth to keep from screaming out in agony.

"You can tell your people that the Coyotes are coming for them..." He nodded and two of his companions grabbed Nik beneath the arms. "If you live long enough to reach them."

Nik couldn't do anything to stop them as they pulled him over to the edge of the bridge. His body was too tired and too broken.

Before he could brace himself, Nik plunged into the freezing water below.

It hit him like solid ice. The current threatened to crush his bones. He struggled to move his limbs, adrenaline fighting with his fatigue. Each movement sent fresh waves of pain through his body.

It couldn't end like this.

Nik's head dipped below the water and he sucked in, the water flooding his lungs. He broke through the surface and inhaled, coughing up water. The stream pulled him away from the bridge, and he watched as the group retreated. They didn't bother to watch if he lived or died. It didn't matter to them.

He swallowed water again. His legs couldn't keep up with treading water. He couldn't breathe. Water filled his mouth, his nostrils, engulfing him entirely. He grasped above the water, desperate for anything to hold on to, but cool, freezing air was all that slipped through his fingers. And then his world went dark.

251

Chapter Thirty-Four

ALI

ALI FELT A HAND on her shoulder, gently waking her from her dream. It had started as a lovely dream. She'd been running through the woods with Nik when they had come upon a waterfall with a secluded pond. She had watched the water glisten on his skin as he jumped in naked. His playful smile tempting her to jump in after him. His muscles had rippled and shadows had danced across his back. He shook his wet head and droplets of water fell around him.

It had been just the two of them, secluded from the rest of the world. In that little oasis, they hadn't worried about anyone else. No one had been there to judge their connection. Nothing to tear them apart. She was free to be his, and he was all hers.

He'd dove under the water and disappeared from her view. The ripples had settled on the surface. She had expected him to pop up again, but he had taken longer than he should've. Too long. Where had he gone?

Before he could reappear, she had opened her eyes.

That feeling still haunted her.

"Ali." Sam's voice was soft, and there was a faint hint of worry. Why was Sam in her cell in the middle of the night? "Ali."

Ali turned onto her back to look at him, and her breath caught when she saw his face. Standing there in the candlelight, she'd never seen Sam look so somber. He rarely let any emotion show. An ominous light flickered across his face.

"What is it? Eli? Nik? What happened?" She rubbed her eyes, struggling to collect her thoughts.

"It's Nik. He's alive, but—"

"Alive?" The severity of the situation was sunk in. That he had to explicitly say Nik was alive meant he almost hadn't been. She yanked on her pants and groped around in the dark for the shoes she kept under her bed. Sam stepped back to allow her room to get dressed.

"Yes. He's..." He bit his lip and ran a hand over his face, too weary to fill her in. "He's in pretty bad shape, but he's asking to see you."

"What happened?" she asked again, this time more frantically. Her throat tightened, and she choked back tears. Her dream was becoming a real-life nightmare.

They hurried through the silent halls of the prison, toward the entrance and out into the night. Her tears froze on her cheeks while Sam explained the situation.

"He was attacked. We don't know a lot about the people who attacked him, but they...they killed Marcus. They call themselves the Coyotes. They almost killed Nik, but he was lucky. He nearly drowned but the other scouts found him floating by the riverbank and pulled him out, resuscitating him. He's got a nasty wound from an arrow, a sprained shoulder and broken arm, lots of bruises and cuts. He looks rough, Ali. I don't mean to alarm you, but you should be prepared."

Ali couldn't swallow. They had killed Marcus. It could've been Nik.

She hurried to keep up with Sam's long strides, and her stomach turned when they made it to the infirmary. It smelled sterile and clinical, and she tasted bile.

It reeked of death.

Ali pushed all that aside when Sam pulled back a curtain to reveal Nik lying on a bed, his face beaten and bruised. Several cuts had been bandaged, but she could see the red seeping through. His breathing was strained, and each heavy exhale felt like a knife in her own lungs.

She stepped forward and grazed his fingers, slipping her hand into his. It was shockingly cold. Much colder than normal, like a corpse, and she shivered. She wasn't sure if he could feel her, but after a moment he squeezed and rubbed his thumb over the back of her hand.

"Hey," he said coarsely. His lips were dry and cracked and a shade of blue that matched the skin beneath his eyes. He attempted a weak smile, and Ali couldn't hold it together anymore.

"Hey, hey, don't cry." He attempted to comfort her but she shook her head.

"I should be comforting you, not the other way around," she sobbed.

"Then comfort me," he joked, and moved his eyes over her body suggestively.

Sam cleared his throat. "I'm going to leave you two alone."

Ali chuckled and wiped at her tears, waiting until Sam disappeared. "How are you so fine with this?"

Nik pulled on her arm, and she sat on the bed next to him. She ran her hand over his chest, double checking that he was real and he was here. He was safe here in front of her and he wouldn't slip through her fingers. This was real.

"I'm alive." He placed his hand over hers and she felt his chest expand, as if providing the evidence she needed. "I'm alive and you're here."

She leaned over, careful not to put any weight on him, and kissed his lips. Gently and slowly, she savored the way his lips fit into hers. She could taste the blood on his cracked skin, but she didn't care. She needed more evidence that he was alive. He moaned when her tongue slipped into his mouth. His hand wandered up her thigh and settled on her hip. His head lifted off the pillow to kiss her more passionately, but then he winced.

Ali reluctantly broke the kiss and brushed the hair out of his face. "You need to rest."

"Stay."

Ali studied him. What were the odds that he would actually rest if she stayed? He gave his best pleading look through swollen eyes, though, and she found it hard to resist him.

"I'll stay."

She settled next to him. The bed was hardly big enough to fit her unless she lay on her side, pressed into him, careful not to jostle him. She stifled the lantern on the bedside table and the room went dark. "You have to promise to sleep."

"Mm, I don't like to make promises I can't keep." He grinned, but he closed his eyes, nevertheless. She tilted her head into his shoulder, and he kissed her forehead. His warm breath blew through her hair and was a persistent reminder that he was still here. He was alive and lying next to her. Everything would be okay.

"Ali?" he whispered softly, his lips moving against her temple.

"You're supposed to be sleeping," she reminded him.

She heard him swallow, felt the ripple of his throat against her forehead. His voice was desperate when he responded. She could hear his pain, and his fear brought tears to her eyes again. "Ali, I don't ever want to lose you."

Something wet hit her hair.

Ali stirred and could barely make out his features in the dark. He flinched when she reached up and ran a thumb under his eyes, wiping away a tear.

"Sorry," she said, remembering the bruises covering his face.

"Don't be." His eyes searched hers for something she couldn't decipher. "Don't leave me behind. When you go, will you take me with you?"

Nik wanted to leave. He wanted to leave with them. He would give up his life here in Rysburg to come with her. The thought rattled her to the core. She could have it all. She could have him.

"Of course."

Chapter Thirty-Five

NIK

NIK SPENT MOST OF the next few weeks in and out of sleep. Sam frequently brought Ali by after she finished work for the day. He tried to sit up and stay awake whenever she was around, but it was hard on his body. He wanted to feel her next to him at all times, but he hated to admit his own body ached when she bumped a bruise or brushed up against a healing bone.

At one point, she called him out on it after catching him clenching his jaw. She stopped sleeping next to him after that, even though she was what his body craved the most. Instead, she pulled up a chair and rested her head on the edge of the bed, holding his hand as he slept.

But today, all of that would change. Today, he would go home.

Nik untied his hospital robe and slid into the clothes that Ali had brought him the previous day. It made him feel human again to be dressed like himself and not like a helpless victim. But a healer had to help pull his shirt over his head, reminding him just how helpless he was. He still had a long journey of healing ahead of him.

Ali would be here any minute. She had promised to walk him back to his house. He had played up his helplessness until she'd agreed to assist him.

The curtain around his bed pulled back. Nik turned around expecting to see her, but instead Jameson walked through. In the years that Nik had worked for the guard, he had never had a personal visit from the head commander. It was a complete shock to see him standing here in Nik's infirmary room.

"Jameson. What can I do for you?" Nik straightened instinctively and winced at the dull pain in his leg. It happened every time he stood upright.

"Actually, I came to do something for you." The commander looked at Nik with sympathetic scrutiny, tallying up his injuries. "How are you feeling?"

"Better." It was the only honest answer he could give. He didn't feel *good*. He'd nearly died, and he hadn't forgotten it. The memory of the ice-cold water piercing his broken body still made him shudder. The darkness of the river consuming him as water filled his lungs. A panic attack threatened, but Nik stilled himself. Forced his focus back to the moment here with Jameson.

He wasn't in the water. He was in a room, safe and sound.

"You've given a lot to protect this town, Nik, and I want you to know just how much we appreciate it. You could've died, but you fought. You held on. And because of you, we can prepare for what's coming."

Nik stared at him, unsure of what this meant. He'd just done his job. It wasn't like he had much of a choice. "What exactly are you offering?"

Jameson cleared his throat. "Take a seat."

Nik's mind buzzed as Jameson made him an offer he couldn't refuse. It was an offer he had dreamed about occasionally but had never been sure it would come to fruition. Maybe years down the road. It felt entirely unreal, and he struggled to focus on the words coming from Jameson's mouth. Nerves fluttered in his gut.

Shortly after Jameson left, Ali entered looking extra cheerful. "Are you excited to go home?" she asked, grinning widely like a ray of sunshine.

His stomach dropped at the thought of going home. Specifically, going home with her. He stared at her, a beacon of light in this dark world. He stared so long that she gave him a questioning look before he smiled softly.

"Ali, I need to talk to you about something."

He sat on the edge of his bed and rubbed one hand nervously on his pants, the other arm held back in a sling. The bone would take a bit longer to set properly.

Her grin slowly disappeared, and she appraised him. "Okay. What about?"

His heart pounded in his chest. If only he'd had more time to prepare for this conversation. He didn't want to say the wrong thing. He knew how he felt and what he wanted, but the deal he made with Eli echoed in his mind. Did Ali really want him? Did she want this? Was he wielding too much power over her?

"Jameson just stopped by. They wanted to give me...something...in exchange for risking my life." His palms were sweating and his heart pounded as he searched for the right words, his mouth as dry as a desert. He'd never felt this nervous before.

"Okay...?" Ali waited for him to continue, clearly unsure where this was headed.

"Well, when I asked for you to come visit...I didn't think. I just wanted to see you. But it turns out that word got around to Jameson that you've been coming here to see me." He ran a hand through his hair and exhaled heavily.

"I'm not following. Am I in trouble? Are *you* in trouble?"

"He started digging for more information about you. And Sam...Sam might've told him about...us. Whatever we are. This thing we have." Nik's face flushed. He sounded like a prepubescent boy with his first crush, stumbling over his words.

He had no practice talking about his feelings and was embarrassed by trying to put a label on their relationship. He suddenly felt very self-conscious that he'd made up their entire relationship and she didn't feel the same at all. He braced himself for her to laugh in his face.

"What does that mean?" Ali asked. "What are they giving you, exactly?"

"Well...you." He reluctantly met her eyes, expecting anger or indignation. Ali stared at him, blank-faced, processing his words. "Jameson said you could come home with me. You don't have to stay in the prison anymore."

She blinked, clearly taken aback by the offer.

This was the part he dreaded the most. He'd made a promise to Eli that he wouldn't force Ali into anything. That she had to know she had a choice in all this. She was free to make her own decisions. And he meant it. But now it felt tainted. How could she turn him down when turning him down would mean turning down her own freedom, too?

"Ali...I don't want you to feel obligated to come with me. You can say no."

"You don't want me to come with you?" she asked, hurt in her voice.

"No, that's not what I'm saying. I...I want you to make your own decision. You have a say in this. I know there's this weird dynamic between us. I just don't want you to feel pressured into staying with me."

"So, I just go home with you? Just like that...I'm free?"

"If that's what you want." His legs shook with anticipation. She hadn't outright said she'd go home with him. And what would happen if she did? Moving in together was a big step for two people who had only known each other for a couple months. "You'd be able to keep your job in the greenhouse, but you'd be paid for it."

She paced in the small space beside his bed. Then she crossed her arms and bit at her fingernails. It was impossible to tell what she was thinking.

"Ali?"

She paused to look at him, but after a moment of silence, she resumed her pacing. It was nerve-wracking.

"Can you say something?"

"Yes."

He shook his head. He needed more than that. "Yes…"

"I'll go home with you."

"I have to ask…and please don't be mad." He stood and cupped her face with one hand. Their eyes met and filled him with overwhelming emotion. "Are you saying yes because you want to be with me or because it'll get you out of that prison?"

"Does it matter?" Her eyes flickered across his face, searching for something.

"It matters. It matters to me, Ali." He stroked her cheek with his thumb, his breaths shallow. He pressed closer to her body, their hips molding together.

"Both."

His shoulders tensed. Of course, it would be both. She'd be crazy not to take the first opportunity to get out of the prison. But she also wanted to be with him.

"You know, you're cute when you're all insecure and vulnerable," she teased.

He rolled his eyes and bent down, pressing his lips to hers. Gently at first, but then she was leaning into him with more pressure and urgency. She slipped a hand under his shirt, and he felt his cock harden. He gripped her ass and rubbed up against her. He felt the smile forming on her lips.

He wanted her to know exactly what she did to him. The thought of having her, of being with her every day, consumed him entirely.

"Let's go home," he whispered, barely taking his lips off hers.

Chapter Thirty-Six

ALI

ALI DIDN'T HAVE MANY belongings to bring with her, which made moving in quite easy. She'd stopped by the prison on their way to his house to grab her things. She came out with a small bag holding her few changes of clothes and some toiletries. Nik made a mental note to take her shopping for her own clothes soon. She probably wouldn't want to live in those old sweatpants and T-shirts for long. They were a reminder of the worst time in her life.

He couldn't help but notice the frown on her face as they left the prison.

"Everything all right?"

"Yeah. I just stopped by Eli's cell to fill him in."

Nik frowned. This couldn't be good.

"He tried to be supportive, but I can tell it's eating at him. It's fine. It's not your problem to deal with."

"Your problems are my problems, Ali."

Still, she dropped the subject. As much as Nik wanted to support her, he was a bit relieved to not have to discuss Eli as they walked home.

He opened the front door and allowed Ali to walk in first. He followed shortly after and shut the door behind him. She stood awkwardly in the middle of the living room, taking it all in. She'd been here before, but this was different. This would be her home now, too, for what little time they had left. He smiled at the thought. His heart ached for something he never knew he needed. She turned around and caught him staring, and the corners of her lips pulled into a grin.

"Should we get you to bed? Don't you need rest? Or I can make you something to eat if you'd like."

"Rest sounds good." Standing for long periods of time left his leg inflamed and irritated. The arrow wound wasn't fully healed yet.

He changed into fresh clothes and let Ali borrow some shorts and a T-shirt to sleep in. She pulled on the shorts but tossed the shirt aside, sliding into bed topless. Devilish woman.

"Ali, I won't rest with you looking like that." His chest constricted, and he adjusted his hard cock in his pants, stroking his length for her benefit.

She licked and bit her lip, then turned to lie on her side, watching with hungry eyes as he gripped his shaft. "I know."

"You minx."

She slid a hand across his abdomen, following the dark hair that led down to his cock. He sucked in a hard breath when she dipped below the hem of his pants. Her fingers slid around him and his breath released through gritted teeth. Her softness felt so good as she pumped his hard cock.

"It would be easier if these were off," she suggested as she sat up and tugged at his sweatpants.

He let her undress him. He could hardly help with a broken arm anyway. She stripped him bare and straddled his body.

"Is this okay?"

Nik nodded enthusiastically, but when she lowered, he flinched in pain.

"You're a bad liar."

She slid to lie beside him and reached down to stroke him slowly.

He gritted his teeth and nudged her face with his nose, finding her lips. Her touch was soft, and he rolled his hips, sliding in and out of her hand. Her tongue was in his mouth and she tasted like cinnamon, hot and sweet.

He moaned into her mouth when she gently bit his bottom lip. She broke from his lips long enough to spit in her hand and grip him tighter.

"My god, you're perfect." She sucked on his neck and tugged at his shaft, giving his head extra attention. Her hair fell across his chest and he reached for her exposed breast, displayed in front of his face. "Fucking perfect."

"You're not too bad yourself." Her lips moved against his skin.

He let out a shaky laugh, "You love my cock. You couldn't wait to undress me and get your hands on me." He playfully bit at her collarbone and she yelped.

Then he inhaled sharply, hissing as the pleasure in his core grew. She was trailing kisses across the top of his chest now. Then back up to his mouth. They embraced in an all-consuming kiss, his tongue exploring every inch of her. They kissed like it was crucial to their survival. Like air, they couldn't live without one another.

He panted heavily when she pulled back. He was on the verge of unraveling now. She sped up, sensing he was near his climax. His legs tensed and the pain from his wound only heightened the sensation.

Ali leaned down and ran her tongue over the edge of his ear. "I love you, Nik."

Nik's eyes rolled back in his head and he surrendered everything he had to her. She kissed his neck as he moaned, trembling against her lips. His muscles flexed and he felt himself throbbing in her hand, pleasure pouring out of him. Trails of white spilled over his abs and Ali rubbed his length gently as he came down from his high.

He was in shock, both from her exclamation and from the earth-shattering orgasm she'd just given him. His mind went blank as he turned to look at her, his heart still racing, his breath still uneven. Her eyes were filled with longing and her lips parted, waiting for him to return the sentiment.

"I think I love you, too." The corner of his mouth curved up in a grin. He'd never felt this way about anyone before. Her happiness was more important than his own. It was exhilarating and scary, but he felt safest with her. With her, he was the most authentic version of himself. He didn't want to go another day without her. If that wasn't love, then he didn't know what was.

She kissed him again, and he slid one hand into her hair, pulling her as close as possible. He wanted to remember the way her lips felt. The way their softness gave way to his. He wanted to remember this moment forever.

After Nik cleaned himself up, Ali slung her arm across his stomach while his good arm drew circles on her skin. They fell asleep holding each other closely.

What was meant to be a nap turned into a full night of sleep. When Nik woke, the sun was rising and the room was a warm shade of orange. Ali looked pretty in this lighting. The sunlight gave her blonde hair a glowing effect, like a halo.

He brushed the hair from her eyes and she stirred, snuggling closer to his swelling chest. Now that he had admitted he loved her, he wanted to scream it in the middle of the town square. His body was bursting with love for her. It consumed him entirely.

She tilted her head and opened her eyes drowsily. "It's morning already?"

"Unfortunately." He kissed the top of her head. "Hey, Ali?"

"Yes?" she whispered into his chest.

"I love you."

He felt her smile against his skin. "I love you, too, Nik."

They watched the sunrise through the window in his room. Their room. Ali was the first to move, pulling back from him.

"No," he moaned.

"I'm starving. Aren't you hungry? You can stay here. I'll make something quick."

"Breakfast in bed? How did I get so lucky?" He threw a wink at her as she tossed a T-shirt on and headed toward the kitchen.

She brought back eggs and toast with a glass of juice and set it on the nightstand beside the bed. He caught her up on everything that had happened during his mission. Until now, he hadn't wanted to relive those moments, but she made him feel safe and cared for. He tried to ignore the pain that was clear on her face, knowing he could've died.

"What are you going to do? What is Jameson's plan?" she asked between bites of toast.

"Jameson wants to fight."

"But you don't?"

"Ali..." He took her hand in his, running his thumb over her knuckles, over her wrists where the metal bracelets had once been. He'd given this a lot of thought. From the moment his body had hit the ice-cold water of the river, he'd been done fighting. Maybe that made him a coward, but Rysburg had slowly stopped feeling like home. It no longer felt like a place worth fighting for. At some point home became a person...the person sitting next to him in bed. "I just want to get out of here. With you."

She dropped the toast. "Where will we go?"

"I'm not sure. I know there are other towns out there, but Rysburg has conquered every one we've come across." He shifted uncomfortably. *He* had conquered. He had helped destroy their neighbors. "We might have to travel quite a ways."

Ali smiled at him. "I'd follow you anywhere."

Chapter Thirty-Seven

ALI

It was quite the adjustment for Ali to move in with Nik. She went from being an unknown prisoner to the woman who had stolen Nik's heart. Every time she walked through town, she could sense people's eyes on her, sizing her up. It was no secret that Nik was attractive and all this time he had remained a bachelor. Who was the strange woman who had finally broken through his icy exterior?

Nik had explained to her how rare it was for a prisoner to assimilate into their population. That explained the wary looks she got as well. It was like people were waiting for her to snap and use her newfound freedom to get her revenge. They didn't trust her.

Eli was speechless when she told him what had happened, his face frozen in shock. He didn't believe it was possible to earn their freedom and up until a few days ago, neither had she. She could sense a longing for his own freedom even though he maintained a stern defiance. He loathed Rysburg and she couldn't blame him. His experience here had been much worse than hers.

She hadn't told Eli that Nik was going to escape with them. That he was helping them. She didn't want to tell him until they had a solid plan in place. She didn't want to get his hopes up prematurely.

The house was quiet when she walked through the front door. Nik was working an extra shift today, so she had the place to herself. She pulled open the drawer she kept her clothes in and added the new pairs of pants and shirts she had just bought. She didn't own much in this home, but she was used to it. Even in Andus, she hadn't owned many things outside of the necessities.

She wasn't even sure she wanted to make this feel more like home. Nik's admission had stuck with her. The idea of leaving Rysburg and starting over with him was a dream she couldn't shake. She pictured a life where they started as equals, chasing their own ambitions and supporting one another. A child or two. She didn't want to raise a child here in Rysburg, but someplace else? Maybe. Escape was feeling like a real possibility.

Ali organized a set of thread and needles she'd bought. She thought it might take her mind off things if she took up a hobby. Something to do in her free time now that she had options outside of staring at the ceiling. Sewing reminded her of her mom. She set some wood in the fireplace and sat down. Grabbing an old pillow from the couch, she practiced her embroidery skills to kill time.

When Nik walked through the door later that night, she had just started cooking dinner. His cheeks were pink from the cold and his eyes glistened. He always smiled when he came home to find her. Always wrapped his arms around her waist and kissed the top of her head. He was so domesticated; it warmed her heart.

In the evenings, they lay together in bed and talked about anything and everything. Tonight was the same. Nik fluffed a pillow and propped his head on his hand, turning to look at her.

"I've been thinking," she started as he rubbed his thumb over her knuckles. "About what you said. About leaving here."

"Go on."

"Are you sure? Are you sure you want to give this up? Your home...I know what it was like to lose Andus."

"Ali, you had people you loved. Andus had positive memories for you." He shook his head before continuing, his eyes filled with sadness. "There isn't anything keeping me here. I...I don't want to do this anymore."

She didn't have to ask to know what "this" was. The violence. The raids. The thieving. She saw his true heart and knew this role wasn't meant for him.

"I think we need to leave soon. I don't want to get caught up in whatever war is coming." She didn't want *him* to get caught up in a war. "I think I've had enough violence to last a lifetime."

"Me, too." He sighed heavily. "I sometimes feel like a monster. The things I've done...I told myself it was to protect Rysburg, but I don't think that's true anymore."

"You're not a monster." She stroked his arm.

He said softly, "I've killed people."

"So have I." He flinched and his mouth dropped open slightly at her confession. "When Andus was attacked."

"That's different. That was self-defense." She could see the guilt in his eyes. He might not have been there that day, but it didn't matter. "I'm sorry you had to do that."

"I don't want to live through that a second time." She didn't know if she could. She wasn't strong enough. The first time had stripped her of so much. What would she lose if they were attacked again?

"I don't want you to live through that again either." He propped up his head with his arm and began to make plans for when and how they could leave. He spoke with such exhilaration that it made her excited for their future, too.

"I do have one question. When we leave here...are you going to be nice to Eli?"

"Absolutely not," he answered without hesitation.

She smacked his chest playfully, and they both laughed.

"I'm serious. I can't travel through the wilderness with you two bickering the whole time. You have to get along."

"What is it with the two of you, anyway?"

She inhaled and rolled onto her back, looking at the ceiling. "He's my best friend."

"Just your friend? There's never been anything else between you two?" His voice was strained. It was clear he didn't want to have this conversation, but he needed to know.

She bit the inside of her cheek. "Well, no."

"No?" His eyes were wide and expectant.

"We kind of thought we would get married one day," she said nonchalantly, as if it wasn't a big deal. And it wasn't. Their inevitable marriage had shattered the day Andus was attacked. It didn't feel real anymore, at least not to Ali.

"Everyone thought it. Our parents...Eli...myself. It's just the way it was. He made the most sense. When you grow up in a small town, there aren't a lot of options, you know."

"No, I don't know. Is this why he's so obsessed with you?" Ali didn't have to look at him to hear the jealousy in his voice.

"I think he might've been in love with me," she confessed quietly.

"You think?" His eyes widened.

She didn't just think—she knew. She recalled the night before the attack when he had confessed. "There might've been some hints."

"Were you in love with him?"

"No. It was never like that for me. He's my best friend, but he's not just that, Nik. He's my family. He's important to me."

"Your family," he mumbled.

They lay together, not speaking for a few minutes. Nik was clearly stewing over her choice of words.

Finally, he broke the silence. "And what happens if I can't get along with him?"

"Don't make me choose, Nik," Ali said in barely more than a whisper.

His eyes bore into her. He didn't have to ask to know what she meant. She wouldn't choose him. She had to choose Eli. Family came first and he would always be in her life. After everything they had been through, after the attack on Andus, she couldn't just run away and start a new life without him.

"Fine. I will play nice with the best friend of the woman I love, who just happens to be in love with her," he said sardonically.

"Thank you." She was eternally grateful to him. He had a good heart, and she knew he would set aside his feelings to do this for her. He couldn't even see that he was so far from being a monster.

Then Nik flinched as if he'd just thought of something. "You didn't...you didn't have sex with him, did you?"

Ali lifted her brow. She'd thought that was obvious.

"No, Ali," he groaned. He covered his face with his hands. "No wonder he's obsessed with you."

She chuckled at his discomfort. "I told you. Small town. What did you expect? I doubt you were celibate before my arrival."

He grinned and pulled on her hand, bringing her body to his. "I was a virgin when I met you."

They both laughed at his transparent lie. The feeling of his laughter rumbled through her core.

Her hands roamed his stomach above the soft cotton of his T-shirt. "There is one thing I've never done before that I wouldn't mind giving a go," she said coyly, biting her lip.

His eyes darkened and he pushed her over, covering her body with his. His arm was mostly healed now, and he could support his weight with minor discomfort. He spread her legs to make room to settle between them. "And what is that?"

Her breath hitched as he placed a hand between her thighs. Her face reddened. She was unexpectedly timid, but she put her hand on his shoulders and gently pushed him downwards. He let her guide him till his face was pressed to her stomach.

A short laugh tickled her skin as he pulled up her shirt. He teasingly kissed above the hem of her pants, using his hand to rub her inner thighs.

Ali gripped the blankets beneath her and relaxed her muscles, surrendering her body to him. He leaned back and grabbed the sides of her pants, tugging them down to her ankles.

His hand slid back to her pussy, massaging through her underwear. "You're so wet. Ali, your panties are soaked." He bit his lip and buried his face, kissing her inner thighs. He alternated between soft kisses, gentle bites, and sucking soothingly.

Ali loved the way it felt to be adored by him.

She brushed a hand through his hair and used her other hand to slip beneath her shirt and cup her breast. When he kissed her clit, she gasped, desperate to remove her underwear. The fabric that separated her from his lips. His tongue was maddening.

It was true. She had never let Eli go there. It had felt like too much to share with him. Too intimate.

"Nik, please," she moaned.

But he wouldn't give into her requests so soon. He hovered over her and pushed her shirt up, kissing the sensitive area just below her breast. He covered her with his palms, massaging breathless groans out of her.

Leaning forward, she pulled the shirt the rest of the way off of her body and wrapped her legs around him. He was too much and not enough.

"You're so fucking perfect. I love the way your body responds to my touch." He pushed her underwear to the side and pressed along her slit, just to demonstrate exactly how her body responded.

She arched her back, shuddering, and her eyes fluttered closed. Her body craved more of him. To stretch around him.

"Look at me. I want to see that longing in your eyes."

She had no trouble obeying his command and looked into his mesmerizing eyes, more gray than blue in this lighting. They were like molten silver, glimmering with lust. His hair softly fell on his forehead.

He pulled her underwear down, kissing every inch of her mound in the process. Quick, tantalizing kisses, long enough to leave her needing more. He moved one leg over his shoulder and spread the other wide.

Ali squirmed in anticipation. His eyes lit up at the sight of her, and it made her heart slam against her chest to feel so exposed to him. Every inch of her belonged to him. She willingly gave it.

The first stroke of his tongue coaxed a whimper out of her. Her throat had gone dry and she swallowed hard, looking down again to meet his eyes.

He held her gaze and gave another long slide of his tongue between her folds and across her clit. She tilted her hips, needing more. He slid his fingers along her entrance, spreading her slickness. He alternated gliding his fingers and sliding his tongue and slowly drove her wild. Just when she couldn't take anymore, he dipped one finger inside.

She let out a heavy sigh, finally feeling a sense of fulfillment. But it wasn't nearly enough. She needed more...more of him. He slid his finger out and then back in again, eliciting a moan from her. Again and again, he teased her, and she gripped the blankets with all her might.

"Fuck, Nik."

He chuckled and pressed two fingers inside, dropping his mouth back to her clit. She squeezed his shoulder with her thigh and her heel dug into his back, not wanting him to pull back this time. He showed no signs of letting up though. She made small thrusting movements as he pumped his fingers in and out of her. He kissed the inside of her thigh again and whispered against her skin, "I love the way you feel. You're so wet and throbbing for me."

"Nik," she whined.

"Tell me what you want."

She could hardly form full sentences. "I want...your mouth. Your tongue." She bucked her hips, letting her body do the talking. She grabbed the back of his head, lacing her fingers through his dark hair, and pulled him close.

He snickered, and his warm breath tickled her most sensitive parts.

Not close enough. She needed him closer. "Please, I can't...I..."

He covered her with his mouth and moved his tongue all the way from her entrance and back to her sensitive bud, sucking ever so slightly. "You taste so fucking good, Ali. Your pussy is perfect."

She felt her legs trembling next to his ears.

"I want to see you unravel. Your pussy fluttering around my fingers. I want it all. I want all of you." He sucked on her swollen clit again. "This pussy is mine. It belongs to me. God, I could worship you."

She rocked her hips harder, his fingers pushing deeper into her. "Nik," she panted.

"Can you come like this? Can you come for me?"

"I...I..." She didn't have to respond to his question. Her entire body shook, and he had his answer. Her vision went black as she squeezed her eyes shut and clenched his hair in her fingers. He used one arm to hold her down while he continued to swirl his tongue over her, prolonging her orgasm. Pleasure rippled through her, and she clamped around his fingers. Her heart raced wildly as she gasped for air.

Then her muscles gave out and she relaxed into the bed, Nik still slowly pushing two fingers inside her. She whimpered and shifted her leg. He relented, licking every last drop of her before placing one more gentle kiss on her sensitive clit. She jolted at the touch.

Nik moved and rested on his elbows, his weight lightly pressing down on her. She could feel how hard he was through his sweatpants. He grinned and brushed a stray strand of blonde hair from her face. "I could do that every night for the rest of my life."

Chapter Thirty-Eight

ELI

LIFE ON THE WALL was every bit as boring as Eli had expected. After a quick two weeks of training, they sent him to sit on top of the wall with nothing but a bow and arrow. His aim wasn't great, but they insisted he'd get better. One day a week was spent training, and the rest of the week he kept a lookout.

Training was his favorite part of the job. He got to learn new skills and move his body. He missed running freely in the woods with Ali. It felt good to use his muscles once more. His strength was slowly returning, as was his stamina. He was getting stronger every day.

Nik was right to suggest this job; Eli could grudgingly admit that. Already, ideas were blazing through his mind. He made mental notes of all the areas of weakness along the wall. Drainage grates were spaced out every mile or so. He went out of his way to make connections with the other men working the wall just in case he would need one of them to turn a blind eye to future plans.

Eli listened intently to every piece of information they unknowingly provided. Like what times the guards would change shifts, when they would be the most distracted, and which areas of the wall were least protected. Of course, those areas also featured the most natural protection. Sharp brambles, marshy land and rough rocks helped protect those places. Still, the marsh wouldn't be too bad to endure in exchange for freedom. He'd been through worse.

The sound of the wooden ladder rattling against the wall attracted his attention. It wasn't time for the next shift change yet.

A blonde head peeped over the top and climbed up to stand next to him. She shivered and rubbed her arms, the friction warming her body. "Sam told me you'd be up here," she explained before he could ask.

"Did he now? And what brings you up here?"

Eli was extremely jealous that Ali had so much freedom these days. He would never take for granted again the ability to walk anywhere he wanted to. He worried that this development would prevent her from taking his plans to escape seriously. Like there was no longer a sense of urgency.

It was a concern that she had stifled when she'd informed him of Nik's near-death experience. Eli should've been happy they were all on the same page about wanting to leave Rysburg but he didn't trust Nik in the slightest. He wouldn't put it past him to leave Eli here on his own to have Ali for himself. He couldn't depend on him. Which was why he spent much of his time devising plans of his own.

"Nik thinks he's found a way to get us out. All of us," she clarified.

Eli gritted his teeth and nodded reluctantly. "How's that?"

"There's going to be another scouting mission soon. He hasn't been assigned to it. With some of the other men out of town, he thinks you'll likely be on night guard, and it'll be easier to sneak you out then rather than removing you from the prison."

"From what I understand, he'd been able to get you out of the prison with no problems." His tone was accusatory. She had recently told him about how Nik had taken her to his home when she was sick. How she had so easily left the prison to go see him in the infirmary. It seemed like Ali had never truly been a prisoner here. Her experience had been so different from his. She didn't understand.

"It's...it's not that easy. He was able to do that because Sam knew about us. He knew Nik was...interested in me. It would draw too much attention if he started asking favors for you too."

"I don't know. I think we could make a convincing argument that we're having a threesome," he joked, and Ali smiled.

"Maybe. I'll run it by him and see what he thinks."

Eli chuckled. He missed moments like this. It reminded him of when things used to be easy between them. Sometimes he wondered if they'd ever return to that level of effortlessness, and instances like this reminded him it was possible. They just needed time.

"Right. So, when is this scouting mission?" he asked.

"They don't have an exact date yet, but it should be the week after next."

"Hmm," he murmured. "Sounds promising."

Ali heard the sarcasm in his voice and rolled her eyes. Hope was a dangerous thing. Of course Eli hoped that Nik's plan would work but he wouldn't believe it until he saw it. It would hurt too much if it failed.

Ali explained how they would leave over the wall and follow the trails southward.

"Why can't we take the tunnel? The one we entered through?"

"I asked him about that. It's locked on both sides, apparently. And they keep the keys separate so it would be too difficult. If one person held both keys, it might've been an option, but we can't risk getting more people involved."

"And what happens when we're out of here?" Eli asked quietly. It wasn't just the escape that concerned him. Where would they go? How would they feed themselves and survive the rest of winter? What if they ran into a group that was even less kind than Rysburg, like the Coyotes? And worst of all, what would it be like to live as a third wheel to Ali and Nik? He could already barely stomach the thought of them together. It would cut even deeper to have it thrown in his face.

Would there come a day when Eli would have to leave them to go off on his own? That future scared him almost as much as the one that awaited him in Rysburg.

"I think we'll have to figure it out as we go." It was a universal answer. The answer to where they'd go and the answer to how they'd cohabitate. She knew just as well as he did that this wouldn't be easy.

Eli nodded and stared at her. Despite the uncomfortable questions, she looked at ease. It struck him just how content and happy she looked, even happier than he remembered her in Andus. Had he missed her entire transformation? Had he missed all the signs that she was changing right before his eyes?

"I should get back," she said as she headed back toward the ladder. "This will work, Eli."

Chapter Thirty-Nine

NIK

"Tell me the plan again," Ali requested for the tenth time. She busied herself with packing three backpacks, one for each of them, mostly filled with clothes and other essentials. She'd seemed like a nervous wreck ever since Nik had gotten the word on the final date for the next scouting mission. Two days from now.

"I've already checked the schedule. Eli is set to work that evening, so that won't be an issue. We'll wait until it's dark out and the town is tucked in bed. The scouts will make their way east, so we'll go west. Once we're confident we're far enough away from Rysburg, we can start heading south. Most of our missions have been up toward the lake, so I think we'll have more luck heading away from the shore."

Nik gripped her shoulders and pressed his thumbs in, rubbing in circles to loosen her tense muscles.

"But you don't know for certain what's out there?"

Nik shook his head. "The furthest I've ever gone on a mission to the south was about four hours. There's nothing in that range. I'm not sure how long it'll take to run into civilization."

"And once we do, there's no way of telling if they're good people or if we're trading one hell for another." Ali's eyes connected with his. They were full of sorrow, pity, doubt, hope. Neither of them had any answers. They just knew they couldn't stay here. Nik would do anything to keep her safe. She caressed his face, the stubbly hairs prickling her fingers.

"Are you certain you want to do this?" he asked.

"One hundred percent."

Time passed slowly over the next couple days. Ali collected non-perishable food to include in the backpacks and Nik bought extra rations of drinking water to take with them. He wasn't sure how long they'd have to survive in the wild, but he planned for the worst. They ate their meals in silence, too nervous to speak, and spent their nights tangled up, distracted from their upcoming adventure.

On the night of the scouting mission, they were ready. It almost felt too right, like there was no way it could be this easy.

The sun went down while they ate dinner. Ali was exceptionally quiet, and Nik could tell by the way her legs shook that she was anxious. "It's going to be fine," he reassured her, although the lump in his throat protested. "Better than fine."

And it would be. He'd spent so much time fantasizing about a future together. The future they could have when they were both given a fresh start. One where he wasn't a shell of a man, the villain in her story, and one where she wasn't stifled, free to be herself.

Free. They could both be free.

"I trust you."

They waited several hours after they normally would've been fast asleep, not wanting to risk running into any night owls. An unnerving silence hung in the air between them. Nik felt like he couldn't breathe, lest someone hear him. He slipped his hand into Ali's as he opened the front door and they left their house behind.

He hadn't expected to feel any remorse about leaving Rysburg. It had been his only home, but lately he'd resented it. Now, though, each step he took felt like a pang of grief for the things he was giving up. The house where he shared memories of his mother as a child. The career he'd made for himself where he was well-respected. Sam, the only person he considered even close to a friend.

But he turned to look at Ali, and he knew he'd give it all up for her. He *was* giving it all up for her. For their future together. It was all that mattered to him.

He smiled at the thought and all his nerves seemed to disappear. Ali studied him and returned a grin.

They turned down a side street toward the post Eli was working. Nik thanked the gods that he'd been assigned one of the side posts. He was still pretty certain they could've made the main entrance work for their plan, but it would've been trickier. Here, there was less chance of a stray person walking by. It would take more time for anyone to realize the post had been abandoned.

The houses sat dark and quiet. Nik could only hear the sound of Ali's heavy breathing next to him. The moonlight was bright enough to illuminate their path, but they stayed hidden in the shadows.

They avoided the town center, just in case there were any night owls heading to or from the tavern. Luck was on their side. They didn't spot a single soul until they were almost to the wall.

A young couple a little older than Nik walked home, hand in hand. The man hummed a soft tune and swayed back and forth while the woman watched him, a huge smile on her face.

Nik felt a pang of jealousy. That these two could walk together, out in the open, without a care in the world. Soon. Soon, he would get to have that with Ali.

The couple moved slowly and then turned down a street to their left. The man's song faded into the night.

"Let's keep going," Nik whispered to Ali.

At last, they could see Eli's post. Nik squeezed Ali's hand, adrenaline pumping through him. He could feel his dinner rising in his throat but forced it down. Instinct told him to proceed with caution, and he was never one to ignore his instincts.

"Wait." He held out a hand and stopped Ali in the shadows of the last house in the row. They were twenty feet from the wall, but he couldn't see Eli. He squinted but couldn't make out a figure at the top.

"What's wrong?" Ali asked.

"I don't know. Something doesn't feel right."

"Can you see him?"

"No. I don't see anyone." He scanned the wall in the darkness. Had he just missed him? "Stay back."

Nik shifted his foot in the pile of snow on the ground and uncovered a small stone. He picked it up and moved into the open. His throw was precise and hit the top of the wall, a clunk echoing into the night sky. He quickly ducked back into the shadows with Ali, peeping out just far enough to see someone stand and look over the edge.

He moved behind the house, pulling Ali with him. "It's not Eli."

"How can it not be Eli?" Panic was rising in her voice; her eyes grew to twice their normal size. "I thought you said this was his post."

"It was." He shook his head. "It was. I checked the assignments three times to be sure." He couldn't comprehend. Everything was falling apart. Their plan that they'd spent weeks on. The image of their future together melted, like a painting that hadn't been left to dry, the vibrant colors he'd pictured dripping together into an ugly mess.

"What do we do now?"

"We can check some of the other posts. Maybe they moved him last minute."

They quietly moved along the outskirts of town, hidden in the shadows of the houses. They first moved clockwise, checking one post and then another. After checking two more posts, they headed the opposite way.

Counterclockwise was more dangerous. The further they moved from Eli's assigned post, the closer they got to the main entrance, which would be more heavily guarded and better lit.

At each post, Nik stooped to grab a stone, throwing it against the wall to draw out the guard on top. And each time it wasn't Eli, his heart sank a little deeper. He never thought he'd be disappointed to *not* see Eli.

They had checked every post except for the main entrance.

Nik paused to gather his thoughts. This was the worst possible outcome.

"We need a distraction. I can't get close enough to the wall in this light."

"What do you need me to do?" she asked.

He had Ali stay hidden behind an old office space where she'd be able to see the top of the wall without being seen herself. The idea seemed a little crazy, but desperate times called for desperate measures.

Several torch lights flickered nearby, keeping the town center lit against the darkness. Nik lit a torch of his own before heading toward the wall. He didn't have to reach the wall itself. Just close enough to catch their attention.

He hid behind another building, hoping they wouldn't see the light emitting from his presence. A quick scan across the top of the wall told him no one was facing inward. They were all facing toward the outside, watching for intruders. *Good.*

A wooden cart sat at the bottom of the wall. They frequently used it on missions, and it stayed parked at the entrance to Rysburg when it wasn't in use. Nik steeled himself, breathing calmly, and braced for what he was about to do.

Before he could talk himself out of it, he ran briskly but quietly toward the cart, tossing his torch into the center. There were still a few broken pieces of wood left in the bottom from past missions. They quickly caught fire as he ran back toward the shadows.

It didn't take long for the entire cart to go up in flames. Shouts and frantic movement stirred from atop the wall while he dashed between buildings, carefully making his way back to Ali.

When he reached her, he was breathless and sweating.

"Well?"

"He's not there. He's not on the wall," Ali said, her voice frail and broken. She was devastated that Eli was nowhere to be found.

She looked at him, and understanding dawned on her face. "We're not getting out today, are we?"

His shoulders slumped, and he pulled her in close. "I don't think we are."

Chapter Forty

ELI

ELI WRAPPED A BLANKET around his shoulders. The night shift was significantly cooler than the day shift. But it was also more peaceful. He gazed out at the forest surrounding Rysburg and praised the gods that they'd soon be on their way, far away from this town. Bringing Nik along was a small price to pay for his freedom.

He fidgeted nervously. He wasn't sure exactly when they'd be coming, but he knew he'd have to wait for night to fall. Dusk still lingered in the sky.

Eli had only been at the top of the wall for half an hour when he heard another guard climbing up the ladder, the wooden steps creaking beneath his weight. His shoulders tensed as the sound set him on edge. He was supposed to be on watch alone tonight.

He'd spent much of his time ensuring that his coworkers found him to be trustworthy for precisely this scenario. It was a bad sign that they'd sent another guard to stay with him. He shifted with unease as he thought of ways to get rid of the second guard. Maybe he'd just strangle him when Ali and Nik showed up. The morbid thought made him shiver, but he knew deep down he would do it. He'd do whatever it took.

The man didn't even bother to greet him. "You're wanted back at headquarters. I'm here to relieve you."

Fear rippled through his body. Did they know? Had they somehow found out about Nik's plan? His heart raced. This couldn't be happening. Their plan began to unravel before him.

"What do you mean? What do they want?"

The man sneered and shook his head. He looked like he would rather be anywhere else than up here talking to scum like Eli. Most of the other guards had warmed up to him, accepting him as one of their own, or at least treating him with neutrality. But others, like this guard, saw him as a captive, property of Rysburg and inferior to them. "How would I know? I was just told to come take your place."

Eli gritted his teeth. He needed to stay calm and stay in control. It wouldn't do any good to panic. He wasn't even sure why he was being called back to base. Maybe he could go quickly and take care of whatever they wanted and be back before Nik and Ali showed up. It was still early.

"Fine," he spat, shoving past the guard.

He hurried down the ladder and headed toward the guard headquarters, attached to the backside of the town hall in the center of the village. He passed several villagers along the way and had an uneasy feeling that they could see right through him, that they knew he was up to something. Did it show on his face?

Eli's supervisor was hovering over a table when he pushed through the large wooden door. Papers scattered on the surface appeared to show a map of the area surrounding Rysburg and little crosses were dispersed across them. Likely the places they'd searched already.

"I was told you needed to see me?" Eli managed to keep the shakiness from his voice.

"Yes." The man ran a hand over his scruffy beard. He looked tired, like he was juggling one too many responsibilities. "A few more people were called in for the scouting mission, so we need to rearrange a little. I need you to help guard the arsenal. They're expecting you, so if you could just—"

"I'd really rather guard the wall if that's okay," Eli interrupted, his nervousness revealing itself in his tone. This wouldn't work. He needed to be at the wall tonight, not in the arsenal. This would ruin their plan and they were so close, *so close* to leaving.

The supervisor looked up from the table and fixed his eyes on Eli with a scowl. "No, that's not okay." There was a hint of challenge in his tone, daring Eli to disagree.

Eli was torn. There was no way to argue his case without it looking suspicious, but he couldn't just give up.

He opened his mouth several times before shutting it, unable to find words that might get him out of this disaster. He couldn't think of a single reason his supervisor should keep him on the wall.

His mind raced to find a way to fix this, but came up blank. All their planning would be for nothing.

So Eli left headquarters and made an impulsive decision. He'd have to find Nik's house first and let them know his assignment had been changed. The only problem was he'd never been to Nik's house before. He knew the general direction from walking home with Ali on occasion. He knew the road she took when he headed the opposite way, toward the prison.

He did his best to look inconspicuous, pulling his shirt over the metal bands on his wrists. This was not the way to the arsenal. Hopefully no one would stop him. One perk of becoming a trusted guard was that he could move around without a chaperone, at least during his shifts.

Eli started down the road he'd seen Ali take several times. He didn't know what he was expecting: that he'd get some sixth sense tingling in his fingers when he passed Nik's house? That didn't happen.

Each house appeared the same as the next. White siding covered single story homes with tin roofs. Plain wooden doors stood between square windows. There were no distinguishing marks.

He would have to ask someone.

A younger couple passed by, and he avoided eye contact. It was only a gut feeling, but something about them didn't seem right. He walked a few more houses and an older woman came out of her front door, a scarf wrapped tightly around her head.

"Excuse me, ma'am." Eli waved a hand in her direction. "Do you know which of these houses belongs to Nik?"

They'd never discussed surnames. He could only hope there weren't many people by the name of Nik around here.

"Nik?"

"Yeah." Eli fumbled over his words. "He's young, about my age. A little shorter than me. Dark hair." He looked expectantly at the woman. Apparently, this very generic description wasn't working for her.

"I'm sorry, son. I'm not sure who you're talking about."

Eli's shoulders slumped. "That's okay. Thank you for your time."

He looked around at the houses along the road. Light poured through a few of the windows and illuminated the interiors so he could see inside, but he didn't catch a glimpse of Ali or Nik in any of them.

He was running out of time. He couldn't take too long searching for them. The guards at the arsenal would expect him any minute now. Finally, he ran his hands through his hair and turned around, giving up on his search. Devastation washed over him as he headed back toward the arsenal.

Two other guards stood chatting when he made it to the arsenal. They took one look at Eli's crestfallen expression and stayed clear of him. Good. He had no desire to make small talk this evening. He was still trying to come to terms with the fact that he would not be escaping tonight.

What were Ali and Nik doing right now? The sky had darkened and the streets were clear of people. They were likely setting out to his post right now. What would they think when they didn't find him there? Would they carry on anyway?

No. He didn't think Ali would leave him behind. Nik, perhaps, but Ali would stick up for him.

Another horrifying thought crossed his mind. What if they got caught? What if they tried to approach the wall before realizing Eli wasn't the guard on duty? Would they be able to talk their way out of it? It would look incredibly suspicious to be sulking around in the middle of the night, headed toward one of the most isolated posts.

Eli's stomach turned and he willed time to move faster. The thought of spending the rest of the night working here was torture, not knowing what Ali and Nik were doing right now.

He picked at loose chips of wood on the table where he sat. The two other guards laughed and talked animatedly, paying him no attention. How unfair, to be so close to freedom only to have everything ruined. He should've known not to trust Nik. Of course, Nik's plan had failed. Eli never should've allowed himself to hope.

It was nearly dawn when one of the other guards left early. "Yeah, I'll cover for you," his friend said as he walked out into the morning fog.

And then Eli was alone with one other guard with only an hour left in their shift. His eyes dropped heavily. He wasn't used to working the night shift, and his body ached for his bed. He wanted to close his eyes and forget this tragic evening had ever occurred.

The other guard continued to ignore Eli, only looking up on occasion when his chair squeaked beneath his weight. After several minutes of silence, the man stood.

"I'm going to go smoke. I'll be right back."

The guard left through the front door, and Eli stared around the empty room.

Maybe this evening wouldn't be a waste after all.

He had to act quickly. The guard wouldn't take much time before he came back. He swiftly grabbed the keys hanging on the wall and walked toward the locked gate that kept their artillery.

There were only four keys on the ring, so he quickly rotated through them, finding the correct one with ease. The gate swung open, and he walked into a large room lined with shelves and more shelves of knives, swords, axes, and more.

Eli could only take inconspicuous items. The ones that no one would notice as he returned to his cell. The corner of the room was lined with smaller weapons. He grabbed a couple modest knives that had wickedly jagged edges. The kind that hurt more coming out than they did going in. If only he could take a full-sized sword. They were gorgeously forged with ornate handles. He could do more damage with one of those, but it was unrealistic to steal one now.

As he turned back toward the gate, he walked by some items he didn't recognize. Curiosity stopped him in his tracks. They were small and round, with a glass-like exterior. He couldn't tell exactly what the glasses contained. It was a dark liquid mixture that he couldn't identify.

Eli brushed the dust off the edge of the shelf to reveal a word as well as a symbol. He couldn't read it but he could make an educated guess from the drawing. It was a circle with sharp triangles bursting from the center.

Explosives.

Smiling grimly, he grabbed one and slid it into his pocket. He would either cause massive chaos or die in the process. Either way, for the first time since arriving in Rysburg, he felt in control of his fate. His fingers tingled with a dangerous sort of excitement.

Eli exited back into the front room and locked the gate behind him, carefully hanging the keys back on their rung. He had just returned to his seat when the other guard came back in from the cold. The man didn't even glance in Eli's direction.

Eli grinned. The guard's standoffish attitude would work in Eli's favor. He praised the gods when the next shift of guards came through and relieved them of their duties.

The night hadn't gone the way he'd expected, but his luck had turned around. He had what he needed to get out of Rysburg, and he didn't even need Ali or Nik.

Chapter Forty-One

NIK

It was nearly impossible to sleep that night. Ali tossed and turned and sighed heavily. The bed shifted under her weight.

"I just don't understand what happened. Do you think he's okay?"

"I'm sure he's fine, Ali. There's nothing we can do about it tonight." Nik turned over and draped his arm over her waist, drawing circles on her skin. "Please, get some sleep."

Her eyes were wide open. There was no way she'd be sleeping tonight.

"I can think of one way to take your mind off of it," he said, sliding his hand between her thighs.

She smacked it away. "Seriously, I'm freaking out over here."

"I know." He pulled himself up, positioning himself between her legs, an elbow on each side of her face. Her gaze bounced back and forth between his mouth and his eyes, unsure where to settle. "Tell me about it. Lay it all on me."

She sighed and her warm breath brushed against his throat. "I'm just worried about him."

"Mm-hmm," he murmured, leaning down to kiss her neck.

Her breath hitched at the touch of his lips. "He should've been there. What if something happened to him?"

"Like what?" He sucked on her neck, trailed kisses up to her ear, and rolled his hips into hers.

Her eyes fluttered shut and she arched her back, sucking in a sharp breath as he reached under her shirt. "Like...like...I don't know. Aren't you supposed to be the one with the answers? These are your people."

"You're my people." He glowered, bringing his head down to kiss her sun tattoo, between her breasts, then just below her navel.

"You know what I mean." She was still talking, but her hands were running through Nik's hair, pulling him in close.

"The most likely explanation is that his assignment was changed. And first thing tomorrow, I will confirm that. Tonight, however, you're going to stop talking and let me fuck you to sleep."

She groaned as he slid her shorts down her legs and spread her thighs wide.

"God, you're already glistening for me. Are you done talking now?"

"Yes." She nodded, finally accepting that there was nothing else to be done tonight.

He kissed the inside of her thigh, gripping her hips tightly. Close enough to tease her, to make her body squirm. She held his hair and pushed him in the direction she needed him, and he smiled against her skin.

"Where do you want me? Show me."

She lifted her legs on each of his shoulders and centered his face.

"Mm, here?" He licked her clit, swirled his tongue all around her and nipped at her, kissed her, then sucked some more. She was gasping for air when he pulled his head back.

"Yes...yes, there."

"And what about here?" He slid a finger into her dripping core and pulled it out at a tormenting pace.

"Fuck yes." Her hips bucked and begged for him to fill her. "More. I want more." Her other hand drifted to her clit, and he smacked it away the same way she had done to him just moments ago.

"This is all mine, Ali."

He slid two fingers inside and felt her clench around him. He resumed sucking her clit while pumping in and out, relishing the way her pussy squeezed his fingers, reacted to his touch. Her legs were quivering already. It was enough to make his cock harden.

She gripped the sheets and watched with him with ecstasy.

"Shall I finish you like this, or would you rather have my cock?"

Her head rolled back, and she mumbled incoherently.

"What was that?"

"I want your cock."

His own pants were off in a heartbeat, and he buried himself in her with one fierce thrust, pulling a high-pitched yelp from her. He pulled back and thrust into her again, her body trembling. Then he pulled her legs back over his shoulders, ankles near his ears and leaned into her. The moan that escaped her lips nearly sent him spiraling. Each thrust sent him deeper and deeper, and she rocked her hips to meet him each time, her wet cunt sliding over him, clenching him in bliss.

She panted audibly and eagerly, completely unabashed by her need for him.

He slid a hand down between them to her sensitive bundle of nerves and massaged her gently, feeling the walls of her pussy clamp tightly around him.

"Oh my god," she whimpered, and he knew she was about to come. Her legs shook as he felt the tremors rip through her. He continued to thrust through her orgasm and came crashing down shortly after, emptying into her and filling her with his seed.

They were both short of breath as he lowered her legs. She was too weak to move them on her own. He slid out of her and fell onto his back.

"Was that it? I was promised to be fucked to sleep and I'm still very much wide awake," Ali taunted as she rolled over, wrapping a leg over his. He could feel the evidence of their pleasure dripping against his thigh, and his cock stirred again. He would need a minute, but the thought of her body being marked with him, filled with him, made him eager for another round.

He chuckled as he pushed her body off him. "On your stomach. Ass up."

A pounding at the door brought Nik out of his slumber. He must've overslept because the sun was shining through the windows in his bedroom.

He slipped out of bed and grabbed a pair of shorts. The pounding continued.

Whoever it was needed to shut the fuck up before they woke Ali. She had finally gone to sleep after several intense orgasms. She was insatiable, and he didn't mind at all. She was his.

The pounding sounded again, and Ali stirred.

"What is that?" she asked softly, half asleep.

"Nothing." He kissed the back of her head. "Go back to sleep."

When he opened the door a moment later, he saw Sam on his doorstep.

"What is your problem?" Nik hissed.

"Sorry to bother you. We have a situation. Jameson wants all hands on deck. Get dressed and meet us at the west end."

Sam looked distressed when he turned to walk away. He didn't give any more details, but Nik knew it wasn't good.

He dressed quickly and tried not to worry.

"You don't think this has something to do with Eli? With our plan last night?" Ali could sense his nervousness and began to panic herself. He had finally calmed her down and now Sam was causing issues.

"Try not to worry, Ali. I'll be home soon."

He met Sam and the other guards on the west side of town. This area was mostly residential and the oldest part of town. Families settled here centuries ago, and the village had expanded from there.

It was eerily quiet. Some guards looked around at each other, unsure of why they'd been called here. Other guards looked somber, some with tears in their eyes.

"What's going on?" he asked Sam.

"It's not good." Sam's eyes were glossed over and dark, like he'd seen death.

Jameson stepped into the center of the court and cleared his throat, preparing for a speech. The guards turned their attention to him and waited with bated breath.

"Last night, Rysburg suffered another attack," he began. "While many of our guardsmen were off scouting, our town was left vulnerable. I take full responsibility for that. Somehow..." He swallowed hard, visibly choking up. "There are people out there who envy us. They want what we have, and they'll take it by any means. We already knew they intended to attack. We just didn't know the nature. It seems they are willing to sacrifice our children. Our women."

The air thickened around them. This was a speech meant to inform them of an attack, but also to unite them. This wasn't at all what the

Coyotes had told Nik when they'd attacked him. They didn't envy Rysburg. They wanted revenge. But this was a better story to sell the guardsmen. It would fire them up and prepare them for battle.

"These *vigilantes* poisoned the water reservoir that feeds the west end. This morning, we discovered the dead, and while many have survived, they are now in critical condition. We don't know the potency of this poison so it's hard to say whether they'll survive."

Gasps and nervous chatter filled the air. Just like that, nearly a third of their town had been wiped out—dead or incapacitated. Nik had underestimated these Coyotes. His stomach flipped.

"What about the other reservoirs? The east and north?" someone asked anxiously.

"Those remain safe. They must not have realized we have more than one and only struck the west side. In addition, there was a fire set at the entrance of town. We're still investigating and aren't sure if it is related. It's possible they set a diversion to draw our attention away from the reservoir."

Sam huffed next to Nik.

"What was that for?" Nik asked.

"He's not telling the full truth. The fire was set from inside the wall. Either they snuck in to set it or we have a traitor in our midst. Neither are great options."

Nik turned back to face Jameson. This was good news for him and Ali. They wouldn't suspect that he had set the fire. They wouldn't be looking for an arsonist amongst their ranks. Did that make him the traitor, though?

"What do we do now?" another guard asked. Nik could see the fear in their eyes. This wasn't just civilians they'd lost. Guardsmen had died here too, or were currently lying in the infirmary, awaiting their fate. They had effectively thinned their ranks and suffered zero casualties in the process. It was unnerving to know they weren't safe in their own homes.

"We remain vigilant. We're securing our borders and adding extra patrols. You'll all be given additional duties for the foreseeable future. We're adding extra combat training for those who need it. In addition, we ask if you see anything, anything *at all* suspicious to speak up. The safety of Rysburg depends on you."

Chapter Forty-Two

ELI

"You did *what*?" Ali exclaimed.

"Shh. Keep your voice down." Eli looked around to see if anyone had heard her. They were sitting in their usual spot in the prison's courtyard. Dating the prison guard had its perks for Ali. She was free to visit Eli as long as Nik was working. The guard sulked over in the corner, pacing and watching them warily. Their friendship clearly still irked him.

It was their first opportunity to catch up after the commotion of the past few days. Ali had filled him in on what happened in the west end. He couldn't believe it. These Coyotes were even more dangerous than he had thought. It was no wonder Nik wanted to get her out of here.

Nik's motivations had become a bit clearer, although Eli still wasn't sure how he fit into it all. He couldn't trust that he was a priority for Nik, that he wouldn't leave him here if it came down to it. That they hadn't left the night of the original plan swayed him a little, though.

Ali had told him their side of the story and he was surprised that Nik had even bothered to go through that much trouble looking for him.

Maybe he'd just been appeasing Ali, but maybe Eli wasn't giving the guy enough credit.

Eli had just finished walking her through everything that had happened the night of their ill-fated escape attempt. How his shift had been changed last minute and he had been assigned to the arsenal instead. How lucky he had been to find himself alone with the keys to all of Rysburg's weapons...and how, in a moment of impulse, he'd stolen an explosive.

"Eli, what were you thinking? You could've been caught. You could *still* be caught. What if they track inventory? And what exactly do you plan to do, huh? Is it just sitting in your cell right now?"

"Well, I haven't thought it through completely. I just saw an opportunity and took it."

Ali's eyes widened. The reprimand there was clear before she even spoke.

He held a hand up to reassure her. "But it's fine. It'll be okay. This is a good thing. With this bomb, we can leave through any point in the wall. Just blow it up. We don't need to wait until I'm assigned to a post."

"Blow it up? Do you hear how insane you sound?" Ali was looking at him like he'd lost his mind. And maybe he had. Isolation and imprisonment could have that effect on people. "And what happens when all of Rysburg hears that and comes after us? We were relying on a head start before anyone knew we were missing."

"Yeah, well, your plan didn't exactly work out, Ali. Excuse me for trying to come up with another one."

Her jaw dropped, and she quickly closed it.

Eli avoided her gaze, a little embarrassed at his outburst. He meant every word, though, and he wouldn't apologize. Nik wasn't looking out for him, and Eli would never feel secure as long as he was calling the shots. Eli had to take the reins.

"I'm sorry, Eli. I know how much you wanted to leave. None of us expected it to fall apart like that." She grabbed his hand and scooted closer to him. Across the courtyard, Nik froze and squinted at them. "But we will get out. You just have to be patient and...think things through. You're so impulsive." She chuckled nervously.

"So now what?" he asked.

"Nik is working on it. We can try again soon."

Eli ground his teeth together. "I'm not waiting on Nik to devise a plan. And what about the outside threat? Do we even know how much longer we have?"

"If they show up while we're still here, you can always just blow them up."

Eli rolled his eyes while she laughed. She might've thought it was funny, but that didn't sound half bad to him. It had been a goal of his since day one to set this place on fire.

"Don't think I won't. It's not off the table for me."

Still, the way she laughed caused him to doubt himself. He had been so excited to finally have some control, and she'd shot him down. Surely, he would make it work somehow. He just needed to give it more thought.

"I need to head back to the greenhouse. My lunch break is almost over." She stood and brushed her hand against his cheek. It felt wrong, the way they touched. What used to feel so intimate now felt like a consolation. And Nik watched them with his arms crossed, clearly displeased. "I'll see you soon."

That evening, Eli lay in bed with his eyes closed, not yet asleep. He tried to formulate plan after plan, poking holes in each of them, the largest of which was being heard by everyone within ten miles. They'd never get far if they alerted the whole town. It would put them all in danger. Maybe Ali was right and he had been a fool.

Footsteps approached his cell, and he reluctantly opened his eyes. He wasn't even sure what time it was. Late evening or past midnight? The hours all ran together.

"I've got good news," Nik said.

Eli grunted in response.

"Always so cheerful. I made sure you're assigned to another night shift in three days. We'll try again."

Eli sank into the bed. It already felt like a failed mission before they even began. Surely something else would come up and ruin their plan yet again. He rolled over, his back facing the cell door.

"Eli," Nik called to him. "It'll work this time."

There was something in his voice. He was pleading for Eli to trust him but also pleading to the unseen gods that it *would* work. That this time would be different. That this time would be a success.

"If you say so."

Chapter Forty-Three

ALI

RAIN PELTED THE WINDOW while Ali rested peacefully in bed with Nik. His arm stretched across her stomach, and she watched his muscles tighten and relax as he brushed against her side. Spring was creeping in on Rysburg and she was thankful for the warmer weather, knowing the venture on which they were about to embark. They'd been lying in bed for hours, but she didn't want to leave his arms. She wasn't sure how long it would be before they could have lazy days like this again.

Tonight would be their second attempt at leaving Rysburg, and she couldn't bear the thought of what would happen if they failed again. It was only a matter of time before their enemies encroached on the village. The attack on the west end had rattled them all and weakened their forces. It was hard to tell who was better fit to win in a battle.

She had seen the ferocity of Rysburg, but they knew very little about their foes. How many of them were there? How well equipped were they? Nik seemed to think they were well prepared based on the few that had attacked him. He'd noted that they all had several weapons a piece and protective gear too. And they were clearly cunning and ruthless after what they'd done to mere civilians.

The scouting mission had been unsuccessful. Whoever these people were, they were good at hiding, even in plain sight. They were one with the woods, and every time Ali looked out into the vast forest, chills ran down her spine, knowing they could be out there, lurking behind the trees.

Nik brushed her arm gently and pulled her close, so close she had to wrap a leg around him. His muscular thigh tucked between her legs. Neither of them wore any clothes and had spent most of the night and early hours of the day intertwined. Again, she had no idea when they'd be able to do this, to have this easy and blissful expression of intimacy.

The corner of Nik's mouth lifted in a playful grin as she rubbed herself against him. She was ravenous. Would this feeling ever leave her? She hoped not.

He pulled her leg further across his body until she was lying on top of him, his hard core pressed against her lower stomach. She pushed herself up to a sitting position while he ran his hands over her body. First across her knees, trailing up her inner thighs. He spent a few moments on her hips, then up her stomach. He paid extra attention to her breasts, biting his lip as he massaged them slowly.

He seemed content to roam her body endlessly, and she grew wetter as the minutes passed, rocking against his length.

The look of adoration that he gave her made her heart positively melt. She'd never wanted something so bad. Something she'd already had. She could never overindulge on this. If only she could freeze this moment, she would stay skin-to-skin with Nik for eternity.

She cupped his face and kissed his lips, delighting in the way he teased her mouth open to taste her tongue. She ran her fingers through his hair, still ruffled from the night before. He wrapped an arm around her, pulling her chest close, and moved his mouth to her neck, to her collarbone.

His labored breathing tickled the skin on her shoulder and his hands moved frantically over her back, over her legs, her arms, any bit of her that he could get his hands on. She was tangled in him.

Ali rolled her hips forward, his cock pressed against his lower abdomen between their bodies. With each motion of her hips, she could feel him gliding along her slit. She whimpered in want.

"Nik." The only word she could form.

"I love you. I love you so much, Ali."

Her arms were shaking, almost too weak to support herself. Nik began to push her over, beneath him, but she stopped him.

"No. I want to fuck you like this," she said with a mischievous smile.

"Please do," he said as she sat back, taking control. He tucked an arm around his head with amusement, giving himself the perfect angle to see where their bodies connected. He used his other hand to thumb her clit.

Ali moaned and rolled her head back. She sat up a little and stroked him a few times before guiding him to her entrance. She slowly eased down onto him, taking him deep, gritting her teeth as she grew accustomed to his girth. It didn't seem possible that she could ever grow tired of the way he filled her.

This man whom she loved.

Every low groan that escaped his lips elicited a strong pulse from her core, clenching him, keeping him all to herself. She ground her pelvis into his and watched his eyes dance across her body, grinning with ecstasy. He alternated between rubbing her clit and rolling her nipple between his fingers.

"I like it when you do all the work, sweetheart."

She giggled, and he groaned from the vibration on his cock. As she picked up the pace, he thrust up into her, pushing against the mattress below them. It hit a spot in her that she wasn't accustomed to and stole her breath.

"Fuck," he growled. He started to wrap both his arms around her waist, but she grabbed them, pinning them above his head. The new angle had her breasts hanging just above his mouth and he reached up to take her in his mouth, his tongue gliding over her nipple.

"You're feisty today."

His lips moved across her chest, devoting equal time to each of her nipples and then the delicate skin between her breasts. She felt like she could hardly breathe between his seductive mouth and his hard cock filling her.

"Tell me how much you love me. How much you love fucking me."

She was panting now, leaning forward on her knees slightly while he pulled back and slammed back in repetitively. "I love you. I love you so much."

"And my cock? How much do you love my dick inside you? I love the way you clench around me, Ali. I can feel you're close."

"It feels so good. I love the way it—" Her breath caught as her muscles tensed. She was gripping his wrist so tightly she was sure it would leave bruises, but the sensation coursing through her body was all-consuming. She couldn't move save for the trembling of her legs around him.

"My god," Nik moaned as he gave a few more powerful thrusts inside her, then let her fluttering pussy pull him over the edge with her.

She collapsed on top of him, listening to his heart pound and the air flow in and out of his lungs. His chest was warm and clammy against her cheek. He made slow and steady thrusts, small movements inside her, and aftershocks rippled through her body. His fingers toyed with her hair, rubbing the strands between his thumb and forefinger.

She must've fallen asleep, because she woke up lying on her back with Nik's arm across her waist, his head resting on her breast. His hot cheek against her chest filled her whole body with warmth.

"Nik," she whispered. "Are you awake?"

"No."

She chuckled.

She couldn't tell how late it was, but they likely needed to get ready for their second attempt to leave. Rain was coming down harder now, and she wondered if they were cursed. Perhaps this was a good sign, though. The first time everything had gone right until it fell apart. Maybe this time it would all appear dismal until they stepped outside the wall, stepping into freedom.

She chose optimism.

Nik tilted his head back to look at her. He stared at her for an uncomfortably long time.

Her cheeks flushed. "What are you thinking about?"

"How lucky I am." He took her hand in his and kissed each one of her knuckles. "Why do you love me, Ali?"

She pondered for a moment, taken aback by his question. How could she describe love? It was a feeling she knew deep in her soul. It consumed her in a way that almost hurt.

"I remember the way I felt when I first arrived here after losing almost everything. I felt like my life was over."

He listened intently, his brows furrowed, and her heart began to race.

"And then I met you and...I don't know." She shook her head, remembering the first time she'd looked into his eyes. The way his voice had seeped through her veins.

"You made me feel safe. You made me feel protected. You made me feel desired. You comforted me, made me smile and laugh. And you did all this in my darkest moments. I didn't even realize it at the time, but you gave me something to hold on to. You made me feel like my life was just beginning."

His lip curled up in a grin, and his steely blue eyes glimmered. "*Our* life is beginning."

Ali smiled back. She liked the sound of that.

Chapter Forty-Four

NIK

ANY LINGERING DOUBT THAT Ali was only with him because she felt pressured to be completely evaporated. He could see that fire behind her eyes that said she was every bit as in love with him as he was with her.

He laced his fingers between hers and drew circles in the palm of her hand.

If it were up to him, they never would've left the bed that day. But as the sun began to set, he knew they needed to get dressed and prepare to leave. He reluctantly pulled away from her and slung his legs over the side of the bed.

His stomach rumbled, and it occurred to him just how little they'd eaten in the past twelve hours. They'd hardly moved since breakfast. He threw on a pair of shorts and left for the kitchen.

Ali was dressed and braiding her hair when he returned to the bedroom with two sandwiches in hand.

"For you, my lady," he said as he extended one to her.

She finished tying off the end of her braid and took it from him, kissing him on the cheek in gratitude.

He ate his sandwich hastily and dressed in black pants with a long sleeve shirt and a thick jacket. It wasn't completely waterproof, but it would help. The rain hadn't let up all day, and he could see puddles of mud forming outside his window.

He tossed in a few extra changes of clothes for the road. If the rain kept up, they'd be grateful for the dry clothes. He was packing the last of their supplies when he heard a low rumble that shook the ground. They both paused.

"Was that thunder?" Ali asked.

Nik waited, listening for another sound to confirm or deny. He furrowed his brow. It had sounded different from thunder, but perhaps his heightened senses were messing with him. Making him hear things that weren't real.

A second rumble ripped through the house, shaking the ground below them so much so that Ali grabbed the nightstand to steady herself.

"What was that?" She panicked. "You don't think Eli would've—"

"Why would he detonate a bomb when we were this close to getting out together?"

"I don't know. He just...he hasn't been very optimistic about our plan. I don't think he trusts you completely." She frantically closed her backpack and slipped her feet into her boots.

Of course he didn't. Eli would be a fool to trust Nik completely. But did he really despise him so much that he'd formulate his own plan without them? Without Ali?

"We need to go." Nik slung his bag over his shoulder and slid the strap of Eli's bag around his arm. "Now."

He grabbed Ali's hand, and they ran through the house and out the door. Although night was falling, the streets were filled with their neighbors who were also curious about where the noise was coming from.

One look to their left and Nik's stomach dropped. Smoke was rising from the entrance to Rysburg. Ali shuddered next to him. This undoubtedly felt like deja vu for her. She'd said she didn't want to live through an attack like this again, and he was determined that she wouldn't. They would get out.

Nik squeezed her trembling hand. "Eli isn't up there. Follow me."

He knew the post Eli was working tonight, assuming his assignment hadn't been changed again.

"The Coyotes. The group that attacked you. They're here now?" Ali's breath was strained as she ran behind him toward Eli's post.

"It would appear so. We need to get out of here as quickly as possible."

Nik tried not to concern himself with the shouts coming from the other side of town. As long as they got to Eli in time, they could escape and run like their lives depended on it. He would leave all of this in the past. There wasn't anything here worth saving.

They made their way down the familiar path toward Eli's post, this time not bothering to hide. Sneaking wasn't necessary when a dozen other people were running next to them. Despite the nightmare of being attacked, the timing presented an opportunity.

They could see Eli standing atop the wall immediately, looking past them in the direction of the entrance. They climbed the ladder with lightning speed and Eli reached out a hand to help Nik up the remaining steps. Nik offered him a bag with belongings they'd packed for him and he threw it over his back, tightening the straps.

"What the hell is happening?" Ali asked as he pulled Ali up the wall. He stared below them as several others began to climb the ladder too. "Who are these people?"

"Rysburg is under attack," Ali said. "They followed us. Everyone is running away from the main gate. It's chaos down there. We need to go."

Eli grabbed a thick rope with knots spaced out every two feet. He tied it on one end and slung it over the other side of the wall. Before they climbed down, he scanned the ground below and the treeline in the distance. They couldn't be sure there was no one waiting to attack this side of town. But there was no one in plain sight, and it was a risk they'd have to take.

"Go on. I'll make sure they all get down," Eli volunteered.

Ali climbed down first. The rough rope burned her hands as she moved too fast. The ground on this side was uneven, and she stumbled when she reached the bottom. It was rocky and sloped downward toward the woods. If anyone was watching, they'd have the advantage.

Nik climbed down after her and she made her way down the large rocks to make room for the remaining refugees. They were slick from the rain, and he watched as she slipped and regained her footing.

"I'm okay," she yelled back when she realized he was watching. She nodded up toward the rope and his attention returned to the men, women, and even a young child descending now.

Nik helped each of them while Ali led the way down the rocky path toward the valley. At last, Eli slid down the rope and he and Nik brought up the rear.

They trudged through the mud that separated the forest from the rocks. Nik's feet were sopping. His shoes did little to keep out the cold and wet.

They walked a few feet into the woods and Nik looked up in time to see Ali frozen in place. It was dark and he could hardly make out her outline in the shadows. Something shifted at her side and his stomach dropped.

They weren't alone.

It had been a gamble and now he knew it had been a losing one. Nik traced her body in the dark and saw with horror that the stranger had a hand on her already, tugging at her elbow.

Nik weaved through the rest of the group until he was in front of them, staring into the man's dark and demented eyes.

"Please," he said roughly, his voice caught in his throat. "Please don't hurt her."

"Ah, he lives."

Nik recognized the voice. The man hadn't bothered with a mask this time, and Nik could see a long jagged scar down the front of his face. It cut from one temple down to the opposite side of his chin. This was the same man who'd directed his men to beat Nik within an inch of his life. Daunting images of Ali facing the same fate flooded his vision. He saw her lying on the ground, bleeding to death. Too broken to fix.

"Please, I'll do anything."

The trees behind the man began to move. More bodies shifted in the moonlight.

The lump in Nik's throat grew. He didn't know how they could get out of this. Not without leaving Ali behind. He turned to Eli beside him and whispered, "Run. Take them. Take the others to safety."

Eli glanced at Nik from the corner of his eye. He was watching Ali just as fiercely as Nik had been. "No. You'll die. You'll both die."

"These people need you, Eli. They need a leader. They've never had to fend for themselves. Please, take them and go. I'll figure out something."

Nik stepped forward, prepared to meet his fate. He would die if it meant freeing Ali.

Behind him, he heard Eli pushing the others back to find a different escape route.

The hidden figures in the background made no move to follow them. They were clearly confident enough they could track them down. If the group had a head start, they didn't care. They were simply waiting for their leader to make the command, but he was having too much fun torturing Nik.

The man had spun Ali to face Nik now, one arm around her neck. A moment away from choking her if Nik tried anything. Her hands gripped at him, trying to loosen his hold.

"Now, what are we going to do with you?"

"Please, take me instead," he begged.

"Oh, I think we'll be taking you both."

Ali's breaths came in ragged gasps, and her terrified gaze met Nik's.

The man's chuckle was sinister as he pulled her forward, stepping closer toward Nik.

It happened so quickly. A dark object, perhaps a bird, flew over their heads, sinking into the middle of their enemies. And then a flash of light blinded Nik, followed by searing heat.

Not a bird. A *bomb*.

Chapter Forty-Five

ELI

THE EARTH QUAKED BENEATH Eli's feet so horrifically that he thought the ground might split in half. He'd never seen a light so bright. It burned his eyes and left him seeing white far longer than the initial blast. His ears rang, and he cupped his hands to them. It felt like they were bleeding, but his hands were clean when he pulled them back.

He felt powerful. And mad. It was the first chance he had to release all the pent-up anger he'd been holding onto for months, and he couldn't think of a more deserving target. Something in him had turned malicious red when he'd seen the man with the scarred face lay his hands on Ali.

Eli wobbled and slumped against a nearby tree trunk. He blinked to clear the haze and saw Ali standing in front of a massive fire. The scarred man had dropped his hold on her in the commotion, turning with anger and horror to see more than half of his men turned to ash.

Ali took a step away from him, but he grabbed for her neck. Her hand reached up just as her necklace snapped in his hands and she tumbled out of his grasp.

Nik reached out as Ali fell into his arms. Both wore identical expressions of shock and terror.

The Coyote hesitated to attack now that he was outnumbered.

With a wicked blaze in his eyes, Eli jogged over to meet them.

"You crazy son of a bitch," Nik shouted with a wild grin on his face.

Eli had to laugh. It was the first genuine smile he'd seen from Nik. Not a sneer or a smirk. Ali just gaped at him in awe. She clearly hadn't thought he had it in him.

Eli turned to the man who had touched Ali and grabbed him by the shoulder, slinging a hard fist into his chin. It felt amazing, unleashing his anger. He let it all out. His knuckles cracked and blood ran between his fingers. He swung three, four times before Ali screamed for him to stop and beckoned him to follow.

Eli looked up. Shadows emerged from the fire. Survivors. The few who had stood through the initial blast were making their way through the flames and smoke. They were like demons, risen from the dead and headed straight toward them.

"Let's go." Eli urged Ali and Nik onward and together they left the light of the inferno.

They weaved in and out of trees, the survivors chasing them through the dark. It was hard work, keeping a quick pace while not stumbling over roots.

At least the others could escape. They had left in the opposite direction, and his antics had drawn all attention to their trio instead. They could lead them away from town and give everyone else a fighting chance.

Nik knew these woods better than any of them, so he took the lead. Eli could tell the ground was sloping downward but had no other way to orient himself. He had seen little beyond the prison walls these last few months, so he blindly followed in Nik's footsteps.

Nik led them to a dirt path, now turned to mud. Eli's boots slid, and it became difficult to keep his footing. They turned right along the road and ran for several minutes before Nik took a sharp left into the woods again. Eli had no choice but to trust that he knew what he was doing.

He dared to look back down the road, and at least five men were hot on their tail. They looked enraged. Furious that he'd killed so many of their men. Furious that they'd escaped their grasp. Fire and smoke rose from the forest behind them.

The ground sloped steeper now, and Eli thought he could hear water running over the sound of their footsteps. It grew louder as they stumbled down the side of the hill until Ali and Nik reached the shore of a river where the ground bottomed out.

This was it. They were almost out. If they could just cross the river, they'd have a chance at freedom. Eli had the feeling the Coyotes wouldn't follow them to the other side. It would waste too much time and effort when the fight in the city was still raging on. They'd have to abandon their chase.

Eli watched as Ali and Nik pulled their backpacks above their heads and began to cross the steady stream. He was almost to them when he lost his footing in the mud, sliding the rest of the way down the hill. A burning pain shot up his right leg as his ankle rolled in an awkward position.

Ali turned her head from halfway across the river.

"Eli!"

Eli saw her mouth move but couldn't hear her over the water. He stepped forward, but the twisted ankle wouldn't support his weight. He hopped a few steps, determined to make it to the water.

"Eli!" she screamed again, pointing.

He knew it before he turned around—they were right behind him. He tried to make it into the water, but he was too slow.

Weapons clanked behind him…and then a sharp blade cut through his side.

He toppled over, landing in the mud facing the river. His side went numb, and the feeling spread to the lower half of his body. His eyelids drooped as he watched Nik wrap an arm around Ali's thrashing body, pulling her to the other side of the river.

Eli smiled, knowing she was safe, and then closed his eyes.

Chapter Forty-Six

ALI

Ali's arms flailed wildly. Nik kept his arm around her waist, pulling her through the river. Water rushed around them, making it difficult for him to navigate the stream. He grunted but didn't release his hold.

All she could do was watch the shore as it shrank, leaving Eli behind.

"What are you doing?" she demanded through gritted teeth, pulling at Nik's arm as he heaved her out of the water. She dug her heels into the sand of the opposite shoreline, fighting him at every step.

"Eli!" She let out a blood-curdling scream.

Nik held her firmly in place against his chest as she pushed against him. She wasn't strong enough to loosen his hold.

"Eli!" she sobbed, clawing at Nik's arm. Why wouldn't he let go?

She watched the opposite shore, illuminated by the moon, with tear-filled eyes. The figures of the other men hovering above Eli's body, and an enraged snarl escaped her lips.

"Let me go!" she screamed at Nik. She broke free and hit him in the chest, but he grabbed her by the wrists, preventing her from entering the water again. She had to get back to Eli. She'd fight Nik tooth and nail if she had to.

Ali wrenched her arms, twisting and turning but it did nothing to break free from his hold. It just burned the skin under his grip. She thrashed against him like a wild animal.

"Ali. Ali, please stop."

His voice was soft. There was no urgency. No fight.

"What's wrong with you? We can't leave him." Her chest was tight; she could hardly breathe. Her voice cracked from the screaming, making it hard to deliver a convincing argument.

"Ali, he's not..." Nik hesitated. "I watched him fall. You watched him fall. That sword..."

"He's not what? He's not *what*?" she screamed, swinging her fists at him, but his grip held firm.

Nik gave her an anguished look. Was it pain she saw on his face? Ali calmed long enough to give him a once over. No blood. No broken bones.

No, that was a look of pity. He was pitying her.

Understanding dawned, and his words finally sunk in. Her stomach turned, and she gripped her sides. It felt like her insides were on fire. He was wrong. He had to be wrong.

"He...he can't be."

She choked on her words. She sought Eli's body on the other side of the river, expecting him to get up at any moment. To move. To make some indication that he was still with them.

But his body was lifeless.

"I'm sorry, Ali. I know...I know how much he meant to you."

Meant. Past tense. Because he was gone.

Nik let go of her wrists, and she began to inch back to the water. She had to see for herself. They couldn't have him. She would get to him and see for herself. He couldn't be gone. He would see her face and crack a joke about her overreacting, and everything would be okay.

"Ali, please don't. You can't help him now. You're just going to put yourself in danger." Tears glistened on Nik's cheeks, and he looked at her cautiously, as if she might break.

The water hit her ankles as she backed up. This wasn't how it was supposed to happen. She looked between Nik and Eli on the other side of the river, sliding further into the water, the cold stream biting at her shins. "I can't leave him."

The water rushed around her; its icy depths comforted her. It understood her. It understood the pain she felt. Its blackness matched the darkness spreading over her heart, taking over her soul. Its roaring waters were a soothing lullaby, telling her it was okay to give in. It was okay to give up. It threatened to swallow her whole, and she was tempted to allow it.

Nik took a step toward her. "Ali, I'm begging you. If you go back over there, you'll die. I can't lose you," he whispered. He reached out a hand, an offer to take hers. "Choose me. Choose us."

Ali had once said if it came down to the two of them, she'd choose Eli. She'd choose her family. But as she looked across the river, she saw Eli's body slumped on the ground, unmoving. The longer she watched, the more she understood. She'd lost him. Her family was gone...had ceased to exist. And Nik was still here, patiently waiting for her to choose him.

She felt numb. The blood rushed from her body and she froze in the water, watching as her best friend lay lifeless on the beach. The person she'd spent nearly every waking moment of her life with. Who knew everything about her and loved her, faults and all. The last remnant of her old life. Everything else felt foggy, her surroundings muffled. It was just the two of them.

A tear rolled down her cheek and touched her lips.

She looked back to Nik, waiting quietly with a hand outstretched. Her lips trembled as another tear fell. She didn't know how she was supposed to carry on. But for him, she would try. She stepped out of the water, her feet like heavy bricks, and back onto the sandy shore.

Nik was speechless. He closed the gap between them and brought his arms around her shoulders, squeezing her tight and stroking her hair. If it weren't for his arms holding her up, she might've collapsed to the ground. His warm body embraced her, but she felt nothing but the cold bitterness of despair.

The men moved and picked up Eli's body, one man carrying him by the shoulders and another carrying his feet. Ali and Nik watched as they disappeared into the woods and out of sight.

Chapter Forty-Seven

NIK

Nik held her in his arms while she shivered. He was afraid to speak, afraid to move. If he disrupted this delicate balance, she might have a full breakdown. For now, she was safe in his arms.

He'd seen that look in her eyes as she had stood in the river. It was the look of someone who had given up. He'd looked into her eyes and only saw hollowness, and it had rattled him to his core. He'd seen many dreadful things in his life, and none had terrified him more than that empty chasm.

A spark had lit when she'd decided to step out of the water.

Over time, her breathing steadied and he could no longer hear the sniffles or feel the shuddering of her cries.

"We should keep moving," he whispered against her hair. She squeezed his waist and sobbed again. "I know it's hard right now. It's going to be hard for a while. Let's take it one day at a time. You can do this."

She rolled her head back and looked into his eyes. Her own were red and splotchy, and she looked exhausted from the emotional toll she had endured. But she nodded.

Nik pulled his backpack around and took out a water bottle. He forced her to take a sip and then took a few himself before replacing it and slinging his bag back over his shoulders.

"We should try to find the others. They won't survive out here on their own. I know they headed north, so we can follow the river that way and scope it out. We'll have to be careful. I'm not sure how many of the Coyotes are in these woods. Stay close."

They could've left, just the two of them. That had been their initial plan. But Eli was now gone and a dozen or so others had accompanied them out of Rysburg. It wouldn't sit right with his conscience to leave them on their own.

Nik walked into the woods, out of sight, and Ali followed, holding his hand. Her silence worried him, but it was probably normal given the circumstances. She was grieving and in shock. He wasn't sure how to cut the tension. All he wanted to do was take her away from here and let her fall apart, but they couldn't do that yet. There was still work to be done. He squeezed her hand instinctively, a signal of comfort.

The rain finally let up, but his wet clothes clung to his body. He longed for his bed and dry blankets, but distracted himself with the treacherous trail. Because they weren't taking a typical path, their trek was filled with fallen tree trunks, overgrown weeds and mud pits.

After some distance, he found the landmark he was looking for: a cement wall that stretched across the river, water trickling over its rim. An old dam that had survived the test of time. If they crossed on the low side they'd be better hidden from enemies.

Nik led Ali down to the water's edge. She carefully hopped down the large rocks with his help. Once again, they moved through freezing water, although this side of the stream only came up to their knees.

"How are you doing?" he called behind him as the water surged around his legs.

"Fine." She didn't sound fine, but the fact that she was speaking again was a good sign.

They reached the other side and wrung the water from their pants.

"We're far enough north now. We can double back and approach from the opposite side. I'm not sure how far they would've gotten. They probably have no idea where to go."

A knot in the pit of his stomach formed when he considered how slow and lost the others probably were. If they hadn't moved far, the Coyotes had probably gotten to them already. Still, he had to be sure.

They snaked through the trees, scrutinizing any sound or movement around them. It was slow-moving work, but at last he saw a flicker of a flame.

They approached it with stealth. As they got closer, he realized it was the remnants of a fight. Eli's bomb wasn't the only thing that had left the woods scorched and burning. The Coyotes had left a blaze in their wake as they'd crossed through the woods, killing everything in their path. Now, blackened tree trunks stood in a lake of smoldering brush.

Nik put a hand to his forehead. Now what? There had been no sign of the other refugees. They seemed long gone. Completely out of his reach.

Ali stood in the firelight, her eyes glazed over. She still hadn't spoken other than the one word she'd uttered in the river. It broke what little fight he had left in him. He hated giving up on the others, but he needed to fight for her first and foremost. He couldn't search forever. It was time to move on.

"Come on," he said softly, placing a hand on her elbow.

He retraced their steps. They would move past the river and further away from Rysburg. The Coyotes hadn't followed across the river; that told him they were headed in the opposite direction. They could stick to their original plan and start making their way south.

They had only taken a few steps when a muffled groan sounded from a few feet away.

Nik looked around for the source of the noise. A handful of bodies covered the ground, but all appeared lifeless.

Another groan.

He scanned the ground and stepped through the field of people, carefully searching for movement, waiting for another sound to steer him in the right direction.

An arm lifted and pointed in his direction. He immediately recognized the face.

"Sam!"

Nik ran to his side and his knees hit the ground, reaching to take his friend's hand. Sam was covered in blood and dirt. He was still alive. Severely injured, but alive.

"What happened?" Nik took a quick look at Sam's body. His leg was twisted unnaturally and weighed down by a large rock.

"Help me," Nik said to Ali. She remained silent, but she stood next to him as they lifted the rock together, freeing Sam's leg.

Sam let out another groan, somewhere between relief and pain.

"They came in through the front gate...took out our guards quickly and quietly. They moved through the front of town and killed everyone they came across. It was...they killed them before they could warn anyone. They moved so quickly...so quietly."

Sam's eyes were wide as he spoke. Nik could practically see the sorrow in his eyes as he relived the attack. It was a struggle for him to recount the tale.

"By the time someone could ring the alarm, it was too late. They had swarmed the city. How did you get out?"

"We heard the commotion. We must've gotten lucky."

"Lucky..." Sam muttered. His eyes glazed over slightly.

"Hey, stay with us. We're going to get you out of here. We were tracking a few other refugees who followed us out. Did you happen to see them?"

"I ran into a few of them...the ones that did this to me. They had a few people bound." Sam had several flesh wounds from sparring with the Coyotes. Nik wasn't sure how he'd found himself beneath the rock, but they had left him for dead after that, assuming he would succumb to his injuries and the elements.

Ali stood behind Nik quietly, taking everything in. When Sam noticed her, he blinked and looked at Nik, a question forming on the tip of his tongue.

"Are you going after him?" Sam asked.

Nik tilted his head, unsure what to make of his question.

"That's why you're looking for them, right? Eli is the refugee you're trying to find?"

Nik's chest tightened, and he glanced back at Ali. To his surprise, she wasn't crying again. Worse...she still looked numb. Unfazed by Sam's questions.

"No. Eli..." Nik glanced at Ali again, wishing she wasn't standing behind him. It would be better to rip off the band-aid. To be blunt and not beat around the bush. To not drag out her pain. "Eli is dead."

Sam stared at him in disbelief, and he heard Ali shift on her feet in discomfort. Then, slowly, he shook his head. "No. He was with them. I saw him. Eli isn't dead."

Ali dropped to her knees next to him and gasped. Her eyes went wide as she studied Sam. "What?"

"He's alive."

"How do you know?" Nik asked, hesitant to believe him.

"He was arguing with one of them. Calling him a bunch of names and saying he would slaughter them in his sleep. The usual."

Ali threw herself onto Sam, crying into his chest. The look of surprise on Sam's face almost made Nik laugh, but he just watched her release tears of shock and unbelievable joy. He rubbed her back as she sobbed, and reality sank in.

Eli was alive.

Chapter Forty-Eight

ELI

ELI WOKE TO THE sound of yelling. A painful, tortured, yelling. The sun was rising, and he wasn't sure how long he'd been passed out. Trees surrounded him, but he couldn't see any distinguishable features. He could still smell the burning forest, though he could no longer see a fire or smoke. A thin blanket was the only barrier between his aching body and the hard ground beneath him.

He vaguely remembered being dragged through the forest surrounding Rysburg, hurling expletives at the Coyotes. It had been the only thing he *could* hurl. They'd injected him with something...some paralytic. One had hit him over the head just to shut him up. His head pounded as a reminder.

Was the battle over? Where the hell was he now?

The yelling continued, and a woman came over, hushing him. The yelling was his own, he realized.

Eli dropped his head to the ground and took deep breaths. The woman pulled back his blood-soaked shirt, revealing a long gash. He watched, half-conscious, as she cleaned it with water and applied a solution, then covered it with clean cloth.

"Drink this," she said, tipping a vial into his mouth. It burned on the way down and he felt his body go numb and light as a feather. Whatever was in that vial knocked him out entirely.

The second time he woke, he blinked and turned toward the other captives. They looked terrified and shivered in their wet clothes. He looked down to find his own body had been covered with a blanket. He didn't feel cold. He actually felt quite hot, feverish even.

"What's your name?" a man asked him. He didn't feel like talking, let alone to one of the Coyotes. The man tapped his shoulder roughly with his foot. "I asked you a question, boy."

"Eli," he croaked.

"Eli," the man repeated. He donned a smug grin. "You got what you deserved. Your type had it coming."

"My type?"

"We know the things you've done. Stealing and killing with no consequences. Well, they're coming to you now." He chuckled and bared his teeth.

Eli could've laughed, perhaps from blood loss. The whole situation was comical. "I'm not from Rysburg. I'm from Andus. I'm a prisoner...was a prisoner."

Now he had no idea what he was.

He pulled up the sleeve of his shirt and his metal shackle glistened in the sun.

The Coyote studied him for a moment. Eli didn't catch what he said next. Fatigue overwhelmed him and he closed his eyes and fell back asleep.

When Eli woke in the middle of the night, his surroundings had changed. They were in an open meadow now, and the other refugees were nowhere to be found. He was alone with the Coyotes. He felt abandoned, and an ache tugged at his chest.

This all felt like a sick joke. Every time he thought things couldn't get worse, they did.

Eli groaned as a healer replaced the bandage on his side. He nearly vomited when he saw the blood oozing from his wound. He was lucky the sword hadn't damaged any organs, but it was deep, and he felt the pain radiating every time he moved. So he lay still.

She checked his ankle, pushing it in different directions and stretching it. The more she moved it around, the less it hurt. Probably just a sprain.

Part of him wished he were dead. He'd seen enough of this world to know he didn't want to see any more of it. He wished his body would succumb to the pain, to the injuries of the past few months. His body had withstood more trauma than most people experienced in a lifetime. But it kept on persevering, and he was forced to mentally persevere with it.

The healer gave him a concoction to drink. It was a concoction he'd grown familiar with. As he downed the vile liquid, he knew sleep would settle upon him in just a few minutes.

"What happened to the others?" he asked her, thinking about the shivering bodies that had sat next to him in the forest. He hadn't recognized any of them, but found it odd that they were now missing.

Her eyebrows scrunched together, and she patted his shoulder tenderly.

"They're gone now."

Acknowledgments

Thank you to my friends and family who've always motivated me to dream big and those who fostered my creativity. I never would've had the courage to write a novel without you!

Thank you to my beta readers who helped mold and perfect this story and who shared in my excitement to release it out into the world. Your words of encouragement mean more than you'll ever know!

And thank you to everyone reading this. I hope you feel as strongly for these characters as I do!

For a list of titles by Rachel Mays, please visit
www.authorrachelmays.com